JOHN

Titles available in this series

Yannis
Anna
Giovanni
Joseph
Christabelle
Saffron
Manolis
Cathy
Nicola
Vasi
Alecos
John

Greek Translations

Anna

JOHN

Beryl Darby

ISBN 978-0-9574532-2-7

Printed and bound in the UK by
CPI Antony Rowe, Chippenham

First published in the UK in 2013 by

JACH Publishing
92 Upper North Street, Brighton, East Sussex, England BN1 3FJ

website: www.beryldarby.co.uk

For the men (in alphabetical order):
Alan, Lambros, Lee, Mike, Phoebus,
Scott, Stuart and Will

Family Tree

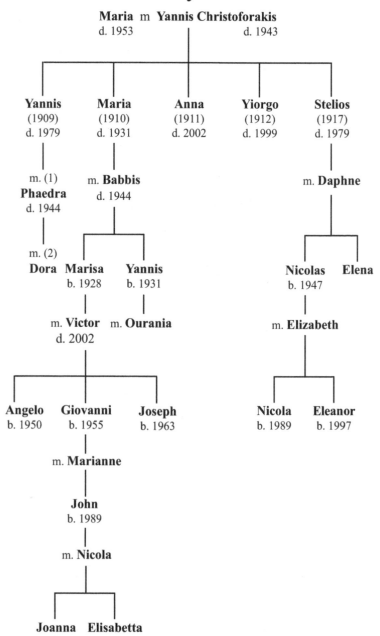

Family Tree

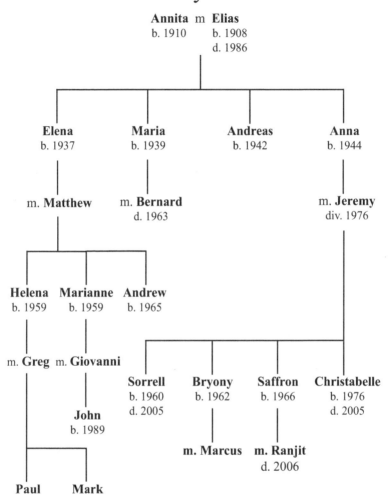

Annita m **Elias**
b. 1910   b. 1908
         d. 1986

Elena
b. 1937

Maria
b. 1939

Andreas
b. 1942

Anna
b. 1944

m. **Matthew**

m. **Bernard**
d. 1963

m. **Jeremy**
div. 1976

Helena
b. 1959

Marianne
b. 1959

Andrew
b. 1965

m. **Greg**

m. **Giovanni**

John
b. 1989

Sorrell
b. 1960
d. 2005

Bryony
b. 1962

Saffron
b. 1966

Christabelle
b. 1976
d. 2005

m. **Marcus**

m. **Ranjit**
d. 2006

Paul

Mark

November 2007 – February 2008

Vasi sat at the desk is his father's study, the computer open before him. He studied the page carefully. He was not poor by most peoples' standards, but he was certainly in debt to the bank. He had only managed to repay half of the loan he had taken out to refurbish the hotel at Hersonissos after Stelios had used it as a brothel. Now the premises were closed until the following year he would still have to continue to pay the bank the arranged monthly amount and also a retainer fee to his manager if he wanted to continue to employ him.

The decision he and his father had made to take their hotel accounts to a different bank meant the loan arrangement he had was not as favourable as before. Having bought Manolis's boat he would not have contemplated the expense of having an echo sounding of the bay with a view to building a jetty had he known he would be forced to purchase the Imperia hotel. He had also promised to buy Yiorgo a scooter so he could travel to Elounda from Aghios Nikolaos to run the boat trips to Spinalonga. The mooring fees for the boat he had paid in advance and he could delay purchasing a licence to carry passengers until the following year, but his expenses added up.

Ownership of the Central hotel had been signed over to him some years ago as a gift from his father and he was loath to approach him for any financial help. Fortunately the Central had made a good profit and should continue to do so during the winter months as the hotel was booked for conferences. To his relief there were no major repairs or refurbishments needed there.

He and his father conducted their accounts in different ways. Vasilis took his percentage from the hotels he owned at the end of each season, whereas Vasi preferred to take a monthly amount and hoped to be able to add a sizeable amount to his bank balance from the final profit when the season finished.

The percentage he expected to receive this year was already earmarked as a repayment towards the loan he had needed to take out for the useless Imperia hotel. He had bought a new car, not knowing how long the police would impound his original one and now he regretted it. He should have had more patience and waited; having had his damaged car re-sprayed the new car sat in the garage totally unused.

His visit to England was booked and paid for. He would only need to have spending money whilst he was there, but John had said he and Nicola had found the city expensive. He closed down the computer with a sigh. He would sell his new car and that debt could be cleared. Once he had returned from England he would look at his accounts more closely and see if he could negotiate a more favourable interest rate for the loans with his new bank.

He stretched and yawned. It was too early to go to bed. He thought about 'phoning Yiorgo and decided against it. If Barbara was not working Yiorgo would suggest that Vasi drove into Aghios Nikolaos and they met up for a drink. That would only cause trouble between Yiorgo and his wife.

The evenings seemed to stretch interminably before him now Saffron had returned to England. Usually when the season ended he was busy making plans to refurbish the hotels, but this year he had made any necessary arrangements earlier, thinking he would be devoting his time to designing and supervising the building of a jetty.

Finally he decided he would go out into the garden and spend some time with the dogs before checking their water bowl and locking the house for the night. Vasi pulled on a jumper and picked up two chewed balls from beside the door. He would play with the dogs for a while and it would not matter how excitedly they barked they would not be disturbing anyone.

An hour later he returned to the house, still feeling restless. The dogs had chased after the balls as he threw them, returning to drop them at his feet until he had become tired of the game before they had. He had filled their water bowl a second time for them and watched whilst they lapped eagerly until deciding they had drunk sufficient.

As he opened the patio door he could hear the telephone ringing. He frowned. Who would be calling the house at that time? It was probably someone trying to sell him something for the hotels. He ignored it and went into the cloakroom and washed his hands to remove the dogs' spittle.

As he returned to the kitchen he heard the end of the answer 'phone message. 'Vasi, do pick up if you're there whatever you're doing. It's urgent.' He heard his father sigh at the end of the 'phone and then the line went dead.

Vasi tapped his pockets. Why hadn't his father called him on his mobile? Where was his mobile? Surely it hadn't fallen from his pocket whist he had been playing with the dogs? He looked around the kitchen wildly. It could be anywhere outside, but why hadn't he realised he had dropped it? He would have to wait until daylight to search for it.

He picked up the telephone and dialled his father's number at the apartment. There was no answer. Obviously his father and Cathy were out somewhere for the evening. He screwed up his face in concentration in an attempt to remember his father's mobile 'phone number, relieved to hear it ring and have his father's voice on the other end.

'Pappa, it's Vasi. What's the problem?'

'Where have you been? I've been trying to call you on your mobile for the last half an hour.'

'I'm sorry. I think it must have fallen from my pocket when I was playing with the dogs. What's so urgent?'

He heard his father take a deep breath. 'I'm at the hospital. Cathy had a fall earlier this evening. I had to call an ambulance. She can't move.'

'What! Has she damaged her spine?'

'We don't know at the moment. They've taken her for x-rays. Now I've spoken to you I'm going back inside to see if they have any results. You can't use a mobile inside. I'll come out and call you again as soon as I have any news.'

'Call me on the land line. I'll wait by the 'phone,' promised Vasi. Now he had to stay up he suddenly had an overwhelming desire to go to bed. He would have to do something to occupy his time until his father had telephoned again.

He walked back into the study. He would open up the computer and look again at the various attractions London had to offer. Already he had a long list, but there could be something he had overlooked. The first thing he saw as he sat down at the computer was his mobile 'phone. He was both annoyed and relieved. Now he could call his father and ask him to use the mobile when he knew the results from Cathy's x-ray.

Vasi sighed with frustration when he was told the number he was calling was switched off. He had no choice but wait up until his father's call came, but at least he would not have to search the grounds for his mobile the following day.

It was almost an hour before Vasilis finally called and Vasi answered with alacrity.

'How is Cathy?' asked Vasi immediately.

Vasilis sighed deeply. 'The doctor says she has broken a bone in her pelvis. That's why she is in so much pain and can hardly move.'

'What can they do for her? Are they keeping her in hospital?'

'They say they'll keep her in tonight and she can return home tomorrow. She will have to stay in bed and rest until the injury has healed. They've warned me that it will take some weeks.'

'Poor Cathy. It could have been a good deal worse, of course.'

His father continued as if Vasi had not spoken. 'I'll need you up here to run the Central. I won't be able to leave Cathy.'

Vasi swallowed. 'How long will you want me to stay in Heraklion? I'm due to go to England in ten days.'

'You'll have to cancel. I'm sorry, Vasi, but Cathy needs me and I need you to be on hand here during the conferences. You can always go to England later. I'll see you tomorrow. Call me from the Central and when Cathy's home you can come over and we'll discuss the bookings and the arrangement requests that have been made.'

'Yes, Pappa,' Vasi answered miserably. 'By the way, I've found my mobile.'

'Good.' The line went dead and Vasi guessed his father had returned inside the hospital to be with Cathy. He dropped his head in his hands. Why did Cathy have to have an accident now? Once he had seen Cathy and spoken to his father again he would have to 'phone Saffron. It was possible that his projected visit to London could take place a couple of weeks later than scheduled.

'Saffie, it's Vasi.'

Saffron felt her heart give a little jump of excitement.

'Saffie, I am so sorry. I cannot come to England.'

'What do you mean? You cannot come? You were told you could leave Crete, that you were no longer under suspicion. It was all arranged. You have your ticket.' Saffron spoke wildly. 'Why have you changed your mind?'

'I haven't. Listen, Saffie, it is not my fault. Cathy has had an accident. It is serious this time. She fell and has broken a bone in her pelvis. She is in so much pain.'

Saffron nodded. She knew the effects such a break could have.

'Oh, Vasi. I am so sorry. Poor Cathy. Is she in hospital?'

'They only kept her overnight to take x-rays and assess the amount of damage. She returned home the next day with orders to rest and move around as little as possible. Pappa is with her, of course, and Rebecca is going to stay with them to help, but I have to manage the hotel.'

'It's the end of the season, Vasi. The hotels are closed.'

'Not the Central. That is open all year round. We host conferences from Athens. I am needed here.'

Saffron felt close to tears. She had not realised how much she had been looking forward to seeing Vasi again.

'You are not cross with me, Saffie?'

Saffron swallowed hard. 'Of course I am not cross with you. I am disappointed.'

'That is good that you are disappointed. I, too, am very disappointed, but you understand that I have to stay, to help my father. He is distraught. I cannot leave Crete until Cathy has recovered.'

'It will take her at least two months,' Saffron frowned.

'So Maybe you could come here?'

'I can't.' Saffron shook her head. 'The winter months are some of our busiest. So many people have falls when it becomes icy. No one is allowed leave between mid November and the end of March.'

'So when will I see you? I want to see you so much and I have something very important to ask you.'

'What's that, Vasi?'

'It is not something that can be discussed over the telephone.'

'Then mail me.'

'No,' Vasi spoke firmly. 'It can wait until we are together.'

'It can't have been that important then,' Saffron replied caustically.

'As soon as Cathy has recovered I promise I will come to England,' continued Vasi. 'Then we can talk about many important matters.'

'Could your father not employ a nurse to help look after her?' suggested Saffron.

'Even if he employed a dozen nurses he would not leave her to come in to the hotel.'

'So what would happen if you were not able to be there?'

'He would probably cancel the conferences.'

'Vasi! You're not serious?'

'I am very serious. Had it happened during the tourist season he would have left the manager in charge, but the conferences we have always supervised whilst the manager has his annual leave.'

'So there is no way you can come to England?' said Saffron miserably.

'It is impossible at the moment. You do understand, don't you, Saffie? You are not cross with me?'

Saffron took a deep breath. 'Of course I am not cross with you. It is not your fault.' She did not add that she thought Vasi's father was being totally unreasonable. If Cathy's mother was staying with them a nurse could be employed and Vasilis could have gone in to the hotel whenever it was necessary. 'Vasi, I have to go. I am already late leaving for work.'

'I am sorry. That is my fault. I will mail you, Saffie, and explain more to you.'

With a deep sigh Saffron closed her mobile 'phone and walked into the kitchen. Despite being late for work she would have to tell Marjorie about Vasi's change of plans.

'Vasi's not able to come to England.'

'Why not?' Marjorie stopped washing their breakfast dishes and looked at Saffron in concern.

'Cathy's had an accident.'

'What's happened to her?'

'She had a fall and has broken a bone in her pelvis. It will take weeks to heal. Her mother is coming down from Heraklion to help look after her, but Vasilis won't leave her. Vasi says he has to stay there to deal with the conferences that are booked at the Central.'

'Oh, poor Cathy. What a shame it had to happen just now. Maybe Vasi will be able to come over in another month or so.'

Saffron shrugged. 'I must go. I'm late and I'll probably get caught in the rush hour traffic now.'

Saffron seemed to be near to tears and Marjorie hoped that Cathy's accident was not being used as an excuse by Vasi. Saffron had seemed so happy when she had returned from Elounda, despite the problems that had besieged Vasi. She had a glow about her that Marjorie recognised as being more than just the aftermath of an enjoyable holiday with her Greek family.

Once home from the hospital Saffron opened her computer and brought up the e-mail from Vasi. *"Firstly, Saffie, I am so sorry that I am unable to come to visit you as we had planned. Please understand that I cannot leave here at the moment. As soon as my father is prepared to leave Cathy at home with her mother and take over the duties here I will contact you and ask if may visit you."*

Saffron smiled to herself. Of course he could visit them at any time.

"I met Yiorgo last week to discuss arrangements for him to take Manolis's boat out during the winter months to become completely familiar with handling her. (I still think of the 'Flora' as belonging to Manolis.) He did not seem very happy and when I questioned him he told me Barbara was expecting another baby. They do not want another and Barbara is thinking of visiting a doctor in Heraklion. I do not like the idea, but I will help him if I can.

My father and I are not terribly happy with our new bank. We still have to repay our business loans to the original one. Before they were flexible with us and sometimes we were a day or two late in making the payment. Now they insist the payment is made on time or we are charged extra interest and the new bank will not send the payment unless our account is well in credit. Five times I have been down to them now and explained that there will always be sufficient money to cover our debts in the account by the end of the week but they have taken no notice of me and held the repayment up. I will have to speak to Giovanni and see if he is having the same problem.

I am planning to sell my new car as I am much happier with my original one. I need to speak to the garage where I bought it and see if they will give me a good price. If they agree I hope I will have time to take a bus down to Elounda next week and drive it up to Heraklion. I wish now I had not bought it.

Dimitra is still living at the Central. She insists she cannot return to her apartment as the doctor may come there looking for her. I went to the police station and spoke to Superintendent Solomakis. He was very unhelpful, of course. All the information I could get from him was that they were looking for Doctor Melanakis to help them with their enquiries. I telephoned the hospital and asked to speak to him and they said he was no longer working there. He has obviously disappeared somewhere to avoid prosecution.

I have suggested to Dimitra that she looks for an apartment in a different part of the town, but she says she is frightened that he will see her. She hardly goes out. When she has finished her duties she retires to her room and spends the evenings alone. I do not think she has made any attempt to contact Alecos.

I have a lot of problems to deal with here at the moment. A booking made by a company for a seminar had been entered under the wrong date. When they began to arrive we had to find an alternative room for them as the conference room was already in use. I persuaded them to wait in the bar until everyone had finally arrived and sent them complimentary coffee whilst we hurriedly arranged for more seating. We had not catered for the extra numbers and I had to call in extra staff. Fortunately they did not realise the mistake we had made or they may have gone elsewhere in future.

We have a difficult company manager staying this week. He had requested a suite and when he found it was on the top floor he insisted he needed to be on the first floor as he had a fear of being trapped in the lift and could not walk up five flights of stairs.

I explained that we had no suites on the first floor and if we had known about his problem earlier we could have arranged for him to have a sitting room in a next door bedroom.

He became very aggressive and insistent so I moved guests from two rooms and arranged for furnishings to be transferred. He is still not happy and said he was disturbed at night by the noise of the lift. I stood in his room and asked a maid to come up. It was just possible to hear the noise of the machinery. He insisted we moved him again to the very end of the hallway. I will be happier when he has left.

At breakfast this morning he said the coffee was not hot enough in the machine and asked for a fresh pot to be brought to his table. He then complained that there was insufficient bacon. I had seen his plate; he had taken at least twelve rashers, along with two eggs and four slices of toast. His company has paid the bill inclusive of accommodation and meals so I cannot charge him any extra.

I have not spoken again to my father about altering his house and providing specialist holidays. This is not the time to bother him. I had planned to speak to you and also to Marjorie when I visited. I have had an idea. Before we make any alterations I need to know if the holidays would be successful.

As soon as my father is willing to come in to deal with the conferences I promise I will book a flight to England, but it is unlikely I shall be able to come until after Christmas. I miss you, Saffie. Once I have finally finished work the evenings seem very lonely now I am spending them alone. Please look into the possibility of visiting me here, even if you are only able to stay for a few days."

Saffron closed the mail and removed her diary from her handbag. Every other weekend she was on call. She had arranged to have an extra weekend free when Vasi was due to visit.

The direct flights to Crete were no longer available. She would have to go from Heathrow and face a long stop-over in Athens airport. Maybe one of the other doctors would be willing to change their shift with hers if she offered to work over Christmas and the New Year. Vince would probably appreciate having more time to spend with his family. Provided there was a doctor on call in the orthopaedic unit it made no difference which one it was.

If she could have two days leave she would be able to catch a late flight on the Friday evening. That would give her the weekend and two full days in Crete. She was sure she would be able to re-arrange her appointments so she did not have to go in to the hospital on the Wednesday and could catch a late night flight back to England.

Saffron replaced her diary into her handbag. She needed to speak to Vince and look at flight schedules before she said anything to Vasi.

Filippos Melanakis, having been forced to give a DNA sample to Inspector Solomakis, had returned to his medical duties in sombre mind. He knew he had at least four days before the DNA results would be back from the laboratory and at first he planned to take a flight to a South American country. As he tried to make a plan he realised it would be impossible for him to obtain a visa at such short notice and that his movements would be traced.

As he had driven home a better plan had come to him. He stopped at a cash point and drew out as much as he was allowed from his account. During the evening he packed his belongings, making sure he had no more than two large cases so he would look like a tourist. He placed them in his car ready for the next day when he planned to call the hospital and claim he was sick.

The following morning he decided to risk a visit to his bank to withdraw his remaining balance. He certainly did not want to use a cash point once he had left Heraklion, but he would need all his money. He had sat nervously before the manager whilst he filled in the form to withdraw all his savings and close his account.

'Are you sure you wish to close your account? Unless you already have another account opened at a different bank you could have a problem when the hospital pay your salary at the end of the month.'

'How large a balance do I have to leave on the account to keep it open?'

'Fifty Euros would be sufficient. Are you sure you wish to withdraw all the remaining balance?'

Filippos nodded. 'I've been rather foolish.' He hung his head as if embarrassed. 'I was tempted to gamble. Small amounts at first and I seemed to win. Like all gamblers I risked higher and higher amounts and needless to say I lost heavily. I've tried to negotiate an arrangement with them whereby I pay off the debt gradually, but they're insisting I clear it immediately in cash. They made it quite clear that if I did not do so I would regret it.'

The bank manager frowned. 'You mean they have threatened you? Have you mentioned this to the police?'

Filippos shook his head. 'I think if I complained to the police I could have even more cause for regret. No, it is wiser for me to pay my debt. I've learnt my lesson. Apart from the odd lottery ticket I shall certainly not be gambling again.'

'It is a very large amount.'

Filippos sighed. 'I know. Thank goodness I had enough on my account to cover it.'

The manager picked up the papers. 'I imagine you would prefer large denomination notes?'

Filippos nodded. He did not care what notes he was given. All he wanted was the cash and then he could be on his way. He waited impatiently until the manager reappeared with a cashier and the money was counted out in front of him and placed into two large envelopes.

'I'm very grateful,' he muttered as he hastily shook hands and left the bank.

Once back in his car he opened his suitcases and placed an envelope in each one. He drove down to the port, purchased a Flying Dolphins ticket for the following day to take him to

Santorini and checked the time the craft would leave. He did not want to be there too early and draw attention to himself.

From Heraklion he had driven sedately to Rethymnon and parked close to his brother's house. He had called earlier, explained that he had the weekend free and would like to visit him and his wife.

'Can I beg a bed for the night?'

'Of course. You don't need to ask. You're always welcome. Stelios can sleep in our room and you can have his. That's no trouble.'

Filippos felt a twinge of guilt. If his brother ever found out the truth about him it was doubtful he would ever be welcome again.

The evening had passed amicably. Filippos had amused their small son whilst Eva had cooked a basic, but appetising meal for them and having put Stelios to bed she joined the men for a short while. Her knitting needles clicked as she worked on a jumper for Stelios, annoying Filippos and he was relieved when she finally placed the wool and needles in a bag and declared her intention of retiring for the night. Filippos hoped Andreas would follow her, but instead he opened a second bottle of wine and sat forward confidentially.

'I'm planning to open my own picture framing business. I've spoken to the bank and negotiated a loan. There are some premises available in one of the side streets and I'm signing the agreement next Tuesday. They're only small, but adequate and the rent is reasonable. I'll take you along there tomorrow and you can tell me what you think. I've put aside a bit for advertising and I'll let slip to our current customers that I'm moving on and give them the address. It will probably take a while for me to be known, but I do a good job and I'm sure I'll be recommended.'

Andreas continued to talk enthusiastically about his plans for his business, but Filippos was not particularly interested. His brother should have made more of his life. He was adept with his hands, able to complete intricate work. He would have made a good surgeon or dentist, but had never expressed any desire for the work. The bottle of wine passed between them, but Filippos made sure he drank sparingly. He did not want to go to bed and fall into a deep sleep. He had other things to do.

Finally Filippos yawned. 'I've really enjoyed this evening, Andreas, but I must go to bed. I've had a busy week at work and the drive was longer than I remembered.'

Andreas nodded. 'Yes, it's a fair distance from Heraklion.' He picked up the bottle of wine and tipped the remainder into his glass. 'I'll finish this; then I'll be off myself.'

Filippos had waited, sitting fully dressed, apart from his shoes, on the edge of his nephew's bed, for over three hours. It had seemed an age before he heard his brother's tread on the stairs, his whispered conversation with his wife and finally the creak of their bed as he lay down. Through the wall Filippos now heard him snoring. Stealthily Filippos had opened the door to his room and crept along the passage hoping his brother and sister-in-law slept soundly. If he woke them he would have to say he needed the bathroom and had mistaken the door.

He turned the handle quietly and gently, hoping the door would not squeak as he pushed it open. He stood there motionless, listening to Eva's rhythmic breathing and Andreas's snores. He looked around the room. Andreas had not closed the shutters or hung up his clothes, not wanting to inadvertently disturb their small son. His jacket was draped over the back of a chair and his trousers and underwear were on the seat.

In his stockinged feet Filippos entered the room, watching the sleeping couple as he moved towards the chair. He ran his hands over the jacket pockets and felt the shape of Andreas's wallet. Swiftly he withdrew it and opened it. He was not interested in robbing him of the few euro notes it contained, he only wanted his identity card and driving licence. Andreas would probably not notice that they were missing for days, maybe weeks and when he did realise he would probably think he had lost them.

With the precious cards in his hand Filippos retreated silently back to his room. He placed the identity card and licence inside his own wallet, picked up his shoes and crept down the stairs. He took the note he had written earlier from his pocket and laid it on the table along with a ten euro note and anchored both with the empty wine bottle.

> *So sorry I had to leave. Had an emergency call from the hospital. Thanks for a most enjoyable evening. We must meet again very soon. Good luck with your business. Buy something for Stelios.*

He unlocked the front door and closed it carefully, walking swiftly along the pavement and around the corner to where his car was parked. Once he had left the suburbs of Rethymnon behind him he began to feel confident that his plan would work.

Filippos arrived back in Heraklion shortly after six in the morning. He avoided the car park and left his car a short distance away from the harbour. Pulling his two cases behind him he pushed open the door of an early morning cafe and ordered coffee and a croissant. He dunked his croissant in the coffee and checked his plans for his journey again. He would spend two, maybe three days on Santorini before taking another ferry to Paros. The following day he would travel to Sifnos and on to Serifos. From there he could ferry to Kithnos and travel by Flying Dolphin to Piraeus. He would give the impression he was a tourist, having travelled around some of the islands and was now making his way home after his holiday.

He smiled to himself. He could be a tourist if he wished. He had no intention of returning to the hospital in Heraklion and his time was his own. All he needed was to evade the police and he was sure they would expect him to fly to Athens. By the time they realised that he had not left the country by air and thought to check the ferries he would not be remembered by the companies as a customer. If they assumed he was hiding on Crete they could search for ever and would not find him.

It was galling that he had had to leave his car behind, but he could always hire one in Piraeus, using his brother's identity. He planned to spend a couple of days in Piraeus investigating the availability of some work. He was not prepared to do manual labour on the docks and could not apply to the hospital, but he was willing to work in an office, taverna or shop for a few months just to have an income. If there was nothing available he would move on to Athens where he was certain there would be something to suit him.

Inspector Solomakis had driven to Filippos Melanakis's apartment with an arrest warrant in his pocket. He had telephoned the hospital earlier and asked to speak to the doctor, only to be told that the man had called in saying he was unwell and hoped to be back on duty within a couple of days. The Inspector was annoyed. They should have kept the man in custody until they had received the DNA results, but he was also aware that he could be sued for wrongful arrest should the DNA samples taken from Dimitra not be a match with the doctor. Both Vasi Iliopolakis's lawyer and father had threatened to sue him when he had kept the man in jail for only a few hours. He could not risk that happening again.

The Inspector had received no reply when he knocked and rang at the doctor's door and he turned his attention to the adjacent apartments, hoping the doctor's immediate neighbours might be able to furnish him with information. The occupants of all four apartments shook their heads. The doctor was a quiet, reserved man, they did not know him well, but one woman did volunteer the information that she thought he had gone away on holiday.

'I was waiting in the lobby for the lift. When it arrived the doctor was in there and had two large cases with him. I thought about asking him where he was going and wishing him an enjoyable holiday, but he seemed to be in a hurry. I just smiled at him and got into the lift to come up to this floor. I think he came back after a short while. I can hear the lift when I'm in my apartment and someone certainly used it about ten minutes later and got out at this level. I didn't open my door and look out, but I'm sure it would have been too early for my neighbours to be returning from work.'

'Did you hear the lift being used again later?'

She shook her head. 'I finished putting my groceries away, then had a shower. I put the television on whilst I was preparing a meal for my husband and myself and I can't hear the lift then.'

Inspector Solomakis made a note of the woman's name and her apartment number. 'Should you see him return I'd be grateful if you would call me at the police station.'

'Is he in trouble?'

The Inspector smiled. 'We just want to ask him some routine questions. Nothing to worry about unduly. If I don't hear from you I'll try to catch up with him in a couple of week's time.'

On leaving the apartment block Thranassis had visited the hospital to see what personal information he could ascertain about the doctor and found he had a brother in Rethymnon. Hoping Filippos Melanakis had taken refuge with him he had driven to the town and paid the man a visit.

Andreas Melanakis was puzzled by the Inspector's visit. He had no idea why his brother should have left Heraklion without sending word to him.

'The last time I saw him he certainly didn't mention to me that he was going on holiday. He came for the weekend and had to leave in the early hours due to an emergency call from the hospital.'

'When was this? Do you remember the date?'

Andreas nodded. 'I can tell you exactly. I signed the agreement for my shop at the beginning of the next week. I've my own business now.'

Thranassis raised his eyebrows. He had not expected the

doctor's brother to be a shop keeper. 'What kind of business are you in?'

'I frame pictures, prints and photographs. Make up the frame myself to the customer's requirements, large or small, antique or modern, gold, silver or coloured; whatever they want to fit in with their decor.' Andreas beamed proudly.

Thranassis took out his notebook and made a note of the date Andreas supplied. 'Maybe I could have the name of your shop also. My wife's been mentioning having some of the grandchildren's photos decently framed.'

'Certainly. It would be my pleasure.' Andreas drew out a pack of cards from his pocket and handed one to Thranassis. 'Why are you looking for my brother? Has he done something wrong?'

'We just want to eliminate him from our enquiries. Here is where I can be reached should he decide to contact you. Thank you for your help.'

Andreas nodded. 'You're welcome.' He took out his wallet. He would put the card safely in the compartment where he kept his identity card and driving licence. As he slipped it inside he realised the compartment was empty. He certainly did not remember moving the important documents elsewhere. He riffled through his notes, but they were not amongst them, nor in the other compartment where he kept his credit card. What had he done with them?

'Something wrong?' Thranassis had noticed the look of consternation on the man's face.

'My driving licence and I.D. are missing.'

Thranassis raised his eyebrows. 'When did you last have occasion to use them?'

Andreas shook his head. 'No idea. I expect I used my licence when I renewed the tax or insurance on my car. I had to produce my I.D. when I approached the bank for my loan for the shop. It was only a formality; the manager knows me.'

'Would you have put them in a jacket pocket?'

'No, I make sure I always have them in my wallet. I was caught out once and had to spend the night in jail. I wouldn't want that to happen again.'

'Not the most pleasant place,' agreed Thranassis. 'Thank you for your help. I'll leave you to your work. Don't forget to call me if your brother contacts you with his new address.'

Andreas nodded, hardly registering the Inspector's words. Where was his identity card and driving licence?

Thranassis Solomakis was thoroughly annoyed with himself. He should have arranged surveillance on the doctor. He had spent valuable police time asking the airports to check their manifestos for a man of his name travelling out of Crete without success. Now he had a suspicion that Filippos Melanakis was using his brother's I.D. to evade the law. He would have to ask the airports to check their lists of travellers again.

If he had no results his only recourse left open was to circularise the police stations and hospitals on all the islands and the mainland with the doctor's description and the reason he was wanted. If another young lady was found to have been viciously raped it would be more than likely that the crime had been committed by the same man, and he could be residing in the vicinity. Men like him could only control themselves for a certain amount of time before they attacked a woman again.

Filippos Melanakis had booked into a cheap bed and breakfast in Piraeus and walked the streets to investigate the possibility of any employment in the area. He could not apply to a hospital for a position without revealing his true identity and producing the certificates he had proving his qualifications. He had no other trade that he was capable of carrying out which limited his options.

He made enquiries at various car hire firms in the hope they needed staff, but was told they needed no one. He visited hotels and asked if they required reception staff assuring them he was willing to work unsocial hours, but when he admitted he had no previous experience he was turned away. At the end of two fruitless days he returned to his room dejected, but determined to take the metro to Athens the following day and hope he would have more luck in the city.

Again he was refused employment at the car hires and hotels and began asking at the tavernas in the vain hope that he could find work as a waiter. Everywhere he asked he was reminded that it was the end of the season in the islands and many of the Athenians who had spent the summer elsewhere would be returning to their winter employment. They would take priority over an unknown and inexperienced applicant. By mid afternoon he was wondering if he should have stayed on Crete, just moving on to Chania until he felt confident the police would have given up their search for him.

He sat in Amonia Square, eating a sandwich and cursing his luck. He had managed to control himself for over a year, sometimes being rather rough with a woman, but he had not had one of his completely uncontrollable outbursts until Dimitra had taunted him unmercifully. Had she succumbed to him earlier she would not have suffered so drastically at his hands.

He watched the tourists dispassionately as they milled around him, much of their conversation unintelligible to him. A couple sat at the table next to his and opened their map. The man placed a cross in a strategic position.

'That's the Acropolis and Agora done, tomorrow we'll go on that trip to Cape Sounion. Thursday we have that other trip booked to Mycenae and that leaves just the museum before we go home.'

'I'd like time to do some shopping,' frowned his partner.

'You have tomorrow morning. We don't go to Sounion until after lunch and I doubt we'll be in the museum all day.'

Filippos lost interest in their plans. He had not thought of approaching the museum or Acropolis to ask if they needed attendants. It would be monotonous and boring sitting in a room all day, just watching people did no damage to any of the artefacts on display, but he could cope with that for a few months. The pay would be poor compared with the salary he was used to receiving, but it would cover the cost of a cheap room. When he decided all interest in him was lost he would take a flight to Canada and be able to claim to have been in regular employment. Once there he was confident he would be able to resume his own identity and be able to apply to a hospital for work.

He finished his sandwich and drank the remains of his beer, leaving the wrapper and bottle on the table as he walked away. The museums would be closed by now, but he could visit the Acropolis and enquire about availability before he caught the metro back to Piraeus. If he succeeded in his application he would see if he could find a cheap room in the suburbs of Athens to avoid the continual travelling on the metro.

Vasi e-mailed Saffron with the news that Cathy was not progressing as quickly as the doctors had anticipated.

"No doubt her previous injuries and her arthritis are hindering her. She says it is not so painful to move around now and is using two sticks, even in the apartment. She is able to get into the car and most days Pappa takes her out for a ride, but the weather has not been good. You have only seen Crete during the summer months, but you would not believe how cold and wet it is here now. We have the heating on and wear thick jumpers and coats when we go out.

Barbara decided not to go to Heraklion. They have accepted that they will have an addition to their family in May. Yiorgo would like this one to be a little girl, but with three boys already he feels it is unlikely. I have been paying him to work on the 'Flora' at the weekends and he says he is saving that towards the cost of the new baby. Barbara's cousin has promised she can have the buggy that is too small for her daughter now and also her cot. That will be a help as they had not saved any of the equipment they had for the boys as they did not plan another child. I am not sure if any of them were planned!

Dimitra has said that when the conferences are finished she is considering going to Athens. She still hardly leaves the hotel and says she does not feel safe any longer in Crete. I cannot make her stay here, but it will make life very difficult for me if she does leave. I had hoped I would be able to rearrange my visit to you for January, but my father is still unwilling to say when he will become responsible for the conference arrangements again.

I am hoping my father will return to the Central very soon. I am continually driving down to Hersonissos or Aghios Nikolaos to check on work that has taken place in those hotels. I do not know if I would be able to manage all the hotels on my own once the season starts. I have good managers that I trust, but they expect me to solve any problems that arise. Of course, the idea that Marjorie had for my father's house I have put to one side. Even if my father was agreeable to turning it into a holiday centre I would not be able to give it my attention at the moment."

Saffron replied to Vasi's e-mails and suggested that Cathy consulted a specialist to see if there was any new drug available that would help her arthritis, telling him that sometimes a steroid injection could be effective. She did not press him to make a definite date to visit England. She was convinced now that Vasi was using his father's attention to Cathy as an excuse to cancel his visit.

Saffron was worried when she was called to the administration offices at the hospital. She hoped no one had complained about the treatment she had given them. A complaint always meant a lengthy enquiry and often the doctor in question had to be suspended whilst it took place. She disliked Sean and was relieved when she was greeted with a friendly smile and asked to take a seat.

'There's nothing at all for you to worry about,' Sean assured her. 'I've been asked to put a proposition before you. Feel free to refuse, but we do need your decision within a day or two. It had been arranged that Janet from the Royal London would visit Nigeria for six months. She would work with the doctors over there instructing them in our techniques for rectifying bone abnormalities and the treatment of difficult fractures. In return their top man would come over here and we would make him conversant with procedures. At the end of six months he would return and take over from where Janet left off.'

Saffron relaxed. If she was asked to take the Nigerian doctor under her wing that would be no problem and meant the hospital were pleased with her work.

'Unfortunately,' continued Sean, 'Janet has just informed us that she will probably be unable to go to Nigeria. Her mother is undergoing diagnostic tests for cancer and she feels she needs to be here to support her if the results are as they fear. The Royal London asked if we could provide a replacement if necessary. We looked at our list of specialists. Vince is married and it wouldn't be fair or practical to ask him to go away for that length of time, Ashkar would probably be refused a passport as he came here as an asylum seeker, the other members of the unit are not sufficiently qualified and are still working under guidance. That left you.'

Saffron gasped. 'Me? Go to Nigeria?' She shook her head. 'I don't know. I can't make a decision like that immediately.'

'Of course not. We can give you a couple of days to consider, but we do need to know as soon as possible. If Janet does have to finally pull out we need to have a replacement doctor immediately available so we can keep our commitment.'

'If I agreed when would I have to go?'

'No definite date is set yet, but towards the end of April or the beginning of May.'

'So I might not return until October?'

Sean nodded. 'Is that a problem?'

'Suppose I was unhappy over there?'

Sean shrugged. 'I don't see why you should be unhappy. You'll be provided with accommodation inside the hospital grounds, the Nigerians speak English so you shouldn't have any difficulties with communication and it is only for six months.'

'Suppose I had a family emergency?'

'We would obviously bring you back immediately and you could return when you had dealt with it.'

Saffron raised her eyebrows. 'I am thinking of my stepmother. If she was taken ill like Janet's mother I would want to be back in England permanently, not just on a quick visit.'

Sean sighed. 'Do you have any reason to believe she may be ill?'

Saffron shook her head.

'Then we would have to cope with that if such a situation arose.' Sean clasped his hands on the desk in front of her. 'I know I have said we need your decision as quickly as possible, but there is always the possibility that Janet may be able to go as originally planned and we will have to disappoint you.'

Saffron continually mulled the proposition over whilst she worked. It was an exciting idea and she was very tempted to agree to take Janet's place if necessary, but she would have to talk to Marjorie.

'When will you know for certain?' asked Marjorie.

Saffron shrugged. 'When Janet's mother has the results of her tests, I expect. If there's nothing really wrong with her then Janet will go as originally agreed. They just want me to be on stand-by. I'm not getting my hopes up or making any plans yet.'

'You'd like the opportunity, though?'

Saffron nodded. 'I'm sure it would be a very worthwhile experience, but if you're not happy with the idea then I'll turn it down now.'

'It's your career. If you were transferred to a hospital in Scotland for six months you wouldn't be able to commute. You'd have to live up there.'

'It would be a bit closer, though.' Saffron smiled wryly. 'At least Nigeria should be warmer than Scotland. So you think I should tell Sean tomorrow that if Janet is unable to go then I can take her place?'

'Suppose Vasi is able to visit just as you are about to leave?'

Saffron shrugged. 'I cannot run my life around Vasi, his father and Cathy. I won't tell him until I'm certain that I'll be going. He may be able to visit us next month.'

Marjorie nodded. She also had a suspicion that Vasi was using Cathy's accident as an excuse not to visit. Saffron had not confided her feelings towards him to her, but Vasi might not wish for the relationship to progress.

'If I am told that I will definitely be going I ought to give you some lessons on the computer. I'll take a lap top with me and that way we'll be able to write to each other every week. Letters could take ages.'

'I could always telephone you.'

Saffron shook her head. 'That could be unreliable. You can't always pick up a signal in some countries. I'm sure I'll be able to give you number where I can be contacted in an emergency and it would be better for you to try that if you needed to speak to me urgently.'

Marjorie smiled to herself. She knew Saffron well enough to know that she had made up her mind to accept the Nigerian exchange appointment should she be asked to take Janet's place.

'If I am asked to go I shall apply for some leave so I can visit my grandmother. She may not be around when I return. I can always tell Vasi my plans whilst I'm there. I'm sure you'll be welcome to go over and stay with the family again this year. In fact you could stay for as long as you wanted. I won't be around and having to be back at the hospital on a certain date.'

'I'll think about it,' Marjorie smiled. 'They may not want me there without you and probably wouldn't want me to stay any longer than two weeks. It must disrupt their routine to have someone else that they have to consider around all the time.'

'I'm sure they wouldn't mind. You're no trouble. You just fit in with whatever they propose doing or sit on the beach and read.'

March 2008

Saffron had debated whether to telephone Vasi and let him know her intention to visit or leave her arrival as a surprise for him, finally deciding it would be more sensible to tell him. She did not want to arrive in the early hours of the morning at the Central only to find he was down in Elounda.

'I will meet you,' Vasi promised.

'There's no need, truly. I can get a taxi.'

'You will not. I will be waiting for you when you have collected your luggage.'

'If you're sure, Vasi.'

'Of course I am sure. I do not want you running down to Elounda to stay with your relatives.'

Saffron bit at her lip. 'I have to go down to see my grandmother.'

'Is there a problem?'

'No, I just need to see her.'

'I will tell my father that I need to visit one of the hotels in the area and I will drive you down.'

'I won't have a lot of time, Vasi. I don't arrive until about six in the morning on Saturday and I have to leave at mid-day on Monday.'

'Would you be able to visit Cathy?'

'Maybe I could do that in the morning before I have to be at the airport,' Saffron answered cautiously. 'I'd like to see how she's progressing.'

As the 'plane taxied to halt Saffron debated the wisdom of her action. It would have been easier to telephone her grandmother and send Vasi an e-mail to say she planned to spend some months abroad. As her passport was checked she caught a glimpse of Vasi standing waiting for her and her heart gave its customary leap of pleasure.

He approached her, his hands outstretched in welcome and took her in his arms. He released her and lifted her small case easily. 'We will go to the Central and I will give you breakfast. Then we will make our plans for the weekend.'

'How is Cathy?'

'She is progressing.'

'Is your father still spending all his time with her?'

Vasi nodded. 'I have an idea that he is using Cathy's accident as a good excuse. He prefers to be at home with her rather than at the hotel.'

'That's fine now, but surely he will be needed at the hotel in the summer months?'

'He says he will return when the tourist season begins, but it will be too late then for me to visit England. I have told him that I am taking you down to Elounda tomorrow to visit your family and I will use the time to call in at the house and the hotels whilst I am there to check that all is in order. It will save me from driving down later in the week. '

Saffron nodded. She felt incredibly tired. Although it was six in the morning in Heraklion her body had not adjusted to the time difference. She closed her eyes as Vasi drove and was surprised when they drew up at the Central.

'That was quick.'

Vasi smiled. 'You have been asleep. Maybe you would like to go to bed for an hour or so and have breakfast later?'

Saffron shook her head. 'No, I actually feel better now I've slept for a few minutes. It's the two hour time difference. My body is telling me I should still be asleep. I can always have a nap this afternoon if I feel the need.'

'You are sure? I do not mind delaying our reunion if you are too tired.'

Saffron glanced at him. What kind of reunion did he have in mind?

'I think we need to sit and talk for a while.'

Vasi nodded. 'When we have had breakfast we will talk.' He opened the car door for Saffron and lifted her hand luggage from the back seat. 'Come, I have booked a room in your name, for respectability, you understand.'

Vasi collected a swipe card from reception and ushered Saffron into the lift. 'We will go to my room first and ask to have breakfast sent up,' he said decisively. 'We can make your room look used as we did before with the suite.' He raised his eyebrows in an unspoken question and Saffron nodded.

Saffron drank the last of her coffee and relaxed back in the chair. 'That does feel better. Maybe having a meal puts your body back into the correct time zone.'

Vasi smiled at her. 'It is good to have you here, Saffie.' Vasi pulled her to her feet and enfolded her in his arms. 'I have wanted to hold you so much.' He kissed her forehead. 'I realised after you left in October just how much you meant to me. I love you, Saffie. I decided when I visited you in November I would speak to you. Will you marry me, Saffie?'

'Marry you?' Saffron jerked out of his embrace. 'Oh, Vasi, why didn't you ask me earlier?' Saffron felt a lump coming into her throat and swallowed hard

'Saffie, you had been married to a man who was sent to jail. I did not know at that time if I would suffer the same fate. It would not have been right to ask you then. When it was confirmed that I had no charge to answer I felt I should be with you when I asked you. To speak over a telephone is too impersonal for such an important question.'

Saffron shook her head. 'No, I mean, I can't, not now, it's too late.' A tear dribbled down the side of her nose.

Vasi frowned. 'You do not care for me?'

'You know I do, Vasi.' Saffron brushed away the tear and gave a deep sigh. 'If you had come to England in November and asked me then it would have been different.'

'You have met someone else?'

'No, there's no one else,' Saffron managed to smile. 'Come and sit down, Vasi. I need to explain why I am here.' She led Vasi to the sofa and pulled him down beside her.

'You are cross with me because I did not come to England? I could not help that, Saffie. Cathy did not fall intentionally.'

'I'm sure she didn't, but it happened nearly five months ago. I would have thought by now Cathy would have recovered sufficiently for your father to let you have two weeks away.'

Vasi took Saffron's hand. 'Believe me, if there had been any way I could have come to England to see you I would have done so.'

Saffron sighed. 'I kept hoping you would come and every week you had excuses that made it impossible for you. I began to think that you did not care.'

'Saffie! You thought I had just had a holiday affair with you? I asked you before to stay for longer so we could get to know each other and you refused. This time we did get to know each other. I did not realise until you left how much I cared for you. I hoped you felt the same.'

Saffron shook her head. 'I can't.'

'Why not? What have I done? Is it because I did not come to England as I intended?'

'No, Vasi, you've done nothing,' Saffron was forced to smile at his anguish. 'I have been asked to go to Nigeria to work for six months.'

'Nigeria? Nigeria in Africa?'

Saffron nodded. 'This is why I have come over this weekend. To tell you and also to visit my grandmother.'

'Why didn't you tell me before?' The hurt in Vasi's voice was not lost on Saffron.

'It was only confirmed last week. A colleague was supposed to go and her mother is ill so she has had to cancel. Until it was certain that I would be going I saw no reason to tell anyone. It is only a six month exchange visit. I'll be back in October.'

'Do you have to go, Saffie? Would you consider cancelling your visit to Nigeria and stay here and marry me?'

Saffron shook her head. 'I have my injections next week and all the paperwork is in order. I can't possibly back out now. Had you spoken to me earlier I would not have agreed to be the replacement doctor for Janet.'

Vasi gazed at her intently. 'Being a doctor means more to you than being my wife?'

'No, Vasi, I admit I've only ever wanted to be a doctor and I love my work. I wish I had never signed that contract.'

'And you would have married me?'

'I'm not sure, Vasi' Saffron hesitated. 'It's not an easy decision to make.'

'What is so difficult to decide? You say you care for me.'

Saffron twisted her fingers together nervously. 'Please understand, Vasi, you've taken me by surprise. At the moment I don't know what I want. I love being here and spending time with you and my family, but it's being on holiday. It isn't a real life. You cannot spend all day taking me out. You have to manage the hotels and what would I do with myself whilst you're working?'

'Cathy did not have this problem when she married my father.'

'The circumstances were very different. Cathy had her friend here with her. They spent time together whilst your father was working and he had only two hotels at that time.'

'You could visit your family.'

Saffron shook her head. 'They are busy. They cannot spend all their time entertaining me, besides, I have to consider Marjorie.'

'Marjorie? She would prevent you from marrying me?'

Saffron shook her head. 'No, of course not, but I cannot leave her alone in England. She made tremendous sacrifices so I could go to Medical School. I had no idea how short of money we were until I began to earn and was able to pay her back.'

Vasi was about to interrupt and Saffron placed her finger on his lip. 'She supported me through my stupid affair with Martin and again when I was married to Ranjit. She is supporting me in my decision to go to Nigeria, although I'm not sure she's happy with the idea. I cannot just turn round and say I am going to marry you and come to Crete to live. It would be abandoning her. I've always promised myself that I would look after her when she became old. I would never let her go into a home unless it was essential.'

'She can come here with you. She would be welcome.'

'She may not want to live in Crete. She doesn't speak the language and she has no real friends here.'

'She would have you.'

'She needs more than me around. In England she has friends she visits, she goes to the Women's Institute and a Bridge club. She is always busy. What would happen to her house? She can't just abandon it.'

'She could sell her house.'

'And suppose she was unhappy and wished to return to England? Where would she live? No, Vasi, I have to consider far more than just giving up being a doctor.'

Vasi sighed heavily and withdrew his hand. 'I am sorry. We will forget I asked you.'

Saffron reached out and took Vasi's hand back in her own. 'Will you give me some time, Vasi? We have this weekend and then I will be away. It will give me time to think. I promise I will give you an answer when I return if you are willing to wait, that is. I don't want to make another wrong decision. I would rather hurt you now by saying no than marrying you and then deciding later I wanted to return to England.'

Vasi drove Saffron down to Elounda on Sunday morning. Saffron had slept during the afternoon and then she and Vasi had talked until late in the evening. Vasi had not tried to talk Saffron out of her decision to go to Nigeria, for which she was grateful. Instead he had questioned her about the work she would do there and how beneficial she thought it would be for the Nigerians. Saffron explained that she would demonstrate the techniques employed in Britain whilst her counterpart at the London hospital would be trained to carry them out. When he returned to Nigeria he would teach his staff how to undertake the procedures. They had spent the night in each other's arms and been reluctant to rise.

'Do you think it would be very awful of me to tell them I didn't arrive until six last night, rather than in the morning?'

Vasi smiled at her. 'What difference does it make?'

'I don't want them to feel hurt that I didn't ask Giovanni to meet me and go straight down to stay with them.'

'It is more convenient for me to take you down. I have to visit the hotels and the house, but I was not able to spend the time to drive down yesterday.'

Saffron raised her eyebrows. 'Really? What was so important that you could not drive down yesterday?' she asked mischievously.

'You have forgotten? Maybe I should take you to my father's house to remind you.'

Saffron shook her head. 'I was teasing. I have to spend today with my relatives and see my grandmother.'

'I am sure I will need to be back in Heraklion at a reasonable time this evening for a business meeting.'

Saffron looked at him. 'Do you mean that?'

'Being back at a reasonable time? Yes.'

'No, having a meeting.'

'I have a very important engagement with a young lady. I plan to take her for a meal and then I shall invite her back to my room where I hope to persuade her to spend the night.'

Saffron giggled. 'I don't think she'll need an awful lot of

persuading, Vasi.'

Vasi removed his hand from the steering wheel and squeezed Saffron's. 'I'm pleased to hear it. I am no good at the small talk that leads to seduction. Now, I must concentrate. This is where Alecos had his accident. I do not wish to follow his example.'

Saffron was not surprised when she reached her family's house to find that everyone was there to greet her except John. She settled herself next to her grandmother and talked exclusively to her for the first ten minutes, whilst Vasi drank the coffee that had been pressed into his hand and arranged to collect Saffron at five in the afternoon.

'Why so early?' asked Bryony. 'You're not leaving until tomorrow.'

Saffron glanced at Vasi. She felt guilty at making excuses. 'My flight leaves early. It makes sense for me to be in Heraklion.'

'I will need to speak my father this evening and it will be an opportunity for Cathy to talk to Saffron about her problems. Saffie insisted I brought her down here to visit you today and this was the only way it could be arranged.' Vasi spoke firmly.

'It really is a flying visit,' Saffron blushed. 'I haven't told you yet, but I'm going away for six months to Nigeria.'

Curious eyes looked at her and Giovanni translated quickly for his aunt, uncle and mother.

'Nigeria?' Marianne looked at Saffron in surprise. 'What on earth are you going there for?'

'It's to do with a hospital exchange.'

Vasi laid a hand on her shoulder. 'I will leave now. You can tell everyone your plans and I will return later. Thank you for the coffee, Marianne.'

'So what is all this about you going to Nigeria?' asked Bryony as soon as Vasi had left them. 'What does Vasi say about it and why didn't you tell us before?'

'It has nothing to do with Vasi,' replied Saffron indignantly and blushed again. 'I didn't say anything because I didn't really think I would be asked to go. Could I have another cup of coffee, please, and I'll tell you exactly how it happened.'

Giovanni translated whilst Saffron talked until she finally said, 'That's it. I'm not sure how I feel about going. I know it will be medically beneficial and I'm very fortunate to be able to have the experience, but I do feel horribly nervous.'

Annita patted Saffron's hand. 'I'm sure you have nothing to be nervous about. I'm going to have a rest now; let me know when lunch is ready.'

'What about Marjorie?' asked Marianne as Annita walked with the help of her sticks to her bedroom. 'How does she feel about you going away?'

'We've talked about it and she says it's no different from me being transferred to a hospital somewhere in England that's too far away from home for me to commute, and it is only for six months.'

'Doesn't she mind being left alone? I would have hated it if Marcus had been sent away anywhere in the States for six months and I wouldn't have seen him.' Bryony shuddered at the thought.

'She has her friends, and I'm not usually around during the day. It will only be evenings and weekends when she's alone.'

'She'll be welcome to come here,' offered Giovanni.

Saffron smiled at him gratefully. 'I'm sure she would appreciate an invitation to come out in May or when it would suit you. I'm planning to ask Cathy if Marjorie could spend a few days with her. It could help pass the time for Cathy whilst Vasilis is at the hotels. Now that is enough about me. Tell me what has been happening over here since I last visited. You are all bad about sending me e-mails.'

Marianne shrugged. 'Not very much. John is away doing his National Service, but you know that.'

'Is he enjoying the army? He seemed quite enthusiastic about the prospect when I was here last.'

Marianne shook her head. 'Not really. He says it is so boring when he has to be on guard duty. He must be freezing sometimes as he just has to stand there. He's already asked if he can have his time shortened as he is the only son and needed in his father's business.'

'Can he do that?' asked Saffron in surprise. 'In England if you enter the services you have to sign to say you will stay in for a certain amount of time and if you hate the life it can be very difficult and expensive to leave.'

'It's different here. You have to enter one of the services and usually you're expected to serve for at least a year. They do make exceptions and shorten your duty if your family depend upon your income or need your help in their business.'

Saffron raised her eyebrows. 'I know John helps out all the time, but you're hardly dependent upon him.'

'Giovanni will say we need him during the tourist season. I think it doubtful that they will believe him; they'll say we can employ extra staff and John will have to serve his full term. I think he's most put out that he won't be around when Nicola comes over.'

'What about the dog they found? Did anyone ever claim him?

Marianne shook her head. 'Dimitris is still looking after him. He's become very attached to him.'

'How is Grandma? I didn't spend as much time with her as I had intended the last time I was here. I know I could have picked up the telephone and told all of you my plans and you would have understood, but I felt I must come and see Grandma. I might not have another opportunity.'

Marianne shrugged. 'No different from the last time you saw her. For her age she's remarkably fit and mentally alert. She gets tired, of course. She insisted on being up early today to see you when you arrived, that's why she's gone back for a nap. She could have had at least another hour in bed.'

'It was good of you to make the effort,' Giovanni smiled. 'Are you sure you can't stay any longer? Not even over night? I could drive you to the airport tomorrow.'

'Thank you, Giovanni, but I've promised to see Cathy tomorrow morning.'

'I thought Vasi said you were going this evening?' said Bryony innocently.

Saffron blushed. 'I have to fit in with Vasi's arrangements. I was fortunate to be able to come just for the weekend. I insisted I had to come to see my grandmother and finally the hospital authorities agreed on the condition that I was back by Monday morning. I need to start having my injections next week and they have to be spaced out. I just hope I don't get any horrible reaction to them.'

'Are you likely to?'

'Some people can be laid low for a week; others just feel a bit unwell for twenty four hours. You never know how you will react.' Saffron did not admit that she was dreading the vaccinations.

'What do you need?' asked Marcus.

'Yellow Fever, Hepatitis A and B and Typhoid. Fortunately my Tetanus is in date, so that's one less to worry about. I shall be living in the city so I shouldn't be exposed to any of the parasitic problems they have in the countryside. I'll have to take malaria tablets, of course.'

'I'm glad we don't have the mosquitoes that carry malaria here. It's bad enough if you just get bitten.' Bryony rubbed her arm.

'You should always be careful,' Saffron warned her. 'It depends where they have been before they bite you. They could give you something nasty that starts up an infection.'

'They never seem to go near Marcus,' complained Bryony.

Marcus smiled. 'I have a tough skin or maybe I just don't taste good to them.'

'I've never been bitten whilst I've been in Greece,' observed Saffron. 'Why are we talking about mosquitoes anyway? Tell me what you have been doing during the winter months. Anything exciting?'

Marianne shook her head. 'Giovanni and Marcus have been repairing and redecorating the chalets ready for the season and Bryony and I are giving the house a thorough clean through whilst we have the opportunity.'

'How are your bookings?'

'Much the same as usual. There's nothing for the first week yet, but enquiries are coming in for later in the season. A lot of people leave it until the last minute to make a decision.'

'How is Uncle Yannis's shop? Are they busy during the winter?'

Marianne smiled. 'They leave a notice on the door with his telephone number. If anyone does want to buy anything they call him and Uncle Yannis makes a special trip in. It isn't worth their while to be there every day when the tourists have left. Aunt Ourania spends the winter months looking at catalogues and deciding what new stock she wants to order. A couple of weeks before the season starts Giovanni and Marcus will go in and give everywhere a good clean and a lick of paint if necessary. Aunt Ourania will rearrange the old stock and unpack the new and then all they have to do is sit back and wait for customers.'

'And Marisa still goes in with them each day?'

'Yes, thank goodness. I don't know what she'd do with herself if she was here at the house all day long.'

Saffron nodded soberly. This was her concern if she decided to marry Vasi and Marjorie came to live in Crete. How would either of them occupy their days?

Marianne and Bryony cleared the table after a late lunch, refusing to let Saffron help. 'You sit and talk to Grandma.' Marianne lowered her voice. 'I know Uncle Yannis and Aunt Ourania are ready to go for their siesta and I expect Marisa will also go to her room. Giovanni and Marcus are working on a new accounting programme and I'm sure they're both desperate to get back to the computer.'

Saffron smiled gratefully. She was relieved that she could have some time alone with her grandmother and wheeled her across to the lounge and took a seat beside her.

'Are you running away, Saffie?' asked Annita immediately.

'Running away? Of course not. What gave you that idea?'

'I've seen the way Vasi looks at you. Last time you were here you spent all your time with him.' Annita held up her hand as Saffron was about to protest. 'I'm not complaining. You should be spending time with people of your own age, not old women like me. Are you frightened that he will ask more than you are prepared to give?'

A slow flush crept into Saffron's cheeks. 'Please don't tell the rest of the family, but Vasi has asked me to marry him.'

'And what was your answer?'

'I haven't given him one yet. I've said I will think about it seriously whilst I am away.'

'So being a doctor means more to you than staying here with Vasi?'

Saffron shook her head. 'There are other problems, Grandma. I don't speak Greek.'

'I went to America with your grandfather and we neither of us spoke the language.'

'You were together and you also knew that if you were unhappy you could both come back. Vasi took me by surprise when he asked me to marry him. I feel I need time to consider and make up my mind.'

'What's to consider? Either you love him or you don't.' Annita felt a pang of guilt. She had asked Elias for time to consider his proposal of marriage to her. She had returned to Crete and persuaded her father to take her to Spinalonga to say goodbye to Yannis before agreeing to marry the microbiologist she worked with and going to America.

'Marjorie. I can't just leave her alone in England. Vasi understands that and has said she would be welcome to come with me. Would she want to leave England and would she be happy here? How would either of us occupy our days?'

'Are you making Marjorie an excuse?'

'I don't want to make any excuses.' Saffron twisted her fingers together nervously. 'I just don't want to make a mistake. I don't want to hurt Vasi. I do care for him.'

Annita sighed. 'Only you know if you care more for him than you do for Marjorie.'

'Grandma! That isn't fair. I care for both of them in different ways. Marjorie was like a mother to me and I can't just leave her alone as she gets older.'

Annita sniffed. 'My girls seemed to have no such scruples and I understood the problems Andreas had with Laurie. Bryony was the only one who bothered with me. I would probably have died during Hurricane Katrina if she and Marcus hadn't taken me away from that care home and looked after me.'

'I'm sure you're exaggerating, Grandma.'

Annita shook her head. 'I'm sure the staff would have done their best, but they would not have been able to move all of us to safety. I'm just grateful they managed to salvage some of my belongings. Are you religious?'

Saffron looked at her grandmother in surprise. The question was completely unexpected. 'Not really. I used to go to church when I was in the Girl Guides, but once I left the organisation I went less frequently and when I was at Medical School I stopped going altogether.'

'Shame. A Priest can be a source of good advice.'

'I have to rely on my own judgement, then I have no one else to blame if I make a mistake.' Saffron gave a shaky laugh. 'You won't mention our conversation to the others, will you?' asked Saffron anxiously. 'It would only embarrass Vasi if he thought I had discussed it with everyone.'

'I'll not tell them. Just make sure you make the right decision and if you do decide to marry him make sure you do it fairly soon.

I'd like to be around.'

'Oh, Grandma, I'm sure you'll be with us for years yet.'

Annita shook her head. 'At my age every day is a bonus.'

Saffron sank back in the seat beside Vasi. 'I'm exhausted,' she announced. 'I'm not used to having so many people bombarding me with questions at the same time.'

'Bombing you?' Vasi frowned. 'They were throwing things at you?'

Saffron laughed. 'Of course not. I said bombarding. It means they were asking me questions non-stop for the first hour or so and I was trying to listen to each one and answer it properly. They were interrupting themselves and me so I could hardly think straight. How have you spent your time? Did you discover any problems?'

'Not really. I wish I had asked you about the colour I decided to repaint the hotel rooms in Elounda. It is the wrong shade of green. I thought they would look light and airy, instead they look cold and miserable.'

'What colour were the rooms before?'

'Yellow. It made them look hot in the summer. Now I have to think again.'

'Everywhere looks cold and miserable at the moment. Why not wait until you have seen them when the sun is shining? You might change your mind then. If you still think the colour is wrong you could paint them cream. That would make them look light and airy, but not hot.'

'As always, you have the good ideas.'

'What about the hotel in Aghios Nikolaos?'

'A few small repairs are needed but nothing to be concerned about. I made a list and asked Yiorgo to give it to his father.'

'How is Barbara?'

'Rather large, complaining of heartburn and wondering why she changed her mind about terminating.'

'I'm sure once she has the baby all will be forgiven.'

Vasi smiled. 'I am sure also. She has just had a scan and been told it is definitely a little girl.'

'Oh, I am pleased. After three boys they must be delighted.

Vasi shook his head. 'Now there is a problem regarding her name. Yiorgo does not get on well with Barbara's mother. He wants to call the child Delphine after his mother with Damara as her second name. Barbara says her mother's name should be first.'

Saffron looked at Vasi in horror. 'Poor little mite. Neither Delphine Damara nor Damara Delphine goes well together. Haven't the grandmothers got a second name that could be more suitable?'

'They are both called Maria.'

'There you are then, that's the answer. Call her Maria. That should satisfy both grandmothers and Barbara and Yiorgo can choose a second name they both like.'

Vasi nodded. 'I will suggest it to Yiorgo. You would not think to name a child could cause so much difficulty.'

'What would you do? Have a number system?'

Vasi smiled. 'I would say call the child whatever you wish, but not after me. It is confusing to have the same name as my father. It would be even worse if I had a child with the same name.'

Saffron gave Vasi a sideways look. Was he hinting that if she married him he would expect to have a family? She was already forty two, not the best age to become pregnant, and she had never had an overwhelming desire to be a mother.

'Did you go to see the dogs?'

'They are fine. They are very polite. They always seem pleased to see me, but they really hardly know me. One day I would like a dog again that can be a pet.'

Saffron nodded. She would settle for a dog rather than a child. She caught herself blushing. She had assumed with that thought that she would marry Vasi.

'I am concerned about my father's house. It is sitting there unused. Lambros goes up and tends the garden and cleans the windows, but inside it is unloved. I had planned to speak to Marjorie when I visited you as it was her idea. I hoped then I would be able to return and persuade my father it was a good idea.'

'Marjorie doesn't know anything about the hotel business.'

Vasi smiled. 'I need to have more information from her. What would the guests be expecting? Would she be willing to come and stay over here and supervise for a few weeks? I would not expect her to do any cooking or cleaning, only have a breakfast ready for them each morning. She would greet the guests when they arrived and explain the arrangements to them. She would be available if there was a problem and I should be staying in Aghios Nikolaos or Elounda by then. If I was not available I am sure Giovanni or Marianne would be willing to help if it involved speaking in Greek or advising her.

'Now you are telling me you are going to Nigeria for six months and Marjorie will be alone in England. If my father will agree this season could be a good opportunity to experiment. As no alterations would have been made to the house there would only be four people staying as Marjorie would be using the other bedroom. If it did not work we would not have to do it the following year.'

Saffron frowned. 'I'm not sure how Marjorie would feel. I know you make it sound like an extended holiday for her, but she may not see it that way.'

'You will ask Marjorie how she feels about my proposal? If she is willing to consider it I will talk to her. Her fare would be paid and she would also be paid a wage for the weeks she spent out here.'

Saffron shook her head. 'You think only in terms of business, Vasi. I'm sure if Marjorie agreed she would appreciate her travelling expenses being paid by you, but I'm sure she wouldn't expect to be paid for talking to people and providing them with a breakfast.'

Vasi shrugged. 'That we can discuss later. I still do not know if my father will agree to the idea.'

'If your father wants to keep it as a house rather than run it as a small guest house why don't you rent it out?'

'Rent it? It is not like an apartment building.'

'I'm thinking of families who would like to come to Crete for their holiday. If they have children a hotel can be far too expensive and the self catering accommodation is not always big enough.'

Vasi nodded. 'It is something else I could suggest to my father.' He switched on the windscreen wipers as the low cloud and mist finally gave way to rain.

'With this weather I could think I was in England,' observed Saffron. 'I never expect it to be dull and miserable over here.'

Vasi smiled at her. 'In the summer we say we would like it to rain. We complain that it is too hot and long for it to cool down and rain. In the winter we say it is too wet or too cold and wish for the sun again. If you look up towards the mountains you will see there is a little snow still left on them.'

'Did you have snow down in the towns?'

'No, that rarely happens. One year it was very bad and the snow came down into Elounda. The Lassithi Plateau is often badly affected and the roads are blocked for weeks, but the people expect this and are prepared.'

Saffron shivered, although she was not feeling cold. 'I would hate that. I would rather feel too hot than be cold.'

Vasi stole a glance at her. 'In a short while you may be wishing you were not so hot.'

After Saffron left Annita retired to her room. She was more tired than she was willing to admit. She picked up the photograph of her late husband and ran her finger across the glass.

'Well, Elias, that poor girl has some difficult decisions to make. She obviously cares for Vasi and I'm sure she would make him a good wife, but is she ready to give up her medical career? I'm sure you would not have given up the opportunity to go to New

Orleans if I had refused to go with you. Your research always came before anything else.

'That was a big decision for me to make. I had to leave my family and I never thought I would see them again. As Saffie said, we had each other for support in a strange new country. At least Saffron could return to England quite easily whenever she wanted. Of course, if Marjorie decided to join her over here she probably wouldn't bother to go back. She's a nice girl to be concerned about her stepmother being lonely. I think she is also worried about being lonely over here; nothing to occupy her all day except running a house and preparing a meal. I remember how unhappy I was when we first had the children and I was at home on my own. I was so bored I thought I would go crazy. If my mother had not been willing to look after the children for me I don't know what would have happened.

'Was it the right thing for me to do to leave them and return to work with you? Did they feel neglected and unloved? Maybe that is why Elena is so unconcerned about me. She has inherited my selfish trait. Maria is different, of course. I'm sure the unexpected death of Bernard affected her mentally. We should have insisted she had some psychiatric help to get over the shock. Andreas is caring, but he would be. I don't know where he inherited his genes. I wonder if my brother was gay and that was the reason he became a priest? Anna was just impossible. I doubt if she ever gives me a thought. How Bryony and Saffron turned out to be such lovely girls I will never know.

'I do wish you were still here, Elias. You would be proud of these three granddaughters. You'd like Marcus as well. I'm not saying you wouldn't be proud of Helena or Andrew. They are certainly not bad people. Helena is selfish, like her mother; only concerned with herself; and I haven't seen Andrew for years. He sends me a card at Thanksgiving with a letter. He never seems to be in one place for very long and no one seems to know exactly what he does for a living. I don't even know if he is married or has the same inclinations as his uncle.

'Paul and Mark are strangers to me now. When Helena writes to me she always mentions them and says they have asked after me, but I think that is from conventional politeness. I must remember to ask Marianne what they are doing. She speaks to her mother regularly, so she should know.'

Annita sighed and closed her eyes. She laid Elias's photograph on her lap. 'I'm rambling again, Elias. I was supposed to be telling you about Saffie. She's going away to Nigeria. She's going to show them some of the techniques used in England to correct birth defects in the bone structure. Six months she will be away, so she won't be coming to Crete again until she returns in October. I hope I'll be around to see her then. I'll want to know what she decides about Vasi.'

July 2008

Filippos had found the work as a guard at the Acropolis during the winter months incredibly cold and thoroughly boring. His only duty was to ensure visitors did not pick up any of the stones or rubble that was lying around and tell people not to climb on the monument to have their photograph taken. He was amazed at their ignorance. Did they have no respect for the site which was both an architectural masterpiece and a place of worship?

Now it was the summer season and he continually tried to find a shady spot where he could stand or place his chair. No one had given him a second glance since he had arrived on the mainland and he felt confident that he had covered his tracks and the police were no longer interested in him. He would risk booking a flight next week to England and then on to Canada, using his brother's identity. He could not bear to think of standing in the hot sun throughout August.

He watched idly as a young girl took photographs from different angles of the Erechtheion to ensure she had photos of all the caryatides. She was wearing shorts, but had a sarong tied through a belt loop. No doubt if she was challenged regarding her immodest dress she would place the flimsy material around her waist. As she drew level with him she stopped and smiled.

'It is alright for me to take photographs, isn't it?'

'No photographs in the museum.'

'But out here there is no problem?'

'Not with tripod.'

She opened her arms, displaying an ample bosom with her camera hanging between her breasts. 'I have no tripod,' she declared. 'I saw you watching me and I wondered if I was breaking the law. I don't want to end up in prison.'

Filippos smiled back. He longed to reach out his hand and grasp her breast firmly, feeling his fingers sink into her soft flesh and hearing the gasp of both pain and pleasure that she would give. She was inviting him. He had managed to keep control of his violent inclinations, using prostitutes who, for a little extra, were willing to put up with a certain amount of rough treatment from him.

'You take many photos.'

'I want to remember this visit for ever more. I may never be able to come back a second time.' She lifted her camera and Filippos stepped to one side out of range of the view finder. 'Where will I get the best view of Athens?' she asked. 'Is the sea visible from somewhere?'

Filippos shook his head. 'Here it is difficult. From the hill with the monument to Philopappos you have the best view. It is possible to see Piraeus.'

'You mean Lycabettus?' asked Beverley.

'No, the hill across the road.'

The girl seemed to hesitate. 'How far away is this other hill?'

'A few minutes' walk.'

She looked at her watch. 'If I come back here when I've been to the museum and seen everything will you give me directions, please?'

'Certainly.'

With a pleased smile she left him and walked over to the perimeter wall. She leaned over to take another photograph and her shorts rode up higher, giving him a glimpse of the flesh at the base of her buttocks. Filippos clenched his hands together and licked his lips; flesh, beautiful, soft flesh that he longed to grasp and pinch so he could listen to her cries of protest and finally her agony as he tore unmercifully into her. He turned to face the wall of the building where he was standing, unable to bear to look at her any longer. There was something irresistible to him about the flesh at the top of a girl's legs. The desire to rip off her clothes and force himself upon her immediately was almost overwhelming. He would have to be patient and give her no hint of his intentions.

Filippos waited in an agony of suspense. He did not want her to return too soon or he would not have finished his duty hours, but nor did he want to wait around until the site closed and she might claim it was then too dark to take photographs. As the time grew closer to him being relieved he began to look anxiously amongst the throng of people for her and finally spotted her ambling towards him, her camera dividing her breasts tantalizingly.

'I hoped you'd still be here. I should have asked what time you went off duty.'

'I am being relieved at any minute. Did you see everything you wanted?'

She nodded. 'It's marvellous. Now, how do I get to this other hill? If I want to take more photos I need to be there before the light goes.'

'You have time. The light will be good for another hour.' Filippos looked at his watch. 'I can leave now and I will show you.'

As they walked across the main thoroughfare he raised his hand to a man hurrying in his direction. The man nodded and took up a position close to where Filippos had been standing. Beverley followed him dutifully to the exit and down the path to the road. He took her elbow and guided her across as there was a break in the traffic.

'We go up there,' he announced and pointed to the wooded hillside.

Beverley frowned. It looked deserted and rather dark amongst the overhanging trees. 'Are you sure?'

'There is the notice.' Filippos pointed to the weather beaten wooden sign.

'Well, thanks. I would never have spotted it without you.'

'I will walk up with you.'

'There's really no need.'

'I will be able to tell you the history of the monument. Also there are many paths that lead off. If you take the wrong one you will be back down on the road. It is only a short climb by the direct route and very pleasant. Often I walk up here at the end of the day.'

They stood to one side as a group of people suddenly emerged from the cypress and olive trees and Beverley felt her apprehension evaporate. There were obviously people walking up and down the hill. She did not exactly mistrust her companion, he was an Acropolis guard, but she had been brought up to be wary of strangers. She began to climb the path that led to the summit of the hill, Filippos following behind the movement of her buttocks acting as an aphrodisiac to him. His enforced wait for satisfaction would only make it more enjoyable for him when the time came. As they climbed they met other couples and groups returning and Beverley also saw the side paths that ran off, often looking like a more direct route than the one they were taking. Had she been alone she would probably have struck off on one and been back where she started.

They emerged on the grassy summit and Beverley drew in her breath. 'Oh, wow! That's wonderful.' She lifted her camera and began to photograph the monument of Philopappos. 'Who built this here?' she asked.

'He was a Roman prince who was exiled to Athens from Armenia. He became a Consul of Athens and a benefactor of the theatre. After he died the people raised the money and built the monument in his memory.'

Beverley moved to one side and looked at the panorama of Athens spread out before her. 'You're right; you can see Piraeus from here.' She began to take photographs, moving her position slightly each time. 'I'm hoping when I get home I can put these together with those from the Acropolis and Lycabettus and I'll have the whole of Athens spread out before me.'

Filippos sat down on the grass and waited patiently. It was far too open and there were too many people around for him to make any overtures towards her. Even when the sun finally disappeared people would stay on the hill to see the lights of the Athenian suburbs.

Finally Beverley turned back to him with a smile. 'Thank you so much. This has really made my day. You didn't have to wait for me, you know. I'm sure I would have found my way back down to the main road.'

'I am sure you would also, but then you would have missed the prison where Socrates was held and the ruins of another theatre. It is down the other side of the hill. You wish to see it?'

Beverley nodded eagerly and followed Filippos as he walked along the brow of the hill before turning onto a path. Within a short space of time the trees gave way to scrub and low bushes and to Filippos's delight there was no one in sight. He stopped and took Beverley's arm.

'You see? It is down there.'

'We'll have to hurry or the light won't be right for photographs any longer.'

'There is no hurry.' Filippos gripped her arm tighter and pulled her backwards onto the grass. He threw himself down beside her and pushed her camera out of the way as he groped for her breasts.

'Hey, no, stop that. Let me up.' Beverley swung a fist at his face, raking her nails down his cheek.

Filippos took no notice of her plea. He grabbed her arms, pulling them down by her sides and knelt astride her, placing his full weight on her wrists. He ripped her T-shirt apart and pulled down her bra exposing her breasts. He gave a groan of pleasure as he felt her softness beneath his fingers.

'Let me go or I'll scream.'

'There is no one to hear you.' Filippos's fingers dug into her breast, making her gasp with pain.

Beverley attempted to wriggle away from him and tried to bring her knee up into contact with his crotch. Filippos's response was to pinch and twist her breast making her cry out in agony.

'Do not make this difficult for yourself,' he admonished her. 'You will enjoy it if you relax.'

Beverley's response was to send a gobbet of spit into his face, followed by a piercing scream. Her scream was cut short as she received a thunderous blow to her face and head. Everything went black for a few moments and her ears were ringing. She could feel his fingers undo the button on her shorts and pull down the zip. His wet mouth was slavering over her naked breasts and she was not sure if the nausea she felt was due to the blow to her head or revulsion at his actions. She had no doubt now that she was going to be raped and if she tried to resist she would also be badly beaten.

A scream burst from her again as he entered her roughly and he placed a hand over her mouth. His eyes closed and a smile of contentment on his face Filippos thrust himself again and again into her unwilling body. The joy; the ecstasy was indescribable as he reached a climax and briefly collapsed onto her, only to pull away as he felt the hot wetness from her bladder soaking him.

Through half closed eyes Beverley watched him as he pulled his trousers up, gratified in a small way that she had succeeded in making them wet. She would feign unconsciousness in the hope that now he had satisfied himself he would have no more use for her and leave. He stood beside her inert body and she steeled herself to remain motionless, finally he raised his foot and stamped on her ribs, the searing pain making her truly lose consciousness.

The light was failing fast as Beverley regained consciousness. Her body was racked with pain and each breath she took caused her agony. She had to get off the hill and find some help before it became truly dark. She attempted to sit up, the pain in her ribs excruciating. With her left hand she tried to cradle them as she eased her wet and dirty shorts up her legs. Sweat stood out on her forehead as she managed to turn onto her knees and pulled them up to her waist to fasten the button.

She pulled her T-shirt across her chest with a shaking and painful hand, hoping she had obtained a semblance of decency. Below her the hillside was dark but she could see lights in the distance. Should she go in that direction or retrace her steps and hope to regain the summit of the hill and find the path that led down to the main road?

She touched the pocket of her shorts and to her relief she could feel the swipe card for her hotel room was still there, along with some euro notes. If she could manage to get to the main road and the entrance to the Acropolis she should be able to wave down a taxi eventually.

Cradling her ribs with one hand she used the other to help her claw her way back up the hill, hoping she would eventually reach the path which led back to the monument. Every step was painful and she had to move slowly, stopping frequently to rest and having to force herself to move on. At the back of her mind was the terrifying thought that the man she had trusted could be waiting for her with the intention of attacking her again.

Finally the track she had been crawling up gave way to the path between the trees and she hauled herself upright, gasping anew with the pain that shot through her side. Her ribs were definitely broken. Using the trees to assist her, she moved slowly, her head down and taking shallow breaths to try to alleviate the pain.

The monument gleamed white in the distance and Beverley resorted to crawling again along the grass. She wished she had some water with her, her mouth was so dry. Trying to crawl down the hill was excruciatingly painful and she managed to turn so she could attempt to crawl down backwards. Unable to see where she was going she continually grazed and cut her already damaged legs on loose stones and the wooden edges of the steps.

By the time she reached the main road it was light, but the

road appeared deserted. She looked at her watch, but the glass cover to the face was so broken she could not see the hands and doubted if it was still functioning anyway. Completely exhausted, bruised and bleeding, she lay on the pavement in a foetal position.

Doctor Eleni Skoufas looked at the patient who had been wheeled in to the accident room of the hospital. There was no information accompanying her arrival. A woman driving to work had seen the girl lying on the pavement and stopped to investigate. She had taken one look at the condition the girl was in, decided she must have been hit by a passing car and called for an ambulance.

Doctor Skoufas had made a brief examination before asking a nurse to remove Beverley's clothes so she could ascertain the extent of her injuries. Now Beverley lay beneath a sheet and the doctor began her examination, hoping her patient would regain consciousness soon so she could question her. Her legs and hands were badly lacerated, she had livid bruises at the top of her thighs and on her arms, one side of her face was bruised and swollen, her eye closed and judging by the discolouration around her ribs they were probably broken. A number of x-rays would be needed to ascertain the extent of the damage to the girl.

Beverley groaned as her body was arranged in appropriate positions for the x-rays to be taken. She could feel hands touching her gently and somewhere in the background there was the murmur of voices. Her head throbbed and it was with a supreme effort that she opened her eye on the undamaged side of her face, only to close it swiftly as the light sent shafts of pain to her brain.

She could feel herself moving, the motion making her feel nauseous and she groaned again. She struggled to sit up, she must not vomit whilst lying on her back or she would probably choke. Hands restrained her, but as her stomach heaved her head was turned to one side and only a dribble of bile ran from her lips and was wiped away.

Doctor Skoufas examined the x-rays. The only breaks were to

the girl's ribs and fortunately they had not penetrated her lungs. She would tape the ribs, but the only other treatment they could give would be pain killers to help with the worst of the discomfort whilst they mended, but she needed to find out how the injuries had occurred.

'Can you hear me?' she asked. 'Can you tell me your name?'

Beverley opened her eye. There was a woman bending over her who was wearing a white coat, but she floated in and out of her focus. 'Drink,' she croaked.

Doctor Skoufas frowned. She had a reasonable knowledge of spoken English, but did have enough confidence in her language ability to question the girl. She motioned to a nearby nurse. 'Give her a drink of water, make sure she takes only a little at a time.' She turned back to Beverley. 'You are English?'

'Ozzie.'

'Ozzie?' Doctor Skoufas was puzzled by the expression.

'Australian. Drink.'

Doctor Skoufas turned away. She needed to find Katerina who had been brought up in Australia before her parents had decided to return to their native land.

Katerina sat beside Beverley holding her hand. 'Can you tell me what happened to you? Were you hit by a car?'

'Raped.'

'You were raped and left by the side of the road?'

'Raped,' repeated Beverley. She felt far too exhausted to go into any details. 'Drink.'

Katerina held a feeding cup to Beverley's lips and allowed her to have some more small sips. 'We're fitting up a drip for you. You'll feel better when that starts to take effect. You're badly dehydrated. I'll leave you to rest for a while. I'll come back in about an hour and see if you can tell me more about your ordeal.'

Katerina went in search of Doctor Skoufas. The doctor needed to know the girl claimed to have been raped.

'You are sure that is what she said?' asked the doctor.

'Certain. She said it twice. I couldn't get anything more out of her. I gave her a drink and thought I ought to come to tell you. She seems totally exhausted.'

'Are you able to stay with her? See if you can find out her name and where she's staying. She probably has friends who are wondering what has happened to her. It might help if one of them could be contacted and asked to sit with her.' The doctor sighed heavily. 'Assuming she has been raped we need to take swabs as soon as possible and check for internal damage, then I'll have to report the incident to the police.'

Katerina nodded. 'I'll stay with her and let you know as soon as I have any information. Of course, it may have been someone she knew and she won't want to press any charges.'

Doctor Skoufas shrugged. 'In that case all we can do is patch her up and send her on her way.'

Katerina sat beside Beverley, talking quietly trying to encourage the girl to confide in her. Apart from asking for an occasional drink or bedpan Beverley lay with her eyes closed, trying to take shallow breaths to alleviate the pain in her chest. She was beginning to feel a little more comfortable and she decided this was due to the tablets she was being given on a regular basis. No doubt that was also why she was feeling so sleepy.

It was three days before Beverley finally felt strong enough to be able to describe her ordeal on the hillside in detail. It was painful to talk and she spoke haltingly whilst Katerina listened without interrupting until Beverley fell silent with tears in her eyes.

'Can you tell me anything about this man? Did he tell you his name?'

'No. I was stupid. I thought he was just going to give me directions. When he said he would show me the way up to the monument I should have refused.'

Katerina patted her hand. 'You mustn't blame yourself.'

'I shouldn't have trusted him. I'd only met him a couple of hours earlier at the Acropolis.'

'Did he speak to you first, ask you to go for a drink with him?'

'No. I asked if I was allowed to take photographs.'

Katerina frowned. 'Why did you ask him? There would be a notice if they were not permitted.'

'He seemed to be watching what I was doing and I thought I may have missed a notice.'

'Was that all you asked him?'

'I wanted to know if I could have a photo with the sea in the background. He said the hill with the monument had the best views. I didn't know where it was and asked if he would give me directions when I had finished looking around. When I returned he said he was just going off duty and would show me the way.'

'Off duty? You mean he was one of the Acropolis guards?'

'I'm sure he was. He was standing by the Erechtheion and when he left he acknowledged a man who went and stood in his place.'

'Can you tell me what he looked like?'

Beverley looked at Katerina with her undamaged eye. The other was still too swollen to open. 'Greek.'

Katerina smiled. 'Young or old?' Most of the guards were late middle age, so if her assailant was young it was unlikely that he had been working at the site.

'Late thirties, early forties. He had that unshaven look.' Beverley gave an involuntary shudder and gasped as her ribs sent a stab of pain through her chest. 'He was slavering all over my breasts and I could feel his beard scraping me.'

'Did he make any overtures to you before he attacked? Any suggestive remarks of any kind?'

'Nothing. He told me about Philopappos and why his monument was built. When I had finished taking my photos he said he would show me the cave where Socrates had been imprisoned. There were plenty of people around still and I thought it would be just along from the monument.'

'You realise Doctor Skoufas will have to report this to the police and they will want to interview you? They will probably ask you very personal and intrusive questions.'

Beverley sighed and closed her eyes. 'I just want the vicious bastard caught.'

Katerina squeezed her hand. 'Good on you.'

Inspector Sikelianos listened carefully as Doctor Skoufas relayed the information about the rape of the Australian girl to him.

'So why have you waited until now to report this to me?'

'I reported a possible case of rape to your department three days ago. The girl was obviously in shock for the first twenty four hours. She said she had been raped and my subsequent examination confirmed that she had been violently assaulted. It is only today that we have been able to get a reasonably coherent account from her.'

'She could have been urging her boyfriend on and when he became rough with her she decided it was rape.'

'No, Inspector, her internal injuries are more serious than you would get from some rough intercourse. I am willing to testify that she was physically assaulted and raped. I have sent swabs for analysis. We have the torn clothing she was wearing at the time and removed grass and twigs from her hair. The injuries to her legs and hands were conducive to someone who had crawled a considerable distance over rough ground. She suffered broken ribs and bruising over most of her body.'

'Can you fax your report over to me? I'll send someone in tomorrow to take a statement from her.'

'She doesn't speak Greek.'

'So how do you know she was raped?'

Doctor Skoufas sighed with exasperation. 'I have a nurse here who speaks both Greek and English fluently. She has gained the girl's confidence and elicited a certain amount of information from her. The girl believes her assailant was one of the guards at the Acropolis.'

Inspector Sikelianos nodded as he made a note. 'If that is so it certainly narrows down the list of suspects. Do you think she would recognise the man again if I brought along some photos of known offenders?'

'I don't know, but I'm sure she would be willing to try.'

Inspector Sikelianos had spent almost three hours questioning Beverley, using Katerina as his interpreter. Now he sat beside her bed as Katerina slowly turned the pages showing Beverley the photographs of men who had been apprehended and questioned about similar offences in the past.

'None of them,' said Beverley finally.

'Is she sure he worked at the Acropolis?' he asked Katerina.

'As sure as she can be. He was standing beside one of the monuments when she spoke to him and he was still there when she returned over two hours later.'

'I'll pay the site director a visit and ask if I can borrow the security photos of his staff.' He eyed Beverley warily. 'If I return this afternoon will she be capable of looking at them?'

Katerina nodded. 'She'll make the effort whatever it might cost her. She wants him caught.'

Filippos Melanakis scanned the newspapers and listened to the news. There was no report of a tourist being raped in the city which gave him a sense of security. She was probably still lying on the hill, but he would certainly not go up there to investigate. For the next few days he would continue with his usual routine and by the time she was found he would have left the country.

It had been a long and uncomfortable walk home looking as if he had wet himself. He was sure one or two people he had passed had sniggered. A pair of wet trousers was a small price to pay for the incredible joy and relief he had experienced. Had they known of his euphoria they would have been envious of him, not viewing him with contempt.

He had showered and scrubbed his body vigorously, washed his hair and cleaned his nails. Now he looked at his ruined trousers in disgust. He decided he would discard all the clothes he had been wearing. It was a sensible precaution to dispose of anything that could possibly link him to the attack. He placed each article in a separate plastic bag and would throw each bag into a different rubbish bin on his way to the metro.

He would work until the end of the week and collect his wages before he left his employment at the Acropolis. Despite having had a weekly wage and living frugally, the cash he had brought with him from Crete was dwindling. He would tell the manager at the Acropolis that he had been called to Thessalonica as his mother had died. In the meantime he would book a flight to Cyprus. He dared not return to any of the Greek islands in the vicinity. Once again he would pretend to be a tourist and fly to England from Cyprus. He wished he was conversant with languages other than Greek and English so he had more choice of destination.

Inspector Sikelianos drove to the site manager's office at the Acropolis and requested the file containing the details of the employees. The manager eyed him warily.

'Why would you want that? We don't employ anyone who has a criminal record.'

'We have reason to suspect that you may have employed someone who has furnished you with false credentials. No blame is attached to you,' the Inspector hastened to assure him.

'What's his name?'

'I don't know a name, that's why I need access to the file that contains their photographs.'

'Most of them have been with us for years.'

Inspector Sikelianos nodded. 'They do a fine job, thanks to your organisation. Do you assign them a permanent position on the site?'

'More or less. I have to change them around if someone calls in sick or applies for a few days off. Occasionally they request a change of scene.'

The Inspector took the folder the manager held out to him. 'Personally, I don't think the man is employed here, but I have to investigate the information I have been given. I doubt if I'll need to keep the file more than a couple of hours. One of my men will return it to you.'

'I want it returned to me personally, not given to anyone else. It's confidential. I would have been within my rights to refuse you access.'

'Quite.' The Inspector tucked the folder securely beneath his arm. 'Had you refused I would have had to apply for a warrant; time consuming and unnecessary. What time do you go off duty?'

'I'm here until we close.'

'In that case I'll make sure I return it to you myself later today.'

Beverley felt exhausted and the photographs seemed to blur and swim before her eyes. Each page held the details of three employees, a passport sized photograph of them with their name and identity number written below, along with their address and the date they commenced working at the site. If an employee had left his photograph had been removed and his details scratched through to make them unreadable. She closed her eyes.

'I can't look at any more.'

Katerina patted her hand. 'We'll give you a break for an hour or so. I could do with one. We might be able to finish looking when you've had a rest.'

Inspector Sikelianos frowned when Katerina told him Beverley needed to rest. 'I've promised to return the file by this evening.'

'I'm sure she'll look at the others later. She needs to sleep for a while. The poor girl was talking to you all morning; she must be exhausted. When you have broken ribs it hurts to talk.'

'I thought she was anxious for this man to be apprehended,'

remarked the Inspector.

'She is, but there's a limit to how long she can be expected to concentrate; she still can't see properly out of one eye. Give her an hour or so and I'm sure she'll be willing to look at the rest of the photos.'

'And what am I supposed to do whilst she's lying there asleep? My time is valuable.'

'You could probably start typing up your report.' Katerina looked pointedly at the Inspector's laptop. 'Why don't you sit at the table and get on with that and I'll go to the cafeteria and bring you back a coffee.'

Inspector Sikelianos glanced at her sourly. He did, in fact, have plenty of work he could complete on his laptop, but he had brought it with him because there were half a dozen men whose details had been sent to him from other islands. If the girl could identify a photograph he would check the details to see if the man was suspected elsewhere.

Katerina woke Beverley just over an hour later. 'Come on, Beverley. Time to wake up. If I leave you any longer you'll not sleep tonight. I'll give you a quick wash to freshen you up, then you can have a cup of tea and some more tablets.'

Still half asleep, but unresisting, Beverley allowed Katerina to wash her hands and face and prop another pillow behind her head. The Inspector remained seated at the table. He felt sure if he upset the nurse by being impatient she would claim that Beverley was not able to look at any more photographs that day.

'Better now?' asked Katerina. 'Shall we try to finish looking at those photographs; then we can send old sour puss on his way.'

Beverley gave a lop-sided smile. 'I'll try.'

Katerina walked over to the Inspector. 'She's willing to look at the remainder now.'

Inspector Sikelianos closed his laptop programme and picked up the folder again, opening it where he had placed a marker. He turned the pages whilst Beverley tried to concentrate. Two pages from the end Beverley raised her hand.

'Let me look at that one again.'

Katerina translated, took the folder from the Inspector and placed it on Beverley's lap, waiting until Beverley placed her finger on a photograph.

'Him,' she said finally.

'You're sure?'

'As sure as I can be without actually seeing him again.'

Katerina handed the folder to the Inspector. 'She says it's that man there.'

'Is she sure?'

'She can't be positive without seeing him, but she pointed him out immediately.'

The Inspector nodded and wrote down the details from beneath the man's photograph. He held the file out to Beverley again and she indicated the same man again.

'Ask her to look at the remaining few.'

Katerina did so and turned the pages again. Once at the end Beverley indicated that she should turn back to the man she had identified. She looked carefully at the photo.

'I'm sure that's him,' she affirmed again.

Inspector Sikelianos took the folder back from Katerina, returned to the table and opened his laptop. He would check to see if the man was wanted anywhere else for assault. He looked from the photograph to his laptop and back again, then stopped. Filippos Melanakis was wanted in Crete. He studied the two photographs. In one the man was clean shaven and in the other he had a fashionable growth of stubble.

He brought up the details on his laptop and scanned the details quickly. Filippos Melanakis was wanted in Crete for assault and also for causing the death of a young woman. He returned to the screen with the photograph and carried his laptop over to Beverley's bed. She looked at the enlargement.

'That's definitely him. He hasn't got any facial hair, but I'm sure that's the same man.' She looked at Katerina. 'You can tell the Inspector I'm certain that was the man.'

Inspector Sikelianos frowned. The man on his laptop was named as Filippos Melanakis with his occupation as a doctor. The man who was working as a guard on the Acropolis site was Andreas Melanakis. He would have to make a telephone call to Crete to ascertain if they could be the same man.

'I'd like to speak to the doctor who reported this to the police,' he said to Katerina. 'I need to check a few details with her.'

Katerina nodded. 'I'll find her and give her a message. I'm sure she'll be with you as soon as possible.'

Inspector Sikelianos spoke to Inspector Solomakis in Crete, telling him that there was a young woman in hospital and she had identified Filippos Melanakis as her attacker.

'The problem is,' explained Inspector Sikelianos, 'we have a man here working at the Acropolis who fits the description, but his name is Andreas Melanakis.'

'Aha! I can explain that! The man we want to catch is Doctor Filippos Melanakis. He knew we were closing in on him and disappeared. The airlines were alerted, but no one had booked a ticket anywhere in that name. I visited his brother in Rethymnon to see if the man was staying with him. I asked for his I.D. and he found both his I.D. and driving licence were missing from his wallet. I requested the airlines to do another search under the name Andreas Melanakis and again I drew a blank. Either he was still somewhere on Crete or he had travelled to one of the islands by ferry. We put out an alert to the police and the hospitals at the time but he's been crafty enough not to draw attention to himself until now.'

'So you think the guard at the Acropolis and the doctor are the same man?'

'Positive. Even if he should turn out not to be the assailant you're looking for we'd certainly like him back on Crete. We have more than enough evidence to charge him.'

Inspector Sikelianos frowned. 'I was going to pick him up for questioning. Until we've a DNA confirmation we can't charge him with anything. It's possible someone else hit the girl over the head, but the last face she remembers seeing is the guard.'

'Put him in the cells until you have the results of his DNA. He'll give you the slip otherwise. If it turns out that you don't want him, we certainly do.'

Inspector Sikelianos met briefly with Doctor Skoufas and requested that the swabs taken from Beverley were tested for DNA.

'We do that as a matter of course,' retorted the doctor. 'They should be due back within the week.'

'If you're able to hurry them up a bit I'd be grateful. I shall be asking for priority on some others and they should take no longer than four days to give a result.'

'Then we'll just have to hope that mine are ahead of yours in the queue.' The doctor smiled complacently, knowing the results she had requested should be with her within the next forty eight hours.

'Let me know as soon as your results arrive.' Inspector Sikelianos collected his lap top, tucked the folder beneath his arm and bade farewell to Beverley and Katerina. He used his mobile to call the station, saying he wanted two officers to go to the Acropolis immediately and wait for him in their car outside the main entrance.

The Inspector used his siren and light to clear a way through the traffic, but turned both off as he neared the Acropolis. He did not want to give advance warning to Melanakis. His men were waiting for him and he gave them brief instructions.

'Spiro, go inside and stand where you can see the Erechtheion. Keep an eye on the guard there, but don't make it obvious that you're watching him. As soon as I join you we'll make an arrest. If he leaves his post make sure you follow him. Costas, you go and stand by the main gate.'

Puzzled, but obedient, the two officers left the Inspector to take up their positions. Inspector Sikelianos returned the folder of photographs to the site manager and thanked him. 'I have two officers with me. One is on site watching the guard we are planning to arrest. He may well try to escape once he becomes aware of our intentions. I'm making an official request that you close the gates and do not allow any of the guards to leave even if they have completed their hours.'

'I can't do that! What about the visitors who are ready to leave? I can't stop them.'

'My other officer is standing at the gate. You stand there with him and between you control the exit of the tourists and ask any guards to wait until I give them clearance to leave. If you hear me blow my whistle close the gate immediately and order the people to move away.'

'Has he got a gun?' the manager paled visibly.

'Highly unlikely. We just want to make sure we pick him up tonight and he doesn't manage to give us the slip. Now, where will I find Andreas Melanakis?'

The manager shook his head. 'He's already left. His duty finishes at four.'

Inspector Sikelianos looked at the man in disbelief. He should have thought to check shift times earlier. 'He's left?'

'That's right. He's due back here at seven thirty tomorrow morning.'

'What time do you arrive?'

'About seven fifteen to unlock the gates and let the workers in.'

'In that case we'll be here at seven. We'll wait in your office. Once he's inside the site we'll arrest him.' Cursing, the Inspector turned on his heel and made his way to the gate. He should have insisted the girl finished looking at the photographs before having a rest. 'Costas, go and find Spiro. The arrest is off. Our man left here an hour ago.'

Inspector Sikelianos drove slowly past the address he had for his suspect. There was nothing remarkable about the apartment block and he guessed by the air of neglect that seemed to hang over it that the rental was low. Cars and motor bikes were parked on both sides of the road and the only space had lines indicating that parking was forbidden. Ignoring the instruction he drew in.

He walked across the road to the main entrance and studied the names beneath each bell. There was no one named Melanakis. He pushed open the door into the large vestibule and began to look through the assortment of post that was lying there, most of it consisted of advertising flyers, but there was a postcard and a couple of letters addressed to people in whom he had no interest. He considered whether to speak to whoever lived on the ground floor and see if they could give him any information, but decided against it. Inspector Solomakis had warned him that the man could easily disappear again if he thought he was in danger of arrest.

It would be more sensible to leave now and arrange for a couple of his men to watch the apartment overnight. If Melanakis decided to leave during the hours of darkness they would be able to pick him up, alternatively if he departed for work as usual in the morning one could follow him on foot and alert the station when the man arrived at the Acropolis. The Inspector returned to his car, just in time to avoid being issued with a parking violation and drove away, passing Filippos Melanakis as he rounded the corner.

Inspector Sikelianos furnished his two officers with photographs of the suspect. 'If he should leave the building during the night I want him arrested immediately. He doesn't know we are looking for him so I am expecting him to go to work as usual in the morning. When he leaves the building I want him followed, but not stopped. Make sure he doesn't realise he has a tail. He will be making his way to the Acropolis and once inside he will have been positively identified as the man we want to question and we'll make the arrest there.'

Theo changed into his own clothes whilst Makkis wore his uniform. It was probably going to be a long and boring night watching the apartment block from an unmarked car. At least they would each be able to catch a few hours sleep whilst the other stayed vigilant.

At six they were both awake and watched as people from the neighbourhood began to emerge from their homes and make their way to work.

'I reckon that's him,' announced Makkis as a man walked out from the apartment block. Theo took a quick look and ducked down to hide his own face from view. 'Yes, I'm sure it is. He hasn't shaved off that beard growth. I reckon he'll make for the station to catch the metro in to work. I'll let the Inspector know we've spotted him and I'll call you on your cell phone if he gives me any instructions for you.'

Theo let himself out of the car and walked along the pavement, leaving a reasonable distance between himself and Melanakis. The man moved at a regular pace, but certainly did not appear to be in any particular hurry. No doubt he knew how long it took to reach the metro station and arrive at work on time.

Makkis followed the Inspector's instructions and drove towards the Acropolis. He parked his car and waited at the main entrance for the Inspector to join him. The two police officers walked up the wide, shallow steps to the main gate which was now unlocked and over to the site manager's office. There were already some men waiting to sign in for their day's duty. The Inspector cursed. He did not want anyone to tell Melanakis there was a police presence on the site and give him the opportunity to evade them.

'Morning, gentlemen.' He nodded to them and opened the door to the office. 'Morning, Babbis. Just come to finish off that job from yesterday,' he announced loudly. 'You carry on. We won't be here very long.' He moved to the side of the room, motioning to Makkis to join him where they would not be seen by those outside.

Babbis nodded and continued to watch the men signing their names and time of arrival, changing the location of two of the guards due to known absentees. Inspector Sikelianos answered his mobile phone and listened to the information Theo imparted. Makkis raised his eyebrows and the Inspector nodded. Melanakis had just started climbing the steps.

Filippos Melanakis signed his name as usual and hesitated at the window. 'I'm sorry, Mr Babbis, but I'll have to ask for next week off. I've had a phone call to say my mother died last night. I'll want to go to her funeral and it will be in Thessalonica.'

'Sorry to hear that, Andreas. When are you planning to leave?'

'I'll work out today and collect my wages tonight; then I plan to catch the train tomorrow morning.'

'I'll have your wages ready when you finish your duty.' Babbis made a note on a pad beside him.

Inspector Sikelianos and Makkis waited a further ten minutes whilst more men arrived and signed in for their day's work.

'Time to move,' the Inspector announced. 'Babbis, close your window and come with us to lock the gate. We shouldn't be long.'

Unwillingly the site manager did as he was instructed and the Inspector and Makkis walked up the steps and across the site towards the Erechtheion. Filippos saw them coming and his mouth went dry. He looked around wildly and began to run. If he ran across the Parthenon he would be able to regain the steps and make his escape through the main gate.

The Inspector guessed his intention and immediately directed Makkis to return to the gate whilst he followed Melanakis. As soon as Melanakis saw the police officer at the gate he doubled back. He would scale the perimeter wall and scramble down the side of the hill to the path below and make his escape that way.

Adrenalin pumped through his body as he jumped and hauled himself onto the wall, the drop the other side was greater than he had anticipated, but he let himself down regardless. The force with which his feet hit the unstable ground dislodged the grass and stones, sending him slithering down the hillside with his ankle twisted beneath him.

Inspector Sikelianos removed his gun from the holster. He had no wish to kill the man, just immobilise him. He waited until Melanakis came to a halt and took careful aim, his first shot ricocheting off the ground. Melanakis crawled behind a bush and the Inspector aimed again, the second shot eliciting a scream from the man as it missed him by a fraction.

Convinced that the man was injured the Inspector raced back to the gate where Makkis was waiting, waving his arms and indicating that the gate should be unlocked. 'Our man went over the wall,' he gasped. 'He'll not get far. I'll call for back up.' The time it took to make the call would give him the opportunity to regain his breath.

Melanakis pulled himself to his feet and began to stumble across the service road to the fence where a gate gave access to a path that led down the hill to an area of Plaka. Both shots had missed him, but his ankle was hurting badly where he had twisted it as he fell down the hill and he knew he would be unable to out run the police. He had to hope that when he reached the houses that were built into the hill he could find somewhere to hide until they gave up searching for him.

The two police officers elbowed their way through the guards who were still waiting to sign in and the tourists who were beginning to congregate.

'Which way?' asked Makkis.

Inspector Sikelianos pointed in the direction of the path that led back to the Plaka area where the small streets and numerous buildings would provide plenty of hiding places. The area where Melanakis had slipped down the hillside was evident from the torn grass and broken bushes, but of the man there was no sign.

They advanced slowly, there was nowhere on the hillside where the man could hide but on the other side of the road was a gate that gave on to a path lined with trees and bushes that led further down the hill.

'Wait here,' Inspector Sikelianos ordered. 'When our back up arrives get them to fan out and search the area. If I find him in the meantime I'll whistle.'

With his gun in his hand the Inspector began to walk cautiously down the path, peering into the trees and bushes, parting the branches with his hands in the hope of finding the injured man. The Inspector reached the bottom of the path and looked around in consternation. There was no sign of their quarry and nothing to indicate the direction he might have taken.

Inspector Sikelianos placed his whistle between his lips and blew two short blasts. Almost immediately he could hear Makkis's feet pounding down the path. He waited until the officer stopped beside him.

'We've lost him for the time being. My second shot can't have touched him or he wouldn't have been able to get this far. We'll have to divert back up and get them to cordon off this side of the Acropolis whilst we do a house to house.'

Makkis looked doubtfully at his superior officer. He thought it very unlikely they would find the man now. He would have disappeared into the rabbit warren of small roads in the area and made his way to Ermou Street where he could have hailed a taxi and been taken anywhere.

'Should we send a car to watch his apartment?' suggested Makkis.

Inspector Sikelianos nodded. 'That would be the obvious place for him to make for unless he has friends locally who would be willing to hide him.'

It was nearly dark when the police found Filippos Melanakis cowering in an outhouse. They hauled him out roughly and he promptly fell over. His ankle had swollen to twice its normal size and was too painful for him to put his weight on.

'Shame,' said Costas as he handcuffed their prisoner and he and Stelios began to drag him towards their car, ignoring his protests.

They pushed him inside the car and radioed to the other men that they could abandon the search of the area.

Inspector Sikelianos rubbed his hands together. At the moment they could only charge Melanakis with resisting arrest, but he would make sure he was secure in a cell until the DNA results were received back from the laboratory. If the DNA swabs taken by Dr Skoufas were confirmed as belonging to Melanakis he would call Inspector Solomakis in Heraklion and ask if the girl he had attacked there wished to press charges.

August 2008

'I'm not sure where she is,' demurred the Thranassis when Inspector Sikelianos telephoned him. 'I know she didn't return to her apartment when she was discharged from the hospital. I sent a female officer round to see how she was coping and the place was empty. The woman below said she'd been asked to pack up her clothes and toiletries and they would be collected. I sent Adrienne around a couple of weeks later and she was still not there. The neighbour said she had seen no sign of her and had no forwarding address. The next time Adrienne called there was a new tenant.'

'Did you visit her employer? If she's still working at the same place he should have her current address.'

'We tried there. He said she was perfectly alright and did not wish to have her address disclosed to anyone. I saw no point in pursuing the matter further.'

'Maybe you could visit him again and see if he is able to contact her?' The question was worded in such a way that Thranassis knew he could not refuse. 'She has a right to know the man has been arrested and she may wish to press charges.'

Thranassis sighed. 'I'll see what I can do.'

Inspector Solomakis visited the Central hotel and asked to speak to Vasi. Wondering what had happened this time to draw him to the attention of the Inspector, Vasi ushered the policeman into his office.

'How can I help you?'

'I wished to ask if Miss Dimitra Artimatakis was still working here?'

Vasi nodded. 'She runs our computer system.'

'Would it be possible for me to have a few words with her? It's regarding the unfortunate incident she suffered.'

Vasi frowned. 'She is still in a very fragile mental state. Is it essential that you remind her of her ordeal?'

'We believe we have arrested her assailant. I need to ask her if she wishes to press charges against him.'

'Where was he?'

'In Athens, working as a guard at the Acropolis.'

'But he's a doctor!'

Thranassis shook his head. 'He could not work as a doctor without presenting his credentials. They would have been checked and we would have found him immediately.'

'How did you find him?' asked Vasi curiously.

'He assaulted a tourist. She said he was a guard from the Acropolis and identified him from their staff photographs. An alert policeman thought to check the computer photograph that we had sent through to all the Greek police stations and she thought it was the same man. We had to wait for the results of the DNA samples to confirm that both assaults were carried out by him. We are now in a position to charge him.'

'So why do you need to speak to Dimitra?'

'Two reasons. I imagine she will be relieved to know the man is in custody and I also need to ask her if she is willing to testify against him.'

Vasi pursed his lips. 'I can't answer for her. I will ask her to come to my office and you can speak to her.'

Thranassis nodded. 'If she is unwilling I thought you might be able to persuade her.'

Vasi shook his head. 'I am not involved and I certainly don't wish to be. Whatever decision she makes is of her own volition. Nothing to do with me.' Vasi dialled Dimitra's extension number and asked if she would come down to his office.

Thranassis rose from his seat as she entered and held out his hand. 'It is good to see you looking so well, Miss Artimatakis.'

Dimitra paled. 'What do you want?'

'I have some good news for you. The doctor who assaulted you is in custody. He attacked another young lady who was able to identify him. He was arrested in Athens.'

Dimitra sucked in her breath. Thank goodness she had changed her mind about moving to the mainland.

'The young lady is determined to press charges against him and I have come to ask if you would also be willing to pursue the case through the courts.'

Dimitra hesitated, then shook her head. 'I just want to forget the incident.'

Thranassis looked at Vasi who shrugged. 'Is there nothing I could say that would make you change your mind?'

Dimitra shook her head again. 'If this other woman is willing to testify you have no need of me. Thank you telling me he has been arrested. If there's nothing else may I go back to work now?'

Thranassis nodded. 'Thank you for your time. If you decide to change your mind please contact me.'

Dimitra closed the office door behind her and Thranassis looked at Vasi and sighed. 'We are able to charge him on the evidence we have and I'm certain he'll be sentenced, but her testimony could have increased his jail sentence.'

Thranassis shook Vasi's hand. 'Should the young lady discuss her decision with you I trust you will tell her that to testify against the man would be in her own interest.'

'I'm quite sure Dimitra will not confide in me,' Vasi replied confidently, 'but should she do so I will support whatever decision she makes.'

Week 1 – October 2008

Abraham Gallagher consulted the letter he had with him and approached the embassy reception desk. 'I'm here to see Adam Kowalski.'

'Do you have an appointment, sir?'

'Not exactly. He is expecting me to call, but I was unable to give him a time. I've only just flown in.'

The receptionist dialled Adam's extension and after a short conversation turned back to Abraham. 'Mr Kowalski will be with you in about ten minutes. Can I offer you coffee whilst you wait?'

Abraham shook his head. He just wanted to get the meeting over and take another cab to his hotel. Flying from the States to London had taken a day, the wait for his flight to Greece had been tedious and then the further four hours in the air had taken its toll. He wanted a hot shower and a few hours sleep.

Adam Kowalski looked at his visitor curiously as he ushered him into a small side room, laid a thick folder on the table and sat opposite him. He held out his hand which was ignored. 'I appreciate you making the journey, Mr Gallagher.'

Abraham grunted. 'I need to sort this misunderstanding out and get my son released.'

'It may not be quite that simple,' Adam warned him. 'Your son has been charged with deliberate arson and when challenged he immediately admitted he had committed the crime.'

'Rubbish.'

'I think you should be made aware of the circumstances under which your son has been detained in custody.'

'I know the owner is saying my son set fire to his property deliberately. He's obviously trying a fraudulent claim on his insurance. My son is innocent.'

'Were you aware that your son was in Crete?' asked Adam.

'He's a man, not a little boy. He doesn't have to ask my permission to go away for a vacation.'

Adam nodded. 'Quite. You are aware, I presume, that he had been involved in two tragic events that had taken place in New Orleans? Firstly the death of his girl friend and being present at a diner when an officer of the law was shot.'

'Neither incident had anything to do with him,' declared Mr Gallagher. 'He wasn't with the girl when she died and he was also shot when he tried to intervene at the diner. It was in the newspapers.'

'Were you aware that your son kept a diary?'

Abraham Gallagher frowned. 'A diary?'

'Apparently it became a habit of his to record his actions and feelings from an early age. During the investigation his lap top was examined and the diary discovered. It is quite a disconcerting document, spanning the previous twelve years of his life.'

'He hasn't had a lap top for that length of time,' protested Adam. 'They weren't suitable for a student when he was young.'

'I understand he began to write a diary in longhand and when he had access to a computer he copied the notebooks. It is a very comprehensive diary of his thoughts and actions.'

'You've committed an invasion of privacy. He could very well sue you for that.'

Adam continued as if Abraham Gallagher had not spoken. 'I believe there was a situation that arose when he was a young teenager. A classmate became pregnant and she claimed he was the father of her child.'

Mr Gallagher's face purpled with annoyance. 'The girl was a precocious little tart. Anyone could have been the father of that child. Todd assured me that all the boys had been familiar with her.'

'According to your son's diary he was responsible. He records that you were furious with him, paid for the family to move away and lectured him on contraception.'

'It was an act of charity. The girl would have been ostracized if she had stayed living locally. That doesn't mean to say I accepted that my son was responsible. As for explaining the facts of life, including contraception, well, that's a father's duty.'

'Of course,' agreed Adam. 'It appears, from his diary, that he took notice of your advice. Sex was obviously very important to him. He took pleasure, not only in the act, but in writing a graphic description afterwards.'

Abraham Gallagher's lip curled. 'No doubt you enjoyed reading the salacious details. You're disgusting.'

Adam shook his head. 'I'm afraid his writing sickened me. I had no interest in reading every entry. I scrolled through to find his more recent entries and one page that was typed in bold caught my attention.' Adam leaned forward. 'Are you aware of the circumstances surrounding the death of the young lady?'

'She fell from her balcony. Todd was devastated.'

'According to his diary he was actually responsible for her death.'

'Nonsense.'

'The lady was already dead when she was deliberately thrown over the balcony. She had told your son that she was expecting his child and he pushed her. She tripped and fell. Unfortunately the fall caused her to break her neck. Your son panicked and decided to make her death appear accidental. He was devastated. He pours out his remorse in page after page of his diary, until a young lady sympathises with his distress and says he is not to blame. From then on he is able to excuse his actions and lay the blame on his girl friend for becoming pregnant.'

'I don't believe a word of it. There was an inquest and she fell whilst waving goodbye to Todd.'

'I'm afraid his diary describes the situation somewhat differently.'

'I don't believe this story about a diary.' Abraham glared at Adam. 'It's fictitious. It's been planted on his lap top to incriminate him. It certainly won't hold up in a court of law. He's innocent. Any confession he may have made was obviously coerced from him under threat.'

Adam shook his head sadly. 'I can assure you he was not put under any pressure when making his statement. It was completely voluntary. He had become totally fixated on this compassionate young girl who worked in the diner he frequented. They attended the same University and he made notes of classes, times of arrival, her clothing, how she spent her time. He would follow her, not with any evil intent, but to ensure her safety. She did not respond to his overtures and he arranged with a fellow student to stage an armed hold up in the diner. His plan was to rescue the girl so she would notice him. Unfortunately the student who was to be the robber decided to take along a real gun and an officer was shot.'

Mr Gallagher's face paled. Todd had made light of the incident to him and there had been no suspicion that he had been anything more than an unfortunate victim.

'I understand that after this event your son asked the young lady to marry him and stay in New Orleans rather than travel to Crete to spend the vacation with her relatives. She refused, but he was so besotted by her that he followed her to Crete and located the self catering chalets where she helped in the family business during the season. He has admitted to the police over here that he set fire to them deliberately, thinking she would have no reason to stay in the country if the business was destroyed.

'The police here are investigating a case of arson where a young man was injured. Fortunately no one died during the event or your son would be facing far more serious charges. The police in Greece are only interested in the recordings in his diary that cover the few weeks before the arson was committed and those entries will be used in evidence against him. I have a full transcript of his diary here.' Adam laid his hand on the folder. 'I thought it could be a good idea if you familiarised yourself with the content and then we could have another meeting. You can then give me your instructions about how you wish to proceed.' Adam pushed the folder across to Abraham.

'Can I see my son?'

'Certainly. He's being held in Crete. I can arrange a flight for you, but I suggest you read his diary before you visit him. No doubt you could also do with some rest. You've had a long journey.'

Abraham Gallagher picked up the folder. 'I'll be back tomorrow.'

Adam Kowalski shook his head. 'I will make you an appointment for Monday. I don't work over the weekends unless there is an emergency to deal with.'

'This is an emergency. My son has obviously been wrongly arrested and is sitting in jail. He needs to be released immediately.' Abraham drew an envelope from his pocket. He had been told this was how one dealt with the authorities in Greece.

Adam shook his head. 'I suggest you put that away, Mr Gallagher I am an embassy official, not an underpaid policeman who has summonsed you for a parking violation.'

Abraham Gallagher read through the transcript of his son's diary. It was alarming. His obvious remorse at the unintentional death of Jennie-Lea showed through. His actions to make her death appear as an accidental fall were inventive and no suspicion or blame had been attached to him. His scheme for a make believe hold up at the diner and wishing to appear a hero before the girl he had become besotted by had gone disastrously awry through no fault of his own.

His detailed plan to burn down the holiday chalets along with his confession would mean that a Greek court would have no option but find him guilty of the act. That would mean any number of years in a Greek jail. He would have to insist that Todd underwent psychiatric tests and ask that man at the embassy for a good defence lawyer who would claim that Todd was suffering psychologically at the time and could not be held responsible for his actions.

Abraham Gallagher was waiting at the door of the American Embassy when it opened on Monday morning and demanded to see Adam Kowalski immediately. He sat in the reception area watching as people entered the various small rooms and leaving clutching papers in their hands. After almost an hour he decided he had been forgotten and approached the receptionist again.

'I need to see Adam Kowalski. I've already been waiting an hour.'

'What time was your appointment, sir?'

'I wasn't given a time. I told him I would be back here on Monday morning. He should be expecting me.'

'Mr Kowalski does have other appointments, sir. If you don't have a time all I can ask you to do is to wait until he's free. I'll let his secretary know that you're here.'

'You should have done that already, then I wouldn't have been kept waiting.'

The receptionist raised her eyebrows archly. 'Had you made an appointment you would not have had to wait.' She picked up her telephone and dialled Adam's extension number. 'Your name, sir?'

'Gallagher, Abraham Gallagher.'

She spoke rapidly in Greek when she was answered. 'I have an Abraham Gallagher here waiting to see Mr Kowalski. Apparently he said he would be here on Monday, but he didn't make an appointment.' She looked at Abraham feeling fairly certain he did not speak any Greek. 'He seems to think he should be getting preferential treatment. Would Mr Kowalski be free at any time later today?'

She smiled as she replaced the receiver. 'Mr Kowalski is a little busy this morning. His secretary suggests you come back at four this afternoon. He should be able to spare you a few minutes then.'

'Four! This is important.'

'Everyone who visits us has important business, Mr Gallagher. If you are able to return at four this afternoon I will add your name to Mr Kowalski's list of appointments.'

'I want a definite appointment.'

'Very well. Four fifteen.'

'What am I supposed to do with myself until then?'

'Why not visit the Acropolis or the museum? The view from Mount Lycabettus is spectacular and they have a good restaurant. You can walk up or take the funicular. There is much to do in Athens.'

Abraham glared at her. Maybe he should have offered her an envelope to enable him to get an earlier appointment, but after Adam Kowalski's reaction he felt wary.

Adam Kowalski approached Abraham Gallagher and held out his hand. 'Good afternoon. I was expecting to see you earlier today.'

'I was told you were busy. This was the earliest appointment I could get.'

Adam looked over at the receptionist and raised his eyebrows. She had the grace to blush and Adam guessed the man had been rude and demanding when he had visited earlier.

'Please come through.' Adam ushered him into one of the rooms and indicated that he should take a seat.

'You've obviously read your son's diary?'

Abraham nodded.

'No doubt you now realise there is no way he can claim that the act was not premeditated. As far as I can see there are two courses of action open to you. The obvious one is that your son goes to court, pleads guilty to the charge and is sentenced to a term of imprisonment. The other is that you request a psychological assessment of his state of mind leading up to the event. If he were to be found mentally incapable of making reasonable and logical decisions the charges would be dropped and he would be sectioned.'

'Let me think.' Abraham closed his eyes and tried to assimilate the information. He did not want his son in a Greek jail for years, but nor did he want him languishing in a Greek mental hospital for an indeterminate amount of time.

Adam waited patiently until Abraham opened his eyes and sat forward. 'If it was concluded that he could not be held responsible for his actions and subsequently sectioned, would he be allowed to return to the States?'

'You would have to apply to the courts for him to leave the country. The decision would be up to them.'

'But if the charges against him were dropped they would have no case against him. Why would they want to keep him here?'

'Personally, I feel sure the Greek authorities would be only too pleased to allow him return to the States, but that is only my opinion. If he was sectioned why should they have the expense of keeping and treating him here? It would make sense that he returned to his own country.'

Abraham smiled. It was quite simple really. He would ask for his son to be sectioned, take him back to the States and install him in a private clinic for a couple of years. He would then be able to join him in his bank and no one would be any the wiser.

'Did you read all of his diary?' asked Adam.

'I skipped through a good deal. All that rubbish he wrote about a girl being his guardian angel and he was her protector. It shows the boy was definitely unhinged, traumatised and suffering from stress.'

'I do have to make you aware that if he returned to the States he would very likely be questioned about previous - er – events that he recorded in his diary. He could well be charged with other offences.'

'But if he was sectioned they would have to take that into account, they couldn't hold him accountable for his actions,' protested Abraham.

Adam shrugged. 'The States may wish to make their own

assessment of his culpability and could come to a different conclusion. It is my duty as an embassy official to point this out to you.'

Abraham frowned. 'If he was sectioned over here and returned to the States that would be the end of the matter. There would be no need for any of his diary to be made over to the police department.'

'The Greek police are in possession of that part of his diary that details his plans for arson. A psychological assessment of his mental state will be conducted as a matter of course. If the doctors feel there are sufficient grounds for him to be sectioned they would no doubt request that the whole diary was made available, to enable them to make a fair judgement. I cannot give you any assurance that the earlier entries will not be passed over to the police in New Orleans. Think about it carefully, Mr Gallagher, before you decide which route is the preferable one to take.'

'How long will this assessment take?'

Adam spread his hands. 'I cannot possibly give you an estimate of the time involved. Nothing moves very fast in Greece.'

Saffron fastened her seat belt and leaned back in the seat. She had not enjoyed her experience in Nigeria. The people had been friendly and welcoming, but she felt no rapport with those she had worked with. She had spent most of her time standing in front of a group explaining various operating techniques and they had listened to her politely. She had selected various unusual cases to operate on personally and demonstrate so they could learn from her. Her fellow surgeons had stood and watched dutifully, but with a disinterested attitude and not asked any questions. When she oversaw their work any guidance she offered was followed impassively and without comment. Although they were accomplished and caring they made it clear that they did not relish instruction from an English woman. She felt her six months in the country had been entirely wasted.

On more than one occasion she had been tempted to contact

the hospital in London and ask to be recalled, but her pride held her back. She did not voice her unhappiness to either Marjorie or Vasi, but she did not wish to spend any more time in the country. To be escorted whenever she wished to leave the medical compound was irksome and it had been impossible to travel around as she had hoped to visit the many interesting places she had read about.

She gave her attention to the safety demonstration that was taking place as the 'plane began to taxi along the runway. Pleased that she was returning to England, she was also filled with trepidation about the decision she would have to make. Did she want to give up being a doctor and marry Vasi, and how would Marjorie feel if she was to leave her alone in England?

Marjorie had turned down Vasi's proposal that she supervised a small group of visitors in his father's house. She had explained to both him and Saffron that she did not feel she was qualified to organise and supervise tourists, nor did she have the inclination to be away from her home for an indeterminate amount of time. She would have to arrive a week before the first visitors to familiarise herself with the house and area, then two weeks with the guests and if someone was to take over from her she would have to spend some time explaining the organisation to them. If no one suitable applied, no doubt she would be expected to stay on if there were further bookings.

Vasi spoke to her at length over the telephone trying to persuade her to change her mind, but Marjorie was adamant, finally telling him that she was too old and although she appreciated his offer she was not interested. Finally Vasi had accepted her decision and had decided to abandon the project.

Saffron had refused to get involved. She made it clear to Vasi that the decision had to come from Marjorie and she was not prepared to influence her in any way. Marjorie was grateful that Saffron did not try to pressurize her. She explained more fully to Saffron that the whole idea terrified her; to be virtually alone in a country where she did not speak the language and be responsible for the well-being of others was a daunting proposition.

Saffron opened her book as the 'plane gathered speed for take-off. She had deliberately chosen a night flight, having found the hours in the air on the journey out tedious. She would read for a while and then try to sleep for an hour or so. If sleep was impossible she would be able to use her lap-top, check for the latest e-mails from Elounda and reply as necessary.

During the time she had been away Bryony and Vasi had mailed her regularly each week. She knew Barbara and Yiorgo now had a little girl to add to their family and had finally agreed that she would be called Maria Tsambika. Yiorgo was happy to be out at sea each day, although he found sailing backwards and forwards to Spinalonga a monotonous journey after being in the navy and used to a vast expanse of sea and no sight of land.

She had been horrified when she had received a mail from Bryony in August telling her about the fire that had destroyed some of the self catering chalets and that John was in hospital suffering from superficial burns and smoke inhalation. She had 'phoned immediately and was reassured that John was in no danger and no one else had been hurt. Since then she had received long mails explaining how a man had become obsessed with Nicola. In his twisted mind he had decided that if the business was ruined Nicola would return to New Orleans and marry him. The man was now in prison in Heraklion and a full investigation was taking place.

When Vasi mailed her she pressed him for more details. He had accommodated as many of the guests as possible at his hotels in the vicinity. Although most of the chalets were usable there was a smell of smoke in the air and the charred remains of those that had been burnt to the ground were depressing and unsightly. He knew that Yannis and Giovanni were busy arguing with the insurance company for compensation and all the other bookings for the rest of the season had been cancelled.

Saffron had smiled to herself when she read about arguments with the insurance company. No doubt Marcus, with his background in insurance, and Marianne with her legal training, were prepared to fight for the compensation they felt the business was owed. She just hoped Yannis and Giovanni would receive enough for them to start the business up again and she was interested to know their plans. Once back in England, and after she had completed the obligatory medical examination she would have to undergo, she would arrange to fly out. Before she did that she must talk to Marjorie and decide upon her answer to Vasi.

Ourania listened to her husband with growing annoyance as he said he planned to sell her shop. He had not mentioned this proposal to her. The shop belonged to her. He had given it to her at the same time as he had given her the ultimatum of moving to Aghios Nikolaos with him or staying in Plaka with her mother. She felt both hurt and indignant. He had no right to make the decision without consulting her. She sat sulkily throughout the rest of the family conference and once they were in the privacy of their room she rounded on him angrily.

'You can't sell my shop, Yannis. You gave it to me. You said it was mine to do as I pleased with.'

Yannis nodded. 'I gave it to you verbally. I still hold all the deeds.'

'And now that it suits you, you're taking it back,' Ourania spoke bitterly.

'You didn't listen, 'Rani. Come and sit down.' Yannis took his wife's hand. 'When I've explained I'm sure you'll agree with me. We've had a good run. Now we both deserve to sit back and enjoy ourselves.'

'And grow senile like Aunt Anna and Uncle Yiorgo did? I'd rather work until the day I drop.'

'You might want to, but I don't. I find it tiring driving you and Marisa back and forth and then sitting in the shop for hours on end hoping a customer might buy something. I'd planned we should sell the shop in a couple of years and I've decided to do so a little earlier. Giovanni wants to build some shops on our land in Plaka and one of those will be yours.'

Ourania pursed her lips. 'And when will these shops be built? Construction doesn't take place over night.'

'I'm sure Giovanni will want to make a start as soon as possible and with luck you could be moving at the beginning of next season. I promise I won't sell the shop in Aghios Nikolaos until you have a new one in Plaka.'

'You say that now, but how do I know you won't change your mind?'

'Think about it, Ourania. Your shop is not on the main thoroughfare in Aghios Nikolaos. If it was down by the pool or in the centre of the town it would be a different matter. We don't get passing trade. Customers come to us because we have been recommended either by their friends or the hotel. A number of gift shops are selling cheap replicas of your goods and our sales have gone down.'

'The local people still come to us if they want a quality gift for someone,' replied Ourania truculently.

Yannis shook his head. 'We can't rely on that for a living. I'll make sure we have a prime site in Plaka. Think of the number of tourists who visit Spinalonga. Once there is a decent taverna and some shops in the village they'll be happy to wander around. That's when they'll find your shop. Trust me, 'Rani.'

John sat with his arm around Nicola. 'Well, that all turned out quite well, didn't it? I was relieved Mum didn't make more fuss about my eye. It was obviously the right time to tell them.'

Nicola moved so she was looking at John. 'You know you said we'd consider getting married when you finished your National Service. Do you still want to?'

'Of course.'

'Sure?'

'You know I'm sure. What's the problem? Are you having second thoughts?'

'I'm pregnant.'

'You're what!'

'Pregnant.'

'When did that happen?'

'I think it was that first night you were home on leave. I should have told you sooner, but with everything else that has happened I thought I should wait. I'm sorry, John.'

John hugged her. 'Why are you sorry? I'm delighted. When do they say the baby's due?'

'John, it's not one baby. I'm expecting twins.'

John looked at Nicola open mouthed. 'Twins!'

Nicola nodded and a broad grin spread across John's face. 'Are they boys or girls? Or one of each?'

Nicola shook her head. 'It's much too early to say.'

John leant over and kissed first one side of her stomach and then the other. 'I don't mind what they are. I love them already. What shall we call them?'

Nicola giggled. 'You are daft. It's much too early to think about names. I've been busy thinking how we'll break the news to your parents and to mine. I doubt if either set of parents will be overjoyed.'

'I'm sure they will be, once they've got used to the idea.'

Nicola sighed. 'We'll see.'

'Who are we going to tell first? Your parents or mine?'

'Yours,' said Nicola firmly. 'I know as soon as I've told mine they'll be on the 'phone and it wouldn't be fair for your parents to be in the dark.'

'So do we just tell Mum and Dad or everyone?'

Nicola pulled a face. 'We might just as well tell everyone at once and get it over with. Tomorrow, after lunch?'

John grinned. 'And then we can 'phone Saff. Bryony says she's back in England. I bet she'll be relieved it happened here and not when we were in London.'

Giovanni looked at his son in horror. 'What am I going to say to Nicola's father? I'm responsible for her whilst she's with us.'

'I'm sorry, Dad. We didn't intend this to happen. We've talked about getting married and we'd planned to wait until we were twenty five. We thought by then I'd be an established photographer and Nick would have had some time to do as she pleased, travel, work, whatever.' John held up his hand as his father was about to interrupt him. 'Please, hear me out, Dad. I realised when Nick came over this time and that awful creep had said he wanted to marry her that I wanted her here, where I could look after her. We were going to suggest that we were married when I finished my National Service. Then the fire happened. I've been invalided out of the army and it's pretty doubtful now if I'll ever make my mark as a photographer. We want to be together so it seemed practical to suggest that we were married now and Nick didn't have to go back to New Orleans. That was before she told me about the babies.'

'Nicola?' Giovanni turned to her.

Nicola nodded. 'John's told you the truth. It's my fault if you want to lay blame.' Nicola reddened. 'I've been taking the pill when I came over here. There was no need when I was in New Orleans. I'm supposed to start to take it two weeks before I need to rely on it. I came here earlier than usual and I knew John wasn't going to be here. Then I forgot about it and only started three days before John came home on leave. '

Giovanni looked at his wife and shook his head. There was no point in being upset with the situation. He had not known about his own son until he was some months old and had not married Marianne until John was over a year old.

'When are these babies due?' asked Marianne.

'They told me April, but being twins they could be early. I hope they are; then I'll be able to help you as usual.'

Marianne shook her head. 'You have no idea how exhausting it is to look after one child, let alone two. You'll be spending all your time feeding and changing them for the first few months.'

Bryony looked at Nicola enviously. She would have loved to have had a child. 'I'll help you,' she offered.

Nicola smiled. 'I'm sure I'll be grateful for all the help I can get!'

'What have your parents said?' asked Marianne.

'I haven't told them yet. We wanted to tell you first.'

'Why?'

'I didn't want Dad on the 'phone and you not knowing what he was talking about.' Nicola looked at her watch, 'I'll give them time to get up then I promise I'll call them.'

Giovanni ran his hand through his hair. 'We could have done without this just at the moment. Now we are going to have to make wedding arrangements. As if we didn't have enough to deal with!'

John shook his head. 'We don't want a grand wedding.' He took Nicola's hand. 'If Nick's parents and sister want to come over that's fine. If not it will be just us, the family. Besides, by the time you had organised a big wedding Nick would probably be too big and unwieldy to get into a boat.'

Giovanni raised his eyebrows. 'A boat?'

'We want to get married on Spinalonga.'

Marisa drew in her breath. 'That would be lovely. I'll never forget my wedding day over there.'

Nicola smiled at her gratefully. She had expected opposition to her idea.

'You don't want to get married in America?'

Nicola shook her head. 'I'm far more at home here, besides, it wouldn't be fair to ask Grandma to make that long trip and I do want her to be with us.'

'What about your aunt in Athens – do you plan to ask her?' asked Marianne.

Giovanni pushed back his chair. 'Those decisions can be made later,' he said irritably. 'I suggest you get on the telephone to your parents, Nicola. You'll have to ask them to send over your birth certificate and you may need other papers from the American

Embassy. You can't make any plans until the legal formalities have been complied with. Once they are completed I'll see how Pappa Lucas feels about making a trip to Spinalonga in the winter.'

Annita picked up Elias's photograph and ran her finger across his lips. 'Well, Elias, what do you make of that? Nicola is expecting twins. She and John seem to be so excited and happy. In our day if such a thing had happened we would have hung our heads in shame and crept away where no one knew us. We felt Anna brought shame on us by her behaviour. Maybe we should have realised the world was changing and people no longer placed such sanctity on their marriage vows. It appears to be accepted everywhere now that young people live together without getting married and have children just as they fancy. Had we been more lenient with Anna her life might have turned out differently. I wish I knew what had happened to her. The money I sent was returned so can only think she has died. I'd like to know what happened eventually to her other girl, Christabelle. I should have asked Bryony to find her before we left New Orleans. It's too late now. I'm sure if I asked Elena she would claim she had no idea where to start and Helena would say she was too busy. I wonder if they will be invited to the wedding and agree to come over? I'd like to see them all again, particularly Andreas, but I also have an idea that I shall be quite happy to wave them goodbye.' Annita shifted her position in her chair slightly. 'Nicola insists she wants to be married on Spinalonga. I'm not sure how I feel about that, Elias. I refused to go over with you when you visited. I didn't want to think about Yannis suffering there all those years. Mind you, I'm not sure how they'll get me in and out of a boat nowadays. I expect Giovanni and John will find a way. Provided they don't drop me overboard!' Annita gave a little chuckle. 'That would make you laugh, wouldn't it, Elias? I'd like to hear you laugh again.' A solitary tear ran down Annita's face and she brushed it away impatiently. 'I mustn't drop tears on your photo. Tears do no one any good.'

'Your Dad doesn't seem at all pleased.' Nicola looked at John for comfort.

John shrugged. 'He'll get over it. He's got a lot on his mind at the moment. Whilst you speak to your parents I'll have a look on the internet and see what legal papers you might require. I doubt if you'll need more than your birth certificate and passport.'

Nicola nodded. She could not put off the telephone call any longer. She keyed in her home number in New Orleans and listened to it ringing. Her heart was beating fast as she heard her mother's voice.

'Nicola, what's wrong? Why are you calling so early? Has something happened with that man?'

'No, Mum. He's in custody in Heraklion. There's nothing to worry about there. I – I've something I want to tell you.'

'You haven't got to stay out there until he's been brought to trial, have you? That could be months. What about your education? You're in your final year and your exams will be important.'

'No, Mum, listen. It's nothing to do with the fire. I'm sorry, but I'm pregnant.'

'You're what?'

'I'm pregnant. It was finally confirmed a few days ago.'

'Nicola! I don't believe you! I thought you were adult enough to behave responsibly. We should never have let you go over to Crete on your own each year. We trusted you and now look what you've done. When are you coming home?'

'I'm not planning to come back to New Orleans. We didn't do it on purpose. John and I had planned to get married in a few years time. This has just brought the date forward.'

'You haven't asked our permission to marry him.'

'Mum, I'm over eighteen. I don't have to ask your permission. All I have to ask is for you to send over my birth certificate.'

Elizabeth ignored Nicola's request. 'I think you should come back home and have the baby and see how you feel afterwards. You don't want to jump into something and find you've made another mistake, you silly girl. How Eleanor will feel I don't know. She won't be able to look the neighbours or her friends in the eye.'

'Mum, I don't need this. Due to me Giovanni's business has been ruined. He could have put me on the first 'plane back to New Orleans. Instead he assured me it was not my fault. I know he's worried to death how he's going to turn the business around. There are all sorts of complications with the insurance and building regulations. Now on top of that we've just told him he's going to become a grandfather.'

'You told him before us!'

'I didn't want Dad on the 'phone to him when he knew nothing about it.'

'And no doubt he's delighted. I know how the Greeks feel about their grandchildren. The more they have the higher their prestige in the village. No, you're to come home, Nicola. I'll get your father to book a flight today, immediately. You can be back in a couple of days.'

Nicola set her mouth in a determined line. 'I am not coming back to New Orleans. Dad can book as many flights as he likes, but I'll not be on the 'plane. Let me speak to him.'

'So you can twist him round your little finger and get your own way.'

'No, so that I can explain the situation and have a sensible conversation,' snapped back Nicola.

'He may have left for work.'

'Then I'll call him on his mobile.'

Nicola heard her mother give a deep sigh. 'I'll hand you over.'

'It's Nicola,' she heard her mother say. 'The stupid girl is pregnant and says she's not coming home.'

'Hello, Nicola. Is it true that you're pregnant?' asked Nicolas in Greek.

'Yes, Dad, and I'm very sorry. We didn't mean it to happen.'

'What are you planning to do about the situation?'

'John and I want to get married now. We want to have a quiet wedding here. You, Mum and Eleanor will obviously be invited over, but no one else. Next year we'll invite everyone and have a big party for the twins' first birthday.'

'Twins!'

Nicola managed a smile. 'Sorry. I should have said before. I've managed a double packet of trouble.'

'Have you told Giovanni and Marianne? What do they say?'

'I don't think they are any happier with the situation than you are, but they've accepted that there's nothing they can do about it. Giovanni says I need my birth certificate so we can apply to get married. Will you send it to me, please, Dad?'

'Will you need anything else?'

'John's having a look on the internet now. If he comes up with anything can I mail you?'

'Of course. I'll speak to Giovanni later, when I've had a talk with your mother.'

'Thank you, Dad.' Nicola felt close to tears. 'You will send my birth certificate, won't you?'

Nicola switched off her mobile 'phone and gave a sigh of relief. She had been dreading her conversation with her parents. She walked into the kitchen and poured a glass of water with a shaking hand.

Marianne placed her arms around her and gave her a hug. 'Rough call?'

Nicola nodded.

'I'll 'phone your Mum later. She's bound to be upset. Mine was when I said I was expecting John. At least you told her who the father is. I refused to say.'

'Dad said he was going to call Giovanni.'

'Yeah, they can man-talk. Don't worry, Nicola. Everything will sort itself out.'

'Mum kept insisting I should go back home.'

'Whatever for? John is here. We're all here to look after you.'

'She seemed to think I would change my mind about getting married if was back over in the States.'

'Why should you do that?' Marianne frowned.

'I won't change my mind. I love John. You know I do.'

Marianne nodded. 'I don't doubt that for a minute. I know you two are inseparable, and I was not so stupid that I didn't know what was going on.'

'I wish I'd been more careful,' said Nicola miserably.

Marianne shrugged. 'Mistakes happen and it often turns out for the best. Cheer up, now. Don't keep blaming yourself. It takes two, you know.'

John walked into the kitchen and raised his eyebrows at Nicola. 'Well?' he asked.

Nicola drew a deep breath. 'Dad was more reasonable than Mum. I've asked him to send my birth certificate. Is there anything else I need?'

'A certificate declaring there is no impediment to us getting married.'

'What do you mean?' Nicola looked puzzled.

'You have to declare that you're not already married to someone else. We'll go into Aghios Nikolaos and check out all the legal requirements. It could take a month or more before we can actually go ahead as you're an American citizen.'

'But I was born in Athens,' protested Nicola.

'That makes no difference. People can be born anywhere in the world. It doesn't make them citizens of the country.' John stopped talking and frowned. 'I was born in New Orleans. How ironic! Mum, am I Greek or American?'

'You're Greek,' Marianne assured him. 'When your father and I married he formally adopted you so you became Greek.'

'Well, that's one problem out of the way. Go and get your coat, Nick, and we'll drive into Aghios Nikolaos and see if they can tell us the details at the Town Hall. Duck and chicken can come with us if they promise to be good.'

Marianne raised her eyebrows. 'Duck and chicken?'

John shrugged. 'They have to be called something apart from 'babies' and 'twins'. Duck and chicken just seemed appropriate.'

'I hope you'll think of some more suitable names later,' remarked Marianne dryly.

John nodded. 'If they're boys they can be Drake and Rooster.'

Nicola giggled. This was the first she had heard of the names John had given to the babies she was carrying.

'John, lovely to hear from you.'

'I thought you'd like a call to welcome you back from Nigeria.'

'It's so good to be home. How is everything in Elounda? Are things getting sorted out?'

'I'm keeping well out of all the business problems. Nick and I have other things on our minds.'

'Such as?'

'You know you told us to be careful? Well we weren't.'

'What do you mean, John?' asked Saffron, feeling her heart sink.

'Nick's pregnant.'

'Oh, Lord. What do your parents say?'

'Mum's okay. Dad's a bit fed up. He's got enough to cope with at the moment.'

'Are you getting married?'

'We were planning to, but Nick's getting sick of all the formalities because she isn't Greek. It might be easier just to live together.'

'I thought she was born in Athens.'

'She was, but her Dad became an American citizen and so did she. That complicates things.'

Saffron frowned. 'How do you mean?'

'We've just come back from the Town Hall. They've told us she has to have a certificate from the United States Embassy declaring there is no impediment to our marriage. An Affidavit has to be signed under oath before a Consular Officer and we'll have to go to Heraklion for that. Then it has to be translated into Greek and a notice published in the newspapers. I had no idea it was such a performance.'

'What kind of impediment would there be?'

'Oh, you know, a criminal record or married before. If she was she has to produce her divorce papers or a death certificate and they have to be translated. We've made a list of everything they say they want and I've just realised we didn't ask them about her American citizenship papers. I'd better add that as well. And Nick also has to apply for a residency permit as she has already been here nearly three months.'

Saffron felt her mouth go dry. She had no idea that to marry a Greek was so involved. 'Does everyone have to go through that procedure?'

'Well, it's easier if both the parties are Greek. There are still formalities, producing certificates and the like, but they don't need to be translated of course.'

'So how long will all this take?'

'It could be months. All we want is to have a quiet wedding on Spinalonga and we can't make any arrangements with the priest or even make a provisional date at the moment.'

'Spinalonga?'

'Yes, that's another thing we have to get permission for and then Pappa Lucas will have to be willing to go over.'

'What made you decide to get married over there?'

'It was Nick's idea.'

'How is Nicola?'

'She's a bit up tight at the moment with all this going on and her Mum was pretty mad with her, but physically she's fine.'

'That's good to hear. I understand the first few months can be the most difficult, with morning sickness and often feeling under the weather.'

'Nick hasn't been sick. I didn't even realise she was pregnant until she told me. Now I know I wonder why I hadn't noticed that she'd put on a bit of weight in the last few weeks.'

Saffron laughed. 'She'll put on a quite a bit more yet. When's the baby due?'

'Oh, didn't I say? They've told her April, but as it's twins she'll probably be early.'

'Twins! You hadn't told me that.'

'Sorry, I just expect everyone to know.'

'Is Nicola there? Can I speak to her?'

'Sure, I'll hand you over.'

'Hi, Saffie. Is it good to be back in England?'

'Apart from the cold weather I'm delighted to be back. John has just told me you're expecting twins. You two don't do things by halves, do you?'

Nicola giggled. 'John has called them duck and chicken.'

'Nicola, you two are taking the situation seriously, I hope.'

'Yes, we are, but we've had a stressful day and need to lighten up a bit. Mum really went off on one at me. Kept saying I had to go back to New Orleans. Marianne spoke to her later and reckoned she'd calmed her down a bit. Dad called Giovanni and I don't know the outcome of that. Finding out about all the paper work that is needed was the last straw. I'm not sure I want to get married now.'

'From what John said about a residency permit you'll have to, otherwise you'll have to continually renew your visitor's permit, and suppose it was refused?'

Nicola sighed heavily. 'It just seems so complicated and such a fuss about nothing. Two people want to get married, end of story.'

'I'm sure it won't be as difficult as you seem to think. Have you told Grandma?'

'Yes, we told everyone after lunch today.'

'What did she say?'

'Nothing. Everyone seemed to leave the talking up to Marianne and Giovanni. Bryony seemed delighted and offered to help me with them.'

'Just take it day by day and don't get all stressed up about the legalities.'

'I guess you're right there. I can't do anything except produce whatever paperwork they ask for. Anyway, when are you coming over to see us? The weather's quite good still. I bet it's better than in England.'

Saffron smiled. 'I have to undergo tests and until I have the all clear on those I can't even go back in to work.'

'What's wrong with you?'

'Hopefully nothing at all. It's a routine thing when you've been to an African country. You can be carrying something that could infect others or make you ill in a few months time. I feel fine, but I can't make any plans until I know for sure. I certainly wouldn't want to come over now and give you something horrible. John says you haven't even been sick.'

Nicola laughed. 'Yeah, I didn't even have that problem to give me a clue. When the Doctor said I was pregnant I didn't believe him. I asked for another test the following month. Now I know it's going to be twins I'm laying the blame firmly on John's shoulders. They come from his side of the family, not mine.'

'Of course, I always forget that Marianne is one of twins.'

'I'm glad John wasn't. Fancy having two like him around!'

'I've no recollection of Marianne's sister. Are they alike?'

'They were to look at when they were children, but not now.' Nicola giggled. 'We may have to pin their names on ours if they're identical.'

'I'm sure you'll very soon know which one is which, besides if you have a boy and a girl you'll have no problem.'

'I really don't mind whether they're boys or girls. Provided they're perfect and healthy, that's all that matters.'

'Exactly. When I get the all clear I'll arrange to come over. I want to be quite certain I won't bring anything nasty with me.'

Saffron closed her mobile 'phone thoughtfully. If Nicola had to produce affidavits and papers to prove that there was no impediment to her marriage to John what would she have to produce if she did marry Vasi? She had been born in New Orleans, taken her father's British nationality when they returned to England, married an Indian who ended up in prison, and was subsequently widowed. Before she gave an answer to Vasi she ought to do some investigating of her own.

Marjorie shook her head when Saffron imparted John and Nicola's news to her. 'They're very young to have such responsibilities.'

'It isn't like England, remember, Marjorie. They have a home and their relatives are all around them to help out with childcare. Apparently Bryony has already offered to help.'

Marjorie shook her head. 'I don't mean like that. They seemed to enjoy going out and around and doing things together when they were here. They won't be able to do as they please once they have the children. I just hope it won't make either of them feel resentful later and cause friction between them.'

'I'm sure it won't. I've said I'll go over to visit as soon as my tests come back showing I'm free from any infection. Are you going to come with me?'

Marjorie shook her head. 'I'd rather wait until the weather is better. I do enjoy lying on their beach and swimming. If I came now I'd be stuck indoors or they'd feel they had to take me places to entertain me. I'm sure they're terribly busy since the fire and wouldn't want to bother with a visitor.'

'If it was a problem I'm sure you could stay with Cathy or in one of Vasi's hotels.'

'No, I'm quite happy here during the winter months.'

'But you didn't have a holiday whilst I was away. I know Giovanni asked you over and Cathy asked you to go and stay with her and you refused both of them.'

'I was busy. I had things to do here,' replied Marjorie vaguely.

She was not going to admit to Saffron that the thought of being at the airport and arriving in Crete alone petrified her.

'I'll feel guilty going away so soon after I've just come back.'

'There's no need to feel any guilt. I have plenty of outings arranged with the Goldsmiths and Henry.'

'Henry?' Saffron raised her eyebrows.

'Yes, I told you in a mail. I met Maurice's brother, Henry, when I went to the Goldsmith's for a meal. I think they asked me to make up the numbers. Henry was widowed about a year ago and decided to move down here to be close to them. I bumped into him at the library a couple of weeks later and we had a cup of tea together. He seemed very lonely. He feels he can't impose on Maurice and Sylvia and expect them to keep him occupied. Well, one thing led to another and he offered to take me shopping at one of the out of town stores later in the week. I really missed going shopping with you each week and having to make two or three journeys in the week to the local shops, and they're much more expensive.'

'You could have gone to a large store on the free bus and had a taxi back,' protested Saffron.

'It didn't seem worth it when I was just shopping for myself. We usually meet once a week, do the shopping and then have lunch in the cafeteria. I encouraged him to join the Bridge Club and he's made some new friends there. A couple of weeks ago we went to the cinema and when the weather improves he says we'll take some drives out into the country and have a pub meal.'

'Do I sense a romance?' asked Saffron.

Marjorie shook her head. 'No, we're just friends. I'm not interested in it developing any further.'

'I wouldn't mind,' Saffron assured her. 'I'd be happy that you had found a companion to take Dad's place.'

'Henry is just a friend. He misses Patricia. They did everything together. He talks about her a good deal. I'm sure he has no romantic inclinations any more than I have.'

'How did his wife die? Was she ill?'

'It was very sudden apparently. They were out for a drive and she complained that she felt nauseous and had a bad headache. By the time they had driven home she was slumped against the door and not responding to anything he said. He went straight to the hospital and the medics came out to the car. As soon as they had moved her inside they pronounced her dead. It turned out she'd had a brain haemorrhage.'

'How awful. Poor man. I'd like to meet him.'

'I'm sure you will at some time. We didn't arrange anything for this week as you were arriving home, but after Bridge he sometimes stops for a cup of tea and piece of cake. I could ask him and the Goldsmiths to supper once the hospital is satisfied with the results of your tests.'

Saffron nodded. 'It should only be three more days. I feel fine, so I'm not expecting them to discover that I have a problem.'

'If they're so worried about you bringing something nasty into the country why do they allow you home? I would have thought it more sensible to keep you at the hospital in isolation.'

Saffron shuddered. 'Don't suggest it! I suppose they think that if I only meet my immediate family anything I pass on can be contained. I had to agree not to go anywhere that I would come into contact with other people, like the cinema or shopping, but they have to trust me to keep my word. For all they know I've been partying and shopping in the West End. As soon as I'm cleared to go back to work I'll ask for some leave so I can go over and see Grandma and everyone. Let me know if you change your mind and decide to come with me.'

Marjorie shook her head. 'I'd rather wait until the spring, besides, Henry and I are in the middle of the Bridge Tournament. I wouldn't want to leave him without a partner.'

Week 2 – October 2008

John walked over to the window and pulled back the curtain. Spinalonga was shrouded in mist and hardly visible. He hoped it would not be like this on the day they chose to get married over there in the tiny church. He looked over at Nicola who still appeared to be sleeping peacefully and smiled. He was looking forward to being a father, not so much whilst they were babies, but when they were old enough to be interested in new experiences and respond. Maybe one of them would be interested in photography and he would be able to pass on his own knowledge.

He looked across to Spinalonga again and as he did so darkness descended before his eyes. He stood completely still, holding the curtain tightly. He would not dare to move until the blackness had cleared. He leaned his forehead against the cool glass, but the darkness remained and he felt panic welling up in him. Was he going to be blind? He blinked rapidly and pressed his hand to his forehead and the darkness disappeared as quickly as it had come. Shakily John walked the few steps to the chair and sat down.

He accepted that his dream of becoming a wild life photographer was over. He could manage well enough with a tripod, to take still shots, but he was unable to hold a movie camera and press his forehead at the same time. He had made light of the problem to his family, but he wished he knew if the sudden blackouts would become more frequent and of longer duration or disappear as his skull fracture healed. It was frightening. There was no way he could not confide his fears to Nicola. He did not want her worrying about him whilst she was carrying their children.

'What's wrong, John?'

He tried to smile. 'Nothing. I just didn't want to disturb you.'

'Is it a decent day?'

'No, it's misty. If it isn't raining now I'm sure it will be in an hour or so.'

Nicola swung her legs over the side of the bed. 'Oh, well, it doesn't really matter. We'll be inside working.'

'You won't over do it, will you Nick?'

Nicola smiled at his concern. 'John, I'm folding bedding and boxing up cutlery. It's not exactly arduous.'

'You won't go up the steps to take the curtains down, will you?'

Nicola shook her head. 'They're down in most of the chalets. Bryony did that yesterday. She says she's left them lying on the bed for me to fold and box up with the bedding. Do you want to shower first?'

John nodded. 'I'll not be long, then you can take your time.' He hoped he would not have a blackout whilst in the shower and suffer a fall.

Saffron entered the London hospital where she worked eagerly. It would be good to be back in the familiar surroundings. To her surprise her secretary, Angela, was not at her desk. It was unlike her to be late. Saffron unlocked the door to her office and frowned in annoyance. The furniture had been moved around, obviously to the liking of the Nigerian doctor. She would have to ask one of the porters to return it to her original arrangement.

There were no case notes or list of appointments sitting on her desk and she hoped Angela had them locked in her cupboard outside. She hung her coat and bag behind the door and returned to the reception area. An unknown girl was sitting at Angela's desk, applying a fresh coat of lipstick.

'Hello,' smiled Saffron. 'Where's Angela?'

The girl shrugged. 'Who's Angela?'

'My usual secretary.'

'Don't know. I'm from the temp agency. I'm Mandy.'

'Oh,' Saffron felt completely nonplussed. 'I'm Doctor Bartlett. Do you have a list of appointments and case notes for me?'

'I've only just arrived.'

'Maybe you could have a look on your computer.' Saffron unlocked the cupboard behind the desk and saw the top shelf was empty.

'What do I look under?'

'Key in Saffron Bartlett and it should come up with my diary. Put in today's date and it will show my timetable for the week. Print a copy off for me and bring it in, please.'

Saffron returned to her office and dialled the extension number for the main reception area of the hospital.

'Hello, is that Fiona? It's Saffron Bartlett here. I seem to have a few problems. My secretary, Angela, is not in and I have a temp who seems clueless. Would you have my appointment schedule for today?'

'Welcome back, Doctor Bartlett. Did you enjoy your time in Nigeria?'

'Not particularly. What's happened to Angela?'

'She's off sick. Has been for over a week.'

'What's wrong with her?'

'I don't know. Not my department to deal with absence. I can find out if you like.'

'No, I'll 'phone her myself.' Saffron sighed. 'It's more important that I know when my first appointment is due and dig out any relevant case notes.'

'Hold on a sec.'

Saffron waited and heard Fiona tapping her keyboard.

'Here we are. Have you got a pen or do you want me to send a copy through to you?'

'Tell me the first two so I can get prepared, then I'd be grateful for a copy. I don't think the temp knows her way around the system.'

'She's not alone there! Jacob Macalister is due at nine thirty followed by John Potter at ten.'

'Thanks, Fiona.' Saffron looked at the clock. She had twenty minutes before her first appointment was due. She went to the filing cabinet and looked for notes on Jacob Macalister. There was nothing relating to the patient, despite Saffron searching under different spellings for Macalister. She decided he must be a new referral, probably with a letter from his doctor. There were no notes for John Potter either and she looked at her clock again. She would have time to telephone Angela.

A somewhat sleepy voice answered her.

'Angela, it's Saffron. I hope I haven't disturbed you too early. I've just found out that you've been off sick for over a week. What's wrong?'

'I've got shingles.'

'Oh, you poor thing. You must be feeling horrible.'

'I am. It's painful and itchy, and the doc says it will be that way for at least another couple of weeks.'

'Just be careful you don't break the blisters. I'll call you when I get home this evening and we can have a proper chat,' promised Saffron.

Jacob Macalister arrived early for his appointment and Mandy ushered him into Saffron's office without knocking prior to opening the door. He was not a new referral and when Saffron had to admit that she did not have his previous case notes he was annoyed.

'I really don't know what the medical service is coming to. If I lost someone's accounts they'd probably sue me. I shall be taking this further. It really isn't good enough. I've taken the morning off work to come here.'

'I do apologise, Mr Macalister. I've only just returned from working abroad and my usual secretary is off sick. I'm sure your notes have been misfiled, not lost. Maybe you could tell me what you were treated for and I could check physically to see if you need another follow up appointment?' Saffron tried to mollify him.

Mr Macalister picked up his coat from the chair. 'I'll not bother. I could tell you anything. My solicitor will be in touch.'

Saffron's face flamed. The inefficiency was not her fault and she could not blame Mr Macalister for being annoyed. She crossed over to her filing cabinet and began another search for John Potter. This time instead of looking under 'P' she began at the front of the drawer where the surnames of patients began with 'A'. She would have to go through everyone as it must have been misfiled. Exasperated Saffron pulled out a number of folders clearly marked with a variety of surnames. Amongst them was Jacob Macalister and further on she found John Potter.

She placed the folders on top of the filing cabinet and slammed the drawer closed. Saffron pressed her intercom button to speak to Mandy. There was no answer after she had buzzed her three times and Saffron rose from her desk and went out to reception. Mandy was sitting in front of the computer leafing through a magazine.

'Why didn't you answer when I buzzed you?'

'I didn't know that was you.'

'Whether it was me or not you should still answer it. Do you have a list of my appointments?' asked Saffron.

Mandy flipped her magazine closed, leaving a finger on the page to keep her place, and handed a sheet of paper to Saffron.

'Is that what you wanted?'

Saffron glanced at it. 'Thank you. How long have you been here temping, Mandy?'

'I started last week.'

'Were you asked to do the filing of the patients' notes?'

'Sometimes.'

'And how did you organise that?'

Mandy shrugged. 'Just put them in the cabinet.'

'It didn't occur to you that there were alphabetical sections and they should have been filed in order using their surname? The whole filing system is a mess. If you are asked to file something you must ensure it goes into the correct place. Mr Macalister was extremely angry that I could not find his notes. He's threatening legal action.'

'Some people!'

'Mr Macalister is quite within his rights. A patient should be able to expect their notes to be available when they attend an appointment.'

Mandy flipped open her magazine again and Saffron could feel anger rising within her.

'And another thing, Mandy, when you bring a patient to my door you always knock before you open it.'

'You didn't have anyone else with you.'

'It's courtesy. It is also a courtesy to the patients to look occupied. Please put that magazine away and keep it to read in your lunch break. In the meantime I suggest you look into one or two of my reports and see how I like them laid out. I will dictate them after each patient and bring them out to you. They have to be typed up on the computer and then a paper copy returned to me for checking. This looks like Mr Potter arriving. Fortunately I have found his notes.' Saffron swept back into her room and Mandy pulled a face behind her back.

At lunch time Saffron read the reports Mandy had printed off and shook her head. Various words were misspelt and the lines were not double spaced. Sighing in exasperation Saffron stood by Mandy's desk waiting for her to return from her extended lunch hour.

As she sauntered across the room Saffron looked pointedly at her watch. 'Lunch hour does mean an hour, Mandy.'

'I was at the hairdresser. She was running a bit late.'

'Then you should have cancelled your appointment and made another for after work.'

Mandy shook her head. 'Couldn't do that. Meeting my mates straight after I finish here and we're having a night out on the town.'

'I trust my reports will have been corrected and reproduced to my satisfaction by then otherwise you may have to meet your friends a little later.'

'I've done those you've given me,' protested Mandy sulkily.

'Not in a satisfactory manner. I have corrected them on the paper copies. You will have to correct them on the computer and run me off another copy to check. When you do the next ones please take more care over your spelling of medical terms. If in doubt use the spell check. The word for the bone in the arm is radius, not radios and a scapula is a shoulder blade – a scalpel is a cutting blade.' Saffron placed the papers on the desk next to Mandy. 'I suggest you make a start and don't forget they have to be double spaced.'

'I'm not a doctor,' muttered Mandy.

'I appreciate that and I spelled out the words I realised you might be unfamiliar with. There's no excuse for these errors.'

Sighing heavily, Mandy took her seat and opened her computer whilst Saffron returned to her office.

At the end of the day Saffron sought out Sean in his office and asked him to spare her a few minutes.

'I've finished reading your reports,' he said with a frown. 'You don't seem to have enjoyed being in Nigeria.'

'I had expected to receive a more positive response from the medical staff. They seemed to resent my presence.'

'That must have been due to your approach. We had no problem with Doctor Zakari.'

Saffron licked her lips. 'I found it very restrictive. I'm used to doing as I please in my spare time. Being virtually a prisoner on the hospital compound was irksome. I appreciate it was for my own safety, but I had hoped to be able to visit different places whilst I was there.'

Sean shrugged. 'It wasn't meant to be a holiday.'

'I didn't expect it to be, but I did think I'd be able to go out and around when I wasn't working. Actually, that's what I've come to talk to you about. I'd like to ask for some leave.'

'You've just had six months away.'

Saffron nodded. 'I know, but as you said, it was not a holiday. I usually visit my relatives in May and September. I wasn't able to do that this year so I have leave owed to me.'

'You've just had two weeks at home.'

'As a virtual prisoner whilst I had to wait for my test results to confirm my health,' replied Saffron bitterly. 'I'd like to arrange to take some time off as soon as possible. My usual secretary is away sick and the girl who has been sent from the agency to replace her is useless.'

Sean frowned. 'We use a very reputable agency.'

'I'm sure you do, but I don't think this girl has any knowledge of medical terms. In two different reports she typed the word radius as radios, amongst other errors. I'd like to investigate the availability of direct flights to Crete, leaving as soon as possible. I want to avoid a long stopover in Athens if possible and I do want to visit my grandmother,'

'It isn't my fault that your relatives live abroad.'

'And it is not my fault that there are no direct flights after the end of October.'

Sean sighed. He had no reason to refuse Saffron's reasonable request. 'That will mean I have to change the work schedule. It's not convenient.'

Saffron bit at her lip. 'I'm sorry to upset your arrangements, but I do have a life outside the hospital. Had my results come back positive you would have confined me to a hospital room until you considered I had a clean bill of health. You would have had to alter the schedule.'

'But as your results came back clear there was no need.'

'I'm very relieved that I haven't brought anything back with me. I wouldn't have considered visiting Crete otherwise. My grandmother is in her nineties and my niece is expecting twins. I certainly wouldn't risk making either of them ill,' replied Saffron stiffly. 'I'm insisting that I take the leave that is owed to me as soon as possible. I cannot work with the incompetent secretary from the temping agency until Angela is well enough to return to work. It makes sense for me to take some leave whilst she is absent.' Saffron folded her arms and challenged Sean with her eyes.

'But I've arranged a full schedule for the next month,' protested Sean. 'I'd like to get all the routine follow ups cleared before the onset of the winter problems.'

'If my test results had shown I was carrying something you would have had no hesitation in suspending me from duty. Someone else would have covered my appointments then so they can obviously do so now.'

Saffron left Sean's office and drove home feeling distinctly aggrieved. She was entitled to a minimum of six weeks' holiday each year. She had booked some time out the previous November expecting Vasi to be in London and then cancelled the days. She had managed a weekend in Crete before leaving for Nigeria and it was unreasonable for Sean to try to deny her a visit to her family when she had been abroad at the request of the hospital for six months.

Marjorie raised her eyebrows as Saffron closed the front door noisily behind her and threw her bag on the chair.

'Something wrong?'

'Angela is off sick. I have the most useless temp imaginable. Someone has moved the furniture around in my office and the filing is a complete shambles. I asked Sean for time off to go to Crete and he tried to tell me I was not entitled to it.' Saffron removed her jacket and threw that alongside her bag.

Marjorie frowned. 'You must be entitled. You haven't had any proper leave this year, just one or two odd days.'

'In his eyes my six months in Nigeria was a holiday. Some holiday! Nothing to do and nowhere to go when I did have free time. He's also counting the time I had to stay home when I returned until my test results were back. It isn't my fault that Nigeria has some nasties and they insist you stay out of circulation until you've been given the all clear. He finally said I could have the last two weeks of this month. That means I'll have to look for flight availability tonight and go at the weekend from Heathrow. It just isn't fair!'

'It's not worth getting worked up over, Saffie. You want to go to Crete and you've managed to get the time off, just be thankful for that.'

'If I do go at the weekend it won't give Marianne much notice,' grumbled Saffron.

'I doubt she'll mind. They have plenty of room at the house. If by any chance she has someone else staying you could always go into one of their chalets or a hotel.'

Saffron shook her head. 'I don't know that the chalets are a viable proposition since the fire. Oh, I'm sure it will be alright. If not I'll ask Vasi if he has a room free at his Elounda hotel.'

Saffron was puzzled by the reception she received when she spoke to Marianne. 'I can't have you here to stay. It's far too difficult at the moment and to stay in a chalet is out of the question. If Vasi has a room free in Elounda it would be far better if you stayed there. Meals are no problem; it's just the sleeping arrangements. I can't get anything organised at such short notice.'

'I understand how difficult it must be for you at the moment.'

'You've no idea!' remarked Marianne dryly. 'You know you're welcome, but everything is completely upside down in the house and it will probably be like that for a considerable amount of time. We're all cramped up trying to store everything from the chalets.'

'I'll speak to Vasi. I'm sure he'll have a room available in his Elounda hotel.'

'That would be best. You can always have a taxi over and Giovanni could take you back in the evening.'

Vasi was delighted when Saffron telephoned. 'I'm so pleased that you are back in England and I can speak to you over the 'phone each day. Have you managed to get some time off work to visit us?'

'I'm flying out on Saturday.'

'This week!'

'Yes, is that a problem?'

'No, no, not really.' Vasi sounded hesitant.

'I've spoken to Marianne and she said it would be impossible to stay at their house at the moment. Would you have a room free in the Elounda hotel?'

'I'm sure I'll manage something. You can't delay your visit for a couple of weeks?' suggested Vasi.

'What's wrong, Vasi? Don't you want to see me?'

'Of course I do. It's just that we are winding down for the end of the season. I am going to be too busy to spend time with you during the day.'

'I understand. I don't expect to have your undivided attention, besides, it will give me more time to spend with my family. It was very selfish of me to pay them such a fleeting visit before I went away.'

'What time does your flight land?'

'I should arrive at mid-day.'

'I will meet you and drive you down to Elounda,' promised Vasi.

'There's no need. I can make my own way down.'

'You will not. I will be coming to meet you. If I am delayed I will call you and you are to wait for me.'

'Thank you, Vasi.' Saffron felt close to tears as she closed her mobile 'phone. Neither Marianne nor Vasi had sounded terribly welcoming.

Week 3 – October 2008

Vasi greeted Saffron with a chaste kiss on each cheek and squeezed her gently. 'I am so pleased to see you.'

'You didn't sound pleased over the 'phone.'

'I will explain as we drive, then you will understand why I am busy and cannot spend the time I would like with you.' He lifted her case and led her to where he had parked his car.

'I honestly don't mind taking the bus down to Aghios Nikolaos and then a taxi.'

'It would be a miserable journey in the rain.'

'I am used to rain in London. It hasn't stopped since I returned.'

Vasi looked at her reproachfully. 'I have arranged my work today so I can have a few hours to myself. I do not wish to spend them alone. I want to be with you.' He placed her case in the boot of the car and opened the passenger door for her.

They drove in silence as Vasi negotiated the congested traffic on the airport road, then he relaxed and smiled. 'So, tell me more about your time in Nigeria.'

'I told you everything in my mails. I'll be happy to put the experience behind me now. Tell me why you are so busy, and how are Cathy and your father?'

'They are both well. Cathy has not improved, but nor is she any worse. My father is the problem. He is still reluctant to leave her alone in the apartment in case she should have a fall. He used to organise the conferences for the winter season, but he seems to have no enthusiasm and makes excuses not to come in to the hotel. He used to enjoy being there and arranging everything to his own liking. Now he asks my opinion and expects me to relay the details and instructions to the manager of the Central. Then he changes his mind and I have to change the arrangements. At the same time I am trying to deal with the accounts instead of Dimitra.'

'Is she leaving?'

Vasi shook his head. 'No, she told me she was considering going to Athens, but now she has changed her mind. She is seeing Alecos again.'

'I thought Alecos had been dismissed from the bank and you and your father had moved your accounts elsewhere?'

'That is true, but I still do not want him knowing anything about my accounts. I do not trust Dimitra to keep my finances confidential now.'

'Is she still living at the Central?'

Vasi sighed. 'I have offered to help her find an apartment but she claims she no longer feels it is safe for her to live alone.'

Saffron nodded. She knew how she had felt when she thought Ranjit was going to be released from prison. 'I'm not surprised. Did Dimitra receive any counselling? She had a very traumatic experience.'

'You think counselling would help her?'

'It could do. Most rape victims tend to think it is their own fault and blame themselves.'

Vasi shook his head. 'In some ways Dimitra does only have herself to blame. She thought the way to interest the man was to provoke him. I saw the way she was dressing. Her skirts were too short and her neck lines too low. She should have behaved with more decorum. That does not excuse the doctor in his violent behaviour towards her, but she had made it clear that she would welcome his attentions. The doctor was not a person to be teased. I think she realises that now and is embarrassed. She is also embarrassed that so many people in the area where she lived know what happened to her. The woman who lives below her old apartment has a daughter-in-law who gossips. Dimitra does not want the gossip to follow her.'

'Where is the doctor now?'

'I understand he is in custody in Athens. Inspector Solomakis called and told Dimitra the doctor had been arrested for raping a tourist. The girl is going to bring charges against him. The Inspector wants Dimitra to press charges also.'

'And will she?'

Vasi shrugged. 'She said she wished to forget the incident. It is not my business to talk to her about it.'

'At least the hotels will soon be closed now the season is finishing.'

Vasi nodded. 'That is true, but always there are problems. Some staff left early to move on to winter employment. I have to check their contracts and decide if any wages are outstanding to them or if we can deduct a severance payment from them. I am giving Dimitra a list of names and dates and she has to work out the payment due to each of them. She is annoyed that I am checking all her work down to the last detail. I will not have her paying more to someone who is a friend when they have not earned the money, nor do I want to find I am paying for someone whose name she has made up and the money is going into her account.'

'Surely she would not do that?'

'I do not think Dimitra would of her own volition, but if Alecos suggested that it would be a good idea and she would not be found out she could falsify accounts very easily. The system can become quite confusing and complicated. It would be very simple for her to insert a name and claim they had worked as casual labour for a few weeks. With many of our employees there is no problem. They will have declared their intended leaving date in advance. It is the ones who suddenly had the opportunity for other work and left immediately. We always need to keep some staff on a little longer to close the rooms down. We have to negotiate extensions to their contracts. Added to that, our suppliers are all presenting their bills at the same time. Some have been outstanding for months due to their lax accounting system and they now wish to charge interest on the payment. There is usually an argument, they say they sent the bill earlier and we say they did not. It happens every year. In the past my father would deal with most of that, but now he says he does not have the time.'

'If you no longer trust Dimitra why don't you give her the sack?'

Vasi smiled. 'I cannot sack her because I do not like her boyfriend. The only way I could get rid of her is if I could prove that she was being dishonest. I have no grounds to suspect that she is and now she knows I am checking all her work I am sure she will make sure that it is completely accurate.'

'Is there any way I can help?' offered Saffron.

Vasi smiled. 'If you could read Greek I would say yes, you would be invaluable. As it is all I can ask is that you understand that I will be unable to spend time with you during the day.'

'Of course I understand, Vasi. I would expect you to understand that I had to go to work if you were staying in London with us. I suppose there is no chance that you will be able to come over later this year?'

Vasi shook his head. 'I cannot see that will be possible at present. How is Marjorie? I tried very hard to persuade her to come over in the summer.'

'She is well and she has a man friend.'

Vasi raised his eyebrows. 'Serious?'

'She says they are just friends and that is all she wants.'

Vasi nodded. That to him was good news. It could mean Saffron would agree to marry him if she was no longer concerned about leaving Marjorie alone in England.

'So have you done anything at all with your father's house?'

'No. He agreed to have four visitors staying there with someone to supervise. Had Marjorie been willing to come over it may have been successful this year. I think he will be agreeable to try again next year, but I will need to find someone suitable for the organisation. He won't consider dividing up the rooms to make more bedrooms.'

'So it's just sitting there gradually becoming a ruin,' sad Saffron sadly.

'It is not a ruin. Lambros goes up and checks for any problems. The heating is on so that it will not become damp during the winter. It is just unused.'

'Why don't you rent it out to a family?'

'What? You mean a Cretan family?'

'Yes, I'm sure someone would be grateful for larger accommodation.'

'Not all Cretans would respect the property. They would say it did not matter what happened to it as it did not belong to them.'

'Then find someone who you know is reliable. What about one of your employees; or your friend Yiorgo might know of someone?'

Vasi nodded. He had never thought about offering to rent the house to Yiorgo.

'What about the trips to Spinalonga? Have they been successful this season?'

'Very. Since that book came out the tourists are pouring into Elounda. The locals are pleased about the increased trade, but the town is impossible during the summer. There are people everywhere. They even bring coach loads down from Heraklion.'

'Really? I read the book, but I wasn't impressed. It is nowhere near as informative and true as the book old Uncle Yannis wrote.'

Vasi shrugged. 'It just caught peoples' imagination. If they have not read Uncle Yannis's book they do not know how much is make believe. There is talk of a television programme being made or a film.'

'That would make the island even more attractive to tourists.'

'A documentary could be interesting but I don't see how they could make a film on Spinalonga. There would not be the space for their large equipment. I have watched programmes about film making. The sets they use are specially constructed.'

'I'm sure they would find a solution if they decided to go ahead. How are the chalets?' asked Saffron. 'Marianne sounded very stressed when I spoke to her.'

'It is not good. I have not been down for a while. One was burnt to the ground and some of the others were badly damaged and will have to be demolished.'

'That's awful. What's happened to the man who caused the fire?'

'I understand he has been moved from Aghios Nikolaos to Heraklion. Eventually a date will be set for his court appearance and his fate will be decided. No doubt the American Consulate will want to have him returned to America to serve his sentence.'

'Poor Nicola. She must feel bad about it.'

'It was not her fault. She did not ask the man to come to Crete.'

'You know she and John are planning to get married?'

Vasi frowned. He felt hurt that he had not been informed. 'As I said I have been too busy to visit for the past few weeks.'

'Nicola is expecting twins.'

'Really? That is good.'

'It would have been better if they were married first,' observed Saffron dryly.

Vasi shrugged. 'No matter. Often couples do not marry until after the first child. It is good to know that your wife will be fruitful.'

'Do you mean that?'

'Of course. Have they set a date?'

'I believe there are problems due to Nicola being an American citizen.'

'I am sure Giovanni will visit the Embassy if necessary and ensure she is given the relevant papers.'

'Is it easy to apply for them?'

Vasi shrugged. 'I do not know. I have never been in that situation.'

Saffron bit her lip. This was not the time to tell Vasi that she could be faced with the same problems should she decide to marry him.

Giovanni drove the short distance to the chalets, Marcus beside him and Bryony, Nicola and John were squeezed onto the back seat. Dimitris was already there and Skele emerged from the open doorway, his tail wagging enthusiastically to greet them and waiting patiently for John to produce his customary dog treat.

At Marcus's insistence, Yannis, Giovanni and he had discussed at length how they would tackle the clearance of the chalets before they were demolished. They had finally decided that the fridges, microwaves, shower trays, basins, toilets and sinks should be disconnected and stored in two of the undamaged buildings along with boxes of china and cutlery. After two attempts to remove shower trays and cracking both of them in the process, Giovanni decided they should be left in situ.

The bedding would be boxed up and taken to the taverna for storage as had been done previously at the end of each season. The mattresses would be moved back to Yannis's house and stored in the guest room that Nicola had occupied when visiting and their frames and other furniture would have to be stored in another two chalets. Once most of the chalets were emptied of their re-useable contents a contractor would clear the site and a start could be made on the construction of the shops.

Giovanni continued driving up the road to where the taverna stood and the fire gutted chalets gave a mournful air of desolation. The area where the carob had grown had already been cleared and the footings were being dug ready for the new self catering apartments. Giovanni sincerely hoped the complex would be completed and ready for business by the next season.

He checked the progress with the site manager and was told all was on schedule. Provided the drizzling rain became no heavier they would be able to finish excavating that day. Inserting the steel rods that were needed for strength and gave stability in the event of an earthquake, and pouring the concrete would begin the following day, but was dependent upon the weather. Satisfied Giovanni returned to the chalets to assist in the manual labour.

John rose from his knees where he had been disconnecting a basin from the waste pipe and as he did so everything went black. He placed his hand on the basin for support and it toppled to the ground with a crash, John landing beside it.

Marcus looked round the bathroom door. 'What's happened? Are you hurt?'

John looked towards the main room, still unable to see clearly. 'I dropped the basin. Careless of me. I hope I haven't damaged it or Dad won't be very pleased.'

Marcus regarded him doubtfully. Why should John be sitting on the floor if he only dropped the acrylic basin? 'Do you want a hand to move it over to the entrance?'

'No thanks, it isn't heavy. It was just off balance.' Now his sight had fully returned John felt foolish sitting there and scrambled to his feet.

'Do you want me to come and help you in the bathroom? I've finished removing the sink.'

John shook his head. 'There's not room enough for two to work in here.'

Marcus nodded. 'I'll move on to the next chalet then.' Marcus covered the sink in bubble wrap and taped it securely. He wrapped the taps and waste fitting in newspaper, placed them inside the sink and covered them with another layer of bubble wrap. Finally he picked up the sink and placed it beside the fridge and microwave that were already wrapped and standing near the door.

'I'll join you as soon as I've finished in here,' John called to him.

Vasi led the way up the stairs to the room in the hotel he had reserved for Saffron.

'I was lucky you had one free at such short notice,' she observed.

'I would always have a room free for you, even if I was fully booked.'

Saffron giggled. 'Don't be silly, Vasi. You couldn't have a room for me if you were full.'

Vasi stopped and regarded her seriously. 'It is very simple to isolate the water supply to each room. I could not expect anyone to stay there if they did not have water.'

'Vasi! You wouldn't!'

Vasi shrugged. 'They would not know I had done it deliberately and I would move them elsewhere to a suitable hotel. They would have no cause for complaint.' He stopped outside the door at the end of the corridor. 'Here is a nice, quiet room. The couple who stayed here were very happy.' He waited a moment as Saffron's eyes widened. 'Their holiday finished on Saturday.'

'Truthfully?'

'Yes, Saffie, truthfully.' He pushed the door open and placed her case just inside, kicking the door closed with his heel. 'Come here,' he said and folded her into his arms. Holding her tightly he began to kiss her neck whilst his hands ran up and down her back, finally cupping her buttocks and pulling her close.

Saffron felt her passion meeting his and she pushed against his chest. 'We ought to get undressed first. You could ruin your suit.'

Vasi let out a sigh. 'As always you are right. Be quick. If you are not undressed when I am I shall rip your clothes off.'

Saffron giggled, and kicked of her shoes. She unzipped her trousers, letting them fall to the floor, and pulled her jumper over her head. 'I shall be ready before you,' she announced as she pulled back the cover on the bed.

'That is not fair. I cannot throw my clothes on the floor. I have to place my suit carefully, but the rest of my clothing does not matter.' Vasi threw his shirt in the air, followed by his underwear and leapt onto the bed beside Saffron.

Saffron wriggled out of Vasi's arms. 'I must shower and go to

Uncle Yannis's. They'll wonder what's happened to me.'

'Did they know the time of your flight?'

'I just told them it would land in the afternoon.'

Vasi looked at his watch. 'It is only four thirty.' He ran his hand across her breasts and Saffron shivered with pleasure.

'No, Vasi,' she said firmly. 'If I don't move now I shall want to stay here all evening.'

Vasi smiled complacently. 'That would be a very pleasurable way to spend the evening.' He reached for her again, but this time Saffron was ready for him and she swung her legs off the bed.

'I really mean it, Vasi. I am going to get showered and dressed. You can stay in bed if you like.'

'I shall take you to Uncle Yannis's house. I am sure Giovanni will drive you back here, if not you can have a taxi. I will meet you here later after I have spent the evening in Aghios Nikolaos with my friend Yiorgo. I, too, need to shower. We will do so together.'

'No, Vasi.' Saffron fled into the bathroom and locked the door behind her. 'I know just what will happen if you come in here with me,' she called. 'You can have the bathroom when I've finished.'

Marianne greeted Saffron with open arms. 'I expected you to be here earlier than this.'

Saffron hoped Marianne did not see the flush that entered her cheeks. 'I'm sorry; I should have called from the airport to let you know I was on my way.'

'It's no problem. You must be starving. Do you want to eat now or will you wait until everyone else is home?'

Now Marianne mentioned it Saffron realise she was indeed very hungry. 'I can wait,' she said. 'I had something on the 'plane. Where is everyone else?'

'Grandma is in her room, Uncle Yannis and the ladies are at the shop as usual. Everyone else is working up at the chalets.'

Saffron frowned. 'I thought Bryony said they were closed due to the fire.'

Marianne nodded. 'Come and sit down. I'll make some coffee and let Grandma know you've finally arrived.'

'I'll go to her room and let her know myself.'

'Tell her I'm making coffee and ask her if she wants to join us in the kitchen. Then I'll show you why you couldn't stay here. It's utter chaos and will only get worse.'

'Will she need some help?'

Marianne shook her head. 'No, she'll take her time, but she likes to be independent and not have help from us if she can avoid it. If you don't come back for a while I'll bring your coffee in and we'll sit with her in her room.'

Annita looked up eagerly as Saffron tapped on her door and entered. Gently she placed her arms around grandmother, conscious of the frail form, and kissed her on both cheeks

'Grandma, you look marvellous.' Saffron regarded the old lady with admiration. Her hair was immaculate and her jumper and trousers were spotless, unlike so many of the elderly visitors to the hospital who had food stains on their clothes.

'So, how was your time in Nigeria? Marianne says you didn't enjoy being there.' Annita ignored the compliment.

'I'll tell you all about it, and I've brought some photographs with me. First, though, Marianne is making coffee and wants to know if you will be joining us in the kitchen or should she bring it here?'

'I'll come along. That way you can tell Marianne as well, save repeating yourself. You go back and tell her I'm on my way.'

Saffron hesitated. Should she do as Marianne said or offer to stay and help? 'Would you like your wheelchair?'

'I only use my chair when I go for family meals. It means I'm put at the end of the table and have plenty of elbow room.'

'You crafty old lady,' smiled Saffron.

'There's no point in getting old and not getting wiser. Off you go,' Annita waved her stick at her. 'I'm quite capable of getting to the kitchen on my own using my sticks.'

Saffron returned to the kitchen with a smile on her face. 'I was almost thrown out. It was as though she read my thoughts. She told me she was quite capable on her own.' Saffron sat down at the table where a cup of coffee was placed along with a plate of biscuits.

Marianne sat opposite and regarded Saffron seriously. 'I'm not going to ask you about Nigeria. I read all your mails. Grandma will want you to tell her about the hospital over there. She kept asking me if you were seeing leprosy patients.'

'I did, actually, but I'll wait until Grandma is with us.' Saffron helped herself to a biscuit.

'I hope I didn't sound too unwelcoming on the 'phone,' apologised Marianne. She sighed heavily. 'Everything is such a mess and so difficult at the moment.'

'Tell me. Bryony told me about the fire and John being hurt. I spoke to him and Nicola on the 'phone and he assures me he's recovered.'

Marianne nodded. 'At first we didn't think it was too much of a disaster. No one had been badly hurt. We sent all the visitors off to stay in hotels for the remainder of their holiday, even if their chalet wasn't damaged. One family lost everything and we gave them immediate compensation, the others we asked to put in claims for any damaged belongings and sorted that out gradually. It was with our own insurance company that we ran into problems. We're not allowed to cook at the taverna and everything has to be rebuilt in stone or concrete.'

'What!' exclaimed Saffron. 'That's ridiculous. You've never had a fire before and it was a deliberate act of arson, not an accident.'

'That was another problem. We had to convince the insurance company we had not arranged to have everything burnt to the ground to make a claim. Luckily the police backed us up as the culprit is in jail having admitted he did it deliberately. Finally they agreed to pay for the fire damage that had occurred but they were not willing to insure wooden structures in future and we had to cancel our bookings for the rest of the season.'

'So what is going to happen?' asked Saffron.

'We had a family meeting and we've decided to build a block of self catering units, in concrete to comply with the insurance regulations. It's already started, actually.'

'That must be costing you a fortune!'

Marianne shrugged. 'The land belongs to the family. We have the insurance money and the bank was willing to give us a large loan. In the meantime the chalets are being stripped of anything that we will be able to use again and being stored. It was Marcus who suggested that. He said it was foolish to throw away perfectly usable items and it would be better to store them temporarily. If they're not used they can be disposed of later. The room you usually have is full of mattresses.'

'At least I would have had something to sleep on!'

'It's slow going as everything has to be packed to protect it from damage and then moved either to the taverna, here or to another chalet. Once that's completed Giovanni will arrange to have the ground cleared.'

'But I thought you said the construction of the self catering units had started?'

'It has, but we decided it was more practical to build it where the carob was. In the meantime it's the storage that's a problem. Giovanni hopes we'll be able to fit the furniture and equipment into four chalets. Once the empty chalets have been cleared Giovanni has plans to build some shops and a new taverna on the land. It will be a prime position on the main road. He'll then rent them out and that should repay some of the bank loan until we're back on our feet with the holiday units.'

'Thank goodness he didn't fire the house. Grandma could have been hurt or worse.'

'If she'd seen him she would probably have attacked him with her stick. Seriously, though, we have to be thankful that the visitors only lost their possessions and not their lives.'

'Is there anything I can do to help?'

Marianne smiled. 'Thanks for the offer, but this is supposed to be a holiday for you. No doubt you'll be spending time with Vasi.'

Saffron shook her head. 'Vasi has to be up in Heraklion at the Central most of the time I gather. His father is still insisting he has to stay with Cathy so Vasi has to be responsible for checking the end of season accounts and organising the conferences. He's not going to be able to spend time with me during the day. I could stay here with Grandma and have a meal ready for all of you when you return.'

'That's a lovely thought, Saffron, but I have to be here to answer 'phone calls and reply to e-mails. I'm still dealing with insurance claims and having to talk to travel firms. I'm trying to persuade them to include the new unit in their brochures for next season and they keep wanting a completion date and photographs. I do the cooking around 'phone calls and e-mails.'

'I must be able to do something useful.'

'Of course she can be useful.' Annita walked slowly into the kitchen, leaning heavily on her sticks. 'Giovanni needs all the help he can get at the moment. She can go up to the chalets with the others. I'm sure Bryony and Nicola would appreciate help with the packing.'

Saffron smiled at her grandmother gratefully. She had had visions of interminably long days spent alone either in her hotel room or wandering around the small town.

'I can find you some old clothes,' offered Marianne. 'We're near enough the same size.'

'I'd be grateful for something to put over my jumpers. I have some jeans with me and it really doesn't matter if they get stained or damaged.'

'It isn't dirty work,' Marianne assured her. 'It's just where you have to kneel on the floor sometimes and when a bed is moved it's often a bit dusty.'

'I don't mind a bit of dirt. It makes a change from blood.'

'I hadn't thought about your hands! You mustn't damage them.'

'If I'm only packing things they're not likely to come to any harm. I shall feel I'm properly part of the family if I'm able to help.'

Yiorgo listened whilst Vasi extolled the virtues of Saffron. It reminded him of the time when Vasi's dog had died and Vasi had talked for hours about how wonderful the animal had been.

'Have you asked her again if she'll marry you?'

'It wasn't the right time today. She was tired from travelling, we had the drive down and then she had to visit her relatives.'

'Stop making excuses, Vasi. You've got cold feet. You're frightened that if you ask her to marry you again she'll say no.'

'What will I do if she refuses to marry me?' Vasi asked miserably.

Yiorgo shrugged. 'Move on and find someone else.'

'I can't. She's not like the Greek girls that I've been out with. She doesn't demand anything of me as they used to. She understands that I'm unable to spend every day with her whilst she's in Crete this time. There was no tantrum, no sulking, just an acceptance of the situation.'

'So what did you talk about as you drove down? Don't tell me you discussed the weather.'

'She told me John and Nicola are planning to get married pretty soon. Apparently Nicola is expecting twins.'

Yiorgo shook his head sympathetically. 'Thank goodness we never managed more than one at a time.'

'I explained that I no longer trusted Dimitra now she was seeing Alecos again and how difficult my father is being at the moment,' continued Vasi. 'She wanted to know how the trips to Spinalonga were going and what was happening with my father's house. She came up with another idea for having it occupied.'

Yiorgo smiled. 'What was that?'

'That I rent it out to a family. It could be practical and I immediately thought of you and Barbara. You could do with a bit more space.'

'Me? Live in your father's house? Don't be silly, Vasi. I'm a poor boatman. I could never afford the rent.'

'We could come to some arrangement. It would be better than leaving it standing empty.'

Yiorgo eyed Vasi dubiously. 'What about my boys? They have to go to school.'

'You could take them down to Elounda in the morning on your scooter. The older ones could catch the bus to Aghios Nikolaos and you take the youngest round to the village school before you go to the boat. Barbara could meet him and the other two could walk home when the bus drops them back in Elounda.'

Yiorgo considered the proposal as he finished his beer. It was certainly tempting. His three boys shared a small bedroom and the baby would have to sleep in their room until she was old enough to spend the nights with Barbara's mother.

'I'll speak to Barbara, see what she thinks.' Yiorgo glanced at his watch. 'I'd better get back. Barbara won't be happy if I disturb Tsambika. She's teething and we're having some bad nights with her.'

'I'll drive you.'

Yiorgo shook his head. 'No need. I'm only down the road. It won't hurt me to walk. It's stopped raining, thank goodness. It was a miserable trip to Spinalonga today. I was surprised anyone wanted to go over there on such a horrible day.' He shrugged himself into his jacket and stood up. 'I'll let you know what Barbara says about the house, and thanks for the offer.'

Vasi was waiting for Saffron when Giovanni returned her to the hotel in Elounda.

'So,' he smiled. 'How are your family and what is their news?'

Saffron removed her jacket and sat on the edge of the bed. 'Grandma is fine and Nicola is blooming. Marianne and Giovanni are stressed. They're clearing the chalets of equipment and storing it all ready for the new units that are being built.'

'New units? They're not replacing the chalets?' Vasi raised his eyebrows.

Saffron nodded. 'Giovanni decided to clear the area where the carob grew and they're building a new self catering block there. The insurance company insists that any new building they do has to be in concrete and comply with the fire regulations. That means they can't just replace the damaged chalets.'

'I'm surprised Giovanni got away with it for so long,' remarked Vasi dryly. 'The companies have begun to tighten up to conform to the European Union regulations.'

'They can't even cook at the taverna because the upper storey and some of the extension for the shop is in wood.' Saffron spoke indignantly. 'According to Marianne they're removing just about everything from the chalets. All the mattresses and curtains are being stored in my usual bedroom and things that won't come to any harm, like the basins and toilets are being stored in the chalets temporarily. Once the chalets are empty Giovanni is planning to have them removed and a row of shops built in their place.'

Vasi sat up straighter. 'Shops? What kind of shops?'

Saffron shrugged. 'Just empty shops. He then wants to rent them out to help towards repaying his bank loan.'

'I hope he'll be successful. He will have invested a considerable amount in the project.'

'Just about everything they have, I think.' Saffron frowned. 'I'm not sure if I'm supposed to tell you this, but Uncle Yannis is selling his shop.'

'Is that to provide more finance?'

'Probably, but Marianne said their shop is not as profitable as it used to be. Tourists don't walk around that part of the town so they have very little passing trade. People have to have been recommended and directed there. He and Ourania are going to move their stock to one of the new shops up at Plaka when they are ready.'

Vasi nodded slowly. 'That sounds like a practical business

move. They can see how trade is next season and always change their mind.'

'They plan to be in Plaka by next season.'

'What? They'll never get all that work done in six months.'

'Giovanni seems to think they will. He said the concrete for the footings of the new unit was poured today.'

'That was risky with it raining.'

'It wasn't raining that hard and it had almost stopped by the time we arrived at their house, remember. He says the forecast for the rest of the week is for dry weather so the builders will be able to get on. Marianne is trying to persuade the travel agents to include the new unit in their brochures for next season so it will have to be ready.'

'That's possible, but I can't see the shops being ready by then.'

Saffron shrugged. 'I'm only repeating what I was told. What are your plans for tomorrow?'

'Unfortunately I have to return to Heraklion. Do you want to spend the day with your family or come with me and go to the museum or walk around the town? You could visit Cathy and my father.'

Saffron shook her head. 'If you have to go to Heraklion you don't have to worry about me amusing myself. I've offered to go up and help with the work in the chalets.'

'You are going to work on your holiday?'

'If I hang around at the house I'll only be in Marianne's way and I can't spend my time on the beach. If I do decide I want to do something else I'll simply tell them I'm not coming that day. I'm sure they'll understand. Tomorrow I plan to get up early and walk up to the house.'

'In that case you should have an early night.' Vasi rose from his chair and pulled back the cover on the bed.

Vasi was showered and dressed by the time Saffron opened her eyes the following morning.

'What time is it?' she asked anxiously.

'Six thirty. There is no need for you to hurry.'

'Why are you up so early?'

'I have an hour's drive, remember. I prefer to leave early before everyone else is late and the traffic becomes heavy and the drivers impatient.'

'Of course. I was forgetting you had a long drive.'

Vasi shrugged. 'It is nothing. I will see you back here this evening. Stay with the family as late as you like. I am sure to have some work with me that I can do.'

'You don't mind driving up and down? Maybe I should have stayed here one week and spent the second in Heraklion.'

Vasi bent and kissed her. 'Provided I am able to be with you each evening I do not mind making the journey. Do not work too hard. I do not want to return this evening and find you are snoring already.'

'I don't snore,' protested Saffron indignantly.

'Do you not?' asked Vasi and placed his arm in front of his face as Saffron hurled a pillow at him. He threw the pillow back and blew her a kiss before picking up his lap top and leaving the room.

Saffron lay in the bed for a further ten minutes, then rose and looked out of the window. There was no sign of rain, and the sky was lightening. It would be pleasant walking up to Yannis's house.

Saffron arrived at the house to find only Marianne in the kitchen.

'Where is everyone?' she asked.

'They've gone up to the chalets.'

Saffron looked at her watch. It was not yet nine. 'I didn't want to arrive too early. Now I appear to be late.'

'They like to make an early start. I'll 'phone Giovanni and ask him to come down to collect you.'

'No way. I walked here. I'm quite capable of walking up to the chalets.'

'You could take John's bike,' suggested Marianne.

Saffron shook her head. 'I've only ever ridden pillion with John. I wouldn't want to risk trying to drive it, besides, John might need it.'

'He's not likely to be going anywhere at the moment. His father's keeping him busy.'

'Did you find an old shirt for me?' asked Saffron.

'Here.' Marianne handed her an old shirt that had belonged to Giovanni. 'It doesn't matter if you ruin it. Giovanni can't fit into it anymore.'

'I'll probably not need it anyway. I put a T shirt beneath my jumper and I didn't really need to wear my jacket walking here. It's windy, but certainly not cold.'

'Coffee before you go?' asked Marianne.

Saffron hesitated, then shook her head. 'I've not long had breakfast. They'll think I've changed my mind about helping if I don't get up there soon.'

Saffron eyed the chalets as they came into view. The ones she could see appeared completely undamaged and it seemed unreasonable for them to have to be dismantled. Giovanni's car was parked a short distance further up the road, but the doors to the chalets that fronted the road were closed and they looked deserted.

She reached Giovanni's car and looked around. There was no sign of any activity taking place. She walked along the path that led between the rows of chalets and was relieved to see an open door.

'Hello,' she called. 'I've finally arrived.'

Skele came to the door to greet her and Dimitris emerged from inside the bathroom. He grinned at her.

'Mr Giovanni, Mr John,' he pointed to the chalets further along and Saffron nodded. She raised her hand and walked past another three chalets. At the fourth she could hear sounds coming from inside.

'Hello,' she called again from the doorway. 'I'm here.'

Nicola looked up from where she was packing plates and dishes into a box. 'Good morning, Saffron, or should I say good afternoon?'

'I didn't realise you would be starting so early or I would have come sooner.'

'Giovanni is a slave driver!' Nicola smiled. 'Actually we've only been here half an hour. Do you want to help me finish this packing? All the cupboards and drawers have to be cleared ready for them to be dismantled.'

Saffron nodded. 'Are you packing in any particular order?'

'No, just however it fits best. I'm sure whoever has stayed here in the past has never used a quarter of this equipment. They would make a breakfast or use the taverna and then they went out for the day. Most people ate out during the evening. They certainly didn't cook.'

Saffron began to fill a second box with saucepans and cutlery. 'Where are you storing this?'

'The furthest chalets have already been cleared of furniture. One is for all the toilets, basins and sinks, the next is for the fridges, microwaves and hobs and the third is for the bed bases and other wooden fittings. The windows will go into the fourth chalet. That way Giovanni reckons we'll know where everything is when it's needed. These boxes just go in wherever there's a space. Mr Palamakis comes up with his van when Giovanni calls him and the men load up. He drives down to the chalets we're using and Dimitris and John meet him there and unload. Whilst they move everything inside Mr Palamakis comes back for another load.'

'Quite a system you have going.'

Nicola pulled a face. 'You know what Giovanni is like for lists. Everything has to be marked to say which chalet it was removed from.'

'Whatever for?'

'They were built and equipped at different times. If cupboard doors are not matched up we could end up with ones that don't fit properly when they're used again. Then we'd have to search through everything to find the right ones.'

Saffron nodded. 'That makes sense. Just tell me when I have to mark anything.'

'All you need to do with this packing is make a list of everything in the box. We don't want to be looking for saucepans and find all the boxes hold china.' Nicola handed Saffron a sheet of paper and a pen. 'When you've filled the box tape it shut, put the list inside a polythene cover and staple it to the top. Don't try to lift it. The men will do that.' Nicola worked swiftly as she talked.

'What is everyone else doing?' asked Saffron.

'The men are finishing the disconnection of the sanitary ware and dismantling the fitments generally. Bryony and I are just packing. I'll go up to the taverna later and make a sandwich lunch for everyone.'

'Would it be more helpful if I did that?' offered Saffron.

Nicola shook her head. 'No. It gives me a break and I can take my time clearing up afterwards.'

'You're not doing too much, are you?' Saffron asked anxiously.

'Don't you start fussing over me like John does! I'm fit and well. I know it would be foolish to lift anything heavy, but apart from that there's no reason why I shouldn't help. After all, it's my fault that it happened.'

'You can't blame yourself. The man is obviously deranged. No one in their right mind sets fire to someone's property.'

'That's what Adam Kowalski told me. He said they have found out he is seriously disturbed and has been since a child. His girl friend met with an accident and died. I should never have spoken to him and sympathised. They think that is what tipped him over the edge and gave him a fixation with me.'

'That's no excuse,' Saffron said firmly. 'I've finished this box, what shall I do now?'

'Move on to the next chalet. You'll be sick of the sight of saucepans and plates by the end of the day.'

Vasi was waiting for Saffron when she returned to the hotel that evening.

'So,' he said, 'how did you enjoy your working day?'

'It was actually quite fun. I worked with Nicola packing up items from the cupboards, then I was given the job of marking the bed slats and bagging up the screws.'

Vasi raised his eyebrows. 'You were marking bed slats?'

Saffron nodded. 'Apparently because the chalets were built at different times the furniture in each one is not always identical. Giovanni wants everything marked with the chalet it came from so that it doesn't get muddled up and cause problems if they want to use it again. Giovanni took me up to see where the new units are being constructed. He's pleased with the progress they're making.'

'How many are there?'

'He told me they plan to build two blocks of twelve units each. Originally they were going to make them just as rooms and the visitors would have to go out for all their meals, but that would mean they became a hotel and would be expected to provide a breakfast. Giovanni says some of their plans depend upon the speed of the rebuilding. He showed me where they want to have the shops and the new taverna will be on the main road with them.'

'He obviously thinks people will become thirsty if they are browsing in the shops.'

'And hungry. Apparently coach loads of visitors come down from Heraklion. After they've visited Spinalonga they usually drive into Aghios Nikolaos for lunch. Sometimes a travel firm would book a meal at his taverna and then go to the island. The premises were not large enough to have more than one coach load a day, but he plans to make the new taverna considerably bigger. It will mean employing some full time staff. There is no way they could manage it between them as they used to.'

'Giovanni, always he has big ideas. I hope he also has the deep pockets.'

Saffron shrugged. 'I'm sure he knows what he is doing. I'm

going to take my swimming gear with me when I go up tomorrow.'

'You will swim? In October!'

'It was beautiful up there today, really warm. I worked just in my T shirt. There's no reason why I shouldn't have a quick swim when we break for lunch.'

Vasi shook his head in disbelief. 'I have told my father I do not plan to work this weekend. Will you want to go to Vai for a swim?'

'I'll be content with a quick dip in the sea opposite if the weather is good,' smiled Saffron. 'Now, I must wash my hair. I had a shower earlier, but I still smell like a bonfire. The chalets look clean, but the smoke probably penetrated all of them and the smell of burning still lingers in the air up there.'

'Tonight you will not lock the bathroom door. I will come and wash your back. When I have washed your back I will wash your front. I will pay particular attention to some parts of your beautiful body.'

Saffron giggled and peeled off her T shirt. 'Is that a promise?'

Saffron arrived early at Yannis's house and joined the family for coffee before Giovanni rose from the table and insisted they went up to the chalets before the morning was wasted.

'Saffron can come with us in the car and John can use the scooter.'

'I don't mind walking up,' offered Saffron.

Giovanni shook his head. 'It just seems foolish to take two cars when John can ride his bike. I'll see you all outside in ten minutes.'

'I could sit in the boot,' said John with a grin.

'That could be terribly dangerous.' Saffron was horrified at the idea. 'If Giovanni braked suddenly the boot door could come down and injure you.'

'No problem. We would have a doctor with us.'

Saffron gave him a scathing look. 'I'm on holiday,' she announced.

'And I am only joking. I'll follow you on the scooter.'

'Bring your swimming gear. I'm planning a quick dip when we break for lunch.'

John eyed her doubtfully. 'I'll bring it, but you might well change your mind when you feel the temperature. You should have said yesterday and I would have got the wet suits out. You could use Nick's. I doubt if she would be able to get the zip done up now.'

Nicola pulled a face. 'Even my trousers are becoming uncomfortably tight. I'll have to get some drawstrings.'

'I'll have a look in Elounda and see if they have any. I could bring them up for you tomorrow,' offered Saffron.

Nicola shook her head. 'They've only got fashion ones. I'll have to go to Aghios Nikolaos and see if they have them there.'

'I could have a look over the weekend in Aghios. Vasi said he would be able to come down for the weekend and asked what I would like to do.'

John laughed and whispered in Saffron's ear. 'He'll have a fit if you say you want to look for maternity trousers. He'll think they're for you.'

'He will not,' answered Saffron firmly. She felt a momentary sadness. Vasi had not asked her again if she would marry him.

'Actually I have a favour to ask him. It involves you as well.'

Saffron raised her eyebrows.

'If Vasi is coming to Elounda for the weekend will he be returning to Heraklion on Monday morning?'

'I expect so. He says he is needed up there at the moment.'

'Would he be willing to drive you and Nick up when he goes?'

Saffron frowned. 'I don't see why not? Why?'

'Nick has to go to the American Embassy in Heraklion to sort out this affidavit thing. She has to swear she's not already married. You're not, are you Nick?'

'Don't be daft. You know I'm not, you big palookas.'

'Palookas? What's a palookas?' asked Bryony looking at Nicola in surprise. 'Do you mean a pashmina or poncho?'

'Sounds like something to do with Eskimos,' commented Marianne as she began to clear the table. 'I'm sure I've heard of a town somewhere called that.'

Nicola gurgled with laughter. 'It means someone who is intelligent but being deliberately stupid.'

John looked at her with mock indignation. 'I am not being deliberately stupid. I asked you a serious question. I would feel very foolish if we were standing before Pappa Lucas and he said "I can't marry you. Nicola Christoforaki is already married to Joe Bloggs."'

'If I was already married I would have sent you an invitation to my wedding.'

'It could have been lost in the post.'

'Well, I'm not already married and you know it, so stop being a palookas.'

John grinned. 'I must remember that word. Is Vasi a palookas, Saff?'

'Sometimes,' remarked Saffron dryly. 'Can we get back to asking Vasi to take us to Heraklion. Why don't you drive up with Nicola?'

'Dad needs me down here at the moment and I'd rather Nick didn't go up alone. If you were willing to go with her it would be great.'

'That's no problem for me,' smiled Saffron. 'We can go to the Embassy, have some lunch, buy some maternity wear and have a taxi back.'

'We could come back on the bus,' protested Nicola. 'We don't need a taxi.'

Saffron shook her head. 'You know how long the bus takes and I'm sure it finds every bump in the road. I'll ask Vasi this evening, but I'm sure there will be no problem. If there is then we'll have a taxi both ways. We'll treat ourselves to a girls' day out.'

'Everyone ready?' asked Giovanni as he re-entered the kitchen and collected the keys to his car.

147

'Five minutes,' said Bryony and rose from the table. 'I just want to say good morning to Grandma.'

'You could have done that earlier,' muttered Giovanni, anxious now not to waste any more time. 'Bring the lunch bag, Nicola.' He picked up a sheaf of papers, checked he had his mobile 'phone in his pocket and walked to the door.

Once again Dimitris was already there working when they arrived and Skele emerged from a chalet looking eagerly for John. Nicola tickled his ears and assured him John would arrive with his treat very soon.

John rode steadily up the road. He looked down at the dials on his scooter. He was getting low on petrol. He would have plenty for getting to and from the chalets that day but he must remember to top up the tank later. As he looked up he could no longer see anything. Instinctively he slowed and braked to a halt. That had been frightening. Had there been any other traffic around he could easily have caused an accident. He balanced himself on the scooter and pressed his forehead, willing the blackness to disappear.

'You took your time,' observed Giovanni when John parked his bike behind his father's car.

'Went back for Skele's treat,' lied John glibly. 'Where do you want me today?'

'You and Marcus dismantle the beds and cupboards before you start on the plumbing fitments. He's in chalet fifteen and has the tools with him. The girls should finish the packing by mid-day. They can mark the beds and cupboard doors this afternoon, otherwise they'll be idle.'

John nodded. 'What's Dimitris doing?'

'He's moving all the packed boxes over to the door and checking there's nothing overlooked in the cupboards. When he's done that he'll make a start on removing the window frames.'

'Are you planning to store all of them?'

'For the time being. I want to keep the patio doors, the small windows may not be of any use, but when the chalets are bulldozed we don't want the land littered with broken glass. Better to spend a couple of days taking them out than having to clear up afterwards.'

'And what are you going to do whilst we all work our fingers to the bone?' asked John cheekily.

'I'm going up to the new units first, then I'll come back and give Dimitris a hand with the windows. It will take three of us to handle the large ones.'

'If the girls have finished packing Bryony and Saff could start taking down the outside awnings,' suggested John. 'That's a two man job and I don't want Nick up a step ladder.'

Giovanni nodded. 'Good idea. Nicola can finish the marking on the beds and cupboards whilst they make a start on those.'

Saffron did find the sea cold, but she was not prepared to admit that to John.

'It's no worse than in England in the summer. Come on, be brave. After all, you dive for the Cross when it's much colder than this.'

John slapped his thighs and arms to improve the circulation and ran into the water to join her. He swam out strongly for a short distance and then turned back.

'Better to stay close to the shore,' he called. 'Don't want to get cramp.'

Saffron nodded. It was very different swimming in the summer when the sea felt like a warm bath, she was already feeling cold. 'I'm going in. We can stay in longer tomorrow if you bring the wet suits,' she called back and struck out for the shore.

'Saff, wait.' There was a note of panic in John's voice as he called to her.

Saffron turned and began to swim to where John was treading water. 'John, what's wrong?'

'Just stay by me for a moment.'

'Have you got cramp?'

'No, I'd just like to swim back in beside you.'

Saffron looked at him curiously. John was far more confident in the water than she was. 'What's the matter, John?'

'I can't see. It's probably where the water is cold.'

'Give me your hand and we'll swim together using one arm each.' Saffron felt thoroughly frightened as she groped for John's hand. She should not have encouraged him to join her. Even young people were known to have heart attacks. 'Have you got a pain in your chest?' she asked.

'No, I'll be alright in a moment. It's where I had that stupid bang on the head. It must be something to do with the way I turn my head.' Still treading water he pressed his forehead and blinked. 'It's clearing now,' he declared.

Saffron held up her hand. 'How many fingers?' she asked.

'Three,' John grinned at her. 'I can see perfectly again now.'

'Sure? Then let's swim in. I'm getting cold.'

'Don't mention it to Nick, will you? She worries if she knows I've had a blackout.'

'I'll talk to you later. Come on, I'm really shivering now.' Saffron released John's hand and swam beside him back to the shore.

Saffron was pleased she had not thought the day warm enough to leave her jumper at the hotel and pulled it over her head gratefully. No doubt she would soon want to remove it when she began to work again. She watched John surreptitiously as he walked back to the chalets with Marcus. There did not appear to be anything wrong, but she would make sure she found some time to talk to him alone.

Removing the awnings that could be spread over the patios of the chalets was more arduous than it appeared. Having cranked the expanding arms out and stretched the fabric taut it became impossible to undo the nylon ties that were threaded through the holes of the metal work. If the arms were not pinned into place as soon as any pressure was put on them they began to fold back against the wall.

'This is impossible,' muttered Bryony from half way up the step ladder. 'I've nearly fallen off twice.'

'Suppose I held the arm firm? Would you be able to undo the first fixings? After that it should be relatively simple,' suggested Saffron.

Bryony shook her head. 'It could come down and hit you. It was one of these struts that hit John on the head. I think these knots will have to be cut undone anyway. I'm going to suggest to Giovanni that we cut the awning free of the supports and if he wants to use them again they'll just have to be re-strung.' Bryony retreated to the ground. 'I'll find him and tell him we can't manage. One of the men will have to come and help and we'll just fold them up afterwards.'

Saffron did not argue. Her fingers were sore where she had struggled to undo the knots holding the awning in place.

'John, can we sort out a wet suit for me?' asked Saffron. 'It was pretty cold in the sea today without one.'

'They're down in the boat house,' replied John, but made no attempt to move.

Saffron regarded him impatiently. 'Come on, then. We've time to get one before Marianne serves our meal. She said fifteen minutes.'

Reluctantly John rose and fetched the key to the boat house. He knew there was no need for Saffron to accompany him and guessed she planned to ask him about the blackout he had suffered whilst swimming.

Saffron leaned back against John's boat. 'Tell me about these blackouts.'

John shrugged. 'There's nothing really to tell. It's where the metal awning arm fell on my head during the fire.'

'How often do they happen?'

'Only occasionally.' John was not prepared to admit they

occurred at least three or more times each day and he had experienced one earlier whilst riding his bike. 'There's no set pattern.'

Saffron looked at him in horror. 'John, this could be really serious. I thought it was just the cold water that had brought one on.'

'Don't tell Nick or Mum and Dad, will you? I don't want them worried. It's bound to clear up within another couple of months.'

'Is that what the doctor said?'

'The ophthalmologist. He reckoned they would stop when my skull fracture has healed and a piece of bone is no longer pressing on my optic nerve.'

Saffron raised her eyebrows. 'John, the blow to your head was in August and it's now October. Your father needs to know. You've been up on a step ladder today cutting free the awnings. Suppose you had suffered one then? You could have fallen off and done further damage. Have you had a follow up appointment for an X-ray or scan?'

John shrugged. 'No one has suggested I should.'

'Well, I'm suggesting it now. I only deal with limb fractures, but a straight forward break in a bone should take no longer than six weeks to heal. I think you should go to the hospital and ask for another X-ray.'

'It's difficult at the moment.'

'Why? I know there's a lot to be done here, but your father can spare you for a day.'

'It would mean going into Aghios Nikolaos.' John regarded Saffron doubtfully. 'Do you really think it's necessary?'

'I certainly do. Please, John, promise me you'll telephone the hospital tomorrow and insist on an urgent appointment. The longer you leave it the more difficult it could be to correct the situation. If you're worried that you'll not understand whatever the doctor tells you I'll go with you to the hospital. I can read X-rays. I also know the right questions to ask.'

John gave a deep sigh and brushed his hand across his eyes.

'We'd better get back in. Mum will be waiting for us.'

'Promise me,' Saffron insisted.

John gave her a weak smile. 'Would you really be willing to come with me?'

'Of course I will. It will be for my sake as much as yours. I want my mind put at rest that there's nothing seriously wrong.'

Week 4 – October 2008

'What is wrong, Saffie? Are you worried about visiting the Embassy with Nicola?'

Saffron shook her head. 'Not a bit. I'm grateful that you are willing to drive us up on Monday.'

'That is no problem. You and Nicola can visit the Embassy and then enjoy your day in town. Cathy and my father will be delighted to see you both later and I will collect you from their apartment and drive you home.'

'Are you sure we won't be imposing on them? Nicola may be tired.'

'They have a spare bedroom. If she needs to rest she will be welcome to use it. Is that what is worrying you?' Vasi took Saffron's hand in his and looked at it in horror. 'What have you done? You are covered in scratches.'

'It's nothing. Bryony and I tried to take down the canvas awnings. We couldn't manage to undo the fastenings and had to ask John to cut them free. He shouldn't have been up a ladder.'

'Why not? I am sure he is more capable of climbing a ladder than you are.'

'He's still having unexpected blackouts where he had that blow on the head. If he had one whilst he was on a ladder it could be really dangerous for him.'

Vasi frowned. 'Giovanni knows this and still allows him to work from a ladder?'

Saffron shook her head. 'John hasn't told him. He's tried to make light of it. I talked to him before Giovanni brought me home and I've made him promise to make an appointment at the hospital for another X-ray. I've offered to go with him.'

'If I can help I will do so.'

'Thank you, Vasi, but you are needed in Heraklion at the moment.'

Vasi sighed. 'When I spoke to my father today I asked if he would go into the Central next week. Just for a couple of days so I could spend more time with you. He refused. I do not know what is wrong with him.'

'Maybe there is more wrong with Cathy than he has admitted,' suggested Saffron.

'It's possible. You could ask whilst you are there.'

'Me!'

'You are a doctor.'

Saffron shook her head. 'I am not their doctor. It would be unethical of me to ask. I can only ask after their health generally.'

Saffron raised her eyebrows to John with an unspoken question.

'I've spoken to Dad and also to Nick. I've said that you feel I should have another X-ray to see how my skull is healing. The hospital won't be open for another hour so I'll have to 'phone them later.'

'You make an appointment and we can have a taxi up.'

'Dad could take us in the car.'

'There's no need for him to do that. See what time you are given for an appointment. It could be a whole morning or afternoon wasted for him. Do you have your original X-rays? I'd like to have a look at them. I'd also like to take them with us so we can do an immediate comparison.'

'I'll get them out for you later. What time are you and Vasi collecting Nick on Monday?'

'Vasi said we would be here at eight thirty. There's no point in being too early in Heraklion as the Embassy doesn't open until ten. Just make sure Nicola has all the papers with her that she needs.'

'You ought to take your passport,' John advised. 'You may be asked to witness something and they would need to verify your identity.'

'I make sure I always have it with me after that incident with the police in Heraklion.'

'Even when you're up here with us?'

Saffron nodded. 'After that experience I feel I can't be too careful. '

Saffron was amused to see that within a very short time Nicola had fallen asleep in the back of Vasi's car. She put a finger to her lips and indicated to Vasi that they should talk quietly.

'So how was your day?'

'Successful, but tiring. We had to wait ages in the Embassy and then we were moved from one department to another until Nicola was finally able to swear an affidavit. I had to swear that she had told the truth so it was a good job I had my passport with me. They still seemed terribly suspicious of us. Apparently they will now check with the officials in New Orleans that all the information she has given them is correct. Only then will they give her permission to marry.'

'I suppose it is a way of keeping criminals out of our country.'

'Oh, I'm sure they have good reason, but when you know you are innocent it all seems such a waste of time.' Saffron spoke uncertainly. She had found the procedure that Nicola had been forced to go through to enable her to marry John daunting. She was convinced that if she had to do the same to marry Vasi she would have permission refused. She might even be forbidden to enter the country when they knew her history and she was frightened by the thought.

Vasi smiled. 'I am sure Giovanni will be able to sort out any difficulties.' He was familiar with Greek bureaucracy and how to solve the problems that seemed to arise from a simple request. 'What else did you do?'

'We had a taxi up to Eleftherios Square and had some lunch, then we went looking for draw string trousers and loose tops for Nicola. We stopped for a drink and Nicola needed something to eat, then I telephoned Cathy and asked if it was too early for us to arrive.'

'I'm sure it was not.'

'We could always have spent some more time looking around the shops if she had sounded reluctant.'

'Did Nicola have a rest whilst you were there?'

Saffron shook her head. 'That's probably why she's asleep now.'

'Did you ask my father about Cathy?'

'I did, and he assured me that she is fine. Her mobility has decreased noticeably due to her arthritis, but she is quite able to get around in the apartment with her sticks. He said that if they go to the local shop she usually walks there holding on to her wheelchair and he pushes her back.'

'That is good.' Vasi frowned. 'So there is no reason why he could not leave her alone for an hour or two and come to the hotel.'

'I think your father may need to have a word with his doctor.'

'Why?' Vasi spoke sharply. 'Is he ill?'

'Not exactly, but I think he needs an examination and some advice. It dawned on me whilst we were there that he was leaving the room about every half an hour to go to the toilet.'

'How do you know?'

'It was very regular. He would get up in the middle of a conversation, mutter "excuse me" and hurry out. I think he probably has Prostatitis.'

'My father has never had prostitutes,' declared Vasi vehemently.

'I didn't say he had,' smiled Saffron. 'I said pros – tat – i – tis.' She broke the word down into syllables for him. 'It's where the opening of the prostate gland narrows as a man ages. It makes you want to pass water more frequently and often very urgently.

It can also be painful. He may have had the odd accident at home and is probably worried that the same might happen whilst he is at the hotel.'

'That would be very humiliating for him. What can he do?'

'Make an appointment with his doctor and be checked. The doctor will know if he needs a small operation or if the condition can be rectified by a change in his diet.'

'Really?' Vasi raised his eyebrows. 'It is so simple?'

'It can be, provided it is treated when the symptoms first appear. It will only become worse if it is ignored.'

'And then?'

'It becomes even more of an inconvenience and an infection can set in.' Saffron did not mention that the condition could also be a sign of prostate cancer. There was no need to alarm Vasi or his father unnecessarily. A diagnosis would be up to his doctor.

'Did you mention it to him?' asked Vasi.

'Of course not. He would have been terribly embarrassed.'

'But you are a doctor.'

'I am not his doctor. I have no right to ask about his state of health apart from the usual polite enquiry. You can speak to him about it.'

'Me!'

'You are his son. It's a man thing. If you think he'll be offended tell him you're having a problem and ask his advice.'

'I have no problem,' Vasi assured her and Saffron sighed in exasperation.

'You do not need to have the problem to be able to discuss it with him. You just say you have a problem. He'll probably recommend you go to the doctor and you ask him to go with you for moral support. You have a quiet word with the doctor and ask him to tell your father it tends to run in families and he needs to be examined also.'

'You think I should do that?'

'Only as a last resort if your father insists there is nothing wrong.'

Vasi nodded solemnly. He wished Saffron had spoken to his father and not put the onus on him.

They drew up outside Yannis's house and Saffron woke Nicola gently. 'Come on sleepy head. You're home.'

Nicola blinked owlishly. 'That was quick.'

'You've been asleep most of the way. Take your time. Vasi will take your bags in.'

Nicola yawned and rubbed her eyes. 'It must be carrying these two around that make me tired.'

'That's quite natural. You may not be that big yet, but it's all extra weight that you're not used to.'

'I'm hungry,' announced Nicola.

Saffron smiled. Despite having eaten breakfast Nicola had eaten two apples during their journey up. She had chosen chicken and chips at a fast food restaurant, cleaned her plate and followed it with a cream pie. She had enjoyed a sandwich later in the afternoon and accepted a large slice of cake when they were at Cathy's.

'I'm sure there'll be a meal waiting for you. We're not planning to stop so you can have our share. I expect Marianne will have cooked enough to feed Elounda. Have you got everything?'

Nicola had a quick look on the back seat of the car to check that she had left nothing behind. 'I really appreciate you coming up with me,' she said, 'And Vasi for taking us.'

'It was an enjoyable girls' day out,' Saffron assured her. 'I've never been shopping for maternity clothes before.'

Nicola giggled. 'Those trousers look enormous. Do you really think I'll fill them out?'

'By the time you're due they'll probably be tight. Come on, I'll just pop my head inside to say hello, then we'll be off.'

It was over half an hour before Saffron and Vasi were able to finally leave. 'I'll see you all tomorrow,' promised Saffron. 'Work tomorrow, then it will be the doctor's visit on Wednesday.'

John nodded. He had deliberately put the impending visit out of his mind. He did not want to contemplate a bad prognosis.

Vasi smiled happily as he slid back behind the steering wheel. 'It will be good to be home early.'

'You think of the hotel as home?'

'Wherever you are is home to me. We will freshen up, then drive to Aghios Nikolaos and have a meal.'

'Why don't we just walk into Elounda?' asked Saffron.

Vasi shook his head. 'Most places are closed now. The season is finished.'

'Really? I suppose I hadn't noticed as I've been leaving early and eating with the family.'

'There is no reason for everywhere to be open. There is very little trade. Many families will spend their days harvesting their olives.'

'Does everyone have olive trees?'

'No, but the villagers will join their neighbours to get the crop in. The owner of the trees will pay them a small amount for their labour. They rely on that to supplement their income during the winter months.'

'What about your olive trees?' asked Saffron.

'It is organised. I do not have to worry about picking them myself.'

'I'm glad of that. Having offered to help Giovanni with clearing the chalets I would have felt mean not offering to help you pick olives.'

Vasi shook his head. 'I would not want you to pick olives. It is hard work for everyone from early morning until the evening.' He drew up outside the dark hotel and took a key from his pocket to unlock the main entrance. 'I have a spare key for you,' he said.

Saffron looked at him in surprise. 'Why will I need it?'

'You could arrive back in the evening before me and you would not be able to enter. The hotel is closed now.'

Saffron frowned. 'So I shouldn't be staying here if it is closed.'

'It is no problem. I have arranged for one of the maids to bring a breakfast for you each day. She has to pass the baker. The maids will be coming in to clean the rooms and the manager will be here, but not in the evenings. I would not want you to be locked out if I was delayed for any reason.'

'When there was no one in the dining room this morning I thought it was because everyone had gone out early. I didn't realise we were the only people there!'

'You did not notice there were only cereals and bread available? No cooked breakfast?'

'I didn't look,' admitted Saffron. 'I only ever have cereal, toast and coffee.'

'This is why we are going into Aghios Nikolaos. I have to ensure that you have a big evening meal as you eat so little in the morning. I do not want you complaining to Marjorie that I did not feed you whilst you were here.'

'I'm more likely to complain that I have put on weight and none of my clothes fit.'

Vasi placed his arm around her waist. 'I will love you however fat you become.'

Saffron felt the colour suffuse her cheeks in the darkness. Was Vasi going to ask her to marry him?

To Saffron's surprise the taverna in Aghios Nikolaos appeared extremely busy. 'I thought you said there was no trade during the winter months,' she remonstrated.

Vasi shrugged. 'This taverna will stay open for maybe another month. Their customers are mainly the olive pickers, they will not spend a great deal of money. The owner is probably paying his pickers' their wages in food and drink. When we have eaten I will telephone Yiorgo and ask him to join us if you do not object. I have to discuss the arrangements for taking care of the 'Flora' over the winter months and one or two other matters. It will not take long, I promise.'

'Of course I don't mind.' Saffron felt her heart sink. The two men would no doubt talk for hours in Greek and she would be thoroughly bored.

Yiorgo joined them and grinned at Vasi. 'Yes? Are we celebrating?'

'Celebrating?' Vasi frowned uncomprehending. 'What should we be celebrating?'

'You mean you have still not asked her? Vasi, what is wrong with you? Look, I will show you. It is very simple.' Yiorgo took hold of Saffron's hand. 'Please, will you marry me? I am in love with you and do not feel I can live without waking up to see your beautiful face on the pillow beside me each morning.'

'Yiorgo, stop.' Vasi spoke sharply.

'What did Yiorgo say to me?' asked Saffron.

'He was being foolish. Take no notice of him.' Vasi glared at Yiorgo. 'I asked you to come here so we could talk business. Thank goodness Saffron does not understand Greek.'

'What could be more important business than asking Saffron to marry you?'

'I could have changed my mind,' answered Vasi stiffly.

Yiorgo laughed. 'Don't try telling me that! I have seen the way you look at her, and let me tell you also, my friend, she looks back at you in the same way.'

Vasi waved his hand as if removing a fly from the vicinity. 'Have you spoken to Barbara about moving to my father's house?'

Yiorgo's face fell. 'She won't contemplate it.' He began to tick off Barbara's objections on his fingers. 'It is too far from Aghios Nikolaos. It is too far from her mother. It is too far from Elounda. It is too isolated. It is up a steep hill. The swimming pool would be dangerous. We couldn't afford it. At least I agree with that.' Yiorgo spread his hands. 'If it was my decision I would manage to find the rent from somewhere.'

Vasi sighed. He would have to try to persuade his father to sell the house or demolish it and build a hotel on the land.

'And the 'Flora'?

'I have a berth booked for three weeks time. She will be taken out of the water and her hull examined. I am sure there will be some re-caulking necessary. Once that has been done I will disable the motor and make her weather proof for the winter.'

'How much will that cost?' asked Vasi.

Yiorgo shrugged. 'I won't know until they've inspected her.'

'Don't agree a price until you have spoken to me.'

Yiorgo raised his eyebrows. Vasi did not usually haggle over money.

'I don't want to find I've paid ten times more than the other boat men through ignorance.'

'I'll ask around,' nodded Yiorgo. 'Would you two like another drink?'

Vasi shook his head. 'I've had half a bottle of wine and I'm driving. Saffron's had a long day up in Heraklion and I know she's tired. We ought to make a move.'

'I'm sure she won't be *too* tired.' Yiorgo pushed back his chair. 'I'll be off as well. I'm working with my father again and he expects me ready by seven. He's forgotten what it's like to have a small child disturb your sleep every night.'

'Still teething?' asked Vasi sympathetically.

'They're always teething, have colic, or a cold. Any excuse to keep you awake half the night.'

Vasi was thoughtful as he drove back to the hotel. Yiorgo was right. He must speak to Saffron.

'We will sit and talk for a while,' he announced and led the way to the lounge area. Saffron suppressed a yawn as she followed him. No doubt he wanted more information about the complaint she believed his father to be suffering from. She was tired after walking around Heraklion most of the afternoon, it was nearly midnight and she would have been happy to go straight to bed.

Vasi sat opposite her and took her hands in his. 'Saffie, before you went to Nigeria I asked you to marry me. You said you could not do so because you were committed to the hospital project and also you would not be happy leaving Marjorie alone in England. You are back from Nigeria. You tell me Marjorie has friends with whom she spends a good deal of her time. I am asking you again, Saffie. Please will you marry me?'

Saffron felt a lump come into her throat. Would Vasi understand her fears? She sat there silently.

Vasi frowned. 'Is it so difficult to say yes or no?' he asked.

'It is very difficult, Vasi.' She squeezed his hand. 'I love you, Vasi. but I'm not sure I would be allowed to marry you.'

Vasi raised his eyebrows. 'Who would not allow you to get married to me?'

'The government. No, listen, Vasi. I did not realise until I went to the Embassy with Nicola today just how they enquire into your background. She had to take her birth certificate and American citizenship papers with her, along with her passport and visitors permit. She had to swear she had not been married before and had no criminal record. They have told her she will be investigated to prove her sworn affidavit is true and only then will she be given permission to marry John. They have told her it could be a matter of some months before permission is granted. She then went to a different department and applied for a residency permit. They wanted the same details from her and agreed to renew her visitor's permit whilst they investigated her background.'

Vasi nodded. 'That is customary. If there is any problem I am sure Giovanni will deal with it.'

'I am not concerned about Nicola. There is no reason why they should not give her permission to live in Crete and marry John, but for me it is different. I was born in New Orleans and became a British citizen due to my father's nationality when we returned from the States.'

'Many people are born outside their own country.'

Saffron shrugged. 'I'm sure that would not be a difficulty;

but I have been married, Vasi and I was married to a criminal.' Saffron looked at Vasi with distressed eyes. 'They could refuse me permission to marry you because of Ranjit. Having investigated me they could refuse me a resident's permit. They might even declare me undesirable and I might not be able to visit Crete ever again.' A tear ran down the side of Saffron's nose and she withdrew her hand from Vasi to brush it away.

Vasi shook his head. 'That is not possible. You have done nothing wrong.'

'I know that, you know that, but will the government believe that I had no knowledge of Ranjit's crime when I married him?' Saffron shook her head. 'The English police know that I am completely innocent. They did not take my passport away. I am free to travel anywhere in the world, but I am frightened that if I make any application to stay over here it may be denied.'

'That will not happen.' Vasi spoke positively. 'I will find the right person to speak to at the Embassy and for a small consideration I will ensure that you have no problems.'

Saffron looked at him incredulously. 'You mean you will bribe someone not to investigate me?'

Vasi shook his head. 'No, you will be investigated, but nothing detrimental will be found against you.'

'Surely that is illegal?'

Vasi shrugged. 'It is paying to have the work carried out quickly and with the correct result. There is no reason why you should be penalised for the behaviour of the Indian you married. You have no criminal record. They will simply accept Ranjit's death certificate confirming you are a widow and declare there is no reason why we should not get married.'

Saffron looked at Vasi doubtfully. 'Are you sure?'

'Of course. I know how the system works in Greece. Giovanni knows also. Nicola will not be waiting for months for permission to marry John.'

'So that was what you meant when you said Giovanni would

sort out any problems?'

Vasi nodded. 'Trust me. You return to Crete as soon as you can, bring all the necessary papers with you and we will visit the Embassy together. Now, I will ask you again, Saffie. Will you marry me?'

Saffron hesitated. She had enjoyed working with her family; being useful and busy during the day whilst Vasi was working, but how would she occupy herself in the future? 'Vasi, I never want to hurt you in any way. I don't want to find that the novelty of living in Crete wears off when I can no longer sunbathe and swim and I have nothing to occupy me. I don't want to greet you with a miserable face and a list of complaints each evening.'

'I am sure that will not happen. Cathy did not have that problem.'

'Cathy had her friend staying here with her, remember. She had a companion whilst Vasilis was working.'

'You will not be left alone, Saffie, I promise. If I have to spend time in Heraklion you can come and stay at the hotel there with me. If my time is to be spent down here then we will be at my father's house. From there it is easy for you to visit your family and spend some time with them. Marjorie can come and stay for as long as she wishes. You will very soon find you have plenty to occupy your days.'

Saffron gave a shaky laugh. 'You make everything sound so easy.'

Vasi smiled at her. 'You make everything sound so difficult! I am willing to take the chance that in a few years time you may say you are unhappy here and wish to return to England. In the meantime we will have had some years of happiness together. Will you take that chance with me, Saffie?'

'I would need to have some work over here.'

'Why?'

'I'm used to working every day. I don't want to be bored and miserable when I'm on my own, besides I will need the money.'

'I will be your husband. It will be my responsibility to provide for you.'

Saffron shook her head. 'I can't be forever coming to you and asking for money. I'm used to being independent.'

Vasi looked at her steadily. 'Is this another excuse because you know how hurt I will be if you refuse me? You will not have to come to me to beg for money. I will transfer an amount to your bank account each month. It will be yours to do as you please with.'

'That won't feel right, Vasi. I will have done nothing to have earned it.'

'You will have looked after the house, done my washing, cooked my meals. It is the allowance a husband should give to his wife. '

Saffron moved towards Vasi and kissed him. 'You are the most kind and generous man I have ever met and I love you dearly.'

'So you will marry me?'

Saffron shook her head. 'I will hand my notice in at the hospital and come back to Crete. I'd like to spend some time living over here to make sure I really can settle into the Cretan way of life. I don't think we should make any plans until I can be certain of that and we know if we will be allowed to get married.'

Saffron waited for Giovanni to arrive at the hotel in Elounda and then drive her and John on to the hospital in Aghios Nikolaos. They had finally agreed that Giovanni would drive them in and they would have a taxi back, rather than have him sit and wait for them. Saffron had examined the X-ray of John's injury and shown him where there were two distinct lines at the front of his skull making a V formation.

'I wish the X-rays were of a better quality. That is where the damage occurred.' She traced the lines with her finger. 'I can't make out whether that is a slight depression in the bone or a shadow. We'll compare these X-rays with the one that is taken today. If there is no sign of it healing that explains why you are still having a problem.'

'And what happens then?'

Saffron shook her head. 'I don't know the procedure in Crete. If it was England you would be referred to a neurosurgeon and he would decide if it needed more time to heal or if an operation to close it would be advisable.'

John looked at her in alarm. 'I don't fancy anyone messing around with my brain.'

'They wouldn't be interfering with your brain. A small metal plate would be inserted and the two pieces of bone would be aligned and held in place. It's the same sort of procedure that I would use on a broken arm or leg that wasn't healing,' explained Saffron.

'So why don't I come to England and let you do it for me?'

Saffron laughed. 'I appreciate the faith you have in me, but I only deal with limbs. I am certainly not qualified to undertake brain surgery unless it was a dire emergency.'

'And I'm not?'

'We'd have to be somewhere completely isolated and it would have to be a matter of life and death before I attempted it.'

'I'll tell you if the doctor wants your expertise.' John winked at her.

'I'm sure he won't. Just tell me exactly what he says.'

'He'll probably speak excellent English,' John assured her. 'You'll probably have less problem understanding him than I will as he'll no doubt use all the technical terms that you're familiar with.'

Saffron nodded. She hoped John was right in his assumption. Although she knew John would do his best with a translation she could not rely on him to be medically accurate.

The wait at the hospital was tedious. Despite arriving early for the appointment John was kept waiting for over half an hour before the doctor called him into his consulting room. John explained that he had been concussed and that he was now having problems with his vision.

'Have you consulted an ophthalmologist?'

John nodded. 'In his opinion the condition would right itself as the bone healed. I'd like to request an X-ray to see how the process is progressing. I'm willing to pay, but I need you to authorise it. My companion is a doctor and when the result is through she would like to compare the X-rays.'

The doctor looked at Saffron. 'She is a brain surgeon?'

'No, she deals in limbs, but she knows how to read an X-ray.'

'I, also, know how to read an X-ray,' replied the doctor stiffly.

'Of course,' agreed John, 'but I don't.'

The doctor shrugged and scribbled a note which he handed to John. 'Take that to the X-ray department. You'll have to wait as you don't have an appointment.'

'Thank you. Will you be available to speak to again later if necessary?'

'That will depend how long you are kept waiting for the results. I have other patients to see who have appointments.'

'Of course.' John pulled a face at Saffron and rose from his chair. 'At least I have the form authorising an X-ray. Today will probably be as boring for you as when you went to the Embassy with Nick. I'm sure you'd rather be back working than spending the day here.'

'I'm staying here with you however long it takes,' Saffron assured him.

She followed John down the corridor to the X-ray department where he handed over the note from the doctor and they took seats at the side of the room. 'I'm not an accident or an emergency so we just have to wait until they have a space,' John informed her. 'If I asked you to go to the cafeteria outside and buy some coffee do you think you could find your way back?'

'I should think so. Even I can read X-ray and follow an arrow. Do you just want coffee or do they sell sandwiches as well? If we're going to be here all day we'll need something to eat.'

'We should have packed a picnic lunch to bring with us. A sandwich is a good idea, but don't get meat or fish. You never know how fresh it is. Do you want some money?' John dug into his pocket and Saffron shook her head.

'I've plenty with me. Up until yesterday in Heraklion I hadn't spend any money since I arrived.'

'Wait until Vasi presents you with the hotel bill.'

Saffron felt a moment of panic, then realised John was teasing. 'I'll pack my case and run away. There's no one there to stop me. See you shortly.'

Saffron wandered down the corridors to the hospital exit. It looked little different from the one where she worked in London. She realised that she would have to confront Sean and give in her notice when she returned next week. She had a moment of misgiving. Was she doing the right thing to give up her career in medicine and make a new life in Crete? Did she want to spend half her time living in a hotel and the other half in Vasilis's large house?

Having made her purchases she walked back down to the X-ray department only to find that John was no longer sitting waiting for her. Momentarily panic assailed her. Had she taken a wrong turn and ended up in a different part of the hospital? She looked up at the wall. The "X-ray" sign was prominently displayed. John had obviously been called in to have his X-rays taken.

Saffron sat down to wait, placing the two cups of hot coffee on the ground beneath her chair and removing the packs of sandwiches she had pushed into the top of her shoulder bag. They did not look particularly appetising and she wished she had thought to ask Marianne to make up a sandwich for them.

By the time John finally emerged with a piece of paper in his hand she had drunk her coffee and John's was tepid.

'It doesn't matter,' he assured her. 'I can always get another cup.'

'Did you look at the X-ray?' asked Saffron. 'You were in there ages.'

John shook his head. 'I had to wait until it had been developed and they had checked to see they had photographed the right area. Then I had to wait for the bill.' He waved the slip of paper at her. 'We have to take this to reception and when I've paid they'll hand over the X-ray to me.'

'I'd like to look at it before we leave.'

'Don't you need that special thing they clip them to with a light behind?'

'Ideally, yes, but I should be able to get a fair idea just by holding it up to the light.'

John picked up his cup of cold coffee. 'I'll get rid of this. No point in carrying it around with me.' He walked through the door with the stylised figure of a man and returned seconds later. 'Now, reception to pay and then we can go. Do you want to stop in the town and have something decent to eat?'

Saffron shook her head. 'We might as well eat the sandwiches I bought. They'll only be thrown away otherwise and it seems a waste.'

John raised his eyebrows. 'You're very frugal suddenly.'

'It's being in Nigeria. It made me conscious of how wasteful we tend to be. Some of the people there are desperately poor and a pack of sandwiches would be a feast to them.'

Saffron waited whilst John paid for his X-ray at the reception desk and he was finally handed the large brown envelope. They walked over to the window and John withdrew the black and white photograph of his skull and handed it to Saffron. She held it up to the light and examined it carefully.

'This is the one that was taken today?' she asked.

John nodded. 'It has the date on the top in the corner. The earlier ones are in here.' He indicated the other envelope he was carrying.

'Take them out and hold them up to the light for me,' she directed. Saffron looked from one X-ray to another. All three looked identical; there was no sign of the fracture having healed. 'I think you need to speak to a neurosurgeon,' she said finally. 'The fracture is still there which must mean the piece of bone is still pressing on your optic nerve. That will be the cause your sight problems and the blackouts.'

'I'll need a letter from the doctor,' frowned John.

'Then we'll ask to see him again before we leave.'

'That could mean waiting here until the end of his working day and he might refuse to see us again without an appointment.'

'So what's the alternative?'

'I'll try to talk my way in,' grinned John and walked back over to the reception desk.

Saffron watched as he waited his turn and then began an impassioned discussion with the girl whom he had paid earlier for his X-ray. She continually shook her head and John spoke more intensely, pointing to his head and his eyes, finally staggering and collapsing on the floor. Saffron rushed over to him.

'Now the doctor has to see me,' he murmured to her and winked.'

Saffron gasped. It had been an act. John had deliberately sunk to the floor to ensure he had his own way. The receptionist, looking quite distraught, began to speak to Saffron in rapid Greek and Saffron shook her head.

'I don't understand. He needs the doctor. Doctor. Medico. Pharmacy.' Saffron searched wildly for a word the girl would understand.

Her companion at the reception had lifted the telephone receiver and was talking to someone whilst watching John at the same time. The other people who were waiting for attention had fallen back, but were regarding the young man who was motionless on the floor with interest. They began to call instructions to the receptionists, offering advice, insisting they called the doctor or at least provided some help. John listened to them and had a desire to laugh.

The doctor who had seen John earlier emerged from his room

and knelt down beside him. 'Can you hear me?' he asked.

'Perfectly,' answered John.

'What's wrong with you? Are you epileptic?'

'No, if I can come in to your room for a moment I can explain.' John sat up and scrambled to his feet. Saffron took his arm as if guiding him across the hallway.

'You'd better sit down,' commanded the doctor. 'Now, what's the problem?'

John smiled easily. 'It's to do with when I had a blow on the head and suffered a fractured skull. I saw you earlier and you gave me a letter to have another X-ray to see how it was healing. I've had that and it hasn't mended. I was asking the receptionist for another appointment with you when I had one of my blackouts.'

'So what do you expect me to do about it?'

'I wanted to ask you for a letter authorising an appointment with a neurosurgeon.' John leaned forward. 'I, and my doctor friend, think I should see a specialist.'

The doctor nodded and drew his pad towards him. 'You'll have to go to Heraklion. We have no specialist unit here.'

'That's no problem,' John assured him. 'We can drive up.'

'Are you proposing to drive home today?'

'No, we'll take the bus to Elounda and then a taxi.'

'I'm glad to hear it. Obviously it isn't safe for you to drive at present.' The doctor pushed the letter towards John. 'Contact the Heraklion hospital and they'll give you an appointment.' He stood up. 'If you need more recovery time I'd be grateful if you would sit outside in reception. I do have my appointments to deal with.'

'Thank you,' smiled John. 'Come on, Saff.'

John placed the letter carefully inside his wallet and shepherded Saffron out of the door. 'Not a word,' he hissed in her ear.

Saffron waited until they were outside the hospital and then she turned to John. 'Did you fake that?' she asked. 'You really frightened me.'

John grinned at her. 'Did you want to sit there for the rest of the day only to be told eventually that the doctor could not see me? How long were we with him? No more than five minutes. That won't have interfered with his appointment schedule. The receptionist was being a pain so I decided I would make the doctor see me.'

Saffron shook her head. 'John, you are truly awful.'

'Not a bit. I was just determined to get my own way. Don't tell Mum and Dad about my act. They wouldn't approve, but Nick will laugh fit to burst when I tell her.'

John imparted his news from the hospital to his parents and Nicola.

'It's a nuisance having to go to Heraklion, but Saff insisted the doctor gave me a letter so I could be thoroughly checked out by a consultant and also have more precise X-rays taken.' John smiled conspiratorially at Saffron. 'The original and the one taken today don't look any different, so the fracture can't have healed yet. I'm not a bad looking chap, am I?'

'Don't be flippant, John. I imagine one skull looks much the same as another in an X-ray,' remarked Marianne dryly. 'I agree with Saffron. You should see a specialist. The injury might be no trouble to you at the moment, but if you happened to hit your head again in the same place it could be serious.' Marianne was concerned that the fracture showed no sign of healing.

'I don't plan to make a habit of it. I'll call the hospital tomorrow and see when they can fit me in.'

Giovanni nodded. 'I'll drive you up and take the opportunity to go to the Embassy. See if I can hurry things up a bit for you and Nicola. If Nicolas and Elizabeth plan to come over from America they need to know a date.'

'I just wish Mum would stop 'phoning me to ask how I am,' complained Nicola. 'Now she's got used to the idea she seems to expect daily bulletins.'

'That's something you'll just have to accept,' smiled Marianne. 'Whenever I speak to her I assure her that you are blooming with good health, but I'm not sure that she believes me. I've promised her that if there is any cause for concern, however slight, I'll 'phone her immediately.'

'I could take a photo of you each day and e-mail it to her,' suggested John. 'That way she'll be able to see for herself how well you're keeping.'

Nicola giggled. 'I'll have to make sure I'm wearing something different each time or she won't believe it's a new photo.'

John ran his hands over Nicola's large stomach. 'Oh, she will. You seem to get bigger every day,' and he ducked as Nicola aimed a blow at him.

John closed his mobile 'phone and looked at it in disgust. 'I don't believe it! I've just spoken to the hospital in Heraklion and they say there is no point in me making the journey up there as they no longer have a consultant. He left last year and they are not planning to replace him.'

'So what happens when someone fractures their skull?' asked Marianne with a frown.

'They do whatever's needed immediately to stabilise the patient and if they feel specialist treatment is necessary then they are flown to Athens. They have no facilities at the hospital for a follow up appointment like the one I am requesting.'

'Then you 'phone Athens and when you have an appointment we'll book you a flight.'

John shook his head. 'I'll not bother. It's no real inconvenience to me and I expect it will heal up given time. It would be better to save the expense and spend it on Duck and Chicken. Nick has been looking at the equipment we'll need, two of everything certainly adds up.'

'You won't need it all at once.'

John frowned. 'Two Moses baskets for whilst they're small, then two cots. Nick will need a double buggy to take them out, not to mention bedding, clothes and nappies. We'll need a mountain of those.'

'We'll help you,' promised Marianne. 'Don't let Nicola worry. Look at brochures and on the internet and make a list of the essentials for the first six months. You could ask Saffron to have a look at the prices in England; sometimes it can be cheaper to have them sent over directly.'

John smiled. He had expertly diverted his mother's attention away from his injured head and extracted a promise of financial help with the children without having to put his request into words.

Saffron was not best pleased when John told her that to see a consultant he would need to go to Athens and that he was not prepared to make the journey.

'They're not going to tell me anything different over there. They'll confirm that the fracture is still there and tell me that it will heal in time.'

Saffron eyed him doubtfully. 'I'm not happy with your decision, John.'

'It's just a waste of money,' he assured her. 'It's really no inconvenience to me, except when I'm trying to take a photo. Now I'm reconciled to taking stills with a tripod I don't even think about it.'

Saffron shook her head sadly. 'Your photography meant so much to you.'

'It still does,' John assured her. 'I also realise that I can't go rushing off all over the world to take wildlife photographs and leave Nick alone here for months on end. That wouldn't be fair to her. I've heard that there's talk of a television series for that book that came out about Spinalonga. If it comes off they'll have to make it locally and I know more about Spinalonga than most people. I could work as a consultant to them or even get a job as a cameraman. I know Dad pays me for working for him, but I realise now that Duck and Chicken are going to cost a small fortune. I shall need all the income I can get.'

November and December 2008

Saffron bade Vasi farewell at the airport with a promise that she would return as soon as she could be released from her contract with the hospital. For the first time since she had become a doctor she was not looking forward to her return to work. She had enjoyed her two weeks of unaccustomed manual labour at the chalets and watching the walls of the new self catering unit grow daily. For the first time she felt properly involved and a part of her extended family.

Marjorie was pleased and supportive of Saffron's decision to return to Crete. 'You really are happy with Vasi, aren't you?'

Saffron nodded. 'He's so kind and thoughtful.' She sighed. 'If he lived in England there would be no problem.'

'Why is it a problem in Crete? Most of your immediate family live there.'

'They all have something to do. Their days are fully occupied. I'm used to being busy and I don't want to find I'm just counting the hours until Vasi returns home.'

'I'm sure you'll find something.'

Saffron shrugged. 'I'm sure Giovanni would employ me as a chambermaid during the season or I could work as a waitress in the taverna. I don't want to do either and I also don't want a job found for me just because I'm a relative.'

'Where will you be living? At the house or in a hotel?'

'Probably both. Vasi said that when he has to work up at the Central I can go up there and stay with him. Once I've made myself familiar with Heraklion I'll have nothing to do up there. I won't be truly on holiday and nor will I be living as an ordinary Greek housewife.'

'So why don't you talk to Vasi about the idea of having specialised holidays at his house? Maybe I was foolish not to go over last season. The project could have been up and running ready for you to take over.'

'I don't know anything about catering,' protested Saffron.

'Nor do I,' Marjorie reminded her, 'But Vasi seemed to think I was quite capable of looking after four extra people and organising their days.'

'You would only really have been giving them breakfast. If they were having Greek cookery lessons they would have provided the evening meal.'

'So why couldn't you do that?' asked Marjorie.

'I suppose I could.'

'Of course you could,' replied Marjorie positively. 'I'm sure Marianne would give you any additional help that you needed.'

Saffron had refused to contemplate Sean's reaction when she gave in her notice and had no intention of telling him the real reason. She would just declare that she was making a career change. She knocked on his door at the end of the day and entered with trepidation.

'I needed to see you,' he remarked as she entered.

Saffron took the seat he indicated and waited. Was he going to ask her to go back to Nigeria or somewhere else for a medical exchange?

'Your contract as a consultant surgeon is up for renewal. You'll have to complete these papers and re-apply.' He pushed a folder across the desk towards her. 'There's no certainty that you will be re-appointed after the amount of time you have had away and there's Mr Macalister's complaint against you.'

'The complaint was unfortunate, but not really anything to do with me,' protested Saffron. 'I've only had the time off that I was allowed, in fact I'm still owed another ten days.'

Sean frowned. 'I hope you're not thinking of asking for that now. After all, you had six months in Nigeria and have only just returned from Greece.'

'I was sent to Nigeria by the hospital. It wasn't a holiday,' Saffron spoke indignantly. 'I'm not here to ask for any more leave and I shan't need to re-apply for my position as I'm giving you my notice. I've decided on a career change.'

Sean raised his eyebrows. 'That's a rather sudden decision. What are you planning to do?'

'Catering,' answered Saffron, she had been turning her conversation with Marjorie over in her mind.

'Really? I didn't know you were an accomplished cook.'

'There are a lot of things that you don't know about me,' replied Saffron. 'I have my letter of resignation here. It gives you the required three months' notice and the date I shall actually leave. I've deducted the ten days still owing to me.'

'How am I supposed to staff your department if you are continually altering the schedule to suit yourself?' protested Sean. 'I'm not at all sure that you can be released on the date you have given.'

'My contract states quite clearly that I have to give three months' notice. I have done that and I can leave at the end of the second week in February. With the deduction of the ten days holiday still owed to me I shall be leaving on February fifth.'

'That's not possible. You know we never grant leave until after the end of March.'

Saffron shook her head. 'I'm not asking for more time off. I am terminating my employment with the medical authorities. If you try to insist that I stay after the fifth of February I shall take sick leave for the remaining ten days. No doubt you will have plenty of applicants for my job and I will ensure that all my work, including the patients' files being in correct alphabetical order, is completely up to date. My successor should have no problems.'

Sean glared at her. There was nothing he could do. She had given the statutory period of notice that was required and was completely within her rights to claim the ten days leave still owing to her. He replaced the folder with the application papers into the drawer of his desk. He did not believe her story of a career change. She had no doubt applied to another hospital and been accepted. The information had just not come through to him yet.

'I shall need the name of the new hospital where you will be working to pass on to the accounts department.' He knew that was completely untrue, but he was determined to find out where she was planning to work in the future and they would receive a confidential report from him saying that she was uncooperative and difficult to work with.

Saffron stood up and shook her head. 'I have told you. I am making a career change. I don't plan to work at any hospital. I will leave you with my letter and if there are any forms for me to complete or my signature needed you know where to find me.'

Giovanni drove up to Heraklion with Nicola and had a few quiet words with the head of the immigration services. Nicola's birth certificate and American citizenship papers, along with her sworn affidavit were examined again before the man looked at Giovanni and spread his hands.

'All appears to be in order, but you know how long these matters can take.'

Giovanni nodded. 'I do. I would also like my son and the young lady to be married before my grandchildren are born. I am sure there must be some way to hasten matters along.' Giovanni drew the edge of an envelope from his pocket.

The man's eyes gleamed. 'I might be able to speed things along a little.'

Giovanni drew out more of the envelope. 'I thought we might be able to collect the necessary papers today.'

'It could be possible.' The official stretched out his hand and swiftly seized the envelope that Giovanni offered. 'If you will excuse me for a short while I will check and see how far along the process is.'

Giovanni nodded. He knew the man would count the money that was in the envelope and if the amount was sufficient there would be no delay.

Ten minutes later the man returned with a smile on his face and papers in his hand. 'They were just waiting for a signature,' he explained.

Giovanni could feel the warmth on the papers where they had just been photocopied and smiled to himself. It was amazing how swift and simple the procedure could be once an envelope had changed hands.

Nicola smiled at him as he waved the papers before her. 'You really didn't need me.'

'I may have done; besides, I have instructions from Marianne to take you to the shop that sells baby equipment. She thought you ought to look at the buggies before you make a final decision and we can collect the Moses baskets and take them back with us. We can't have these two arriving early and have nowhere to put them.'

'It is only December! They're not due until April at the earliest,' Nicola reminded him.

'Need to be well prepared, just in case.'

'They're still talking about making that television series,' John announced to Nicola. 'As soon as they arrive I'm going to see if there's any opportunity for me to work as an advisor.'

Nicola frowned. 'Surely they'll have their own advisors, besides they're working from a book. It would be different if they were filming the true history.'

'No harm in me asking. I'm sure to know far more about the island than they do. After all, my great uncle lived there, my grandmother was married there and I was conceived there. What more could they want?'

Nicola shrugged. She could not get excited about film crews and actors coming to the area. Although she felt perfectly well, everything was becoming an effort as she seemed to grow larger and more unwieldy every day.

'If they arrive soon I could also ask if they want a pregnant woman for any of the scenes. You could end up as a film star,' continued John.

'I wouldn't contemplate the idea, besides by the time they've finished talking about making a film I will have had these two. There's nothing attractive about me at the moment. I wish I hadn't chosen grey trousers. They make me look like an elephant,'

'I think you look like a beautiful elephant.' John ran his hand gently over Nicola's enlarged stomach. 'How are these two today?'

Nicola smiled complacently. 'I think I felt one of them move last night.'

'Really? Which one? Duck or chicken?'

'Idiot! I've no idea.'

'How did it feel?'

'Just sort of fluttery.'

'I wish I could feel it.' John spoke longingly.

'You'll be able to later on. As they get bigger their movements become stronger. I've been told that towards the end you become sick of being kicked around inside and can't wait for them to be born.'

'Do you want me to be with you when you have them?'

Nicola smiled at him. 'Of course, but the choice is yours. The doctor told me that the fathers often faint. You'll be alright, won't you?'

'Of course I will. Fainting is for wimps.'

'If I need to have a Caesarean you probably wouldn't be allowed in the theatre anyway.'

John frowned. 'Is that likely?'

'We'll have to wait and see. It usually depends how they are positioned.'

John patted her stomach. 'You two be good. I want to see you the moment you make me a proper father.'

Giovanni looked at the new self catering unit with a feeling of satisfaction. The builders had now turned their attention to the taverna and in another week the footings for the first half dozen shops would be completed. The rebuilding schedule was going to plan, despite the lack of work that had taken place over the Christmas holiday. He just hoped he would not run out of money before it was finished.

It had taken Marcus a considerable amount of time to convince Giovanni that it was practical and made sense to salvage everything that could be useful in the new buildings. Now he was pleased he had taken his advice. Re-using the glass patio doors had saved him a small fortune. He was now saving more money by having the old fitments installed, rather than buying new ones. There were still new shower trays to be supplied and some of the mattresses needed renewing, but provided the shower units, fridges and microwaves worked when they were tested he would make a further saving in the region of three thousand Euros.

He had calculated that the saving he was making would cover the cost of the decoration and landscaping the grounds. Once the basic work had been done he could call on John and Marcus for help with the finishing touches. He might even find that Saffron was willing to lend a hand again now she was returning to Crete to be with Vasi. Once she had settled in she could easily find herself with very little to do each day whilst Vasi was working. It was a nuisance that Dimitris had been called for his National Service and was no longer available. He had been willing to work long hours for a minimum wage.

He had taken out another loan from the bank to cover the wedding costs for John and Nicola and help with the basic necessities the twins would need when they were born. He had not been amused when he was told that the interest rate for a new loan was considerably higher and warned that the rate he was paying on his original loans would be increased in the next financial year.

Giovanni began to make notes of the various jobs he must check on during the following day. The family still laughed at his copious lists and the instructions he left in strategic places for the builders, but he found the system worked well. He did not forget an outstanding job and the builders, carpenters and plumbers had no excuse to say they did not know what he had wanted and done it their way. Even Uncle Yannis had finally realised that his system of labelling and listing made sense. As he and Ourania carefully packed up each item of glass or china ware from their shop the box was marked with a description of the goods. In the previous years when they had packed items away whilst decoration was taking place they had no idea later what the boxes contained

Yannis had been insistent that his new shop should be built opposite the taverna. 'We don't want people to notice our shop just as they are getting on the bus to return to Elounda. They will be able to see us whilst they are eating or drinking and will no doubt come over out of curiosity. John can take some photos and you can have a small brochure advertising the shop that you give to people along with the menus. People need something to occupy them whilst they are waiting to be served.'

Giovanni smiled. So many years ago when Uncle Yannis had the hotel in Athens he would have scorned such obvious publicity.

Vasi checked his accounts. The money he owed the bank had hardly reduced due to the high rate of interest being charged on his loans and there was still an enormous amount outstanding. He wished he could solve the problem of the Imperia Hotel. It was costing him a great deal of money standing there empty, but it would need another massive loan from the bank to repair the structural damage and put it into good repair.

Dimitra had been an additional drain on the income of the Central. He had agreed to let her occupy a suite there at a nominal rent when she was released from the hospital, expecting it to be for no more than a few weeks. She had now been living there for almost two years and her rent had remained the same, not increasing in line with his increased expenses. He must no longer delay a confrontation with her. She would be far more likely to be able to find an apartment at a reasonable rent during the winter months if she was prepared to move on.

He would have to pay the annual retaining fee to the manager of the Hersonissos hotel, but fortunately this year there was little in the way of maintenance needed. He closed his accounts with a sigh. Due to the increase in charges for the utilities his financial position was no better than it had been at the same time last year and now he planned to buy a small car to give Saffron her independence when she returned to Crete.

January 2009

Nicola looked out of the window and across to Spinalonga and groaned. 'John, it's awful out there.'

John stood at her side. There was no way they would be able to get over to Spinalonga for their wedding. 'Maybe we could postpone it? Have it tomorrow.'

'There's no guarantee the weather will be any better then. We just chose the wrong week.'

'It may have calmed down by this afternoon. Let's have a look at the weather forecast.' John switched on his computer. Nicola looked at the screen over his shoulder and shook her head.

'They're predicting high winds for three days. We can't put it off for that long. My parents are booked to fly home before the end of the week. Dad and Eleanor can't have any more time off from school. The authorities weren't happy to release either of them as it was.'

'We'll see what Yiorgo says. If he's willing to go over we'll know there's no problem.'

'I doubt that Pappa Lucas will be very happy, and what about Grandma?'

John put his arms around Nicola. 'I'm convinced that Grandma would survive anything. I'm more concerned about you with Duck and Chicken. Don't worry. I'm sure something can be sorted out if we really cannot get across.'

'I did want to get married over there,' said Nicola sadly. 'Your grandmother was looking forward to it. She said it would bring back memories of her wedding day.'

'I'm sure she has plenty of memories of that. If the conditions really are impossible we'll ask Pappa Lucas if he'll conduct the service in the church at Plaka. After all, my grandmother was married there as well as on the island.'

Vasi took one look at the weather and his face blanched. There was no way he could go out in a boat on such a day. He felt sick and his hands were shaking at the thought. He would telephone his father and ask him to declare an emergency at the Central that needed his immediate attention. He would drive Nicola's parents and sister along to Yannis's house and explain that regretfully he would be unable to attend the wedding.

'So what are you going to do?' asked Elizabeth. 'I can't allow you to go over to Spinalonga in this weather. The boat could capsize.'

Nicola looked at her mother in amusement. If she decided that she was going to risk the trip there was no way her mother would be able to stop her. 'It could calm down later. John is going to ask Yiorgo what he thinks. We may have to postpone it until next week.'

'Nicola! You can't do that. We've come all this way to be with you at your wedding. You should have made proper arrangements and held it in the church at Elounda. It would have been more convenient for your father and Eleanor to come over during the Christmas vacation.'

'We couldn't arrange anything until I had permission, then it was the Christmas break over here. You know nothing ever gets back into routine until after the first week in January. You could always stay on. I'm sure Vasi wouldn't mind you staying at his house for an extra week.'

'It was very good of him to allow us to stay there in the first place rather than have to go to a hotel. We mustn't take advantage of him, besides our flights are booked.'

'I'm sorry, Mum. I know I'm a disappointment to you, but you can't blame me for the weather.'

'That's it, then.' John closed his mobile 'phone. 'I've spoken to Yiorgo and he says the boats are forbidden to leave port and he certainly wouldn't want to take Nick and Grandma over in such a rough sea.'

Giovanni nodded. The news came as a welcome relief to him. He had been worried about getting Annita in and out of the boat safely, even if it had been a calm day. Yannis, Ourania and Marisa were also a responsibility at their ages and he had no desire for his son's wedding to be spoilt by a catastrophe. 'I'll let Pappa Lucas know that he won't be needed.'

'Oh, no,' remonstrated Nicola. 'John suggested that we asked him to conduct the service in the church at Plaka.'

'Plaka?'

Nicola nodded. 'There's no reason why we shouldn't have it there provided Pappa Lucas agrees. It's the next best thing to having it on Spinalonga.'

Vasi listened to their conversation and breathed a sigh of relief. If the service was to be held in a church on the mainland he would be only too happy to attend. He wished Saffron could be there with him to enjoy the day, but he understood that her contract with the hospital did not finish until the following month.

Giovanni picked up his mobile 'phone. 'I'll speak to Pappa Lucas. If he agrees we'll have to go up this morning and clean the church.'

Pappa Lucas was as thankful as the wedding party when he was told the journey to Spinalonga had been cancelled. It was no day to be out on the sea, however short the journey. When Giovanni asked if he would be willing to come to Plaka and take the service he hesitated.

'Why don't you come into Elounda?'

Giovanni shook his head. 'Nicola had her heart set on Spinalonga. She's willing to compromise in view of the weather, but she would like it to be at the church at Plaka.'

Still Pappa Lucas demurred. 'The church there is not open.'

'I have the key,' Giovanni assured him.

'But it will not have been cleaned.'

'We'll go up this morning and do everything that's necessary. I'm sure it will be spotless by the time you arrive.'

'The guests will all have to be notified. As you cannot get to Spinalonga they will be expecting it to take place in Elounda.'

'Most of the guests are our family and they are here with us at the house. It is no problem for us to contact the others. Shall we say three thirty at Plaka? Will that be convenient for you? It's the same time as we had arranged for on the island.'

Pappa Lucas sighed. There was no way he was going to be able to change the man's mind and have the wedding in the comfort of his own church. 'Very well, but I will need to be collected from Elounda.'

'Just a moment.' Giovanni turned to Vasi. 'Are you able to collect Pappa Lucas at three from his church in Elounda?'

Vasi nodded. 'No problem,' and Giovanni relayed the arrangement to the priest.

'That's settled then. We'll have to go up and clean the church this morning and the service is at three thirty. The same as it was to be on the island.'

Marianne immediately began to open her cupboards and make a pile of furniture polish, brass and silver cleaner along with a pile of dusters.

'What's happening?' asked Elizabeth.

'Cleaning the church,' replied Marianne.

'What!'

'Oh, I forgot you didn't understand. Pappa Lucas has agreed to hold the wedding ceremony in the church at Plaka. It is only open on special occasions so it will need to be cleaned. Do you want something old to wear?'

'You mean we are cleaning the church?' asked Elizabeth incredulously.

'Who else? You can have one of Giovanni's old shirts to put over your clothes. I seem to have a number of those. You're getting fat, Giovanni.'

'I am not,' he replied indignantly and pulled in his ample stomach. 'My shirts shrink in the wash. Now, you and Nicola will stay here with Grandma. I'll take Bryony, Marcus and John in my car and Vasi can bring the others. Don't tell the elders about the change of plan until we come back. They'll only want to come up and help and they'd be useless and get in the way.'

'I'll tell them I need them here to help me prepare the meal for when we return from church after the ceremony. Uncle Yannis can sort out the wine and set out the glasses. I'll have plenty to keep them occupied.'

'What are we doing, Mum?' asked Eleanor.

'We're going up to help clean the church ready for Nicola and John to be married this afternoon.'

'You mean you expect me to work as a cleaner!' exclaimed Eleanor.

'If I can, you can,' replied her mother tartly. 'It won't hurt you.'

'I didn't come over here to work,' complained Eleanor. 'I've got to wash my hair and do my nails this morning.'

'I suggest you leave both until we come back or you'll probably have to do them again.' Her father spoke to her firmly. 'Ask Nicola for some old jeans and a top that can go in the wash. You've got ten minutes.'

'But, Mum, if I have to do cleaning I'll be too tired to go to the wedding later,' protested Eleanor.

'Then you can have a rest this afternoon and forgo painting your nails. Ten minutes as your father says. If you're not back here I shall come and get you.'

Sulkily Eleanor flounced out of the room. Nicola suppressed

a smile as she followed her. At last her parents seemed to realise that Eleanor was bone idle and played on having had glandular fever to shirk from any arduous work.

Brooms, buckets and scrubbing brushes were added to the pile of items Marianne was gathering together. 'Anything else?' she asked, wrinkling her brow.

'Some old towels. We can kneel on them and if we need to dry anything off they'll be useful.'

Marianne nodded. 'I'll get some, oh, soap and detergent, Bryony. Take a fresh pack of each from under the sink.'

John returned to the kitchen. 'Dimitris's on his way up. He'll help. We might even find a use for Skele.'

'Such as?' asked Nicola scornfully.

'If we wanted to send a message down to you we could tie it to his collar.'

Nicola raised her eyebrows. 'It would be quicker to use your mobile.'

'Then we'll just tie a duster to his tail.'

'Idiot. Go on, the sooner you start the sooner you'll be back. Make sure you're back in time to have something to eat before you shower and change.'

'That won't be necessary. I won't get dirty.'

'John! I am not marrying you unless you've showered and put on a respectable suit.'

'You have to.' John took her in his arms. 'Pappa Lucas is making a special effort for us today. He's being chauffeured all the way from Elounda to Plaka to say a few words over us to make you my legal wife.'

'I'll tell him I've changed my mind. I don't want to marry a man who's unwashed and in dirty clothes. I'll say I want to marry Dimitris instead.'

'I think Dimitris would be delighted.' John bent and kissed her. 'I'll make sure I'm clean and respectable enough for you. What are you wearing?'

Nicola pulled a face. 'I haven't got a lot of choice. My elephant trousers. I can't fit into anything else.'

Annita was relieved when she was told of the change of venue for the wedding. She had never been ashore on Spinalonga and was not sure she wanted to do so even all these years later. She had also been dreading the boat trip when she saw the weather. She did not fear being sick, having been a fisherman's daughter and gained her sea legs as a child, but she had no wish to be pitched overboard at her age.

Marisa let out a wail. 'I was so looking forward to going to Spinalonga. It was so lovely when Uncle Yannis walked down to the altar with me.' Tears filled her eyes. 'I do wish Victor could still be with us. I know he would have insisted that we went over regardless of the weather.'

Yannis looked at his sister scornfully. 'Victor had more sense. He would have realised it was impossible. We'd all arrive soaked with spray and end up with pneumonia. You'll just have to remember when Uncle Yiorgo escorted you into the church at Plaka.'

'I'm pleased we're not going over there,' remarked Ourania. 'I'm sure I'd be sick and what it would do to Grandma I dread to think. The journey would probably kill her. Then we wouldn't be celebrating a wedding we'd be attending a funeral.'

'Don't be such a pessimist, Ourania. It wouldn't be comfortable for her, but I doubt if it would kill her. I'm sorry Nicola can't have her wish, but it really makes little difference which church you get married in.'

'Didn't you want to get married on Spinalonga?' asked Marisa of her brother.

Yannis shrugged. 'There was never any suggestion of it. The island was closed and Uncle Yannis was in Athens. There didn't seem to be any point in going out there to get married when there was a church just up the road.'

Nicola looked at herself in the mirror. She had waited until John was in the shower before putting on the pair of black drawstring trousers and emerald green top that she had bought whilst in Heraklion with Saffron and kept hidden away. She smiled to herself. So much for the grand white wedding that her mother had suggested took place after the birth of the twins.

'Wow! You look terrific.' John emerged from the shower towelling his hair dry.

'Will you be warm enough?' He touched the fabric with his hand. 'It isn't very thick.'

Nicola smiled. 'I've a jumper underneath, but these two are marvellous insulators. They keep me warm all the time. I'm glad they're not due in August. I'd probably melt.'

'I need a photo of you. I'm taking the tripod and my camera up to the church, but I've got to rely on Vasi to take the video.'

'You really like it?' asked Nicola anxiously. 'It was difficult to know what to wear.'

'I love that sparkly top.'

'It's not too flamboyant is it? I could change it for a plain white one.'

'You're perfect as you are. Don't change a thing. Stand there and pretend to brush your hair.' John set his camera on the tripod and looked through the view finder and pressed his forehead to enable him to focus. 'Now another, turn to the side, fine, now look straight at me and smile.'

'Did you finish cleaning the church?' asked Nicola as John lifted a sandwich from the plate his mother had prepared.

John nodded, his mouth full. 'Marcus and I cleaned the windows whilst Dimitris and Dad scrubbed the floor. Your Mum and Eleanor polished the chairs whilst Bryony polished the altar. Then they cleaned the brass and the silver and put new candles in the holders.'

'You must have worked hard. Fancy having to do all that on your wedding day.'

John grinned. 'We'd had a trial run when we cleaned the church on Spinalonga last week. These sandwiches are good. Have you had some?'

Nicola nodded. 'It was your mother's idea. It was easier than making a proper meal for everyone. It meant that my family and Vasi could take them back to the house and eat them whilst they were getting ready. Whilst I made them she prepared everything else for when we return.'

Nicolas took his daughter's arm and gave her a squeeze. 'Ready? Bryony is taking up your bouquet and I've checked that John has your ring.'

'You're not mad with me anymore, Dad?'

Nicolas smiled. 'I never could stay cross with you for long. It's your mother who's disappointed. She wanted you to have a big white wedding.'

'That would have been a bit hypocritical when you see the size of me! My ring won't even fit on my finger and I'll have to wear it on a chain round my neck until I've had this pair. We'll have a big party next year to make it up to Mum, and I'll make sure it's at a convenient time to suit her.'

'I'm sorry you couldn't go to Spinalonga.'

'No matter. I only said I wanted to go there because I knew how much it would mean to John. I hadn't thought through the practicalities of getting in and out of a boat or that the weather could be this bad. It would have been freezing going over, even without this wind blowing. It would have been horrible for everyone.'

Giovanni drew up outside the house and Nicolas opened up his large umbrella. 'I'll do my best to keep you dry.'

Nicola flung her old waterproof over her shoulders. 'A bit of rain won't hurt me. I wish John hadn't forbidden me to wear my wellingtons, though. I hate wet feet.'

February - March 2009

Marjorie watched sadly as Saffron packed up her belongings. She would not spoil her step-daughter's happiness by telling her how much she had missed her whilst she had been in Nigeria. At least she had known she would return at the end of her duty over there. Now, if she decided to stay with Vasi she would only see her when she visited England or if she was invited over for a holiday. Marjorie desperately hoped that Saffron would be happy in her new life in Crete and if she finally decided to marry Vasi there would be no obstacles put in their way by the Greek government.

'I'll arrange to have these boxes collected by courier,' announced Saffron. 'I'll just take my winter clothes with me. I know I won't need summer dresses until at least April or May. If I pack up my books and other things that I want to keep, may I leave them here?'

'You can leave anything you want. I can always send it on to you if you change your mind.'

'I doubt if I shall need anything urgently. If I do you can always bring it out with you when you come to stay with us. I'm hoping we'll both be able to come back and visit you at the end of the season and I can always go through things again. Some of it should probably be thrown out anyway.'

'Just store it for the time being. If you throw it now you could regret it later.'

'I am making the right decision, aren't I, Marjorie? I haven't always been very sensible in the past.'

'I just hope you won't miss being a doctor. It was all you ever wanted to do.'

Saffron nodded. 'I'm sure I will miss it, but I'm not sorry to be leaving. I've never got on well with Sean. He took a great delight in telling me I would have to re-apply for my position and that he thought it unlikely I would be re-appointed. I think he had every intention of trying to influence the medical panel against me.' Saffron frowned. 'I do wish I could speak Greek. I'd be able to work as a doctor in Crete then.'

'You could always learn.'

Saffron shook her head and laughed. 'It would take years for me to become proficient. I might eventually know enough to be able to understand a conversation, but certainly not to work in a hospital.'

Vasi breathed a sigh of relief as he saw Saffron walk through passport control with her luggage. He had been frightened that she would change her mind at the last moment, despite her having told him she had resigned her position at the hospital and he had already received two large boxes of her belongings.

He took her cases and smiled. 'How was your journey?'

Saffron pulled a face. 'The flights were fine. It was just the long stopover in Athens.'

'You should have 'phoned me. We could have chatted to pass the time.'

'For six hours! My mobile battery would have run out and it would have cost a fortune using an airport phone.'

'No matter. You are here now. We will go to the Central tonight and drive down to the house tomorrow.'

'Separate rooms?' Saffron raised her eyebrows.

Vasi shook his head. 'I have told the staff that my wife is arriving.'

'That is a bit premature, isn't it?'

'I have also bought you a pre-wedding present, but you will

have to wait until we go to the house tomorrow to receive that.'

'Wedding present! I haven't actually said I will marry you yet.'

Vasi shrugged. 'So, it is a present in advance for when you do agree to marry me.'

'That sounds like bribery to me,' Saffron tried to speak sternly. 'Besides, we don't know if I will be allowed to marry you.'

Vasi smiled easily. 'I am sure there will be no problem. I spoke to Giovanni regarding the procedure. He had no trouble when he visited the Embassy with Nicola. Within an hour they came away with the necessary permission. We will deposit your papers and ensure all is in order. If, after six or seven weeks we have heard nothing we will pay them a visit to ask after the progress of your application. I will have a small incentive with me that should make the whole process be completed very swiftly.'

Vasi opened the electronic gates that led to his father's house and parked behind a small car that was outside the garage.

He turned to Saffron and smiled. 'I hope you will like your present.'

Saffron frowned. 'My present?'

'The wedding present I spoke about. If you do not like the model it can be changed.'

'Vasi!' Saffron gasped. 'Do you mean that car is my wedding present?'

Vasi nodded. 'You will need it. Sometimes I will be delayed in Heraklion and you will wish to go somewhere. It could be cold or raining and you would not want to walk down the hill and back in such weather.'

Vasi did not admit that he had discussed keeping Saffron occupied with his father and it was he who had suggested that if she had a car it would give her the freedom to go wherever she wished. He had taken out a further loan to finance the purchase. He should never have allowed Alecos to blackmail him into purchasing the worthless Imperia hotel, his finances were now stretched to the limit.

Saffron shook her head, completely speechless.

'You do not like the colour?' Vasi asked anxiously. 'It can be re-sprayed.'

'Vasi, I just don't know what to say. I was expecting a piece of jewellery.'

'You would prefer some jewellery?'

'Oh, no. It's the most wonderful present I've ever been given.' Saffron's voice trembled. 'I'm not sure if I will dare to drive it. Suppose I scratch it?'

'I will accompany you for the first few journeys you make.'

'I can't think of anywhere I will want to go, apart from my family and maybe on to Plaka.'

'We can visit them this afternoon and you can show off your car.'

'What can I give you, Vasi?'

'If you are happy to stay in Crete and be my wife you will have given me everything I could possibly want.'

'You always said you'd like a pup to train and make into a pet. Would you like me to give you one? You'd have to choose it, of course, but I'd pay for it and all the vet's fees and things.'

Vasi shook his head. 'I would love that as a present, but not at this moment. I do not have the time to spend with a dog. When my father is well again and takes some of the work load off me I may remind you of your offer.'

'I won't forget,' promised Saffron. 'Is your father showing signs of improvement?'

Vasi frowned. 'He says he is better, but I am not so sure. The doctor placed him on a diet that should help him. He was not pleased when he was told to give up coffee and reduce his wine each evening. He is still having more tests and he has been warned that he may need an operation.'

'The operation is quite simple.'

'Simple, maybe, but operations are expensive.'

'Doesn't he have insurance?'

'He was always healthy. He saw no need to insure himself in case he was ill. Also, when he married Cathy and wanted to have insurance cover for her he was refused.'

'So any medical treatment has to be paid for unless you have insurance?'

'That is so.'

'I wonder if John is covered by insurance,' mused Saffron. 'I know he had to pay for his X-rays, but they were taken at his request.'

Vasi shrugged. 'He probably has the basic insurance like most people. He would still have to pay for his hospital treatment and claim it back later. If he wants private treatment he will have to pay in advance and it is doubtful if he would be able to reclaim that.'

'I imagine that was why John refused to go to Athens for a consultation. I know he said it would be expensive and it would be better to spend the money on the babies. I thought he just meant the flight and staying there for a couple of days.' An awful thought struck Saffron. 'Do you think Nicola has insurance? Suppose she needed a Caesarean? How much would it cost?'

'Some thousands of Euros. I expect Nicola has thought of that. They have the same system for medical treatment in America. I am sure that now she and John are married her insurance would be recognised in Greece.'

'I certainly hope so. I'll have to ask her this afternoon.'

'You are planning to visit your family this afternoon?'

Saffron looked at Vasi, puzzled. 'You suggested that I did.'

'I know, but since we have arrived here we have sat and talked about health problems. I thought maybe you wished to stay sitting in the car all afternoon. You have not even looked at your present yet.'

'Oh, Vasi, you make me sound terribly ungrateful. I'm longing to look at the car, my car, we just became side tracked when I offered you a dog.'

Marianne greeted Saffron and Vasi joyfully when they arrived. 'I was so pleased when you told me your news,' she said as she hugged her cousin. 'Welcome to the family, Vasi.'

'Where's Nicola?' asked Saffron.

'Resting. I insist that she has at least an hour each afternoon on her bed. If she heard your car draw up she'll no doubt be out in a few minutes. If she's asleep I don't want to wake her. You're able to stay, aren't you?'

'Of course we can. I just wish I could have been over here for her wedding.'

Marianne smiled. 'That was quite a day, wasn't it, Vasi?'

Vasi nodded. 'One does not usually spend the morning cleaning a church before attending the wedding in the afternoon. Where is everyone else?'

'Up at the unit. Everything is finally coming together and we'll certainly be ready for opening at the start of the season. The men have just started decorating and Bryony is cleaning up after them and doing any odd jobs.'

'Would Giovanni mind if we drove up and had a look?' asked Saffron.

'I'm sure he wouldn't. He'd probably like to show it off to you and tell you all the other ideas he has.'

'What about Grandma? I could pay her a quick visit, then if Nicola isn't around we could go up to the unit and come back later to see everyone properly.'

Saffron left Vasi in the kitchen with Marianne and tapped on her grandmother's door. She peered inside the room to see Annita sitting on her sofa engrossed in the news that was showing on the television.

She patted the seat next to her. 'Sit down and let me just finish listening to this.'

Saffron sat silently until Annita switched off the television. She gave a deep sigh. 'It is not good news.'

'What's happened?'

'It is the Euro. We are being told that Greece has no money. We have always told them that we are a poor country but they did not believe us. Anyway, enough of our problems. How are you? Marianne tells me that you have given up being a doctor and are planning to stay in Crete.'

'I finally decided, Grandma. I want to be with Vasi. He means far more to me than broken arms and legs.'

Annita nodded. 'I'm pleased to hear it. He's a good man, gentle and considerate.' Annita regarded Saffron's stomach. 'Are you expecting?'

Saffron's face flamed and she shook her head. 'No, I'm too old now to think of going down that route.'

'Rubbish. These days women often have their first child when they're in their forties. It isn't like it used to be when you expected to get married young and start a family straight away. Wouldn't Vasi like to be a father?'

'We've never discussed the possibility.' Saffron smiled. 'Vasi gave me a car of my own as an early wedding present and I have offered to buy him a dog,' she said quickly to divert the conversation.

'A dog? Why should he want a dog?'

'He had one as a boy and would like another to treat as a pet.'

Annita sniffed. 'I hope he won't let it in the house. Filthy creatures. John insists on taking that mongrel into his room to see Nicola before he walks it back to the village. It isn't healthy.'

'I understand that Skele saved John's life.'

'He still shouldn't be allowed in the house.' Annita spoke firmly. 'It's bad enough that Ourania has that cat of hers back here now. It never comes in my room, thank goodness. I'll throw a jug of water over it if it does.'

'She couldn't leave it alone at the shop for days on end. That would be cruel.'

'I'm not suggesting that, but it should live outside. That's the proper place for animals, not treated like humans. If you saw the way some people in the States pampered their animals. They spend more money on them and give them more attention than they do their children. Are you sure you're not pregnant?' Annita eyed Saffron's stomach again.

Saffron shook her head. 'I'm sorry to disappoint you, Grandma, but I'm definitely not expecting. Don't be greedy. You'll be a great great grandmother very soon when Nicola has the twins.'

'Duck and Chicken! I shall be glad when they have proper names. Have they told you what they plan to call them?'

'I think they're waiting to see if they're boys or girls. I'm sure they have suitable names planned.'

'I certainly hope so. Duck and Chicken indeed!'

Saffron was bored. Her first week back in Crete had been spent unpacking her belongings at the house and then packing half of them up again to return to the hotel in Heraklion to be with Vasi. The weekly journey to and fro, trying to remember what clothes she had in each location and not forgetting to take anything she considered essential back and forth was becoming irksome.

Whilst Vasi was working she had revisited the museum, wandered around Heraklion to get her bearings, taken the bus to Knossos, visited Cathy and Vasilis, sent long e-mails to Marjorie and read a number of books. She had bought a book to try to teach herself Greek and disciplined herself to spend an hour each morning and afternoon trying to recognise the letters of the alphabet and memorise short sentences. Now she had nothing to occupy her until Vasi returned to their suite that evening and they decided where they would go for a meal.

On a number of occasions she had broached the subject of running the specialist holidays at his father's house and he had presented her with the practical problems that would confront her. She would need to speak to a couple of women in the village and ask if they would teach the guests cooking and ask another about weaving. The village women did not speak English. She did not know the countryside well enough to advise artists where they should go to have the best views or help walkers to choose a route that would not be too arduous.

'Wait a while, Saffie. Learn a little Greek, become known in the villages. Once you are officially my wife you will find the villagers accept and respect you. They will listen to your ideas and be willing to help.'

She wondered if Vasi would agree to her driving her car up from Elounda to Heraklion. If she had her car with her she could drive to some of the outlying villages and explore them. If her idea met with his disapproval she would say she wished to spend the following week down in Elounda and drive out to some of the villages there. She did not relish the idea of staying in Vasi's father's large house on her own, but that would also give her the opportunity to visit her family more often, or even help Giovanni with any last minute work that was needed at the units.

Vasi shook his head sadly when she broached her idea. 'I know you have little to do whilst I am working. I am sorry. I should not have persuaded you to give up being a doctor and come to Crete.'

'I'm not unhappy, Vasi. I know I will settle down. I'm just used to being busy all day and not having to amuse myself. It's different when you're on holiday. You know you have a limited amount of time and want to see and do everything. That's why I thought if I drove my car up I could go off during the day and see some new places.'

'You would be confident driving alone over here? So far you have driven no further than Plaka and I have been with you.'

Saffron nodded. 'I was terribly nervous the first few times I drove, but it isn't as difficult as I thought it would be. It seems foolish to have a car sitting down there not being used and for me to be sitting here with nothing to occupy me.'

Vasi sighed. 'Saffie, I cannot stop you. I want only your happiness, but I will ask you to tell me where you plan to go each day. If I know the drive to be difficult I can warn you or suggest a different route.'

'I will be sensible, Vasi. I'll only do short journeys at first. I'll go down to Elounda by bus tomorrow, visit the family and drive back here in the afternoon.'

'You will telephone me as soon as you have returned to the hotel?'

Saffron squeezed his hand. 'You really do not have to worry about me, Vasi. I'm used to driving in London and the traffic there has to be seen to be believed.'

April – May 2009

John had managed to have one quick glimpse of his daughters as they slithered into the world one swiftly followed by the other, then his legs buckled and he keeled over in a faint and lay on the floor totally ignored by the nurses. When he regained consciousness Nicola was sitting up in bed a baby cradled in each arm and she was looking from one to the other.

He scrambled to his feet, brushed his hand across his eyes and blinked. He pressed his forehead and blinked again. His vision improved, but everything was blurred.

'Sorry, Nick, I fainted.' He stroked her damp hair. 'I'm such a wimp.'

Nicola smiled wearily. 'You're not a wimp and I was too busy to notice. Have you seen them?'

John nodded. 'They're beautiful. Two little girls just like you.' John did not admit that he could not see them clearly. 'Duck and Chicken.'

'Do you want to hold them?'

John looked at Nicola aghast. 'Hold them?'

'Why not? They're your babies too.'

'Suppose I drop them?'

'Why should you? Sit down on the chair and I'll ask the nurse to give them to you.' Nicola looked down at the babies in her arms. 'This is Joanna Helena,' she nodded towards her left arm 'And this is Elisabetta Maria.'

'How do you know?' frowned John, wishing he could see them clearly, everything was so blurred.

'Joanna has one identity bracelet as she was born first and Elisabetta has two.'

John picked up his camera and fitted it on to the tripod. 'I need to take photographs,' he said, hoping he would be able to focus successfully. 'I'll hold them afterwards.'

'Not too long,' the nurse warned him. 'The babies need to be bathed and settled, and their mother needs to rest.'

'Well, Elias, two little girls added to the family. I'm sure Nicola is relieved that is all over. Joanna Helena and Elisabetta Maria. Pretty names. I was a bit concerned they would choose something modern and stupid. No doubt John will shorten them to Jo and Lisa, but that's acceptable. Nicola should be home tomorrow and I'll be able to see them for myself. I'd quite like to hold them, one at a time, of course. I couldn't cope with two. I remember what it was like when our Elena had her girls and she put both of them in my arms. I felt helpless and didn't dare to move. I wish you were here to see them. You always liked babies more than I did, but then when our first ones were small you were at the laboratory all day and only saw them in the evenings. You hadn't had to spend all day washing and feeding them and trying to get household jobs done in between. At least Nicola won't have to worry about running a house and cooking and Bryony will always be willing to keep an eye on them if Nicola does want some time to herself. A shame she and Marcus never had any of their own. Too late now, of course. I wonder about Saffron and Vasi. Saffron was very quick to deny that they planned a family, and she doesn't look pregnant. I think she would have told me if she was. After all, she told me Vasi had asked her to marry him before she told anyone else in the family. She still hasn't given him a definite answer. She says she wants to see if she can adapt happily to living in Crete. I don't see why she shouldn't. I'm expecting them to arrange their wedding for September. Maybe when Saffie has a ring on her finger they'll think again. Mustn't leave it too much longer, though. Age catches up with you. I just wish I didn't feel so tired all the time. I'm the last of the old ones. Who would have thought that a fisherman's daughter would have lived so long and done so much in her life?'

Annita placed Elias's photograph back on her bedside table and closed her eyes. The doctor had assured her that she had nothing medically wrong with her, but her body was wearing out. It was only to be expected when you were nearly a hundred. It was incredibly frustrating.

John walked along the road towards Elounda, Skele at his heels. Whilst Dimitris was doing his National Service his sister had agreed the dog could still live at their house, but John had to be responsible for his keep and his exercise. It was no hardship to John. He just wished Ourania was not so frightened of dogs, so he could have been able to keep the mongrel at the house.

He walked deep in thought. There was something wrong, something very wrong with his eyes. He would turn and as he did so everything would go black. He could still press his forehead, blink rapidly and bring his focus back, but it was unnerving not having any warning. As his sight came back to him he would feel a burning pain in his head for a moment and would thrash out wildly.

The sight problem he could deal with, he had become used to his vision being blurred, but the uncontrollable rage was something else. He was frightened it would happen whilst he was helping Nicola with the babies and began to make excuses not to touch them. Suppose it happened in the night and he hurt Nicola? He sat down on the bank and hugged his knees.

'What am I going to do, Skele? I'm sure I've developed a brain tumour. What else could be causing my problems? I was so happy a few months ago. I was looking forward to my babies, now I wish I didn't have them. At least I could tell Nick I didn't love her anymore and go away somewhere on my own.' At the thought John felt scalding tears come into his eyes. 'Everyone seems so excited about their baptism and I'm dreading it. Suppose I have to hold them and I have one of my blackouts?'

Skele licked his hand and John automatically pulled at the dog's ears. 'At least having to take you home is a good excuse to be out of the house all evening.'

Saffron watched as Bryony and Antonia deftly undressed the two little girls and wrapped them in a towel. She had been expecting a service similar to the Christenings she had attended in England and was totally unprepared for the ornate decoration in the church and the number of people who had pushed their way inside along with the invited guests.

She wished she had been brought up in the Greek Orthodox religion so she could have acted as a godmother to them, although when Bryony had explained her responsibilities that would have to be taken seriously and last forever she felt quite daunted. She had insisted on giving Bryony and Antonia a monetary gift each when she found out they would be responsible for the babies' clothes for before and after the service, the church fees, candles and a small gold crucifix for each child to wear.

Bryony held Joanna, her naked body slippery having been anointed all over with oil. The priest said something inaudible to Bryony who gave a nervous giggle. Holding Joanna firmly the priest immersed her into the water whilst he chanted the liturgy. Joanna gave a gasp and seemed to accept her fate, but as the priest dipped her body in a second time she gave out a piercing cry. Totally oblivious to her distress the priest immersed her a third time before handing her back to Bryony who wrapped her in the towel and cradled her gently.

Antonia followed suit with Elisabetta who had begun to cry in sympathy with her sister and continued to whimper as Antonia patted her small body dry. Both girls were laid on their white towels whilst the priest cut four small strands of hair from each of them and followed this by blessing their clothes.

Once they were dressed, Bryony and Antonia carried each baby down to the door of the church, followed by Dimitris and Vasi, who had also been asked to be godparents. They made slow progress as everyone wished to touch and admire them. Twins were something of a rarity in the community and as such were regarded as a novelty.

John set up his camera outside the church and began to take photographs, it seemed that everyone who had attended the service wanted to have a photograph to remember the occasion. Finally Vasi took a photograph of John standing with his arm around Nicola whilst she held both the girls. He was relieved he had been able to avoid holding them himself. It was almost an hour later when Nicola was finally able to climb into the car and have her babies handed back to her.

'There was a time when I didn't think I would ever see either of you again,' she smiled. 'You behaved beautifully. I'm proud of both of you.'

Marcus waited until Bryony was in the car and then began to drive away slowly. Bryony sank back against the seat. 'Thank goodness that's over. I thought John was never going to stop taking photos and my feet are killing me.'

'Is everything ready at home?' asked Nicola.

'Saffie drove back earlier to do any last minute jobs There's less than twenty of us, so there should be no problem. It will be different next year if we have the big party you've talked about; all our American relatives will be here.'

'I wish my Mum and Dad could have been here today,' said Nicola wistfully.

'I'm sure you do, but at least they were able to come to your wedding.'

'Yeah, Dad would probably have lost his job it he'd asked for any more time off and Eleanor has missed enough schooling. Will you be able to help me with these two when we get back? They'll need a feed and I'm sure Joanna's leaking.'

'I'm not used to putting on a cloth diaper,' protested Bryony.

'Nor am I,' Nicola assured her. 'At least it's only for three days then we can go back to the disposables. I just wish I could bath them as usual. Just giving them a wash won't be the same.'

'You'll have to tell Antonia when she can come up to the house. It would be symbolic somehow if they were both bathed at the same time.'

'Why don't you arrange that with her?' suggested Nicola. 'After all, you're both godmothers.'

Bryony smiled. Once she had removed her shoes she would be completely happy.

Saffron e-mailed Marjorie and described the Christening of the twins to her in detail.

"I do wish you had arranged to come over. I'm sure you would have enjoyed seeing the difference between an English Christening and a Greek one. Here it is so much more elaborate. The service was all in Greek, of course, so I didn't understand anything the priest said.

I am really enjoying exploring in my own little car. I wish you were here with me so we could go off together for the day. I look at the map in the evening and decide where I would like to go; then I ask Vasi if it is a practical journey and how long it will take. Sometimes he does not know the area and other times I do not take his advice and drive there anyway. I do find it rather disconcerting. The map often makes a village look quite close, but the roads are so narrow and winding that it can take me all morning to get there.

I am planning to drive to the memorial next week, although Vasi says it will take me a long time due to the traffic in Rethymnon. If I decide it is too far I do not have to continue, but can turn around and come back to Heraklion.

I'm not sure how I will occupy my time when I have driven everywhere around here. I have talked to Vasi about your idea of

having people to stay at the house and learn Greek cookery or
weaving, or to use it as a base for a walking or painting holiday,
but he is finding all sorts of reasons why it would not be practical
or possible. I don't think he likes the idea of having strangers
around when we are living there. It would also mean I had to be
down here in Elounda every day and he would either have to drive
up and down to Heraklion or stay up there alone.

If Vasilis would return to working at the Central as he used
to it would be easier. I am not sure if he is not well enough or if
he is still using Cathy as an excuse to stay at home. Poor Vasi is
quite exhausted on occasions. I just wish I was able to help him.

I am trying to learn a little Greek and the locals often laugh
at me when I try to use it. They usually speak to me in English
and I do not laugh at them when they are confused about their
tenses or plurals. The families who live in Pano Elounda and
Kato Elounda speak very little English and I usually just say
good morning. They often say something back to me but I do not
understand and just smile."

Marjorie smiled as she read the e-mail, despite Saffron's
concern that she would have nothing to do in the winter months
she seemed to be settling down happily.

Giovanni opened the door to the self catering apartment and
ushered his first guests inside. 'You're our first visitors this season.
We've only just opened up so if you find any problems please
tell us immediately. My personal telephone number is written on
the information brochure. The taverna is open and also the shop
where you can buy basic food stuffs. Someone will come to give
you room service each day, probably mid morning so that you'll
not be disturbed too early.'

The man nodded and placed his suitcase on the floor. He had
not been impressed when he had seen the building work still being
undertaken further along the road where the construction of the
first shops was nearly completed.

'What time do the builders start work?' he asked.

'About seven thirty, but they should be no inconvenience to you. Most of their work is inside now. I had hoped it would have been completed by the start of the season so the shops could be open, but the work has fallen a little behind schedule. The general store and taverna are open of course.'

Giovanni did not admit that he was short of money. The bank had refused him a further loan until the self catering units and taverna were bringing in some revenue. Only two shop keepers had shown any interest in renting the premises and he sincerely hoped he had not made a disastrous financial mistake.

He smiled at the couple. 'I'll leave you to get settled in. As I said, any problems please feel free to call me.'

Giovanni walked back over to the taverna where Bryony was waiting for him. 'Have you everything you need? They may come over for a quick lunch.'

'I brought up calamari, sausages, steak and chicken and it's in the freezer along with some chips. Stop fussing, Giovanni.'

'I'm not fussing,' snapped back Giovanni. 'It's always difficult to get the catering requirements right at the beginning of the season. I don't want to find we've wasted food.'

'If I don't use the salad or bread I'll bring it back with me this evening. Everything else will be fine in the fridge for a few days.'

'I need them to tell their travel company that everything was perfect. A bad report from the first guests could ruin the bookings for the rest of the season.'

'I can't think of anything they could complain about. The units are equipped exactly the same as the chalets were. You even made sure this couple had one of the new mattresses you bought. Any problems they have will be of their own making.'

Giovanni nodded. 'I know I've done all I can and so has Marianne. Fortunately we have a good reputation, but word of the fire spread amongst the agents. Until they're sure the new units are up to standard they'll hesitate to recommend us. At the moment we've only three bookings for the rest of the season.'

'Don't worry. It's early yet. I'm sure your bookings will increase. They always have in the past.'

'I certainly hope so.'

'What's wrong, Nicola?' Saffron looked at the young girl anxiously. Her previous sparkle seemed to have disappeared and she looked miserable most of the time.

Nicola shrugged. 'Nothing really. Baby blues, I suppose.'

'It's more than that. You can tell me. I'm a doctor, remember. Whatever you tell me has to be in confidence.'

'You're not my doctor.'

'I'm not a gynaecologist either, but I can see when someone is unhappy and it's more than baby blues. Tell me what's troubling you.'

A solitary tear ran down Nicola's nose and she brushed it away with her hand. 'I've just made such a mess of everything for everyone.'

'A mess? What? Do you mean the babies? From what I've heard everyone is delighted.'

Nicola shook her head. 'I'm sure they're only saying that because they feel they should.'

'John means it.'

Nicola gave a small smile. 'Does he?' She sighed deeply.

Saffron looked at her sharply. 'Are you regretting marrying John? Do you think you should have gone back to America to your parents?'

Nicola shook her head. 'I love John. I always have. When I used to come over here as a kid I thought he was wonderful. I really looked up to him and respected him. He was so much better at everything than I was, but he never made me feel stupid.'

'So what is the problem, Nicola? If you're just feeling low due to lack of sleep that will go as the girls get older and sleep through the night.'

Nicola smiled shakily, but the tears still ran down her face.

'That could be part of it, I suppose, but it's John. It's since I had the babies. He doesn't get involved with them at all. He'll stand and look at them and give them his finger to grip, but if I ask him to hold one of them he refuses. If I lay them on our bed he'll watch over them, but if I ask him to help me bath or dress them he refuses. He wouldn't even have a photo taken of him holding them at their baptism.'

'He's probably frightened that he'll hurt them. A lot of men think they'll be too rough whilst they're tiny.'

Nicola shook her head. 'It's more than that. It's almost as though he tries to avoid us. During the day he's working with his father. After our meal be brings Skele in to see me before he walks him home and then he often doesn't come back for hours. When I ask him where he's been he says he's been talking to friends in Elounda or makes some other excuse. He told me once he had been with Dimitris. I saw Antonia the following day and she said Dimitris wasn't due for leave until the following weekend. John got quite cross when I mentioned it to him and told me it was none of my business and to stop nagging at him. Why is he lying to me? John has never lied. He can be devious, but he's not a liar. It can only mean he's met someone else.'

Saffron looked at Nicola in horror. 'He can't have. That isn't like John.'

Nicola shrugged. 'It's the only explanation. He hasn't been near me since the girls were born and they're six weeks old now. There's no reason why we shouldn't, well, you know. He even takes a duvet and pillow into his dark room and sleeps in there. He says the girls disturb him too much.'

'Have you spoken to Marianne?'

Nicola shook her head. 'It's between John and me. I wouldn't have told you except you caught me at a weak moment.'

Saffron placed her arms around Nicola. 'I'm sure there has to be some explanation. Maybe John doesn't realise that you can resume a normal married life and that's why he seems to be avoiding you. I'll see if I can manage a time alone with him and have a word.'

'You won't tell him I've spoken to you, will you?' asked Nicola anxiously.

'Of course not.'

'It's just that he gets so angry sometimes.'

'John, gets angry?'

Nicola nodded. 'Very angry. Apparently he had a row with his father the other day. I heard Giovanni telling Marianne. Giovanni said he was dripping paint on the floor and John threw down his brush and walked out, telling his father that if he wasn't happy with his work he'd go somewhere else. He returned a few minutes later, cleared up the mess and apologised, making the excuse that he'd been up in the night helping me with the girls.'

'And he hadn't?'

'He's never given either one a bottle or a cuddle if they're crying. I don't think he loves them.' Nicola began to cry again. 'Maybe I should go back to New Orleans. Maybe Mum was right when she tried to get me to go back home.'

Saffron rocked the distraught girl in her arms. 'Don't even think of that at the moment. I'm sure everything will sort itself out very soon.'

Saffron left Nicola feeling distinctly worried. John had been delighted when Nicola had first told him she was expecting twins and throughout her pregnancy he had been attentive and had given the impression that he was overjoyed at the prospect of becoming a father. What could have happened to bring about such a drastic change in his attitude?

'It's no business of yours. Who asked you to start interfering?' John rounded on Saffron angrily.

Saffron stood her ground. 'I'm concerned about Nicola. She's exhausted looking after the babies and you never seem to be around to help her.'

'Bryony is always willing. She's a proxy mother. Satisfying her own need to have had a child.'

'Is that the problem, John? Do you feel excluded? Fathers often do at first. It's quite natural.'

'Natural. How would you know what's natural?' John hit the wall with his fist. 'Maybe I'm not natural. Just go away and leave me alone.'

'John, there's something very wrong. Please, forget I'm a relative and think of me as a doctor. Tell me what's troubling you.'

John pounded the wall again with his fist. 'Get out. Get out. Get out. It's none of your business. Nick and I will sort out our own problems.'

'I don't think you can without help. I think you're ill in some way. The injury to your head has affected you more than was realised at the time.' Saffron began to walk towards the doorway. She had hoped to be able to talk to John and he would realise how much Nicola needed his help and support. Now she seemed to have made matters worse.

'Saff, Saff, I'm sorry. Please, don't go. I didn't mean it.'

Saffron turned and John had his hand outstretched, but not in her direction.

'John?'

John tilted his head in the direction of her voice.

'John, can you see me?'

'Of course I can.'

'Then where am I?' Saffron moved swiftly to the side.

John pointed in the direction from where he had heard her voice. He blinked rapidly and pressed his forehead.

Saffron walked forward and took his arm. 'I think we need to have a serious talk. You've got a problem with your sight, haven't you?'

To her horror John's eyes filled with tears. 'I'm going blind,' he said desolately.

'What makes you think that? Have the blackouts become

more frequent?'

'Most of the time everything is blurred and I have such a headache.'

'Blurred?'

John nodded miserably. 'Everything is fuzzy round the edges. Sometimes it will clear and I can see properly again and a short while later I have a blackout. My head feels as if it is on fire and I get so angry that I just hit out. I don't mean to. It just happens.'

'Is that why you won't help Nicola with the girls?'

'I can't. I mustn't. Suppose I had a blackout and then hurt one of them? I'd never forgive myself.' The tears began to run down John's face. 'I love them so much. They're so precious and so tiny. I want to hold them. I want to hold Nick and tell her how much I love her and how proud I am of her, but I dare not. I wouldn't want to hurt Nick for the world.'

'You're hurting her now. She doesn't understand why you won't go near her. She thinks you've found someone else.'

'Never.'

'You have to tell her, John. She has a right to know.'

'She won't want to be married to a blind man.'

'John, Nicola loves you. Even if you did go blind Nicola wouldn't stop loving you.'

'She wouldn't want to spend all her time looking after me and making sure I was safe. I'm frightened, Saff. I don't want to be blind. I want to be able to see my girls and watch them grow. I don't even know if I've taken any decent photos of them.' John spoke bitterly. 'I had such plans. Now I'll never be able to take them swimming or out in the boat on my own. I can't even work alone up at the taverna. Suppose I had a blackout whilst I was cooking?'

'Oh, John,' Saffron's heart went out to the distraught young man. 'When did you notice that your sight was worse?'

'The day the girls were born. I was with Nick. I'd been holding her hand and talking to her. The doctor told me to sit down and

I ignored him. It finally happened so quickly, first one and then the other. I turned to look back at Nick and I fainted. Pretty stupid of me. When I came round everything looked a bit distorted. I thought it would soon go, but it hasn't.'

'Did they give you any medical attention?'

'I'd only fainted. Apparently a lot of men do. When I came round everyone was still busy with Nick and the babies. They gave them to me to hold and I was petrified that my sight would go completely and I'd drop them.'

'But you didn't drop them. There's no reason why you shouldn't hold them. You have to tell Nicola. Provided you're sitting down with them they should be perfectly safe.'

'Are you sure?'

'Of course. Why don't I drive you home now and you sit and have a chat with Nicola? Explain the situation to her and make her a promise.'

'What's that?'

'You'll get some medical advice. You should have gone to Athens months ago and seen the neurosurgeon.'

When Saffron arrived at Yannis's house the following morning she found Nicola white faced and distraught.

'Is John really going blind?' she asked immediately, her eyes filling with tears. 'He says he can't see properly.'

'I don't know,' Saffron answered honestly. 'He really does need to go to Athens and see a neurosurgeon.'

Nicola shook her head. 'I agree he needs to see someone, but it's difficult. You can wait for months for an appointment.'

'So why doesn't he go privately? He should be able to get an appointment quite quickly if he's willing to pay.'

Nicola snorted in derision. 'Once the doctor knows you are willing to pay the cost of the treatment doubles and the waiting list for a private appointment gets longer until you've made it worth his while to see you.'

Saffron looked at Nicola in horror. 'You mean bribe him to see you?'

'Of course. You'll forever go to the bottom of the list otherwise.'

Saffron sighed. 'All right, let's move on from there. Suppose John goes to Athens and sees a specialist. Have you any idea of the cost of an operation if it was necessary?'

'No, but the same thing applies to get you to the top of the waiting list for a non life threatening operation. It's also difficult at the moment. If John did need an operation there would have to be someone in Athens with him so they could look after him at the hospital. I can't go and Marianne and Giovanni need to be here.'

'I'm sure John would like someone to be there with him, but he wouldn't be in for more than a week.'

'Someone has to take food in for him and anything else he might need.'

Saffron frowned. 'Surely they feed you whilst you're in hospital?'

Nicola shook her head. 'You get basic medical care. They'll take your temperature and change your bandages. You're expected to have a relative with you who will wash and feed you.'

'What happens if you don't have any relatives?'

'A good friend or neighbour, otherwise you have to pay for additional care.'

'Suppose I contacted a neurosurgeon in London. Do you think John would agree to see him?'

'Will he know what's wrong with John?'

'Not without scans being taken and examining him.'

Nicola looked doubtful. 'How much will that cost?'

'A considerable amount, but it could be quicker and cheaper than going to Athens.'

'I'm not sure we could afford it.' Nicola frowned. 'Our parents have been very generous to us, but we'll need that money for the girls. They've already grown out of their first clothes.'

Saffron took Nicola's hand. 'I'm sure you want the very best for them, but whilst they are growing so quickly you can buy cheap clothing. Go to the market and see what's available. I'll ask Vasi to speak to Yiorgo and find out where they bought clothes for their daughter. I'm sure they didn't have any money to spend on designer outfits bought from exclusive shops.'

Nicola smiled shakily. 'I'm so glad you have come over here, Saffie. No one else realised John had a problem. Giovanni and Marianne thought he was bad tempered because he was missing his sleep and I thought he was interested in another woman. Poor John, we misjudged him so badly.' Nicola brushed away a tear. 'After he took Skele home last night he came straight back and gave Jo a bottle whilst I fed Lisa. He didn't know how to bring up her wind, but he'll soon learn.'

Saffron smiled delightedly. 'I'm so pleased.' She peered into the two Moses baskets where the girls were sleeping peacefully. 'How do you tell them apart?' she asked. 'They look identical to me.'

Nicola stood beside her. 'That's Joanna. Her face is just a little rounder and I think her nose is slightly bigger. The easiest way is to look at their ears at the moment. Elisabetta's is crumpled at the top. It may straighten out as she grows, but it's no big deal. They're both perfect in every other way.'

'I've never had any great urge to be a mother, but when I look at these two ....' Saffron shrugged.

'You and Vasi?' queried Nicola.

Saffron shook her head. 'We have no plans. I'm forty four. It's not a good age to think about starting a family. I'll leave it to you young people. I'm going to spend half an hour with Grandma, then I'll go up and see John. I'll ask him how he feels about me consulting a neurosurgeon in London. I don't want to make any 'phone calls or arrangements before I know he's agreeable. He may prefer to go to Athens.'

Nicola hugged Saffron. 'What can I say except thank you?'

Saffron opened her mobile 'phone and began to tap in the number for the hospital in London. Half way through she realised she had forgotten the extension number she would need to get through to her department. She consulted her address book, amused that she should have erased the number from her mind within such a short time.

When she was answered by the main reception desk she did not give her name, just asked to be transferred to the orthopaedic department and was relieved when she heard Angela's voice.

'Hello, Angela, it's Saffron Bartlett here.'

'Saffron! Lovely to hear from you. Where are you? Can we meet for lunch and have a proper chat? It's not the same without you here.'

'I'm not in London at the moment, but I promise I'll contact you and we'll have lunch together as soon as I can. I'm really 'phoning to ask if you can give me Dr Gharcia's extension number.'

'Hold a sec.' Angela scrolled down her list of extension numbers on the screen. 'Here you are seven two eight six. Got that? What do you need to see him for?'

'I don't. I just want to make an appointment for a friend. I thought it might be quicker if I made it myself.'

'You haven't got a problem?'

'No, definitely not. I have to go, Angela. I'm baby-sitting and one of them has just started to cry.'

'Don't forget your promise.'

'I won't.'

Saffron closed her 'phone in relief. She had not wanted to get involved in a long conversation with Angela who would no doubt relay details to her ex-colleagues so that it finally reached Sean's ears. She took a deep breath. This next call could be difficult.

'This is Dr Bartlett here. I'd like to speak with Dr Gharcia please.'

'Dr Gharcia is engaged with a patient. Please call back later.'

The line went dead and Saffron sighed in exasperation before dialling the number again.

She spoke acidly when the telephone was answered again. 'Please do not put the 'phone down on me again. I am Dr Bartlett and I need to speak with Dr Gharcia. I appreciate that if he has a patient with him it would not convenient. If that is the case please give me a time when he is free and I will call again then.'

'Who's calling?'

'Dr Bartlett.'

'Are you from the hospital or a medical practice?'

'The hospital.' Saffron hoped the woman would not realise that she had left some months earlier.

'I'll put you through.'

'Thank you.' Saffron hoped she would not be forced to listen to the annoying canned music for too long.

'Matteus Gharcia here.'

'Good morning, Dr Gharcia. This is Dr Saffron Bartlett here. I'd be grateful for a few minutes of your time.'

'Saffron Bartlett from orthopaedics? I heard you'd left under somewhat unpleasant circumstances. You're being sued, I understand.'

'That's the first I've heard of it!'

'Something to do with some missing case notes. The patient is suing for negligence.'

'Who told you that? The case notes weren't missing. They'd been misfiled by a temp. I found them shortly after the patient left. I resigned from my position for personal reasons and worked out my notice.'

'Where are you working now?'

'I'm not. I'm spending some time with my relatives. That's what I wanted to speak to you about. My nephew has a problem and I wanted to ask if you would be willing to see him.'

'Why shouldn't I? Just make an appointment through my secretary.'

'It isn't quite so simple. We're in Crete. I'd like to give you the background to the problem before we fly over. You might decide you are unable to help.'

'Are you asking me to waive my fees for a private consultation?'

'Certainly not,' replied Saffron immediately. 'I just don't want him to spend money coming to England if you feel there's nothing that can be done.'

'Why doesn't he go to Athens?'

'A number of reasons, besides, I trust you to give an honest diagnosis and prognosis.'

'Make it as short as possible. I'm due in the operating theatre in fifteen minutes.'

'Thank you. My nephew had a blow on the head last August. His X-ray showed a small cranium fracture. Since then he's had trouble with his vision. He had another X-ray taken in December and the fracture showed no sign of healing. He had another slight blow on the head in April and his vision has deteriorated alarmingly. He has a number of blackouts each day and when they happen he is also quite violent for a few moments.'

'What does the neurosurgeon say?'

'He hasn't seen a specialist. The hospital told him the situation should right itself when the fracture healed.'

'So what do you expect me to be able to do?'

'I'd like you to authorise an MRI scan and see if there is any other damage that could be the cause of his problem. If it means he needs an operation I'd be willing to pay.'

'He doesn't have medical insurance?'

'Not for anything like that.' Saffron did not wish to admit that John had no insurance at all.

'It could be expensive,' demurred Dr Gharcia.

'It would be if he went to Athens. I really would appreciate it if you would agree to see him.'

'Does he speak English?'

'Perfectly.'

'Well, I suppose I can make him an initial appointment and arrange a scan. I'll see what I can do about reducing my consultation fees.'

'I'm terribly grateful, Dr Gharcia. I do need a definite date before I look for flight availability. Any follow-ups need to be as soon as possible afterwards. He doesn't want to be away from home for too long. He became a father two months ago.'

'Good time to be away I would have thought. Avoid the sleepless nights. I'll tell my secretary to make him an appointment. Phone her back in five minutes. I'll tell her to expect your call. What's the man's name?'

Saffron heaved a sigh of relief. 'Pirenzi. John Pirenzi.'

'Vasi, I have to talk to you. I need to go back to England.'

Vasi's face blanched. 'You are not happy? What can I do to make you happy here? I love you Saffron, please do not leave me. I hoped you would agree to marry me at the end of the season. What has happened to make you change your mind? What have I done?'

Saffron leant over and kissed Vasi's cheek. 'I'm not leaving you. I need to go back to England and take John with me.'

Vasi frowned. 'So you are not leaving me? You are not unhappy?'

'Of course I'm not unhappy. Now I'm able to speak a little bit of Greek I feel much more at home. I enjoy being able to spend more time down in Elounda now the season is under way and also going off wherever I please in my car.'

'So why are you going back to England with John?'

'He needs to see a neurosurgeon.'

'He cannot do this in Athens?'

'He would need to go to the hospital here and get a referral letter. It could take weeks before he received an appointment. Depending on the results he could need brain surgery and then he would have to go on a waiting list. That again could leave him waiting for weeks before they called him and would mean another trip to Athens. If he went privately he would be seen immediately but have to pay for his flight and also for somewhere to stay. He would have to pay for a CT scan, possibly an MRI, consultations and any treatment that is prescribed. If I take him to England we can stay with Marjorie. I've spoken to a neurosurgeon at the hospital where I used to work and he's willing to see John. I explained that he is a relative and Dr Gharcia has agreed to reduce his fees for a private consultation so it makes sense to go to London.'

'How long will you be away?'

'That will depend upon the doctor's findings. If he says he can't help then we'll come straight back.'

'You will need some money?'

Saffron shook her head. 'I have plenty in my bank account here and I kept open the one I have in England. I thought it could be sensible in case Marjorie ever needed any money in a hurry. I'll just transfer some funds back. John can always repay me later in Euros.'

'You are sure? You would tell me if you needed more in your account?'

'Thank you, Vasi, but at the moment there is no problem.'

Secretly Vasi was relieved by her words. The government were talking about raising taxes yet again and introducing further austerity measures to meet the requirements of the European Union to enable the country to receive more funds to keep the Greek economy afloat.

Week 1 - June 2009

John sat in front of Doctor Gharcia nervously.

'I've spoken to Dr Bartlett, but I'd like you to tell me exactly what happened that caused you to have a cranium fracture.'

'Well,' John took a deep breath. 'My father has self catering holiday chalets. Someone set fire to them and when I tried to stop him a metal strut from the awnings fell and knocked me out.'

'You were actually knocked unconscious?'

John nodded. 'I think so. I vaguely remember my friend hauling me away from the burning building and telling him I couldn't see.'

'You couldn't see clearly or you were seeing double?'

'Everything was black. I couldn't see a thing. I think I may have passed out again as the next thing I remember is waking up in hospital. I had a terrible headache and I thought my bad vision was due to that.'

'Did your sight improve when the headache subsided?'

'I thought it had, but sometimes everything went completely black again. I had trouble focusing my camera and found if I pressed my forehead it helped. It also seemed to clear away the blackness if I blinked rapidly and pressed at the same time.'

Doctor Gharcia nodded. 'How often did this lack of vision occur? Once a week or more often?'

'Sometimes it was three or four times a day,' John admitted.

'Did you seek any advice? Did you return to the hospital?'

'The hospital recommended that I went to an ophthalmologist.

226

He said it should clear up when my fracture healed.'

'And it hasn't done so?'

John shook his head. 'Saff, Doctor Bartlett, insisted I had another X-ray taken in October. She compared both X-rays and according to her the fracture hasn't healed yet.'

Doctor Gharcia made a note on the pad in front of him. 'Have you had a more recent X-ray taken?'

'I've been a bit busy so I thought I'd wait a few more months.'

'Busy?'

'Helping my father, then there was Christmas and the wedding.'

'So you are still having these blackouts?'

'It's worse now. I seem to have a permanent headache and most of the time everything is blurred. Sometimes it clears completely for a few moments but then I have another blackout and when that happens I also have an uncontrollable rage for a few minutes.'

Doctor Gharcia nodded. 'Is there any reason why your sight should have become worse? Have you banged your head again?'

John grinned sheepishly. 'I was with my wife when she was giving birth and I fainted. I probably hit my head on the floor when I fell.'

The doctor smiled back at him. 'I understand that happens to a lot of fathers. Why did you not return to your local hospital? Why come over to England?'

'After the X-ray in October I asked to see a specialist. I was told I would have to go to Heraklion, but when I 'phoned I was told I needed to go to Athens. The doctor in Heraklion had left and they hadn't replaced him.'

Doctor Gharcia sighed. He knew the economic situation in Greece was giving cause for worldwide concern and cuts to government services were being made, but it was unforgivable to cut back on the medical services. 'So why didn't you go?'

'At that time I'd become used to having just the blackouts and could cope with them. I still thought they would go when the fracture healed.'

Doctor Gharcia rose. 'I'm going to make arrangements for you to have an MRI scan tomorrow. That will be more detailed than a CT scan. When I've looked at it we'll talk again and I'll tell you my conclusions.'

'It can't be today?' asked John, disappointed.

'I cannot disrupt today's appointments. Be here tomorrow morning at eight thirty and as soon as the staff arrive you will be seen. It should take no longer than forty five minutes, if that. I should have the results for you within two or three days. I'll ask my secretary to telephone you with an appointment.'

'Do you want to look at my X-rays?'

'I will, but I think the scan will tell me considerably more.'

John left the doctor's consulting room pleased that he was to have a scan so promptly, but nervous of what it might show.

'I have to be here at eight thirty tomorrow morning,' he declared to Saffron. 'The doctor's going to ask them to scan me first. He said he would 'phone with another appointment in a few days once he has the results.'

Saffron nodded. 'We'll make sure we're early.'

'You don't have to come with me, Saff. I know the tube station where I have to get out and I'll take a taxi from there to the hospital.'

'We can go on and do something else afterwards. There are two photographic exhibitions on at the Victoria and Albert Museum. One finishes in a few days and I thought you might like to go and see those.'

John smiled. 'I'd like that. I just wish I could see a bit better. You don't think I have a tumour, do you?'

'I think it very unlikely, but I honestly do not know.' Saffron did not say that she had been worried that could be the case since she had discovered John had problems with his vision and uncontrollable outbursts of temper. 'Dr Gharcia is very thorough and very honest. If you have he'll explain the treatment available and a likely prognosis.'

'What else could it be?' John looked at Saffron as everything went black around him. Without warning he flung his arm out and knocked over the chair he had been sitting on earlier. He aimed a kick in the same direction before pressing his hand to his forehead. The receptionist half rose from her desk as John picked up the chair.

'I'm so sorry,' he said. 'That was an accident. I hope I haven't damaged anything.'

Saffron looked at him in consternation. On occasions she had experienced the sudden flashes of uncontrollable temper that John had shown, but she had never seen him react so violently. No wonder he was frightened he could inadvertently injure his children or Nicola. She took his arm and could feel him trembling beneath her touch.

'I think a cup of tea is needed,' she said firmly. She smiled at the receptionist. 'We'll be back tomorrow morning.'

The receptionist grimaced as they walked out. She was not sure the incident with the chair had been accidental and hoped there would be no repetition of the behaviour the following day.

'I am sorry, Saff. That must have been embarrassing for you. A fine way for me to show you how grateful I am for all the trouble you have taken.'

Saffron continued to hold John's arm. 'If Dr Gharcia says this is a condition you have to learn to live with there could a medication that would help.'

'You mean keep me doped up with a vegetable existence!'

'No, I don't. Just something to keep you a little calmer when these attacks happen.'

John took a deep breath. 'I begin to know when it's likely to happen. I can see perfectly for a few seconds, then it's black again and something erupts inside me.'

'That's definitely progress.'

'Is it? I looked at you and could see you clearly. The next thing

I knew everything was black and I'd knocked that chair over.'

'There was no harm done. Don't dwell on it, John. It won't do any good. What would you like to do now?'

'I thought you said we were going for a cup of tea.'

Saffron smiled. 'I could do with one, but I meant after that. It's only just eleven thirty. We can go back to Marjorie's and sit and do nothing for the rest of the day or go somewhere that interests you. I know there were a number of places you didn't manage to visit when you were here before.'

'I wish Nick was here now.'

'I'm sure you'd like her to be here, but you'll have to put up with me, I'm afraid. Tea or coffee?'

'I'd rather have a fruit juice. English coffee is pretty awful and I'm not fond of tea.'

'Go and find a seat. I'll bring it over.'

'Saffron! Are you back with us?'

Saffron turned to see Vince's smiling face.

'Hi, Vince. How are you and the family?'

Vince nodded. 'Good, all good. So, are you back here working with us?'

Saffron shook her head. 'I'm only visiting. Come and meet my nephew. He's trying to decide where he would like to spend the remainder of the day.'

'He's spoilt for choice. What's he interested in? The Science museum is fascinating. I can spend hours in there.'

'We'll avoid that one if you don't mind. I'm not interested in science and technology. I admire the minds who invented these things but I have no desire to know how they work. He can always go there another day without me.'

Vince placed his cup of tea on the table and Saffron handed John a bottle of fruit juice. 'This is Vince,' she said. 'We used to work together.'

John nodded. 'I'm John.'

'So,' continued Vince, 'what are you up to now?'

'I'm living abroad. I decided I wanted a complete change.'

'Caribbean?'

'No, whatever makes you think that?'

'You've got a fabulous tan.'

'The weather's been good in Greece since April. It doesn't take long to get a bit of colour.'

'What are you doing back here if the weather's so good over there?'

'Visiting Marjorie, tying up a few loose ends.' Saffron shrugged. 'Nothing much.'

Vince eyed John speculatively. Was he really her nephew or the reason she had left so suddenly to go to Greece? He would have a word with Angela. She might know.

'What about you John? On holiday?'

'Just for a few days.' Saffron answered quickly before John could say a word. 'He's visited London before and we were just deciding where to spend the afternoon.'

'What about the British?' suggested John. 'I saw they have an exhibition of Pacific native shields. That could be interesting, besides I'm sure I could spend a week in there and not see everything.'

'Good choice,' approved Vince. He looked at his watch. 'I'd better get back. Let me know next time you're coming in Saffron and I'll grab a few extra minutes between appointments so we can catch up.'

Saffron nodded, having no intention of telling her ex-colleague when she would be in the hospital again.

Dr Gharcia scrutinized the MRI scan carefully. He was thankful there was no sign of a tumour, but there was a need for cranial surgery where the fracture had not healed. Although he was willing to reduce his consultation fees the operation would be expensive due to the use of a theatre and essential staffing along with nursing care afterwards. He wondered if Saffron and the young man realised just how much the final bill would be.

John sat in front of the specialist nervously. He had spent long hours awake during the night convinced he was to be told he had an inoperable brain tumour and only a few more weeks to live. He had shed tears as he imagined Nicola's distress when he told her and wished Saffron had not insisted he saw a specialist. Even if he could have an operation it was possible that he would end up in a vegetative state eventually and be a burden to his family for as long as he survived.

Dr Gharcia smiled at him. 'I have good news and bad news.'

'I've got a brain tumour,' said John dully.

Dr Gharcia shook his head. 'That is the good news. I can see no sign of any malignant growth.'

'Really?' John spoke incredulously and felt his eyes fill with tears of relief.

Saffron let out the breath she had been unconsciously holding and squeezed John's hand.

'The bad news,' Dr Gharcia continued, 'is that the fracture has started to close, but the piece of bone is still depressed. It has tried to grow back, but in the attempt the bone has thickened.' He pointed to the scan. 'Can you see there? That's the fracture line. It's slightly shorter than in your X-rays where it is gradually knitting together, but below it there is an extra growth of bone. It's minimal, but enough to put extra pressure on your optic nerve. That is what is causing your vision problems and your blackouts.'

'So there isn't really anything wrong with me?'

'I wouldn't go so far as to say that. It's a difficult situation. Many people have a fracture in their skull that never completely heals and it causes them no problem whatsoever. In your case the bone could stop thickening and your problems never get any worse. On the other hand, if the bone does continue to grow there will be even more pressure on your optic nerve which means the blackouts will probably become more frequent and your sight will deteriorate further.'

John frowned. 'So what are you saying? That I will go blind eventually?'

Dr Gharcia shook his head. 'Not necessarily. The choice has to be yours. You can take a chance and leave things as they are with the risk of losing your sight at some future date, or allow me to operate, remove the offending piece of bone, shave it down to its original thickness and replace it in its correct position. After that if your vision doesn't improve I would recommend fenestration.'

'What's that?'

'Small slits are cut in the sheath surrounding the nerve to allow the cerebrospinal fluid to drain into the orbit and disperse. There's always a slight risk that such a procedure could make your sight worse, but that could be discussed at a later date depending upon your initial decision.'

'If John decided against the operation now and the bone continued to grow, would he be able to have the operation later?' asked Saffron.

'He would, but the longer you leave something like this the more unsatisfactory the result is likely to be. The pressure could be removed, but his sight might not improve, too much damage to the optic nerve would have taken place. Would you like time to talk it over and let me know your decision tomorrow?'

Saffron nodded. 'You ought to have the operation John.'

John attempted a weak smile. 'It's not your head on the block. How much is all this going to cost?'

Dr Gharcia spread his hands. 'If the procedure goes ahead without any problems you're talking in the region of seventy thousand pounds.'

'Seventy thousand!' John gasped.

'Any complications like a blood clot or haemorrhage would mean going in again to rectify the situation and an increased cost. Assuming none of those problems arise you would be in hospital for about a week. During that time you'd be given another MRI scan and if all was well you'd be fit to fly home the following week.'

'Seventy thousand.' repeated John. 'I can't ask my father for that amount. Not at the moment. It isn't possible.'

'As I said, think about it and telephone me with your decision as soon as possible. My bill for consultations to date, along with the scan, is with my secretary. If you decide to go ahead I can fit you in next week.' Dr Gharcia rose and held out his hand to John. 'It has been a pleasure meeting you.'

John looked at the bill that Saffron paid immediately. 'No wonder he said it was a pleasure meeting me! He must get a lot of pleasure out of a week's work!'

Saffron smiled. 'That's just the cost of the MRI scan. He hasn't charged you for his consultation time.'

Saffron and John returned to Marjorie's house in a sombre mood. Marjorie raised her eyebrows as they entered and Saffron shrugged.

'John needs to speak to his father. Dr Gharcia says he needs an operation. The piece of bone that is pressing on his optic nerve has thickened.'

'He also says it's going to cost about seventy thousand pounds,' said John miserably. 'How can I ask Dad for that amount? He's struggling to get the business back on its feet and he's three staff short. Nick can't help, Dimitris is doing his National Service and I'm over here. I'll just have to wait and have the operation in a few years time.'

Saffron shook her head. 'Speak to your father first. You could find it isn't a problem.'

John looked at her sceptically. 'Unless he has the units full for the season and is able to let the shops it is a problem. He's already paying a massive amount of interest on the loans he's taken out.' John sighed. 'I'll 'phone him and tell him it was a waste of time and we'll be home as soon as we can book a flight.'

'Don't be foolish, John. At least tell him what Dr Gharcia said and the amount the operation will cost. If he says it's out of the question then we'll make arrangements to return.'

Marjorie hesitated. 'Suppose I enquired at the bank about mortgaging the house?'

John looked at her in surprise. 'You would do that? For me?'

'I'm sure I could come to some arrangement with your father whereby he repaid me as soon as possible.' Marjorie did not relish the idea, knowing that all her pension would be needed to make a monthly repayment and she would have to dip into her savings for everything else she needed.

Saffron shook her head. 'You can't do that, Marjorie, although it's a lovely idea on your part. Your house is your security. I've some savings, not enough to cover John's operation, but I could loan what I have to him. I'm sure Vasi would help also.'

'You need your savings.' Marjorie spoke firmly. 'You're not working now so they are all you have to fall back on if things went wrong between you and Vasi.'

John swallowed hard. 'I appreciate the offers you're both making, but there's no way I could accept. I'll speak to my father. If he says it's out of the question we'll telephone the doctor and book a flight home. I'm longing to get back to see Nick and the girls.'

'I want to speak to your father, John.' Saffron spoke firmly. 'I want to explain exactly what the operation involves for the cost.'

'I can tell him that.'

'You'll no doubt speak in Greek. I want to be sure you've told him the truth.'

'Don't you trust me, Saff?'

'On this occasion I don't. Your father has a right to know the risks you run by delaying the operation. If you just tell him that you can have it at a later date it would be understandable if he agreed to that proposal. Suppose the growth of that piece of bone accelerated and you lost your sight? It could be too late to rectify it in a couple of years' time. Dr Gharcia said the longer the operation was delayed the less satisfactory the outcome would probably be.'

John glowered at Saffron. She had guessed correctly the

information he had planned to pass on to his father.

'I'll 'phone him now from the landline. It will be cheaper than using our mobiles.' Saffron picked up the telephone receiver and dialled Giovanni's mobile number. 'You can talk to him after I've told him what Dr Gharcia said and then I'll have another word with him.'

Giovanni spent the remainder of the day studying his accounts. Having spoken to Saffron he had immediately insisted that John had the operation, but now he had the problem of raising the money. Even if the bank did agree to him having a further loan he did not have the money coming in to cover the repayments. He would have to swallow his pride and ask Vasi or Vasilis if they were willing to give him a temporary loan. Before he went down that route he needed to have a family conference. There was a chance that his Uncle Yannis still had some savings and would be willing to use them to pay for John's operation.

Yannis spread his hands. 'If I could sell the shop premises in Aghios Nikolaos I'd willingly lend you the money, but until then I've nothing spare. Ourania insisted we needed to invest in some new stock for the shop in Plaka, but at the moment we're struggling for custom. I'm beginning to wonder if it was a mistake to move. At least we were known in Aghios.'

Giovanni nodded. 'I'll approach the bank and ask for another loan. If I can persuade them to lower their interest rates on those I already have I could probably manage. If they refuse me I'll have to speak to Vasi and see if he or his father would come to a private agreement with me.'

'If it helps you don't need to pay me any wages,' offered Bryony.

Marcus frowned. They had no savings. They had invested their money in purchasing and renovating their house that had been destroyed by Hurricane Katrina. The small amount they had retained they had used to move to Crete. Although Annita had insisted on passing Bryony's share of her inheritance to her a year ago they had added the amount to the capital needed to rebuild the self catering unit, relying on a share of the profits at a later date.

Nicola felt the tears coming into her eyes. 'It's all my fault. If that awful creep hadn't set fire to the chalets John wouldn't have been injured and you wouldn't have had all the expense of rebuilding. He's the one who should pay for it.'

Marianne looked at her daughter-in-law. 'Nicola's right. He should pay for it.'

Giovanni shook his head. 'We should have tried to claim earlier before we had the insurance money.'

'I'm not talking about the rebuilding. I'm talking about John's operation costs.'

Marcus nodded. 'If you were in the States the first thing you would have done would have been to engage a lawyer and sue for damages.'

'So why don't we do that now? I'll 'phone Adam Kowalski and tell him we want to sue for the cost of John's operation.' Marianne looked at her husband, hoping to have his approval for her idea.

Giovanni looked at his wife doubtfully. 'Do you think it would work?'

'We can try. We claim three hundred thousand.'

'Why so much?' questioned Bryony. 'John said his operation was seventy thousand.'

'Compensation for his ruined career as a photographer,' answered Marianne firmly. 'We ask for three hundred thousand. If he refuses we'll tell him we're taking the compensation claim for John to court as a separate issue from the arson charge where we'll be asking for compensation for our ruined business.'

'Suppose he hasn't got that kind of money?' asked Bryony.

'His father owns a bank. He'd have no difficulty in raising the money. He offered to put up bail money as soon as he heard Todd had been arrested. Speak to Mr Kowalski, Marianne. It's a brilliant idea.' Nicola was full of enthusiasm.

Giovanni nodded slowly. 'It's worth a try. Is it too late to 'phone him now?'

Marianne looked at her watch and grimaced. 'He's not likely to be in his office now, but I can try.'

Marcus shook his head. 'Even if Mr Kowalski says you have a good case it could take months, even years to get a settlement if it goes to court.'

'I tell the bank that a settlement is imminent and I just need the loan for a couple of months,' said Giovanni confidently.

'Won't they investigate, want proof?' asked Marcus doubtfully.

Giovanni smiled. 'A little envelope in the right direction should mean they accept my word.'

Adam Kowalski had only met Mr Gallagher once when the man had visited the Embassy and requested his son be released from custody and repatriated to the States.

Now Adam listened to Marianne's reasoned argument for asking for compensation from Todd Gallagher's father. 'It could be a question of proving liability.'

'There's no disputing that he was the cause. He's admitted firing the chalets. John was taken into hospital at the time and an X-ray showed a fractured skull. He's had problems with his sight ever since and it has ruined his chances of becoming a photographer. A second X-ray was taken before Christmas and showed the fracture hadn't mended. Now he's in England and the MRI scan confirms there's a piece of bone pressing on his optic nerve. If it isn't operated on quickly there is the likelihood that he'll lose his sight altogether. He needs that operation now and with all the rebuilding we've had to do we just haven't got the money to finance it.'

'Even if Mr Gallagher agreed to settle out of court it could take a considerable time before you received the actual money,' warned Adam.

'We know that, but if the bank knew there was a settlement

pending and the amount we were expecting to receive they would allow us another loan. John's sight is priority and in hindsight we should have taken proceedings much earlier. Even if we had only asked for a quarter of the amount it would have been compensation to John for the injury he sustained.'

'And no doubt helped with the finance needed for the twins he had fathered,' thought Adam. 'What exactly are you asking me to do?' he asked.

'Contact Mr Gallagher and advise him of our intentions. E-mail a letter to my husband now to say that you have informed Mr Gallagher we are taking the case for compensation to court, asking for three hundred thousand dollars plus costs. My husband will take that letter to the bank tomorrow and he's sure they'll allow him a loan to be settled in full when the compensation comes through.'

'Suppose you do take him to court, are unsuccessful, receive nothing and have to pay the costs yourselves?' asked Adam anxiously.

'By the time the case reaches a court John will have had his operation, the self catering business will be back on its feet and we'll have the money. If the court decision goes against us we'll appeal. As you know, there are ways to ensure that a judgement goes in your favour. There is, of course, another option that you could put before Mr Gallagher,' continued Marianne, dropping the strident tone from her voice. 'You could suggest that he settles out of court. If the amount he offered was sufficient Mr Pirenzi would consider dropping the charge of arson. As a lawyer speaking on behalf of Mr Giovanni Pirenzi, I know Mr Pirenzi will be asking for an award between one and two million in compensation for lost business along with the court costs. Mr Gallagher could save himself a considerable amount of money.'

For a moment Adam was speechless; then he laughed. 'Mrs Pirenzi, I'd forgotten that you had studied international law and were conversant with the Greek system. It is a great shame you decided not to pursue it as a career. You have a most devious mind and, I'm sure, you would have made your fortune. Send me an e-mail with the medical facts that you outlined to me and details of the claim. Send me a separate statement itemising the reasons you will be asking the court for compensation for loss of business and I'll see what I can do.'

'It is very urgent,' insisted Marianne. 'John needs to have the operation next week. My husband has to go to the bank as soon as possible so the money can be transferred to England.'

'You'll have to give me a while to compose my initial letter to Mr Gallagher. I'll mail you a copy. I'll not mention any conditions for additional compensation or an out of court settlement at this stage. We'll see what his reaction is. There's a chance he may offer an immediate settlement. I'll mail you a copy of Mr Gallagher's reply as soon as I receive it. There's just one other thing, Mrs Pirenzi, do you have a lawyer should the case go to court?'

'If necessary I will conduct my own case and thank you, Mr Kowalski. Thank you very much.' Marianne gave a huge sigh of relief.

Abraham Gallagher opened his e-mails and saw he had one from Adam Kowalski in Athens. Did this mean a date had finally been set for his son's trial? He was aggrieved that the man had refused to recommend bail for Todd. There was no way he should have been sitting in a Cretan jail for nearly a year. Had Kowalski accepted the envelope he had been offered Todd would have been back in the States and the matter of the fire forgotten.

He shook his head. The boy was a fool. To have kept a diary with the details of Jennie-Lea's death recorded was the height of stupidity. If the knowledge became available to the local judiciary it was likely Todd would be facing manslaughter charges when he was finally allowed to leave Greece. All Todd's talk of this other girl being his guardian angel and him being her protector was a load of rubbish. If he continued down that route he was likely to be sectioned.

Sectioned. That was the answer. He must speak to his lawyer. If Todd was declared psychologically unfit he would be unable to stand trial in Greece and be deported back to the States. He would arrange for him to have a couple of years in a private treatment centre. That would be preferable to him being tried for murder or as an accessory to the robbery at the diner and serving a prison sentence.

He blamed his wife. The quiet, biddable woman he had married and expected to dominate had turned out to be a nymphomaniac. It had soon become clear to him that he was totally incapable of satisfying her insatiable desire and had turned a blind eye to the number of committee meetings she had to attend or sick friends she had to visit during the evenings. Their son had obviously inherited her excess of sexual genes.

When she had first told him she was expecting their child he was doubtful that he was the father. It was only as the boy grew and developed that the physical likeness between father and son became obvious and Abraham had doted on him. Even when Todd was accused of fathering a child at the age of thirteen he had excused the boy, saying it was due to his innocence and the girl had encouraged him to experiment. It had been costly for him to pay all the expenses for the family to move to a different State, but at least Todd had emerged with his reputation intact.

He opened the e-mail from Adam Kowalski with a feeling of trepidation and drew in his breath sharply when he read the contents. A brief message from the Embassy official told him that the family of the young man who had been injured in the fire was pressing for damages and his lawyer's letter was attached.

Abraham Gallagher read through Marianne's carefully phrased document. He had no doubt that she had medical reports to back up her claims of the injury sustained and the cost of private medical treatment in England. The claim for a ruined photographic career he would dispute. There was no evidence that the man had been more than a taverna keeper.

He keyed in the number of his lawyer and demanded an immediate appointment. Before he replied to Adam Kowalski he needed professional advice.

Abraham sat in his lawyer's office and waited whilst Eli Lambert read the missive through. Finally he raised his eyes. 'I need the details of the incident your son was involved in. Am I able to speak directly to him?'

Abraham shook his head. 'He isn't in the States.'

'Does he have a mobile?'

'It isn't possible to contact him at present.'

Eli raised his eyebrows. 'Where exactly is Todd at the moment? I cannot give you any advice or act for you unless I know his version of events.'

Abraham sighed and ran a hand over his forehead. 'The stupid boy became infatuated with a local girl. When she went over to Crete he followed her. He thought if he ruined the family business where she was working she would return to New Orleans with him. He was arrested, of course, and is waiting for a trial date.'

'He will plead not guilty, of course.'

Abraham shook his head. 'He confessed immediately that he had set the fire deliberately. He insisted that he hadn't meant anyone to be hurt and I believe him.'

'Could his confession be blamed on him suffering from shock at the time of his arrest?'

'Hardly. He kept a diary and he had detailed his proposed actions.'

'And this happened when? Nearly a year ago? That's rather a long time to be kept in jail before being tried for a crime you have admitted to having committed. Have you applied for bail?'

'It was refused.' Abraham sighed. 'He's undergoing psychiatric tests.'

Eli raised his eyebrows. 'Is his defence claiming that he is schizophrenic?'

'I don't know what conclusion will be reached, but I'm hoping he'll be sectioned. If he is he'll be allowed back to the States and they won't be able to charge him with the crime.'

'Really? Apart from arson are there any other reasons to think he may be unstable?'

Abraham hesitated and then nodded. 'His diary shows that he is somewhat prone to mood swings and fantasy.'

'Then before we discuss any liability claims I think you'd better familiarise me with the contents of this diary. Have you any proof that it was written by your son?'

'It was on his lap top. When I contested the accusations I was shown a transcript covering the entries for the last two years. I know he wrote it.'

'Do you have a copy?'

Abraham shook his head. 'I saw no need to have one. I only came here to ask your advice regarding this letter claiming compensation.' He was not prepared to own up to having a full transcript of Todd's diary sitting in his safe at home. He did not want his lawyer probing into the death of Jennie-Lea or the shooting incident at the diner. 'The diary was originally about his fixation with this girl, how many times a day he saw her, what she was wearing, things like that. Then when he went over to Crete he had this ridiculous idea about setting fire to some holiday chalets and wrote down how he planned to set about it.'

Eli raised his eyebrows. 'You say his plans for committing arson are laid out in there and he has confessed that the act was deliberate?'

Abraham nodded miserably.

'If, as you say, he is undergoing psychiatric tests it may be possible to claim he was creating an imaginary event that he never intended to carry out. Due to some mental aberration, brought on by heat or stress, the fantasy took over and he put the plan into action. As regards his confession, well, that can be claimed to have been misunderstood due to the language.' Eli leaned back in his chair, pleased with the scenario he had conjured up.

'What shall I reply?'

'Just acknowledge receipt of the communication and say it is in the hands of your solicitor. I'll give some thought to a suitable reply. The chances are that we'll hear no more from this Greek lawyer.'

'So what would you like to do this weekend, John? We've been to the Royal Academy and the Natural History museum. Marjorie suggested you might like to visit Hampton Court. You didn't go there with Nicola when you were here last time.'

'I'm game for anything. You've taken me wherever I've wanted to visit. What about you? Surely you'd like to visit somewhere you haven't been before.'

Saffron smiled at him. 'I haven't been to Hampton Court in a long time. When you've seen enough inside we could walk around in the gardens and you can take some photos.'

Saffron had been delighted at John's reaction to the ornate decor and furnishings. Whilst they ate their lunch in the cafeteria John insisted that Saffron told him as much as she could remember from her history lessons regarding Henry VIII.

'I need to know so I can tell Nick.'

'History really wasn't my thing,' protested Saffron. 'It always seemed to consist of dates, wars and politics. I just wasn't interested.'

'Henry must have loved Ann Boleyn very much to actually defy the Pope and break away from the recognised church.'

Saffron smiled. 'I believe he thought he did, but he was also a man who was used to getting his own way. At that time whatever the king said was law. If you opposed him or upset him you were likely to find yourself imprisoned in the Tower. Once you were sent there it usually meant you would be beheaded.'

'Don't remind me.' John pulled a face.

'You're not going to be beheaded,' replied Saffron with a smile. 'What is it Nicola calls you? A palookas?'

John grinned. 'I wish I knew a suitable Greek expression that I could use when she says something daft.'

'Why don't you buy a guide book?' suggested Saffron. 'That will have pictures of the main exhibits and also a short history of Henry VIII.'

'Good idea. Would I be allowed to take some photos inside?'

'I'm not sure, but we can always find out before we leave. We mustn't be too late. Marjorie is arranging for an early meal for us. After that I'm afraid you can't have anything else to eat until after your op.'

John pulled a face. 'Suppose I'm hungry?'

Saffron shrugged. 'You'll just have to put up with it. You won't starve. It's better to feel hungry for an hour or two than be violently sick after the anaesthetic.'

'I'll come to the ward with you, John, and wait whilst they prep you.' Saffron led the way along the hospital corridors.

'Prep me?'

'They'll need to shave some of your hair away so they have a clear view of the area they wish to open up.'

'Yuk! I don't really want to think about it.' John swallowed nervously.

'There's really nothing to it. As I said, I'll wait with you and then I can also bring your clothes home. There's not a lot of space in hospital lockers. I'll find out what time I can 'phone to know that you're back on the ward and then I'll phone Nicola and your Mum.'

'I can do that.'

Saffron shook he head. 'You won't be allowed to use a mobile 'phone on the ward and there's no way you will be able to go outside today. I'll 'phone them with another update when I've seen you this evening. They may allow me to escort you out into the grounds when I visit tomorrow and you can speak to them both then for a few minutes.'

John turned away. 'Tell Nick how much I love her.'

'John? What's wrong?'

'Saff, I'm petrified. I've never been so frightened in my life. Suppose I don't come round from the anaesthetic? Suppose I end up blind or completely paralysed where the doctor cuts a nerve accidently?'

Saffron placed her arms around him. 'That won't happen. You're worrying and frightening yourself unnecessarily.'

'You sound very confident!'

'Of course I am. Dr Gharcia performs hundreds of similar operations every year. There's really nothing to worry about. He told you exactly what he plans to do. It truly is a simple operation. It shouldn't take more than an hour.'

John shuddered. 'Drilling little holes in my skull and then sawing a piece out! It doesn't bear thinking about.'

'Then don't think about it. Think about the positive. You'll be able to see clearly again. In a couple of weeks you'll be back home in Crete, looking at Joanna and Elisabetta, taking photographs of them. You won't have to worry any more about having a blackout and hurting them.'

John sighed. 'Do you think I'll see a change in them when I get back? Nick has been sending photos to me, but I can't tell one from the other and they don't look any different from when I left.'

'You're sure to see a difference in them. By the time we get home you will have been away a month.'

'I ought to buy something to take back for them and a present for Nick.'

'What have you in mind?'

John shrugged. 'I haven't the faintest idea. What do women usually like apart from jewellery? It would be stupid to buy something in that line over here. It's much cheaper and better quality in Crete.'

Saffron frowned. Nicola was not interested in clothes, being quite happy in a pair of jeans with a T-shirt or jumper. She was a difficult person to buy anything for. 'I'm sure Nicola would be more pleased with a gift for the girls than anything for herself.'

'Do you think so?'

Saffron nodded. 'I do,' she said firmly. 'It will show that you have been thinking of them whilst you've been away.'

'What could I buy for them?'

'Well,' Saffron considered. 'You could get a rattle or teething ring for each of them. When babies start to cut their teeth they like to bite on something.'

John nodded. 'Where would I get that?'

'There are plenty of shops that sell baby goods. You need to get something that is well made and won't break. Don't get anything that is painted, that gradually comes off, and whatever you buy needs to be suitable for sterilising.'

'I should have thought of it before.'

'You'll have time to go shopping before we fly home,' Saffron assured him. 'We'll go up to Harrods and Selfridges and see what they have on offer, then we'll have a look in the baby departments of other shops and find something similar at a reasonable price.'

Saffron wished she did not have John's holdall containing his clothes with her. It was not heavy, but cumbersome and she would have liked to take advantage of the beautiful day to walk through the nearby park. A walk would also have passed the time before she could logically telephone the hospital and ask how John's operation had gone and when she would be allowed to visit. She had always sympathised with relatives whilst they had to wait for operation results, but now she truly realised how stressed and nervous they must be.

Marjorie was waiting for her when she arrived home and asked how she planned to spend the remainder of her day.

Saffron shrugged. 'Just waiting around, I suppose.'

'I thought you might like to come over to the Goldsmiths with me. You don't have to stay long, but they did say they'd like to see you whilst you were in England.'

'Can I wait until I've 'phoned the hospital before I make a decision? I want to know what time I can go in to visit John, and I'll have to 'phone Nicola and Marianne. It would be rather rude if I spent the afternoon on my mobile.'

'I'm sure they would understand, but there's no pressure on you to come. You can always drop in to see them another day whilst John's in hospital.'

Saffron nodded. 'That could be a better idea. I can't spend all day sitting there with him and I shall need some other things to occupy me. I thought I'd arrange to meet Angela for lunch one day, but I haven't any other plans.'

'You do whatever suits you best. I thought it would be practical if we had a take away this evening. It's too warm for a casserole. Which would you prefer – Indian or Chinese?'

'Indian. Depending what time I get back I could order it whilst I'm on the tube and collect it as I come past. I'm sure I won't be very late.'

'Good idea. I'll have my usual chicken jalfrezi.' Marjorie reached for her purse and Saffron shook her head.

'I am definitely paying for this. I know I gave you some money for food, but John has a big enough appetite for two.' As Saffron said it she made a mental note to suggest that John bought Marjorie a gift before they returned to Crete to thank her for having him to stay.

Saffron ate her lunch whilst her eyes continually strayed towards the clock. John's operation had been scheduled for ten that morning and she knew she had to allow time for any delay that might have occurred. He was not likely to be out of the theatre until eleven thirty. No one would appreciate her telephoning until after lunch had been served to the ward and cleared away. She insisted Marjorie left her the washing up to do as it would occupy her for a few minutes.

As the local news started on the television Saffron slipped into the kitchen and telephoned the hospital, waiting an interminably long time before she was finally put through to the ward where John would have been taken, and then having to wait again whilst someone who had authority could talk to her.

Her heart pounded whilst she waited. She knew this was the correct procedure and a junior nurse, part of whose duties would be to answer the 'phone, would not be allowed to disclose patient information, whether it was good or bad.

'Hello, Dr Bartlett, Matteus Gharcia here.'

'What's happened? What's wrong?' Saffron felt sick with apprehension.

'Nothing at all. I just happen to be doing a ward round so I thought I would speak to you personally. The operation on your nephew went exactly as planned and he's resting comfortably.'

Saffron let out a long breath of relief. 'Thank you, Doctor.'

'I'm sorry if I gave you cause for concern by taking your call myself. It was thoughtless of me. I should have let the ward Sister report to you and spoken afterwards.'

'That's quite all right,' replied Saffron, her voice shaking. 'When may I visit him?'

'I imagine he'll be properly awake by about five. Half an hour will probably be long enough for him. He'll still need more sleep, but you know that, of course.'

'I'm very grateful, Doctor.'

'What for? It's my job.'

'For agreeing to see John and treating him so quickly.'

'No problem. I'll see you again no doubt after he's had his next MRI scan.'

'Yes, of course, and thank you again.' Saffron could not wait to curtail her call and telephone Nicola.

Marjorie raised her eyebrows as Saffron returned to the lounge. 'Everything all right?'

Saffron nodded and sat down heavily on the sofa. 'I actually spoke to Dr Gharcia. I thought something awful had happened when I heard his voice, but he was doing his ward round. The operation went as planned and John's sleeping off the anaesthetic. I can visit him about five.'

'You'll feel better still when you've seen him, no doubt.'

'I'll leave here about three thirty. I thought I'd get a photographic magazine for him. I don't imagine he'll feel much like reading it tonight, but it will be something to keep him occupied tomorrow morning. I'm going to call Nicola and Marianne now. I promised I would and then I'll call them again when I've actually seen him. Give the Goldsmiths my apologies and you have a nice afternoon.'

Nicola answered her mobile as soon as it rang. 'Saffron?' she asked immediately.

'Reporting as promised,' replied Saffron cheerfully. 'John's op went well and he's back on the ward. I'm going in to visit him about five. I'll call you again when I leave the hospital and be able to tell you exactly how he's feeling. Listen out for your mobile at about seven thirty.'

'I've hardly put it down all day. Thank you, Saffie.' Nicola's voice broke. 'I was so worried.'

'Of course you were. It's only natural. How are the girls?'

'They've been restless and grizzling all day. Not a bit like their usual selves.'

'They probably picked up on the tension in you. I'm going to call Marianne now. She's probably been having a bad day as well.'

Saffron repeated her news to Marianne, promising to call her again that evening when she had visited John. 'How's Grandma?' she asked finally.

'She's been so crotchety all day. Nothing Bryony or I could do was right. I'll go and tell her that John's fine and that might improve her temper.'

'Where's Giovanni? I ought to 'phone him.'

'I'll do that. He's up at one of the new shops. A man from Agios

Nikolaos has shown interest. He says he wants to open a boutique. Provided he pays his rent Giovanni doesn't mind what he sells.'

'I hope he clinches the deal.' Saffron spoke sincerely. The shops had been completed at the end of May, but only the one Uncle Yannis had earmarked for himself was occupied and she knew Giovanni was worried that he had made a mistake in building them. 'I'm going to 'phone Vasi now. I hope he won't be available to talk or I shall be on the 'phone for hours. I'd rather just leave him a message for now and then talk to him properly this evening.'

'Why don't you send him a text?'

Saffron shook her head although Marianne could not see her. 'No, I said I'd 'phone. I can always make the excuse that I have to get to the hospital at a certain time and must leave immediately. I'll call you again this evening.'

Saffron walked into the small ward where John was to spend the week and looked in surprise as he waved to her. He was sitting up, watching a programme on a small television screen that was mounted above his bed.

'It's great,' he announced. 'I can actually see properly again.' He turned off the television. 'I'm so glad you've come. I'm bored and they won't let me out of bed yet.'

'Your vision's fine?'

'It may not be perfect yet, but at least the awful fuzzy edges have gone. I expected to wake up with a terrible headache, like I did after the accident, but I haven't.' John beamed in delight.

'Once the anaesthetic has fully worn off you may find you have one,' Saffron warned him. 'Don't forget, you can always ask for some pain killers if it's bad. I've 'phoned Nicola and your mother and I've promised to call them again when I leave here. I'll be able to give them a good report on your progress.'

'How is Nick? When I spoke to her this morning she sounded tired.'

'She'd probably had a disturbed night with the girls.'

'I'll be able to help her properly when I go back. I'm really looking forward to bathing and playing with them.'

'And the night time feeds, I hope.'

John grimaced. 'I'm not so sure that I'm looking forward to that. At least Nick is able to catch up on her sleep a bit during the day when Bryony looks after them. Dad will expect me to go to work as usual.'

'I'm sure you'll cope. I brought you a magazine.' Saffron handed it to John and he immediately opened it. 'No, you're not to look at it tonight. It's something for you to look at tomorrow.'

'Aren't you coming in to see me tomorrow?' asked John anxiously.

'Of course I am, but I can't spend all day with you. We'd soon run out of conversation, besides, you might be feeling fine, but you will still need to rest. If I was here visiting you'd feel obliged to stay awake and talk to me.'

'Will I be able to go outside tomorrow? You said I couldn't use my mobile in here and I do want to speak to Nick.'

'I'll ask when I come tomorrow afternoon. Provided you're given permission I can take you out in a wheelchair.'

'A wheelchair! There's nothing wrong with my legs,' protested John.

'I'm not taking any chances. If you tripped over you could break an arm or a leg and then you could be in here for a lot longer.'

'Yes, Doctor,' John answered her solemnly. 'If you say so, Doctor.'

'I do. You obey the rules and you'll be out in no time. Start thinking you can run before you can walk and you'll find yourself in trouble, not only with me and the nurses, but Doctor Gharcia as well. He nearly frightened me to death when I 'phoned to see how you were. The surgeon only usually speaks to a relative if there's a problem.'

John frowned and winced at the same time as the action pulled the stitches in his head. 'Is there a problem?'

'No, he just happened to be doing his ward round. He assured me that the operation had been successful. You wouldn't be sitting up in bed and talking to me if there was anything wrong.'

John's stomach rumbled and he rubbed it with his hand. 'I'm starving. You haven't brought any food with you, I suppose, Saff?'

Saffron shook her head. 'You'll be given some supper in about another half an hour.'

'They didn't give me any lunch,' complained John.

'That would have been intentional. You hadn't been back from the theatre long enough to be properly awake. They won't starve you. I'll bring you a packet of biscuits tomorrow.'

'I suppose Marjorie hasn't made any cakes?' asked John hopefully.

Saffron shook her head. 'Not that I know of. She was visiting the Goldsmiths this afternoon and I'm collecting a take away on my way home.'

'I wish I'd arranged for you to bring one in for me. You know what I'd really like? A large pepperoni pizza and salad.'

'Well you would have been disappointed because I'm getting an Indian.'

John wrinkled his nose. 'I don't like Indian.'

'That's why we're having it whilst you're in here. We'll celebrate with a pizza when you come home.'

'Promise?'

'Of course. Give me that magazine and I'll put it in your locker ready for tomorrow, then I'm going home. I'll be in to see you after lunch tomorrow.'

'I wish you'd stop talking about food! It's making me feel even hungrier.'

'On my way out I'll ask them to give you large portions.'

John squeezed Saffron's hand. 'Thanks, Saff. Thanks for everything.'

Week 3 – June 2009

'Sit down, Mr Gallagher.' Eli shook his client's hand. 'I have a letter drafted that, with your approval, can be sent to the Embassy. Read it through and let me know if you are happy with the content.' Eli Lambert handed Abraham a sheet of paper and sat back whilst the man read it carefully.

I, Abraham Gallagher, refute the claims made for compensation as stated in your letter.

Any confession that Todd Gallagher may have made would have either been under duress or due to ignorance of the language and should be disregarded.

I understand that my son is undergoing psychiatric tests and I am sure that when these have been completed you will understand that my son cannot be held responsible for his actions at the time and he will be free to return to United States.

I sympathise with you over the injuries your son sustained but refuse to accept any liability.

'It's very brief,' commented Abraham.

Eli shrugged. 'Brief and to the point. You're not writing to a friend.'

'Do you think their lawyer will accept it?'

'That depends. If the family are advised they have firm evidence that your son is responsible they could well pursue the claim even if he is declared psychologically unfit to stand trial.

Of course, if they are just trying to extract some money from you, hoping you'll pay up on a threat, they'll realise you are not a man to be trifled with and fade away.'

'This man, Kowalski, from the Embassy, says they have medical evidence.'

Eli wagged his finger at Abraham. 'He *says* they have, but has he seen it?'

Abraham handed the draft of the letter back. 'Very well, give me a copy to sign and send it. Hopefully that will be the end of the matter.'

Each day Saffron tried to learn a little more Greek vocabulary and decided it was an ideal time for her to enlist John's help. He was allowed to sit out in the grounds whilst she visited, but after four days and no change of scenery they were both running out of conversation.

John sat down and took Saffron's book in his hand. He looked at the page. 'This is only fit for the kindergarten. Shall I teach you some swear words?'

Saffron shook her head and took her book back from him. 'That's just about the stage I'm at and kindergarten children should not know swear words. Ask me a simple question in Greek and I'll try to answer or translate it into English to show I understand.'

John grinned. 'Suppose I asked you something in Italian? Would you know I wasn't speaking Greek?'

'Yes, I wouldn't understand anything. At least when you're all speaking Greek I can recognise a word here and there.'

'If we refused to speak English to you you'd learn more quickly.'

Saffron shook her head. 'That would be too frustrating. All I really want to know is how to speak politely to people. I felt really foolish the other week when I found I was in Kyparissos and wanted to buy some petrol. The man I asked didn't understand English and I thought he had directed me to the supermarket. I didn't understand that he was trying to tell me to turn left at the supermarket and there was a garage just down the road. I asked three other people before I found it.'

'You were lucky they had one. You should make sure you always have a full tank before you start out and a spare can with you. What made you go down there anyway?'

'I'd planned to go to Varthypetro. There's a Minoan settlement there and I thought it could be interesting to visit. I missed the turning and instead of going back I thought I'd be able to cut across and find the road.'

John frowned. 'Saff, you must be careful when you go off driving alone. You're safe enough on the main roads, but if you start trying to find short cuts you could end up just about anywhere.'

'There's bound to be someone around. I'll show them the map and they can tell me where I am and they can direct me to the main road. If I ever get really lost I'll 'phone Vasi.' Saffron spoke confidently.

'If you don't know where you are how could you tell him where to find you?'

'I'd be able to tell him roughly where I was by the name of a village I'd passed through.'

'Just remember you can't always get a mobile signal due to the mountains,' warned John.

'I'm sure I'd manage to find my way to a village anyway. The roads have to lead somewhere,' reasoned Saffron.

'Once you're in the countryside they often only lead to a farmer's field.'

'Then I'd have to turn round and go back.' Saffron smiled.

'By the time you realised you needed to do that you could have a puncture or be out of petrol.'

'Stop being so pessimistic, John. You've seen very little of England. If I drove out into the countryside here I could have the same problems.'

'At least you'd be able to speak the language.'

'Exactly. That's why I need to learn enough to ask directions and understand the answers. Now, are you going to help me with my Greek or continue to lecture me about the dangers of driving alone?'

'Where will I find a garage to mend a puncture?' asked John in Greek.

'What do I need a garage for?' Saffron had seized on the Greek word she was familiar with.

John grinned and repeated the question in English.

'That's easy,' declared Saffron triumphantly. 'I would point to the flat tyre and say the word garage.'

'Suppose it was your carburettor or a problem with the sparking plugs?'

'John, if it was a mechanical problem like that I wouldn't have a clue what was wrong. I would just have to ask for a garage – whether I was in England or Crete. Ask me sensible questions, like directions or the time.'

John grinned at her again. 'What time is my appointment with Dr Gharcia tomorrow?' he asked in Greek.

'Easy. Ten thirty,' answered Saffron.

'Why am I going to see him?'

Saffron frowned. 'Why are you what?'

'Why am I going to see him?' repeated John.

Saffron shook her head. 'You'll have to ask me that in English.'

John complied. 'Why am I going to see him?

'That's cheating,' exclaimed Saffron. 'I don't know how to change the tense of verbs depending upon the sentence. It's hard enough trying to remember when I use masculine or feminine. There doesn't seem to be any logic behind it.'

'There doesn't have to be logic. It's Greek.'

'I thought the Greeks invented logic,' replied Saffron caustically. 'I'll bring your clothes with me when I come tomorrow morning. Assuming Dr Gharcia is happy to discharge you after he's looked at your MRI scan we'll have a taxi and should be home by twelve thirty.'

'You still haven't answered my question,' complained John. 'Why am I seeing Dr Gharcia tomorrow?'

'The nurse removed your stitches this morning and he'll want to check the incision is healing properly. It's the procedure after any surgery. If the hospital just said you could leave without seeing a doctor and later you were found to have an infection in the wound or it wasn't healing as it should you'd be suing them for negligence. They want to avoid that, of course, and they do care about their patients' well being.'

'Now tell me in Greek,' grinned John.

Saffron looked at him seriously. 'Honestly, John, I wouldn't know where to start.'

'Have you packed everything?' asked Saffron.

John nodded. 'I appreciate all that has been done for me whilst I've stayed here, but I can't wait to get out. Can we look up flights when we get home?'

'Of course.' Saffron did not admit that she had already looked for a direct flight to Crete that left and arrived at reasonable times.

'I've told Nick I'll be leaving the hospital today.'

Saffron raised her eyebrows. 'That was a bit presumptuous of you. You should have waited until you'd seen Dr Gharcia to be sure.'

'I'm fine. I know I have to wait another week before I'm allowed to fly, but at least Nick knows I'm on my way. I'll take that.' John took his holdall from Saffron and walked across the ward to bid farewell to the nurses.

Saffron followed him, hoping John's MRI scan would be satisfactory and his hopes for leaving within the next half an hour would not be dashed.

John punched the air. 'Freedom! I feel as if I've been cooped up inside for weeks.'

'You've been out in the gardens every day.'

'I've still had to go back inside when you left. I've missed taking Skele for his evening walk home. Is this our taxi?'

'I'll check, but there's no one else waiting at the moment.' Saffron spoke to the driver and opened the rear passenger door, ushering John inside. 'Seat belt,' she reminded him and buckled her own.

'When can we go shopping?' asked John. 'You said we could look in Selfridges and Harrods for baby things.'

'I think you should have a quiet day tomorrow. You'll find that just coming home tires you more than you would expect. There's plenty of time for shopping.'

'I saw this in a magazine at the hospital. I pulled the page out. Tell me what you think.' John bent down and opened his holdall.

The van that unexpectedly impacted the taxi on the driver's side threw them both off balance. John's head hit the car door handle with a sickening smack and Saffron fell against the door on the opposite side, feeling an excruciating pain shoot through her arm as it twisted beneath her. She gasped and righted herself. John was slumped against the door and the driver was collapsed over the steering wheel.

'John. John, are you alright? Are you hurt?' She felt for John's pulse, which to her relief, was beating strongly. 'John, speak to me.'

There was no response and Saffron looked around wildly for her bag that had fallen to the floor at her feet. She fumbled to release her seat belt and tried to reach down for her bag with her right hand. As she did so the pain in her arm gripped her. Biting her lip she groped for her bag with her left hand and pulled out her mobile. The taxi door opened and a woman looked in.

'Are you hurt?'

Saffron shook her head. 'John's unconscious. He needs to get back to the hospital as quickly as possible.'

'Someone's already called an ambulance. The paramedics will

assess him and then take him to be checked over.'

'You don't understand.' Saffron began to punch in the numbers for the hospital they had left so recently. She did not want John taken to the nearest casualty unit, but back to Doctor Gharcia.

The ambulance arrived whilst she was still waiting to be connected to the doctor's extension. The paramedics placed neck braces on both John and the taxi driver and began an assessment for broken bones before they attempted to remove either of them from the cab.

'We have to go back to the hospital,' Saffron said to one of them urgently.

'Don't you worry, miss. We'll take all three of you to the hospital. Just need to check for broken bones before we move any of you. Don't want to do any further damage.'

'No, you don't understand. John has to go back to see Doctor Gharcia. He had brain surgery last week.'

The paramedic withdrew his head and spoke to his companion. He pointed to John's head where the recently healed wound was oozing blood; the surrounding area was already turning a shade of purple from the bruising and swelling around his eye. His nose had bled and the front of his shirt was stained.

'Dr Gharcia? This is Saffron Bartlett. We've been involved in a car accident. John hit his head and he's unconscious. The ambulance is here. Please will you speak to them and ask them to take him directly to your unit at the hospital?'

Saffron handed her mobile to the paramedic who listened to the doctor and frowned. 'It isn't normal procedure, sir. We always take the casualties to be assessed at accident and emergency before they are transferred to any specialist unit.'

'I am insisting that young man is brought directly to me. If you are not able to comply I will request another ambulance to attend the scene.'

A police car drew up and two constables walked over to the taxi. 'What's the damage?'

'One walking and two stretcher cases. The driver definitely has a broken leg and is concussed. The woman in the back appears unhurt but is insisting that we take her companion to the neurology department immediately. I've just had the doctor from there on the 'phone and he says the same. He's sent for another ambulance.' The paramedic handed Saffron back her mobile.

The police constable nodded. 'You move the driver as soon as you can and I'll see if the young lady can tell me what happened whilst we wait for the second ambulance.' He bent and looked inside the back of the taxi where Saffron was holding John's limp hand and imploring him to answer her.

'Are you able to tell me what happened?' he asked.

'A van hit us,' Saffron answered briefly. 'John needs to taken back to the neurological unit immediately. He had brain surgery last week and was only discharged an hour ago. Where's that ambulance going?' she asked as the paramedics drove away taking the taxi driver with them.

'I understand there's another on the way. Can you give me a description of the van? The size or colour? Was there a firm's name on the side?'

Saffron ignored him. 'Doctor, are you still there? Is there another ambulance coming? The one that was here earlier has left.' Tears began to pour down Saffron's cheeks.

The policeman took the mobile 'phone from her hand. 'The young lady is very distraught. I don't know the condition of the young man but if you have a way of speeding up that ambulance I think it could be advisable. We'll follow on and when the lady is a little calmer we'll take a statement from her.'

The second ambulance arrived, the siren blaring and lights flashing. A crowd was beginning to gather around and the policeman waved them away. 'Keep back, please. There's nothing to see.'

As the new paramedics began a cursory examination of John for broken bones he stirred. 'Saff?'

'I'm here John.' Saffron held his hand. 'A van hit our taxi and you've bumped your head. We're going back to the hospital for Doctor Gharcia to examine you.'

'Great!' John blinked. Everything was black. He blinked again. Surely it would clear in a moment and he would be able to see again. 'Saff, I can't see.' There was a note of panic in John's voice.

'Right, sir, we're ready to move you now. You don't seem to have any limb fractures, but you tell us the moment you feel any pain in your arms or legs and we'll stop. If you'd let go of your friend's hand, miss.'

'I can't see!'

'You've had a bit of a bang on the head. You'll be fine when we get you to the hospital.'

'Saff. Don't leave me, Saff.' John tried to find Saffron's hand.

'I'm coming with you in the ambulance. I won't leave you, I promise.'

'My head.....'

'Don't try to talk, just close your eyes and try to relax. I'll hold your hand all the way so you'll know I'm with you.' Saffron waited until John had been settled into the ambulance and strapped to a stretcher before she turned to the paramedic. 'Could you place his holdall in the ambulance for me, please.'

He nodded and pushed it towards a spare seat at the back and Saffron climbed in.

'I'm here, John. I'm sitting right opposite you, but I can't reach across to hold your hand. The driver has just got into his cab and we're about to leave. Doctor Gharcia is expecting us so you'll not be kept waiting. He'll see you straight away. There's a little bit of blood where your stitches were taken out but nothing worse. Your shirt's a bit of a mess as you've had a nose bleed.'

'Just stay with me.' John's eyes flickered open. Everything was still black.

'Of course I will.'

The siren sounded and Saffron knew John would be unable

to hear her above the raucous sound, but she continued to talk to him, reassuring him that there was little wrong and he would receive medical attention the moment they arrived at the hospital.

Doctor Gharcia looked at his recent patient with concern. 'Any pain in your back or limbs?' he asked.

'No. I just can't see.'

The doctor patted his hand. 'I'm sending you off straight away for an X-ray, just as a precaution, you understand. You could well find that by the time you've had that you can see again. Where you banged your head it has probably just shaken you up a bit. It's possible your cheek bone is fractured and you may have broken your nose. Doctor Bartlett can go with you and wait outside with the technicians. She'll be able to talk to you whilst you're waiting.'

Saffron smiled at Doctor Gharcia gratefully. Whilst John was being prepared for his X-ray she would slip outside and call Marjorie. She would appreciate hearing her comforting voice.

'Marjorie, we won't be home for a while. The taxi we were in was hit by a van.'

'What! Are you either of you hurt?'

'John hit his head. He says he can't see.' Saffron's voice broke. 'We're back at the hospital and he's having an X-ray.'

'I'm on my way,' announced Marjorie.

'No, really, there's no need,' protested Saffron.

'Rubbish. You need someone there with you if only to pass the time. I'll call Henry and ask him if he can drive me over. You can tell me exactly what happened when I arrive.' As she spoke Marjorie collected her cardigan from the chair and picked up her handbag. She checked she had sufficient money for a taxi should she need it and then dialled Henry's number on the land line.

'Henry, it's Marjorie. I have a favour to ask. Are you able to drive me to the hospital?'

'What time's your appointment?'

'It's not for me. Saffron and John were involved in an accident.

John has been hurt. I don't know how badly. Saffron said he couldn't see. She's terribly distressed. She needs to have someone with her.'

'You need to go now?'

'If it isn't convenient I'll take a taxi.'

'Start walking down the road. I'll meet you,' promised Henry.

Saffron waited anxiously until Doctor Gharcia emerged from his consulting room where he had been examining John's X-ray. Doctor Gharcia sucked in his breath when he saw the extent of John's new injury. The small triangular piece of bone that he had so carefully removed and thinned before replacing was perfect, but no more than two millimetres away from it and running down John's forehead to his eye socket was a new line denoting a hair line fracture. It was going to be a delicate operation to repair the eye socket due to his fractured cheek and nose without causing any further damage to the optic nerve and this time he would not be able to rely on bone cement for the repair. The new break was too close to the original. He would add two small titanium plates and screw them into place.

Marjorie hurried in to the reception area of the neurological department. 'Where can I find Doctor Saffron Bartlett?' she asked.

The receptionist frowned. 'We don't have a doctor of that name working here.'

Marjorie passed a shaking hand across her forehead. 'She was involved in a car accident. She called me from here.'

'She would be in the accident and emergency department if she has been hurt. This is a surgical unit. You need to go back to the main building ....'

'No,' Marjorie shook her head impatiently. 'You don't understand. The young man who was in the taxi with her was hurt. He has been brought back here. He was only discharged this morning. You must have a record of him. John Pirenzi. Doctor

Gharcia's patient.'

'Have a seat and I'll see what I can find out for you. Are you the young man's mother?'

'I'm Mrs Bartlett. I need to see my daughter. She said she was here with him.'

'Just a moment.' With a bright smile the receptionist dialled Doctor Gharcia's extension. 'Really?' Marjorie heard her say. 'I'll 'phone down and see if a message can be given to her.'

'Mrs Bartlett, I understand your daughter is waiting whilst her friend has a X-ray taken. I'll ask one of the technicians to let her know you are here.'

'Thank you.' Marjorie sat on the chair, twisting her fingers nervously. It seemed an age before Saffron finally appeared and rushed towards her.

'Oh, Marjorie, have you been waiting long? I'm sorry. I should have explained when I was on the 'phone.'

'It was no problem. I've sent Henry back home. There was no point in him hanging around and clocking up parking fees. Now sit down and tell me exactly what happened to you both.'

Saffron shook her head. 'I'm not really clear. I've told the police as much as I can, but I was too concerned with John to take much notice of anything else. One moment we were talking and then there was an almighty bang as a van hit us on the driver's side. John hit his head on the door handle and was concussed for a while. When he came round he said he couldn't see. The wound on his head was bleeding a bit and his face is rather a mess.'

'Oh, how awful. To be discharged and then that happen to him. I presume an ambulance crew attended to you?'

'They wanted to send us to A and E along with the driver, but I called Doctor Gharcia and insisted John was brought straight back here for him to see. Had we gone to A and E we would still be waiting our turn no doubt. Doctor Gharcia was so good. He sent John down for an X-ray immediately. Doctor Gharcia looked at the X-ray as soon as it was developed and showed me where there is a hairline fracture in John's cranium above his eye socket and he also has a broken cheek bone. John's on his way down to the operating theatre now.' Saffron lifted her tear stained face to Marjorie. 'What am I going to say to Nicola and Marianne? They're expecting a call from John to say he is safely home.'

Marjorie frowned. 'Did John tell them what time he expected to be home?'

Saffron shook her head. 'I don't know, but if he doesn't call they'll know something has happened and be worried sick.'

Marjorie glanced at her watch. 'It's just gone one thirty. How long will John be in surgery?'

'I'm not sure. It could be around three hours. Doctor Gharcia told me that his cheek bone will have to be plated, that will be done through his mouth. He'll also need a plate below his eye socket to hold his eye in place.'

'We can still wait a while before we telephone. Provided he isn't in the theatre too long we can tell them about the accident and the outcome of this operation at the same time. Now, you won't have had any lunch. Why don't you check out with the receptionist and we'll go over to the cafeteria. I could do with a cup of tea.'

Saffron looked at Marjorie doubtfully. 'I ought to stay here. I want to speak to Doctor Gharcia as soon as he returns.'

Marjorie shook her head. 'You've just said the operation will probably take about three hours. That's more than enough time for us to have a cup of tea. You can always bring a sandwich back with you.'

'I don't feel much like eating.'

'Better to have something with you in case you change your mind. I'll tell the receptionist that we're going to the cafeteria and will be back in about half an hour.'

Saffron felt her resistance slipping away. Now John was in surgery and Marjorie had arrived to support her she felt incredibly weary and nauseous. 'Delayed shock,' she said to herself. 'A cup of tea and something sweet to eat and I'll be fine.'

Marjorie unloaded two cups of tea, a packet of sandwiches and a bar of chocolate from a tray. 'Eat the chocolate first. You need a shot of sugar and I know you don't like it in your tea.'

Saffron picked up the chocolate bar and went to unwrap it. 'I can't do that,' she complained and rested her arm in her lap. 'That really hurts where I twisted it underneath me.'

'Did the paramedics check you over?' asked Marjorie.

'No. I told them I was a doctor and there was no need. I was far more concerned with getting John back here as quickly as possible.'

'Saffie, you know that however minor an accident is you should always be checked out. How often have you come home and complained that people thought they had sprained their wrist and struggled on for a couple of days only to find it was broken?'

Saffron smiled guiltily and looked down at her hand. It was very tender beneath her thumb and she had a deep, dull ache in her arm. She tried to pick up the chocolate bar again with her right hand and was unable to get a grip. She pushed the chocolate bar and cup of tea away from her.

'When I've spoken to Doctor Gharcia I'll nip in and see if Vince is around. He'd be able to rush an X-ray through for me. I expect it's just badly bruised. I hadn't realised how much it hurt until I tried to take that wrapper off.'

'Shall I do it for you?'

Saffron shook her head. 'I'm not taking any chances. I won't starve by waiting another couple of hours before I eat anything. I can always have it after the X-ray.'

Marjorie looked at her stepdaughter steadily. 'You think it's broken, don't you?'

'It could be. Better not to risk eating or drinking anything until I know. I wouldn't want to have to sit around for hours waiting for treatment.'

Marjorie placed her empty cup back on the saucer. 'Are you really not going to drink your tea?'

Saffron shook her head. 'You have it. I can always have a sip of water.'

'I think you should go over to see if Vince is around now.'

Saffron shook her head. 'I must find out about John. They'll obviously keep him in and I'll need to know where to take his holdall. I promise I'll go over and have my arm looked at after that.' She looked at her watch. They had only been in the cafeteria for twenty minutes.

'You could well have seen Vince by the time John is ready to be admitted to a ward.' Marjorie placed the sandwiches and bar of chocolate in her bag. 'Do you want to use my cardigan as a sling?'

Saffron hesitated. 'I suppose that would be sensible,' she admitted.

'I'll go back and speak to the receptionist. You see if Vince is around and I'll meet you over in the orthopaedic department.'

Vince grinned when he saw Saffron waiting outside his consulting room. 'Hi, you obviously can't keep away from us. Killing time before you visit your friend? How's he doing?'

'I've come to ask a favour, Vince. I think I may have broken my wrist. Any chance you could rush me through?'

'Come in and tell me what's happened.'

Whilst Saffron related the accident in the taxi to Vince he felt her arm. She winced under his touch and he nodded. 'I'm pretty certain that's a fracture. I'll call down to X-ray and tell them you're a priority. Come back up to me and once I've seen the damage I'll arrange for you to be plastered. Have you eaten recently?'

Saffron shook her head. 'Not since breakfast, about eight. I was going to, then I realised how much my arm hurt and decided against it, just in case it needs to be reset.'

'Sensible. I'll see you in about twenty minutes.'

Feeling thoroughly miserable Saffron walked back down to the X-ray department, hoping she would not bump into Sean whilst she was in this area of the hospital. She certainly did not want to have to explain to him how she had hurt her arm.

Marjorie was waiting for her upon her return and Saffron nodded. 'It's a fracture. It looks straight forward. Once Vince has seen the X-ray he'll send me off to get it plastered; then I can have that bar of chocolate. Any news of John?'

'You can't expect any yet. As soon as you're finished here we'll go back to neurology.'

'I'll have to 'phone Nicola soon.'

'You can leave it another hour at least. It would be better for her to be wondering why you haven't called than know John is in surgery without knowing the outcome. That would really worry her.'

Saffron sighed. 'You're right, but the longer John spends in the theatre the more serious his injury must be.'

'Not necessarily. Doctor Gharcia is bound to be meticulous. He's sure to take another X-ray before he lets John out of the theatre to ensure he hasn't missed anything. That takes time.'

'If only it hadn't happened.'

'It wasn't your fault, Saffie. You weren't driving the van or the taxi.'

Saffron frowned. 'I ought to go down to A and E to ask after the taxi driver. I heard the paramedics tell the police he had a broken leg but he was still unconscious when they took him away.'

'Vince might know. He may well have treated him and he's probably sent him home by now.'

Saffron looked at her arm, encased in plaster it felt heavy and unwieldy, but it was certainly no longer painful. Six weeks was the statutory time before the cast would be removed. Provided John was in hospital no more than a week or ten days he would be able to fly back to Crete a week later. She had every intention of accompanying him, even with a fractured wrist encased in a plaster cast..

She handed Marjorie her cardigan. 'Thanks. That certainly helped whilst I was waiting. Back to neurology now. What a horrible afternoon you've had.'

'At least I'm not hurt. Why don't you try eating that sandwich now?'

Saffron shook her head. 'I'm really not hungry. I'll wait until we get home.'

To Saffron's surprise Doctor Gharcia had already returned to the neurology department. There were five patients waiting for him. As he ushered a woman out he saw Saffron waiting for him and walked over to her.

'Fractured?' He raised his eyebrows at the sight of her plastered arm.

Saffron nodded. 'How's John? How did the operation go?'

'I've put a small plate across the hairline fracture. It's a safety precaution more than necessity. The hairline should heal perfectly well without assistance, but I wanted to ensure that nothing moved whilst Peter Sheridan plated his cheek and repaired his eye socket. He's the expert in that department. We won't know about any permanent damage to his sight for a couple of days. Give him another hour then you can see him for five minutes. After that you go straight home and get some rest. Doctor's orders. Now, I must see to my patients.'

'Thank you, Doctor. Thank you very much.' Saffron felt quite faint with relief.

Doctor Gharcia turned to his waiting patients. 'I'm so sorry I'm running rather behind time with my appointments. I was called into the operating theatre urgently. I believe my next patient is Mr Pargeter? If you would like to come in, sir.'

Saffron sat down beside Marjorie again. 'I can have five minutes with John in about an hour.'

'And?'

'Doctor Gharcia was cautious. He's plated John's skull in two places, but said that was just a precaution against any further damage whilst his cheek was plated. Peter Sheridan, the ear, nose and throat specialist is doing that, but they can't be sure if John's sight will have been affected.'

Marjorie nodded. 'Well the first news is positive. I'll 'phone Henry and ask him if he can be here to collect us in about an hour and a half.'

'He really doesn't have to. We could take a taxi.'

'I don't feel like travelling in a taxi today. I think I could be considerably safer with Henry.'

When Saffron spoke to Nicola she had tried to convince her that John had not been seriously hurt and explained the procedure that Doctor Sheridan had carried out. 'It isn't unusual. Cheek bones always break in three places and plating them holds the bone in place until it has healed. If John didn't have a plate beneath his eye it would sink backwards and give him double vision, he'd also have a flat side to his face which would give him a bit of an odd look.'

'What about the skull fracture?'

'Doctor Gharcia assured me that was nothing to worry over. He has fixed a plate over the new one and another over the original fracture. He said he wanted to make quite sure nothing moved whilst Doctor Sheridan operated. I saw John for a few minutes when he returned from the theatre and he's obviously a bit bruised. I'll go in tomorrow morning and call you when I've seen him. I'm sure he'll be allowed out in the garden again in a couple of days and you'll be able to speak to him yourself.'

'I ought to be there with him.' Nicola sounded desolate and Saffron guessed she was crying. 'I was so looking forward to him coming home.'

'I'm sure you were. It was most unfortunate, but it could have been considerably worse.' Saffron's arm was throbbing and she forced herself to continue listening to Nicola's unhappiness and comment with sympathetic words. She took a mouthful of water and swallowed a pain killer. 'I must call Marianne now. I have to tell her and Giovanni what has happened.'

'I could do that,' offered Nicola.

'No, it's better that I speak to them. They may want some details from me that I haven't thought to tell you.'

'Like what?' asked Nicola, immediately suspicious.

'I don't know, maybe how fast we were going, was it the fault of the taxi driver. That kind of detail. I swear I've given you every bit of information I have about John.'

'You will call me tomorrow, won't you?'

'I promise. Just remember you're two hours ahead of us so it will probably be about three in the afternoon.'

'We should never have allowed him to go to England for an operation,' complained Giovanni. 'Now look what's happened.'

'It was an accident. It could have happened anywhere.'

'Accident, maybe, but who's going to pay for a second operation? We haven't got the money, Marianne. I had to really work on the bank manager to get the latest loan. I can't see him letting me have another.'

'Could you ask Vasi? If he would underwrite a loan the bank would surely agree.'

'I don't like to ask him.'

'Do you have a choice? The hospital in England will have to be paid somehow.'

'Could you approach Adam Kowalski? See if you can get him to put a bit of pressure on that boy's father so we get a quick reply.'

'I can try, but you know these things take time. I showed you the e-mail from Adam acknowledging receipt of my letter. I told Adam to inform Mr Gallagher that we were definitely going to take the case to court. No doubt Mr Gallagher has consulted his lawyer and is waiting for him to suggest a suitable reply.'

Marjorie insisted that once Saffron had called Nicola and Marianne she had something to eat and went to bed. She had fallen asleep virtually immediately, only to wake up just after midnight. She closed her eyes and tried to get back to sleep but all she could see was John's damaged face. If he hadn't been bending down just at that moment to retrieve something from his holdall he would probably only have banged his head on the window and consequently suffered no more than a headache.

Saffron looked at the clock every half an hour. She was unable to get comfortable. She could not lie on her arm and if she laid it across her abdomen it felt like a lead weight. She tried lying on her stomach with her arm at her side, but that gave her a pain in her shoulder. Finally she gave up and turned on her light. Three fifteen. Maybe if she made herself a cup of tea it would help her to get back to sleep.

She opened her door quietly and tiptoed across the landing not wishing to disturb Marjorie. Without switching on the light and holding the banister carefully she walked slowly down the stairs and felt her way along the hall to the kitchen. It was more difficult than she had realised to make a cup of tea using your left hand when you were naturally right handed. She carried her mug into the lounge and returned to switch off the kitchen light. She settled herself on the sofa, a cushion beneath her arm and waited for her tea to cool. It was there that Marjorie found her sound asleep when she came downstairs at seven thirty, the mug of cold tea untouched.

Saffron walked into the ward and looked for John. He was propped up in bed, but appeared to be asleep. The side of his face and his head were bandaged and the bruising had spread all the way across and down his face. His nose was swollen and he looked far worse than he had the previous evening when she had seen him briefly.

'John,' she said quietly.

His eye opened a little and he tried to smile. 'Saff! I'm so glad you've come.' His voice was hoarse and soft. 'Why am I here? The nurses keep telling me I'll be perfectly all right in a few days, but what's happened? Why is my mouth so sore and my head all bandaged up?'

Saffron swallowed. 'There was an accident and you bumped your head.'

Beneath his bandages John frowned and winced. 'That was ages ago.'

Saffron sat down on the edge of his bed and took his hand. 'John, do you know where you are?'

'In hospital. That's pretty obvious.'

'Do you remember coming to England with me?'

'Of course. I had an operation on my head, but you told me I was fine and we were going home.'

'That's true. Do you remember seeing Doctor Gharcia yesterday?'

'I was sure I'd seen Doctor Gharcia and he had said I could go home, then everything is a jumble. The next thing I really remember is waking up in here. I thought I must have been dreaming.'

Saffron shook her head. 'You didn't imagine it. Do you remember getting into a taxi? Doctor Gharcia said you could go home and I ordered a taxi to come to collect us.'

'When was that?'

'Yesterday morning.'

John looked at Saffron blankly. 'If I was able to go home yesterday why am I still here and covered in bandages?'

'Whilst we were in the taxi there was an accident. A van ran into the side of us and you hit your head on the door handle.'

'Did I?' John sounded surprised. 'Have I cut myself?'

'You've broken your cheek bone and your nose. Doctor Sheridan has put in some small plates to repair your cheek. The bandage is probably to keep it everything in place until it begins to heal.'

'Why does my mouth hurt?'

'They insert two of the plates through your mouth. It will be sore for quite a while.'

'Does Nick know? About the taxi accident I mean.'

'I spoke to her yesterday evening and I'm going to call her again in a while and tell her how you're progressing.'

'I bet she called me ... what is it she calls me? Saff, why can't I remember things?' There was a note of panic in John's voice.

'You have traumatic amnesia.'

'Amnesia? You mean I've lost my memory?'

Saffron shook her head. 'No, you have temporarily lost your recent memory. It often happens when you've had a blow to the head. You were concussed for a short while. Your memory blanks out the events leading up to the accident and it's called traumatic amnesia. If you had truly lost your memory you wouldn't have known me or remembered Nicola.'

'Why didn't the nurses tell me what had happened? I've been lying here trying to puzzle it out.'

'They probably didn't realise you couldn't remember the accident. Your memory as such is not impaired; you've just wiped out an unpleasant experience.'

'So when can I go home?'

'Where you hit your head you broke your cheek bone and that caused another small skull fracture above your eye. Doctor Gharcia had to operate on you again. I don't know how long you'll be kept in, a week possibly, but you'll have to wait until you've spoken to him.'

'Another week! Nick is expecting me home.'

'Nick understands that you cannot fly home until Doctor Gharcia discharges you and gives you a certificate declaring you fit to fly.'

John groaned. 'I feel terrible. My face hurts, my head aches and I can hardly see.'

'I'll ask them to give you something for the pain and a fresh ice pack for your face. That will bring the swelling down beneath your eye and then you'll be able to see better. I'll see the charge nurse now; then I'll leave you to sleep for a while and come back later.'

'If you say so.' John felt far too weary to argue for Saffron to stay with him. He had not even noticed that Saffron had a plaster cast on her arm.

As a formality Saffron went over to the orthopaedic centre to have her cast checked. Her hand was not swollen and the plaster did not feel tight, but it was a safety precaution. When she had done that she would search out Doctor Gharcia and see if he had time to update her on John's condition. He saw her waiting and shook his head.

'I'll have to deal with my patients before I can speak to you.'

Saffron nodded. 'I understand.' She knew he had given John preferential treatment the previous day; she could not expect that every time she wished to speak with him.

She turned over the pages of the magazines that were on the table and wished she had brought a book with her as it was over an hour before Doctor Gharcia beckoned her into his room.

'How's the arm?' he asked.

'Just a nuisance,' smiled Saffron. 'I went to see John a while ago and he has traumatic amnesia. Did you know that?'

'No, I haven't done any ward rounds yet. I can't say I'm surprised. He took a very nasty blow.'

'He doesn't remember being in the taxi.'

'Provided he only has memory loss of no more than twenty four hours I'm not unduly concerned.'

'How long will he be kept in this time?' Saffron was worried that she would have to ask Giovanni to send over another large sum of money to pay for the second operation and subsequent nursing.

'I'd like to keep him in for at least five days. I want the ophthalmologist to have a look at his eye before I discharge him. He'll need another MRI scan a little later to ensure none of the plates have come adrift. Once I'm satisfied that all is well he can finish recuperating at home.'

'Home as in Crete?'

Doctor Gharcia shook his head. 'I certainly wouldn't want him to fly for at least two weeks after discharge. He would find it far too painful.'

'How much is this going to cost, Doctor? I shall have to ask his father for some more money and I don't know how long it will take to be transferred to me.'

Doctor Gharcia raised his eyebrows. 'Didn't you take out travel insurance when you booked your flights?'

'Yes, but I'm not sure if John's covered for a second operation. I had to declare that he was coming to England for neurosurgery and there is a clause that says he isn't insured for that.'

'This was an accident and the damage to his face had to be rectified immediately. It was not neurosurgery. Contact the insurance company and ask them to send you claim forms. When you've completed them I'll add the medical report and sign them. There shouldn't be a problem.'

Saffron felt a huge weight lifted from her and tears came into her eyes. 'I'm so grateful to you and I know John and his family will be.'

'Are you planning to claim for your fractured wrist?'

'I hadn't even thought about it.'

'You should. You're a surgeon. A badly damaged wrist could wreck your career.'

Saffron bit her lip. 'I've resigned from the hospital.'

'I know, but suppose in six months time you wished to work as an orthopaedic surgeon again somewhere else and found your wrist wasn't strong enough?'

'I'm not likely to do that.'

'You would still be wise to make a claim. Why pay insurance and not take advantage of it when you have a legitimate claim? I'll be visiting the wards after lunch. If you want to wait around and have a word with me again then you're welcome.'

Saffron smiled gratefully at the doctor. 'I'll be with John.'

Abraham Gallagher was furious. So much for taking the advice of his lawyer and expecting the Cretan lawyer to disappear! A further e-mail had been forwarded from Adam Kowalski with a letter attached. It stated quite clearly that if the compensation was not received the case would definitely be taken to court and a far higher figure of recompense would be requested.

Abraham called his lawyer and read the letter to him.

'So what do you want me to do?' asked Eli Lambert.

'Advise me. That's what I pay you for,' snapped back Abraham.

'Well, you have two courses of action open to you. Ignore the letter and take your chance in court or pay up as requested.'

'If I do pay there's no guarantee these people won't ask for more. I don't trust them.'

'I suggest you forestall them. They're asking for three hundred thousand U.S. dollars for their son's injury and if you don't settle they'll take you to court and no doubt up the figure. I think they could need this money urgently and would be only too happy to agree to an out of court settlement. I propose you settle for three hundred thousand dollars on the understanding that they will make no further demands on you for compensation for their son's injury.'

'That's extortionate. I'm not made of money.'

'Think about it, Abraham. It could be to your advantage. The final amount awarded by a Greek court could easily be double that or even more. You'd need to have a legal agreement drawn up. You would have to guarantee to pay the agreed amount and they would have to sign to say they would drop the injury claim. The documents would be signed by both parties. If you default they would obviously proceed, but if you have their agreement in writing and have kept your side of the bargain they have no grounds to persecute you for more.'

'Can you do that for me?'

Eli hesitated. 'I don't feel confident. I'm an American lawyer and I'm not familiar with Greek litigation law.'

'Can you recommend a colleague?'

'Not really. Why don't you give that chap at the Embassy in Athens a call?' suggested Eli. 'He must deal with these sorts of situations all the time. He should know of a lawyer attached to the Embassy who could work on your behalf.'

'He'd probably be Greek and prejudiced in their favour,' protested Abraham.

'Insist that he's American. Don't employ a local man or you could be right in your assumption.'

'So you won't help me?'

'As I said, I'm not qualified. I wouldn't want to draft a document for you to sign only to find that I had left you open to legal abuse in any way due to my ignorance of procedures.'

Abraham sighed heavily. 'I suppose I'll have to speak to this man at the Embassy.'

'Mr Gallagher, I think you could have made a very wise decision to settle out of court on condition that no further claims for injury compensation will be made against your son. The amount awarded by a court could easily have been double the amount you are agreeing. I will contact Mr Pirenzi's lawyer and say you have accepted the proposal. We will then be able to proceed with drawing up an agreement.'

'I want an American lawyer, not one of those crafty Greeks.'

'Mr Pirenzi's lawyer is American, qualified in International Law. I'm sure you will have no cause for complaint.'

Week 1 – July 2009

Marianne opened her computer and scanned her list of mail, gratified to see that some of them were booking confirmations. Despite a slow start to the season business had definitely picked up in the last few weeks. It usually did at this time of year, when parents decided at the last minute they wanted to take their children away for some sun before they had to return to school. If only some more of the shops were occupied there would be some rent being paid to add to their income.

She opened the mail from the travel companies and printed off the reservation requests before going in to her accommodation list and allocating the rooms. She had three requests for ground floor rooms and had only two available during the specified dates. She would have to look at the other bookings and see if she could move someone to a higher floor. Unless the visitor was disabled it was often pure laziness that made them want ground floor accommodation.

Opening the accounts Marianne sighed; as the tourist numbers had increased it had become necessary to employ more staff. Bryony could no longer cope alone up at the taverna as more coach parties were booking a visit to Spinalonga and requesting lunch either before or after their visit. Three more chambermaids had been employed and Marcus was kept busy in the shop whilst Giovanni made endless trips to the wholesaler to keep him stocked.

Uncle Yannis's shop in Aghios Nikolaos stood empty and no

one seemed inclined to want to buy it from him. His new shop in Plaka was doing a small amount of business but people appeared unwilling to part with their money for holiday souvenirs, even if they were exclusive designs with certificates proving their origin. Two other shops stood empty but the one that had been rented and called itself a Beach Boutique appeared to be making a profit.

Rather than reducing their overdraft it was increasing and there was no extra money available to repay their loan for John's operation. She was so thankful that Saffron had had the foresight to take out insurance when she booked their flights and John had been covered for his subsequent accident. She wondered if John would be fit enough to work when he returned. At the moment if a small repair job was needed at the self catering apartments Marcus had to close the shop to attend to it or they had to pay a local man for the repair. Neither system was financially practical. If John could relieve Marcus in the shop it would be a help.

Marianne made some notes on the pad beside her. Last month's bill at the wholesaler must be paid this week and also the outstanding one to the garage for repairing the handle to their mini bus. That would leave her with just over one hundred and fifty Euros to provide food for all nine of them until the travel companies settled their outstanding bills at the end of the month. There was the formula milk to be bought for the girls and their endless supply of nappies to be replenished. Marcus would bring back any unsold perishable or out of date items from the shop and she would make use of them as best she could, but it was not easy. They were struggling now as they had been when they first started the self catering business.

The icon flashed to say she had another incoming e-mail and she entered the programme again, hoping it would be another booking confirmation. When she saw it was from Adam Kowalski her heart sank. No doubt she was now going to be embroiled in long communications with Mr Gallagher's lawyer whilst he tried to argue that his client had no case to answer. Although she had pursued Abraham Gallagher for compensation she also realised that it was not truly his responsibility. It was his son who should be made to pay.

She read Adam's brief mail. *"I am attaching the reply from Mr Gallagher's solicitor. I believe you will be happy with the outcome."*

Marianne opened the attachment and read it rapidly. She then read it again more slowly and sucked in her breath. The man had agreed to pay the sum of three hundred thousand dollars on condition that no further charges for injury compensation were made.

Marianne read the e-mail a third time. She could hardly believe it. Mr Gallagher had not contested her claim. He either had a very inefficient lawyer or he was desperate to keep his son out of court. She wondered what else the Greek police might be planning to charge the young man with. She smiled to herself. She would accept the offer of compensation for John's injuries, but if the man thought that would enable his son to avoid a Greek trial and probable imprisonment in the country he would have to think again. She had nothing to lose. She could at least speak to Adam Kowalski and suggest a further negotiation.

Marianne called the American Embassy and asked to speak to Adam Kowalski. The delay before she was finally connected to him was frustrating, but it enabled her to get her thoughts in order and make some notes on the pad before her.

'Good afternoon, Adam. Yes, I have received your e-mail, that's why I'm calling. Mr John Pirenzi's lawyer is willing to accept the three hundred thousand dollars as compensation and I'll put that in writing to you. I'll draft an agreement and send it to you. If Mr Gallagher and his lawyer are happy with the wording I see no reason why it should not be signed immediately and the money transferred to the bank over here at once.'

Adam smiled, knowing full well that Marianne was acting as a lawyer for her son. 'I thought you'd be pleased.'

'I was expecting to have a fight with his lawyer. I certainly didn't expect him to agree immediately. It took me by surprise.'

'You draw up an agreement; I'll have a look at it and send it on to Mr Gallagher. Provided it's straight forward and his lawyer doesn't raise any objections we could be looking at completing the settlement within a couple of weeks.'

'There could be a problem,' Marianne frowned. 'John is still in hospital in England. We don't know yet when he will be fit enough to fly back to Crete.'

'I'm sure a fax with his signature authorising his father to sign on his behalf and countersigned by his lawyer would be acceptable.'

'I'll 'phone him and arrange it. There is, also, another option that you could put before Mr Gallagher,' continued Marianne. 'If the amount he offered was sufficient Mr Pirenzi would consider dropping the charge of arson against Mr Gallagher's son. As a lawyer, speaking on behalf of Mr Giovanni Pirenzi, I know Mr Pirenzi will be asking for an award between two and three million dollars in compensation for lost business along with the court costs. Mr Gallagher could save himself a considerable amount of money if he decided to settle that charge out of court. It could also mean his son avoided a lengthy jail sentence.'

Adam whistled through his teeth. 'Are you sure? It could mean you have to disclose the amount of income from the business for the previous year.'

'No problem at all.' Marianne spoke confidently. 'Our accounts are open to scrutiny and if the case went to court we would have to prove the amount we were claiming. I'll send you two separate mails; one accepting the compensation for John and the other a proposal to put before Mr Gallagher.'

'I have been asked to put another proposal forward to you, Mr Gallagher. I understand that Mr Giovanni Pirenzi would consider an out of court settlement for compensation for his ruined business.'

'I'm sure Todd will be found innocent, or not responsible for his actions at the time.'

'Mr Gallagher, having read your son's diary it shows quite clearly that the act of arson he committed on Mr Pirenzi's property was premeditated and he also admitted liability when he was arrested. The psychologists can find nothing at present to indicate that he was suffering from a psychological condition at the time or that he acted on impulse. I think it is highly unlikely that your son will be declared incompetent and unanswerable for his actions. If they are given access to his diary from the previous years that might influence their decision. Those entries indicate that he had sexual problems from quite an early age.'

'The earlier entries are those of a boy and an immature young man. They have no relevance.'

'That decision may not be in your hands when the case does go to court. I'm sure the entries he made as a boy would be disregarded, put down as the wild imagination of a pubescent youth, but those, shall we say for the previous two years, could be illuminating. I'm sure a good defence lawyer would claim that the more recent entries shed light on the stress he was suffering due to the death of his girl friend and the pressure of University; that he was in a confused state of mind and incapable of reasoning logically at the time. They would not be grounds to section him, but could be classed as mitigating circumstances.'

'Is there no way to invoke a privacy law to prevent that?'

'That would be suppressing evidence.'

'I don't want my son spending years in a Greek jail and nor do I want to get embroiled in a court case that drags on for months.' Abraham was not prepared to admit that he did not want the details from his son's diary revealed. It was perfectly clear that Todd had planned exactly how he was going to set fire to the chalets. He was also concerned that the New Orleans authorities could re-examine the cause of Jennie-Lea's death and the details of the shooting at the diner should they become aware of the diary.

'As things stand at the moment I don't see how it can be avoided. Personally I feel it would be far better for you to offer to settle with Mr Pirenzi out of court. It could be to your advantage. You could find the final amount of a court case far outweighs any compensation figure that was claimed at the moment.'

'I'd be admitting my son was responsible.'

'Mr Gallagher, your son is responsible. He has admitted as much. Due to his actions Mr Pirenzi's business has been ruined. Assuming a court judgement went in favour of Mr Pirenzi, as in my opinion is inevitable, you would be liable for the costs involved and the court would be bound to grant compensation.'

'What figure do they have in mind?' Abraham licked his dry lips.

'The lawyer mentioned a figure of two million dollars. I was only asked to put the suggestion to you. A complete breakdown of the income they would have expected to receive during the remainder of the season and any other expenses that were incurred could be provided if you think the sum is excessive. Mr Pirenzi had to compensate the visitors who were staying there at the time of the incident and pay for alternative accommodation for them.'

'Wasn't he insured?'

'He was insured for the buildings, but not for loss of income or visitors' personal possessions. I could be wrong, but I would estimate you could be looking at three million dollars and expenses if it goes through the courts.'

Adam Gallagher felt the sweat beading his forehead. He had nowhere near that amount of money available. He was extremely wealthy, but most of his collateral was in the bank he owned and long term investments.

'Is there any way I could stop them from bringing the court cases?'

'Not unless your son was certified and as I have told you already that is most unlikely.'

'If, and I'm only speculating now,' Abraham hastened to add,

'I offered them one and a half million dollars as compensation for their ruined business would they be willing to drop the arson charges against my son?'

'I'm not able to answer that without referring to their lawyer. I'm sure they would be only too pleased to avoid a court case that could drag on for months or even longer. Do you want me to make them an offer?'

Abraham Gallagher frowned. 'If they agree to one and half million they would have to give me an assurance that they would drop all charges against my son and I would also want Todd back on American soil.'

'Assuming your proposal was acceptable to them and they withdrew the charge the Greek police would have no reason to keep your son in custody. He would be persona non grata in Greece and as such refused entry to the country ever again, but apart from that he would be free to return to the States.'

'I'll speak to my lawyer and get back to you.'

'And in the meantime, as the settlement you have offered and the conditions are acceptable for Mr John Pirenzi's compensation I have asked his lawyer to draw up a draft agreement. As soon as I receive it I will send a copy through to you and you could run that past your lawyer at the same time to make sure all is in order.'

'How do I know I can trust them? Once they had their hands on the money they could retract.'

'I would not expect them to do that. They are an old and respected family. As a safeguard the money could be paid into an Embassy holding account. They would know the funds were safe and could not be withdrawn by you so they would have no reason not to keep to the terms of the agreement.'

Giovanni looked at Marianne in disbelief. 'He's going to pay three hundred thousand if John drops his case for compensation against his son? Didn't he try to bargain? What's wrong with the man?'

'That's right.' Marianne smiled triumphantly. 'I've accepted it and I have to get John to send a fax to Adam authorising us to sign the agreement on his behalf as he's in England. I've also asked for an out of court compensation settlement for our business losses. In return we agree to drop the charge of deliberate arson.'

'I don't know about that,' frowned Giovanni. 'The man's a criminal.'

Marianne shrugged. 'I agree, but a court case could go on for years. No doubt his defence lawyers would keep coming up with reasons to delay the trial. Better for us to take a settlement now. Provided he's deported from Greece I really don't mind if he's in jail or allowed his freedom in the States.'

'How much should we ask for?'

'I've told Adam Kowalski that you'll be asking him for two million dollars and you would expect the court to award you three.'

Giovanni gasped. 'That much? He'll never agree.'

'It depends how desperate he is for his son to avoid being put on trial. Think about it, Giovanni. We lost the remainder of our summer bookings – nine weeks – we lost about six hundred and fifty thousand Euros. We had to pay hotel bills for the visitors who were here at the time and compensate them for the loss of their belongings. Our reputation for reliability and service was damaged with the travel agents. We're struggling to get that back. I'm willing to negotiate down to one and a half million. It's not an unreasonable sum and I'm sure the courts would award you double that amount and he'd have to pay the costs of the case.'

'Suppose we have to produce our accounts to prove we lost that amount? I don't want to give him the accounts I show to my accountant.'

'I'm sure you and Marcus can work on those if necessary,' smiled Marianne. 'Vasi will always produce bills for the accommodation he provided. We just give him the names of the visitors and how long they were supposed to be staying with us. Even if they went elsewhere he can say they stayed at one of his hotels.'

'Suppose Gallagher's lawyer decided to check up and found the people hadn't stayed with Vasi?'

'A mistake. There was so much confusion at the time that mistakes were bound to be made. Trust me, Giovanni. This man is trying to hide something in relation to his son and he's willing to pay to keep that information away from the authorities. He's not likely to start prying into the accounts for the sake of a hundred dollars or so.'

Abraham Gallagher read through the agreements he had been sent by Adam Kowalski. There was a copy of a fax from John Pirenzi accepting the compensation and authorising his lawyer to sign any necessary papers on his behalf whilst he was undergoing hospital treatment. Also enclosed were the details of the American Embassy's international bank account. The monies would sit there until the agreements had been signed by all parties and then transferred to the relevant bank account in Crete. There was no mention of a date for Todd's release and return to the States.

Abraham checked the time and realised he would have to wait at least another couple of hours for the American Embassy in Athens to open and he could speak to Adam Kowalski. Before he agreed to pay two million dollars he wanted to know a definite date when his son would be freed from custody and also have that information in writing.

'Well, Mr Gallagher, the release date for your son really depends upon you. Once the money has been deposited into the Embassy's account Mr Pirenzi will be agreeable to drop the charges. Your son will be released into your custody and you will be responsible for his departure from Greece.'

'Me?'

'Yes, Mr Gallagher. Someone has to escort him to the airport and ensure he boards his flight.'

'Surely that would be the responsibility of the police?'

'Once your son has been released from custody the police will have no further interest in him. He will have to report to the Greek Embassy in Heraklion. His passport will be stamped with the date by which he is to leave the country and the information that he is to be refused admittance at any subsequent time in the future. Unfortunately I don't feel he can be trusted to do that voluntarily.'

'It isn't convenient for me to travel to Greece again at the moment,' protested Abraham.

'I'm sure we can make arrangements so that your son stays in prison until such time as you are able to make the journey.'

'An innocent man should not have to spend time in jail.'

'Mr Gallagher, your son is not innocent. He committed a very serious crime and he should be very thankful that you have been willing to negotiate for his release. I suggest you contact me again when you have a suitable date for your journey and I will ensure the relevant papers are sent to the Embassy in Crete and also to the police. Now, you will have to excuse me. I have a call coming in on my other line and an appointment waiting.' Adam cut short any further protests by Abraham Gallagher by curtailing the conversation.

John punched the air as he looked over Saffron's shoulder at the computer. 'Yes. Going home at last. You don't think there'll be any problems, do you?'

'Such as?'

'Not giving us our tickets or boarding passes; bad weather delaying the flight or another accident.'

'They have no reason to refuse to give us our tickets. I've paid for them and they've accepted my money. The weather forecast here is good and there is no reason to think there might be another car accident. If there is, just make sure you're sitting well back in your seat, not bending over to get something from your bag.'

John smiled sheepishly. 'I know, I'm just being neurotic. I promise I will sit quite still all the way to the airport. If I'd done as I was told by the nurse and stayed sitting down when Nick had the girls I wouldn't have hit my head again.'

'In retrospect it was probably a good thing. Your operation could have been a good deal more complicated in a few years' time. That piece of bone would have continued to grow. Banging your head and dislodging it a bit more simply speeded up the inevitable. Maybe you should wear a crash helmet if you're going to make a habit of banging your head.'

'I didn't intend to bang it in the first place,' replied John indignantly. 'There is one thing, though. I'll wear my crash helmet when I ride the bike and not hang it on the handle bars anymore.'

'I'm glad to hear it. Maybe some sense has been knocked into you.'

'I'll make sure Nick wears hers as well.'

Saffron looked at her nephew in concern. 'John, will you promise me something?'

'Saff, for you, anything.'

'It's not really for me. I want you to promise that when the girls are older you'll not take them on the bike standing in front of you as many parents do. That is so dangerous. If they fell or you had an accident they are so vulnerable.'

'I wouldn't drive into Aghios Nikolaos with them, but there's no problem if I'm just taking them along the road to school in Elounda.'

Saffron shook her head. 'I'm serious. I want a promise, John. Even to take them from the house to the end of the drive is dangerous. You were sitting innocently in a taxi when your accident happened, remember. Think of the awful injuries they could receive if they fell off your bike; they could even be killed.'

John's face blanched at the thought. 'Don't even think anything so awful.'

'Then promise me, John, and keep your promise.'

John sighed. 'Alright, Saff, I promise. I'll make everyone else promise as well.'

'And whilst we're on the subject of safety, if you or anyone else plans to take them out in the car they must have their own safety seats. I know it's expensive and you have to keep getting larger ones as they grow, but it's worth it to keep them as safe as possible.'

John smiled. 'That compensation money I've been awarded; I'm planning to put a hundred thousand into bank accounts for each of the girls. Each time they need a larger car seat I'll charge them. That's pretty fair, isn't it?'

'If you take the money from their account each time they need a new pair of shoes or the next size in clothes they'll soon have nothing left,' remarked Saffron dryly. 'What are you planning to do with the rest of it?'

'Pay Dad back, of course, for the operation, and then pay for us to have a have that large family party we've spoken about. I can't expect Dad to foot the bill for that after all he's done for us. Then I want to take Nick and the girls to New Orleans the following year.'

'You talk as if you're a millionaire. The money will soon go if you're not careful. You ought to invest as much as possible.'

John shrugged. 'I'll be working for Dad at the taverna. What about you? You're used to working and having a large salary at the end of each month. Are you happy to spend your time trotting around after Vasi?'

'I am at the moment. I have some ideas for next season.'

'I'm sure you could help at the taverna.'

'There's enough of you there and I've never done that sort of work.'

John frowned. 'I'm not sure I want to run a taverna for the rest of my life. I'm hoping I'll be able to take decent photographs again.'

'What will you do with them? Sell them?'

'I'd try National Geographic first or a wildlife magazine to see if I could get a regular assignment with them.'

'You could try selling them to tourists.'

'That would mean having to have somewhere to display them and the general store isn't really suitable for art work. You need a shop.'

'So why don't you use one of the new ones that your father has built?' suggested Saffron.

'I wouldn't want to be cooped up in a shop from morning 'til night. I wouldn't have the time to take the photographs. At least at the taverna I have plenty of time to myself during the day to do as I please.'

Saffron frowned and fell silent. Should she confide her idea to John?

'John,' she said eventually, 'If you wanted to display your photos and sell them you would need a shop that sold other things to bring in the customers. Suppose there was a shop selling quality items like Uncle Yannis sells, not the usual tourist souvenirs, do you think it would be successful?'

'I don't see why not. Why? Are you thinking of opening one?'

Saffron nodded. 'I could be. I've been thinking about it whilst we were in England."

John raised his eyebrows. 'Tell me more. What has given you that idea?'

'I suppose it was when I was driving around the villages. There's always a shop where you can buy local hand made goods, pottery, something embroidered, T-shirts with slogans, but there's nothing of real quality. I didn't see anything I would have wanted to take back for Marjorie.'

'So what kind of souvenirs are you thinking of?'

'Well, your photos for a start; you could have a variety showing Spinalonga, some of the churches, the market, sunset, the fishermen.' Saffron shrugged. 'There's no end to the list of possible subjects. They'd have to be properly framed, of course.'

John nodded. 'You'd need more than just photos to make money from a shop.'

'I know that. I'd want silk scarves, silk ties, some evening blouses that had been hand embroidered, not done by machine. Maybe some jewellery, I'm not talking about the really expensive items like they sell in a jeweller's shop, but in the hundred euro range.'

'You can buy those things in Aghios Nikolaos.'

'Yes, but you can't buy them in Elounda or Plaka. Visitors come to see Spinalonga and they wander around the area for a while, get back on their coach and return to Heraklion. We want to encourage them to spend their money with us.'

'Have you spoken to Vasi about opening a shop?'

'Not yet,' smiled Saffron. 'I thought I'd wait until we were home to talk about it. I'll need to ask your father if I can rent one of his shops and also to Uncle Yannis and Aunt Ourania. I wouldn't try to sell the same goods as they do, but I'm sure they would know the suppliers I would need to contact. I've crossed perfume, alcohol and cigarettes off my list. They would probably buy those at a discount at the airport, but I need to think of something that would bring people in. Once shoppers start to browse around they nearly always see something they decide to buy.'

Week 3 – July 2009

Todd lay in his bed in the hotel room listening to his father snoring loudly. His father had lectured him on the foolishness of keeping a diary and had made him swear to erase it from his computer and never write one again. He was relieved that he was no longer incarcerated in the prison at Heraklion, conditions there had been more unpleasant than in Aghios Nikolaos, but he was irked by the restrictions that his father had put upon him. He was being treated like a little boy.

He was to leave Crete and return to America immediately with his father. Once there he was to live with his parents again and would be given a junior position in his father's bank. He would have to prove his worth before he was given any form of promotion. He would not receive a salary, but his father would give him a monthly allowance and he would have to account for every cent. There would be no car available to him and he would have to ask permission before going out to meet friends at the weekends or during the evening.

Already he was planning to continue to write a diary. It would have to be in notebooks hidden away, but he needed his diary to be able to express his thoughts and feelings. To have to leave Crete immediately was the worst punishment his father could have inflicted on him. Todd had pleaded with him to allow him to make one last visit to see Nicola. He could not leave Crete without seeing her and making a final attempt to persuade her to return to America with him. Somehow he had to evade his father the following day and he knew his father would be loath to let him out of his sight.

Quietly Todd slipped off his bed. If his father woke he would have to make the excuse of needing the bathroom. His holdall was packed, but he needed to ensure all he needed for tomorrow was on the top of his rucksack and within quick and easy reach. It was annoying that the embassy had stamped his passport with his exit date and his father had locked it in his case. Had it been in his possession he might have been able take a ferry to one of the islands and return to Crete at a later date, pleading ignorance if he was refused entry.

As his father snored he unzipped the bag, holding his breath, and waited for another snore to be emitted before he dared to place his hand inside. He felt around carefully and drew out a pair of jeans, a cap and a red T-shirt. He folded them carefully and placed them on the top of his belongings in his rucksack. His father's wallet was lying on the bedside table and Todd had seen earlier the quantity of one hundred dollar notes he was carrying. He would not miss some of those until he was back in the States. Keeping a careful eye on his father he pulled out most of the notes and placed them inside the pocket of the jeans in the rucksack before refastening the straps.

When Abraham Gallagher woke he immediately looked over at the bed where his son appeared to be still asleep and drew a breath of relief. He had alerted the hotel staff that if they saw his son attempt to leave the building during the night he was to be notified immediately and the boy restrained. They had looked at him curiously when he made his request and he had explained that Todd, although appearing to be a healthy young man, had the mental age of a ten year old and would not know his way back to the hotel if allowed to wander around Heraklion on his own. Although Todd appeared biddable and reconciled to returning to the States Abraham did not feel he could fully relax until they had boarded their flight.

'Time to get up, Todd.'

Todd rolled over and blinked. Despite having spent most of the night awake going over and over his plan in his head he felt alert and clear headed.

'What time is it?' he asked.

'Seven thirty. Plenty of time for us to shower and have breakfast before we leave for the airport. I've ordered a taxi for nine thirty. I've been assured it's no more than a fifteen minute drive so we'll be towards the front of the queue to check in.'

'What time is the flight?' he asked.

'Eleven fifty.'

Todd nodded. He knew precisely the time the flight was due to leave. 'I'll get ready then.'

He left the bathroom door ajar. He had no intention of showering. He wanted to make sure his father did not inspect his rucksack whilst he was out of the bedroom. He shaved carefully and washed his face before pulling the shower curtain across and turning on the water. He placed the shower head into the base and stood and watched his father from behind the slightly open door.

Abraham allowed himself the luxury of a few more minutes in bed before stretching and placing his feet on the cold marble floor. He unlocked his case, removed their passports and placed them in the pocket of the jacket he planned to wear. He pulled his clean underwear from his case, took his slacks and shirt from the wardrobe where he had hung them the night before and waited for Todd to emerge from the bathroom.

Todd turned off the water and mopped some of it up with a bath towel that he tied around his waist. He pulled the curtain back noisily and stepped back into the bedroom clutching his toiletries.

'All yours. I've tried not to make a mess, but the shower's quite small.'

Abraham nodded. He picked up his jacket and walked into the bathroom with it. He closed and locked the door. Silently Todd cursed. There had been no need for him to get up in the night to move some clothes into his back pack, but there had been no guarantee that his father would not have left the bathroom door wide open. He took the opportunity to check the amount of money he had placed in the pocket of his jeans and felt satisfied when he saw that he had eight hundred dollars. That would be sufficient.

He placed a flannel and deodorant into a pocket of his rucksack hoping he would be able to freshen up a little later and the other toiletries he placed in his holdall. By the time his father exited the bathroom Todd was dressed in a pair of fawn slacks and a white T-shirt.

'Will you be warm enough without a jacket?'

'I've a jumper in my rucksack.'

'May as well go down then if you're ready.'

Todd picked up his holdall and slung his rucksack over one shoulder. He was not at all sure he would be able to eat any breakfast due to the way his stomach was churning.

To Abraham Gallagher's annoyance and Todd's delight they were not the first to arrive at the airport. A coach party were milling around in the entrance, claiming their luggage and being directed towards the correct check in. The company representative held them back at the door.

'If you can just let this party through, sir. They're running a little late for check in.'

'Can you tell me which desk I need?' asked Abraham. 'We're on the eleven fifty to Heathrow.'

She shook her head. 'I'm sorry. You'll have to look at the departure displays.' She turned back to the party of tourists who were her responsibility. 'Yes, sir. You will need your passport. If you have packed it in your case please get it out now.'

Abraham waited until she was speaking again to the group who could not find their passports, touched Todd on the arm and signalled him to move inside the airport building with the other travellers. Abraham studied the departure information and wished people would stop pushing him.

'Desk twelve,' said Todd and pointed to where there was already a queue of people.

'Are you sure?'

'Certain. Follow me.' Todd began to elbow his way through towards the check in desk that suited his purpose. He dumped his holdall on the ground and looked around. The Gents' toilet was a short distance away and only a few yards from some kiosks and an exit.

Abraham looked at the milling throng of people. 'We'll miss our flight at this rate.'

Todd shook his head. 'They're not actually open yet. They know how much time they need to get everyone boarded. Don't fuss.'

Abraham looked at his son, who seemed very calm and reconciled to leaving the country. No doubt he was relieved to be out of jail and on his way home rather than facing a long sentence. Todd bent over and clutched at his stomach.

'I've got to get to a toilet,' he announced.

'I'll come with you.'

'There's no point in losing our place in the queue. They're just opening up. I'll be back as soon as I can.'

Abraham hesitated. Todd was not a little boy to be escorted to the toilet. 'You can leave your bags with me.'

'I'll take my rucksack. I might need a fresh pair of shorts.' Todd clutched his stomach again. 'I must move,' he announced and began to push his way through the passengers.

Todd entered a cubicle and immediately removed his trainers, followed by his slacks. From his rucksack he took his jeans and the T-shirt and cap. Within minutes he was ready to return to the departure hall, but looking very different. He placed his sunglasses on, checked the dollars were safely in the pocket of his jeans, picked up his rucksack and walked out of the cubicle. He hesitated at the doorway. There were plenty of people around and with his change of clothing he doubted if his father would notice him amongst them.

He walked swiftly to the exit and once outside hurried across to where the coaches sat awaiting the new arrivals.

'Where's the taxi rank?' he asked and the coach driver pointed to the other side of the car park. Without stopping to thank him Todd sprinted across the tarmac and threw himself into the first taxi in the row.

'Elounda,' he gasped and ducked his head down as if dealing with his rucksack. 'I'm in a hurry. Quick as you can.' Whilst in prison he had learnt a rudimentary amount of Greek.

The driver shrugged. 'I need a full taxi.'

'No, I need to leave now. I'll pay double.'

The driver shrugged again. If the man was willing to double the fare he had nothing to lose. He placed the taxi into gear and began to draw away.

As they left the airport behind them Todd sat back and relaxed, a pleased smile on his face. It would be a while before his father left the queue and went in search of him. When he realised Todd had given him the slip he would no doubt guess he had gone down to Elounda, but by the time he had tracked him down he would have seen Nicola. If she could be persuaded to return to New Orleans with him he knew his father would not refuse to pay her fare.

Abraham Gallagher looked at his watch. Todd had only been gone just over five minutes. Not long if the boy had an upset stomach and had needed a change of underwear. The queue moved forward and Abraham pushed his case forwards. He could always get the luggage booked in and then go in search of Todd.

Abraham looked at his watch again. It was nearly a quarter of an hour since Todd had left. Had the boy really been taken ill or was he wandering around the kiosks before rejoining the queue? He looked around trying to see him amongst all the other young men.

'Please put up your case.'

'Oh, yes, sorry.' Abraham lifted his case onto the scale and had a sticky label placed around the handle.

'Ticket.'

He dug into his pocket and produced his own and Todd's ticket.

'Where are you travelling to?'

'England. Heathrow.'

'Wrong check in. You need check in five.' The man ripped the sticky tape off the handle of the case.

'No, I was told to come to this one.'

'Check in five. Next.'

Abraham moved out of the way. He had taken Todd's word for it that they were in the correct place. He squinted up at the departure notice. The Heathrow flight due to take off at eleven fifty was clearly marked as check in five. Had Todd realised the mistake and gone to the other end of the airport to meet his father? It was most unlikely. Hampered by the case and Todd's holdall Abraham began to make his way over to the Gents' toilet. He stood just inside and called.

'Todd. Todd, are you there? Are you all right?'

There was no answer. Abraham banged on a cubicle door. 'Todd are you in there?'

Someone answered him in a language he did not understand and he banged on the next one. It opened and a man emerged looking at him suspiciously. Abraham stood and looked at the other cubicles. He was certain Todd was not in any of them. The boy had gone off somewhere.

Abraham sighed. Should he continue to search for his son or go to check in five and rely on Todd joining him there? Dragging his case behind him and carrying Todd's holdall he returned to the departure lounge. There were less people around now and he stood and looked around anxiously. Two security men stood chatting together over by the entrance and he pushed his way over to them.

'Have you seen my son?'

'Son? Boy lost?' The security man pulled his walkie-talkie off his belt. 'How big?' A child separated from their parents was always a concern.

'Six foot near enough. He's wearing fawn slacks and a white T-shirt.'

The security man frowned. 'How many years?'

'Twenty three.'

'Twenty three?' The security guard checked he had heard correctly and Abraham nodded.

'Not little boy?' He tapped his forehead. 'Problem?'

'No, he said he needed the toilet about half an hour ago. I waited in the check in queue and he hasn't come back. I've checked the toilets and he's not there.'

'Moment.' The guard looked around and saw a girl carrying a clip board with the name of the travel company on it. He touched her arm. 'Please. Moment. Help.'

She looked at Abraham and smiled. 'Is there a problem, sir?'

'My son has gone missing. He said he needed the toilet and he hasn't returned.'

'How old is he?'

'He's not a little boy, but I need to get us checked in or we'll miss our flight.'

'Have you looked in the toilets?'

'He's not in there.'

'What about the shops? He may have gone to buy something to read or a bottle of water.'

'I've looked. He's not there.'

'I'm sure he won't have gone very far; maybe outside for a cigarette?'

'He doesn't smoke.'

'Don't worry, sir. I'm sure he's around somewhere and you just haven't seen each other. I'll ask for a call to be put out requesting that he meets you at the car hire desk. There aren't many people around there so you should spot each other easily.'

With a bright smile she whisked away and Abraham dragged himself over to the car hire desk she had indicated. He stood there scanning the passengers, becoming more convinced as each moment passed that somehow Todd had given him the slip, but where had the boy gone?

Twenty minutes later, despite announcements having been made there was no sign of Todd. Abraham sighed. The boy had been released into his custody, with the assurance that he would be responsible for taking him back to America. Now that Todd had disappeared he would be in trouble with the police. He pulled his mobile from his pocket and searched for the number of the American Embassy. As soon as it was answered he gave his name and asked to speak to Adam Kowalski, impressing upon the receptionist the urgency of his call.

'What's the problem, Mr Gallagher? The paper work for your son is all in order.'

'He's disappeared.'

'Disappeared?' Adam frowned. 'What do you mean? He's disappeared?'

'I'm at Heraklion airport,' Abraham Gallagher tried to speak calmly. 'We were queuing to check in our luggage and he said he needed the toilet. He didn't come back. There's no sign of him and he's not responded to the messages that have been put out.'

'What!' Adam was aghast. 'Are you sure he isn't in the airport? There are a lot of places where he could hide in there.'

'I've looked everywhere I can think of.'

'Have you still got his passport?'

'Yes.'

Adam gave a sigh of relief. At least the boy wouldn't be able to get very far without that, particularly with his exit date from the country clearly stamped inside. 'Stay where you are Mr Gallagher and leave it with me. I'm sure we'll soon locate him.'

Adam picked up his outside extension 'phone and dialled the

number for the controller of Heraklion airport. 'I need a search made of the airport. A young man who was being deported to America has disappeared. I think he's probably trying to avoid being put on the flight.'

He listened to the disgruntled voice of the airport controller.

'Yes, I realise you may have to shut the airport down for a while. I can't help that. This man needs to be apprehended. He could be dangerous. His father is waiting by the car hire desk. He should be able to give you a full description. Yes, I know it's unorthodox not to have a police escort, but the criminal charges against him had been dropped. You put the procedure in place and I'll call you back immediately if he turns up.'

Adam did not truly believe that Todd was dangerous, but he did not want to have to spend time explaining the circumstances to the controller and then have his request for a full search turned down. He tapped his teeth with his pen. There was always a chance the young man was making for the Elounda area to try to make contact with the girl again.

'Eva, get me the police station in Aghios Nikolaos, Crete. Yes, Crete. Quick as you can.'

The voice that answered him sounded sleepy. 'Inspector Christos here. What can I do for you?'

'Adam Kowalski here from the American Embassy. Remember that fire at the holiday chalets last year? The man responsible was being deported today. He's absconded from the airport and we believe he's going to the owner's house. He needs to be apprehended.'

'Where does the owner live?'

'That big house between Elounda and Plaka. The name's Pirenzi.'

'Oh, you mean Yannis Christoforakis's place. I know it.'

'Get there as soon as you can and stay there until he's been located.'

Christos was about to argue that he could not spend the rest of the day down at the house in case the young man turned up as the 'phone went dead. He picked up his cap. 'Antionis, you'd better come with me.'

The passengers in the airport looked at each other in consternation as the message in various languages was relayed to them over the loud speakers and security staff began to usher the women and children to one end of the terminal building and requesting that all the men went to the other end.

'What's happening? Is it a bomb scare?' asked a woman who was heavily pregnant and had two small children by the hand.

'No madam. It is a young man who is trying to avoid deportation. Come with me and I'll find you a seat. I'm sure the security check will be carried out very swiftly and your husband will be back with you.'

'You're sure there isn't a bomb?'

'Quite sure. If that danger had arisen the terminal would have been cleared.'

The women, along with their young children, had been shepherded to the left end of the terminal and the men kept apart on the right. The rope aisles to the check in desks had been moved to enable a long line of men to form. Standing at the head were two security officers and Abraham Gallagher.

At first Abraham had protested at having to accompany them, thinking he was being arrested. The security officer sighed.

'We have no reason to arrest you, sir. If you stand at the head of the line with us you are likely to recognise your son immediately and the other passengers can then proceed with their business normally.'

Abraham sighed. What had Todd been thinking he would gain by disappearing at the airport? As the men reached the front of the line Abraham shook his head and the security officer did not attempt to check their passports. The swifter the line moved through the quicker the airport could get back to normal. Every so often his walkie-talkie crackled into life reporting that another area, off limits to passengers, had been searched and found to be clear of any intruder.

'Nearly home,' smiled John as the 'fasten seat belts' sign flashed up. 'As soon as we're allowed I'll call Nick and tell her we've landed. Vasi will be there waiting for us, won't he?'

'Of course. You can rely on Vasi. I told him the number of our flight and the time of arrival. He's sure to be there.'

John settled back. 'I'll feel so much better when I'm home.'

'Does your face or head hurt?' asked Saffron anxiously.

'Not a bit. Doctor Gharcia is amazing. You can't even see where he put the plate in my forehead as he made the incision just above my hair line My hair's a bit short where it's growing back, but that won't notice in another month or so. I've told him if he and his family want to come to Crete for a holiday they only have to pay for their flights. Everything else will be at our expense.'

'Did he say they would come?'

'He said he would talk to his wife and think about it for next Easter. They're already booked this year for a fortnight in Spain just before their children go back to school.'

'I thought you and Nicola wanted to arrange a big family party next Easter so all your American relatives can come over.'

John shrugged. 'That's no problem. They can join it.'

Saffron raised her eyebrows. She had an idea this party was going to end up costing John far more than he envisioned. She swallowed hard to try to clear the pressure in her ears as the 'plane descended and felt the familiar bump as the wheels touched the tarmac. She looked at John, but he seemed to be totally unconcerned as he looked out of the cabin window as they taxied to a halt. He undid his seat belt and stood up.

'Let's go.'

'There's no point in trying to be the first person off. They haven't put the steps up yet and you'll have to wait for the bus.'

The captain spoke from the cockpit. 'Ladies and gentlemen, please remain seated. Unfortunately the airport is not ready to receive us yet and all passengers have to stay on board. Hopefully the delay will be minimal and we apologise for any inconvenience this may cause. Rest assured that if you have transport booked to take you on to your accommodation it will wait for you. May I remind you that you are unable to use your mobile 'phones until you have disembarked.'

John groaned and sat back down in his seat.

Vasi waited in the queue of cars that wanted to enter the car park. There seemed to be a tremendous number of coaches around and none of them were unloading their passengers or the luggage. He finally found a parking space and walked up to the entrance of the airport. He was surprised when the automatic doors did not open for him and a security guard waved him away.

'What's going on?' he asked a man who was standing nearby.

The man shrugged. 'No idea. Must be a bomb scare. They're not letting anyone in or out.'

'Bomb scare!' Vasi was horrified. By now Saffron and John should have landed and could be in danger inside the airport. 'I need to find out if my fiancé is safe.'

Vasi banged on the glass of the entrance door and the security guard waved him away. Vasi continued to bang until the guard finally opened the door a crack.

'You can't come in. The airport is closed.'

'Just tell me what's happening. My fiancé is in there. Is it a bomb scare?'

'The premises are being searched for an illegal immigrant. There's no danger.'

Vasi felt limp with relief and before he could ask for any more details the door was closed again. He looked back at the man who had suggested the closure was due to a bomb scare and shook his head. 'They're searching the airport for someone who's arrived illegally. There isn't a bomb. Any idea how long they've been closed down?'

'I've been here about half an hour. It will be chaos when they open up again.'

Vasi nodded understandingly. The schedules for the outgoing flights would have been delayed and those due to arrive could well have been diverted elsewhere. For all he knew Saffron and John could be sitting at the airport in Athens. He pulled out his mobile 'phone and tried calling their numbers. In both cases their 'phones were switched off.

He tapped in the number for his father, sighing with frustration when he was told that 'phone was also switched off. Of course, his father was at the hospital for an appointment to discuss his prostate condition and no doubt Cathy was with him and her 'phone would also be off. He hesitated, should he return to the Central and look for details of John and Saffron's flight on the computer or should he call Dimitra and ask her to look for any information?

Nicola laid her babies in their buggy and fastened a cat net securely over them. Ourania's cat eyed her balefully and there were always stray cats around. She was not prepared for one of them to get in the buggy with the girls. She pushed the buggy around to the patio outside the kitchen and parked them in the shade where she could keep an eye on them whilst she helped Marianne in the kitchen.

'Your Pappa is coming home today,' she told them. 'That's exciting, isn't it? We haven't seen him for almost six weeks. You'll have to show him your beautiful smiles. You can lie there in just your diapers until you've had your lunch, then we'll have to put one of your new dresses on to make you look 'specially pretty. I shall want you to be very good for me this afternoon. No soiling your diapers as soon as your Pappa says hello. I want you to be all clean and sweet smelling for him. Have a little sleep now or you'll be grouchy this afternoon.'

Nicola pushed the buggy backwards and forwards gently,

pleased to see their eyes were already closing. She wished she could lie down and go to sleep for a couple of hours also. Bryony was no longer able to look after them during the morning as she had to spend the time up at the taverna cooking and attending to the shop. Whilst her babies slept after lunch she was often able to have a short siesta but today was different. She had promised Marianne that she would help her prepare the food for their evening meal; it was going to be a big family meal, with Saffron and Vasi there to celebrate John's return.

She applied the brake to the buggy and turned to go into the kitchen. She would start to make the dolmades, it was time consuming rolling the leaves around the meat; then she would prepare the mixture for the keftedes before dicing the chicken and placing it on the kebab sticks along with the peppers and onions. She wanted to get all the preparation done during the morning so she could leave the cooking to Marianne without feeling guilty. John should be home by three and she wanted to be able to spend some time exclusively with him.

'Nicola!' She heard her name spoken softly and spun round. Her eyes widened in horror a she saw Todd standing there. How long had he been watching her? Instinctively she stood in front of the buggy, shielding her babies from his view.

Her hand went to her throat and she swallowed rapidly. 'What – what are you doing here?' She heard her voice trembling.

Todd took a step closer and Nicola held up her hand. 'Don't you dare come near me.'

'I had to see you, Nicola. All the time I've been in jail I've thought only about you. Forget this crazy idea you have of marrying this Greek man and come back with me. I can make you happy, I know I can. You'll not want for anything.'

Nicola took a deep breath and shouted as loudly as she could. 'Marianne! Marianne! Help me!' She hoped Marianne was not closeted with her grandmother and unable to hear her.

Todd shook his head. 'There's no need for you to call anyone.

I'm not going to hurt you. I couldn't hurt you, Nicola. All I want is for you to agree to return to America with me. That's where you belong. You're American, not Greek.'

Nicola tried to keep her voice steady. 'I'm happily married.' She thrust her hand out so he could see her wedding ring. 'I don't want anything to do with you. You belong in prison for the rest of your life.'

Todd shook his head sadly. 'I only set fire to the chalets so you would come back to America with me. Please, Nicola, forgive me for that and come away with me now.'

Nicola felt herself shaking. 'My husband was injured during that fire. He was a photographer and now he can't see properly.' Where was Marianne? Why didn't she come out to the patio?

'I truly didn't mean to hurt anyone.'

'You didn't even consider that someone could lose their life,' replied Nicola scornfully.

'Oh, I did,' Todd assured her. 'I waited until all the visitors had left. I could have done it at night, but I decided that was far too risky. People could have been trapped inside. I didn't want that to happen.'

Marianne heard Nicola's distressed call and rushed into the kitchen. Had something happened to one of the girls? She was about to go out on the patio when she saw Nicola was engaged in a conversation with a young man. There was something about the way she was standing there that made Marianne feel uncomfortable. Something was not right. She moved away from the window and pulled her mobile from her pocket. She pressed Giovanni's number and hoped he would pick up straight away.

'Yes?' she heard him say. 'Has John arrived home early?'

'Giovanni, get back to the house as quickly as you can. It's an emergency.'

'What's wrong?' Giovanni was already signalling to Marcus to return to the car.

'I don't know. There's a man here talking to Nicola. Just get here.' Marianne closed her 'phone and wished for the first time in years that she was in America; she would have had a gun at her disposal then.

Marianne stepped out on to the patio. 'Are you troubling my daughter-in-law?'

Todd shook his head. 'We're old friends. I just came to talk to her.'

'It's Todd, Marianne. The man who set fire to the chalets.' Nicola's eyes were wide with fear.

Marianne raised her eyebrows. 'Oh, is it! What have you come back here for? Are you thinking of starting another fire?'

'I needed to see Nicola. She has to come home with me.'

'Nicola is home. This is her home.'

Todd shook his head. 'No, you don't understand. She can't be happy here. She needs to be back in the States where I can look after her.'

Marianne nodded towards the house. 'Get inside, Nicola and take the girls with you.'

Nicola needed no second bidding. She released the brake on the buggy and wheeled it swiftly across the patio and into the kitchen. Now her babies were safe she felt very much braver. She could not leave Marianne out there alone to face the deranged young man. He could suddenly turn violent. She closed and locked the patio door, slipped the key into her pocket and walked back to where Marianne stood confronting Todd.

Trying not to let her voice waver Nicola looked directly at the man she disliked and had come to fear. 'Todd, listen to me. For the last time I am telling you that I am not returning to the States with you. I'm married. I'm a mother. This is my home and this is where I intend to stay. I don't know how it is that you've escaped from prison, but I'm sure the police will find you very soon.'

Todd shook his head. 'They won't be looking for me down here. They'll be looking at the airport in Heraklion.'

'I suggest you have a taxi to Aghios Nikolaos and report to the police station there. They'll give you a free ride back to Heraklion.'

'You come with me, Nicola. You can explain to them that it's all a misunderstanding. I can wait whilst you pack a bag and get your passport. My father will pay for your flight. You don't have to worry about a thing.'

Nicola shook her head in despair. 'Todd, you haven't listened to a word I said. I am NOT going back to New Orleans with you. Now, if you don't leave the premises immediately I'm going to call the police.'

'I'm a free man, Nicola. The charges have been dropped.'

Nicola's mouth set in a straight line. 'You're trespassing. This is private property.'

'I'm not doing any harm.'

'You're being a nuisance and you're harassing me.' Nicola pulled her mobile from her belt. 'I mean it, Todd. I'm calling the police.'

'Please, Nicola...' Todd reached out his hands towards her and Nicola took a step backwards. From the corner of her eye she saw Annita wheeling herself around the corner and on to the patio.

'Grandma, go back,' she called. 'Go back to your room.'

Annita took no notice but continued to propel herself forwards until she was beside Nicola.

'Who are you and what do you want?' the old lady demanded.

'I'm Todd,' he smiled naively. 'I've come to take Nicola home with me.'

'I'm not going anywhere with you,' shouted Nicola, close to tears.

Annita looked at the young man in disgust. 'Well, you just listen to me. Nicola is happily married, she has twin babies and has no intention of going anywhere at all with you. Her place is here with her family. You have no claim on her at all. I suggest you go back to wherever you came from and get on with your life.'

Todd shook his head. 'I can't. I'm her Protector and she's my

Guardian Angel. We need each other. We belong together.'

'Utter rubbish!' snorted Annita. 'You're suffering from delusions. Are you on drugs?'

'I've never taken drugs.'

'Well there's certainly something wrong with you. Are you under a psychiatrist?'

'I don't need a psychiatrist. I just need Nicola. Then my life will be complete.'

'If you haven't left these premises by the time I could to ten your life will be ended, young man.' Annita pulled a carving knife out from beside her seat and Todd looked at her warily.

'No, Grandma. Giovanni and Marcus are on their way. They'll deal with him.'

'I'd rather deal with him myself. I learnt how to fillet a fish from my father. I haven't forgotten how to do it. First you slit the belly open, then you pull out the intestines.' Annita glared at Todd and pointed the knife at him, moving her wheelchair a little closer.

Marianne could not believe that her grandmother was physically capable of attacking the man, but she also knew the old lady would be prepared to give up her own life rather than see any of her family harmed.

'Grandma, please, give me that knife. You could hurt yourself.'

With a squeal of brakes Giovanni turned into the driveway and stopped within a few feet of them.

'What's going on?' asked Giovanni.

'This is the man who fired the chalets and he's escaped from prison.' Marianne could hear her voice trembling.

Todd shook his head. 'I haven't escaped from prison. You agreed to drop the charges against me if my father paid you compensation. He's done that so I've been released.'

'We'll see what the police have to say about that.' Giovanni moved forward and took a grip on Todd's arm. 'Hold him, Marcus.'

Marcus took hold of Todd's other arm and he made no move to

resist them. 'Get inside Marianne and call the police. We'll hold him until they arrive. Nicola, take Grandma back to her room.'

Marianne stood her ground. 'I'm not leaving you alone out here with him.'

'I'm staying here,' Annita insisted.

Giovanni looked at his wife in exasperation. 'Call the police.'

'I already have. It's ringing.' Nicola's voice had an edge of desperation. 'Why don't they answer?'

'Nicola, I beg you. See reason and return to the States with me. I'm your Protector, remember, and I need you as my Guardian Angel.' Todd pleaded with her.

Nicola's lip curled in disgust. 'You are not my protector and I am no one's guardian angel. You had no right to come down here and approach me.' She still held her mobile 'phone to her ear, frustrated that the telephone in the police station was not being answered.

'I'll use mine,' said Marianne. 'There may be a fault on yours.'

'What's Grandma doing with that knife?' asked Giovanni as Marianne pressed in the numbers on her 'phone.

'Preparing vegetables,' Marianne snapped back at him as she also listened to the telephone at the police station ringing.

'No I'm not,' argued Annita. 'I'm going to slit that man's belly open if he takes one step nearer to any of us.'

Giovanni wiped the sweat off his forehead. This was a situation that could very quickly escalate and get out of hand.

'Try again in a few minutes,' suggested Marcus as Marianne shook her head, indicating that no one had answered her. 'They may be on a break.'

'They have no right to leave the station unmanned whilst they take a break,' remonstrated Marianne. 'We've been trying to contact them for at least ten minutes. I shall complain to Inspector Christos. It's probably his day off and the men are taking advantage and sitting in the back playing cards.'

'Shall we put this man in the car and take him to Aghios

Nikolaos ourselves?' suggested Giovanni.

'No.' Both Marianne and Nicola spoke at once.

'Why don't you tie him to the back and make him run behind,' suggested Annita and Marianne was forced to smile.

'We could tie him to the railings,' suggested Marcus. 'That way we wouldn't have to hold him, but we'd be able to watch him until we can contact the police.'

'Good idea,' agreed Giovanni. 'Marianne, find some rope.'

'Where am I supposed to get rope from?'

'Get some belts,' suggested Nicola. 'You can fasten the buckle end round his wrist and tie the rest to the railing.'

'You go and get them. You know what you want.' Marianne was unwilling to leave the scene. If the young man decided to fight he could probably overpower Marcus and Giovanni. She must prevent her grandmother from using the carving knife at all costs.

A car swung into the drive and parked behind Giovanni's.

'John,' cried Nicola joyfully, then realised she was mistaken as Inspector Christos appeared, followed by Antionis.

The Inspector walked swiftly down the drive, taking in the tableau before him. A young man was pinned back against the railings by two men whilst the old lady in the wheelchair was threatening the captive with a knife.

'Madam. please put that knife down,' ordered Inspector Christos.

Annita shook her head. 'Not until you've handcuffed him.'

'We shall certainly be doing that and removing him from your premises. Please put down the knife.'

'Give it to me,' Marianne urged her.

Annita hesitated, finally handing the knife to Marianne who placed it on the ground.

Inspector Christos moved forward, his hand on his holstered gun. 'I believe you are Todd Gallagher?'

Todd nodded. 'You know I am. I spent a couple of weeks in your jail.'

'I understand you were returning to the States under your father's custody today. You left the airport and decided to come down here.'

'I came to fetch Nicola. She's coming home with me.' Todd smiled as though his statement would explain the situation.

'I am not,' shouted Nicola. 'I'm staying here.'

Inspector Christos nodded to Antionis who stepped forward and seized Todd's wrists, cuffing them behind him. Marianne let out a sigh of relief and Giovanni and Marcus moved away, Marcus rubbing his hands down his trousers as if removing something dirty.

'What happens now?' asked Giovanni.

'We'll report to the Embassy that we have the suspect in custody. No doubt we'll be asked to drive him up to the airport and I imagine he'll have a police escort until he's left Greek territory.'

'Suppose he escapes again?' asked Nicola fearfully.

'That is most unlikely, miss. Once in the car he'll have ankle cuffs and when we drive him up to the airport he'll be firmly secured in the police van. An armed officer will be with him and any attempt on his behalf to escape will be dealt with appropriately.' Inspector Christos glared at Todd. 'You understand? If you try to escape you'll be shot.'

'How much longer do you think we're going to be kept sitting here?' asked John fretfully. 'Nick's going to wonder what's happened. She'll think we've met with an accident on the drive down.'

'I'm sure Vasi will have 'phoned and explained the situation,' Saffron tried to calm him.

'We should have been home by now. I wanted to spend time with Nick and the girls. Do you think Nick will like the clothes I bought for them?' asked John anxiously.

'I'm sure she will. It was clever of you to find T-shirts, jumpers and trousers with duck and chicken motifs on them.' Saffron smiled, remembering how proud John had been to find the clothes adorned with the motifs he considered appropriate for Joanna and Elisabetta. Left to his own devices he would have purchased every one the shop had in stock.

'It will be the only way I'll be able to tell them apart,' grinned John. 'Do you think I'll see a difference in them?'

'You're bound to. They will have grown whilst you've been away.'

'Nick's sent me photos, but it's hard to tell just by looking at those. I'll be able to take some decent photos again.' John smiled delightedly at the thought. 'And I'll be able to go for a proper swim. I'd hoped to be home in time to fit one in today. I've missed the sea.'

'It won't hurt you to go another day without a swim,' remarked Saffron. 'When you do go swimming remember what Doctor Gharcia said – no diving.'

John grimaced. 'It's not much fun just paddling around on the surface.'

Saffron shrugged. 'I shall just be paddling until this cast comes off. The choice is yours, but if you undo all his good work by disobeying his instructions he'll probably charge you double to put it right next time.'

'I'm a man of money now,' John announced.

Saffron shook her head. 'Not that kind of money. In fact from what you were saying to me about putting two thirds into accounts for the girls, repaying your father, paying for a big party and taking Nicola and the girls to New Orleans you've just about spent it all.'

John shrugged. 'I can always get a loan from the bank.'

Saffron sighed in exasperation. 'You can't live on loans from the bank forever.'

'Of course you can,' replied John scornfully. 'How do you think we finance our businesses over here? No one admits to having any savings or spends their own money on a project. Oh, look, something's happening. They're attaching a gangway to that aircraft up ahead of us. Maybe we'll be next.'

Vasi was frustrated. He had spent almost three hours at the airport waiting for it to reopen. This particular week was one of the busiest of the summer season and his time would have been better spent at the Central. He had called Dimitra and asked her to check if Saffron and John's flight had landed and she had eventually called him back to say it was on the runway, but was unable to give him any more information. He had tried to telephone Nicola and then Marianne to advise them of the delay, but their 'phones had been continually engaged. Giovanni had not answered his and he did not know the numbers for Marcus, Bryony or the taverna. There was nothing he could do but wait.

Abraham Gallagher had spent the time at the airport sitting miserably in a small side room. He had been offered food and drink, but asked not to leave the area. It had seemed an interminable amount of time before a police inspector had informed him that his son had been captured in Elounda and would be transported up to the airport.

'We have had to change your flight. You will need to go to Athens and wait there for a connection to Heathrow,' he was informed.

'Why? I have tickets that take me directly to Heathrow. I have to make a connection there for the States.'

The Inspector had eyed him dispassionately. 'Your son will be travelling under police escort. There are no extra seats available on the direct flights.'

'I'm sure that isn't necessary,' blustered Abraham. 'Todd is not dangerous.'

'He is a nuisance. He has caused great disruption and inconvenience to hundreds of people today. Flights have had to be cancelled and rearranged. We are not prepared for this to happen again. One of our Cretan police will escort you to Athens where an Athenian officer will take over and escort you to Heathrow. The British police will take responsibility for you from there until you reach your final destination.'

'You're treating him like a criminal!'

The Inspector shrugged and left. Abraham Gallagher would see for himself that his son was being treated like a criminal when he arrived handcuffed and with ankle restraints that he would be forced to wear until he reached the States.

John paced up and down waiting for their luggage to arrive in the terminal whilst Saffron 'phoned Vasi.

'We're just waiting for our luggage. We've been here for ages just sitting on the 'plane and we weren't allowed to use our mobiles. I'm sorry, Vasi. We should have arranged to have a taxi down to Elounda.'

'Now I know you are safely here I do not mind having had to wait. Do you want to stop at the Central for something to eat and drink before we drive down?'

Saffron smiled. 'I think if you suggested that to John he'd start walking. No, I'm sure they will have an enormous meal prepared ready for us. Do they know we've been delayed?'

'I couldn't get through to them for some time. When I finally spoke to Marianne she sounded very strange.'

'Strange? What do you mean?' asked Saffron.

'I can't explain. She didn't ask how John was after the flight or what had delayed you. She seemed not to want to speak to me and in a hurry to get off the 'phone.'

'She's probably worried that all her cooking will be spoilt. I think I can see John with our cases. It's terribly congested in here, oh, no, we're being held up again.'

'Don't worry, Saffron. It will not be for very long.'

The airport security guards had closed the doors of the arrival lounge to stop anyone leaving and they shepherded the waiting passengers in departures back towards the walls as Todd was brought through, shuffling where his feet were fettered and handcuffed to a police man on each side. Murmurs of apprehension went through the waiting crowd, none of them wishing to be on the same flight as an obviously dangerous criminal.

Abraham looked at his son in horror as he was pushed inside the room. 'What have you done?' he asked.

Todd shook his head. 'Nothing. I only went down to Elounda to speak to Nicola.'

'You were released into my custody. You had no right to sneak away. How did you get down there?'

'I took a taxi.'

Abraham looked at his son in disbelief. 'You haven't any money on you.'

'I borrowed some from your wallet whilst you were asleep last night. I'll pay you back.'

'What was the point of going down there?'

'I wanted to ask Nicola to come back with us,' replied Todd mutinously.

'You stupid, stupid boy. Why should she want to go anywhere with you after the trouble you've caused? The airport had to be closed whilst they looked for you, people have had their flights delayed and we have to fly via Athens instead of direct to Heathrow.'

'I didn't mean to cause anyone any problems at the airport. I just thought you would have to wait for me.'

Abraham glared at his son. 'Now you are here I suppose I'd better try to find out how much longer we'll be detained.'

Vasi held Saffron tightly to him. 'I'm so relieved you're safe. When I first arrived a man told me there was a bomb scare, then the security guard said they were searching for an illegal immigrant. He must be dangerous as they shut the whole airport down.'

'We just spent a frustrating few hours sitting on the 'plane. We weren't told what the problem was.' Saffron took a deep breath. 'I love the smell of Crete.'

Vasi raised his eyebrows as he lifted her case into the boot and John placed his inside the car.

'You don't notice it when you've been here a while, but all you smell when you arrive in England are traffic fumes,' explained Saffron. 'I didn't think I would miss Crete so much.' She looked at Vasi and smiled. 'I feel I have come home.'

Vasi slid behind the steering wheel, a delighted smile on his face. If Saffron felt that Crete was home that must mean she intended to stay and marry him.

John had the car door open before the vehicle had finally stopped when they drew into the driveway of Yannis's house. Not waiting for Vasi or Saffron he ran round to the patio.

'Nick, Nick, I'm home. Where is everyone?'

'Oh, John.' Nicola flung herself into his arms, tears pouring down her face. 'I was so frightened.'

'Frightened? There was no need to be frightened. We were only held up at the airport.'

Nicola gulped. 'Todd was here.'

'What!' John was aghast. 'Did he touch you? Are the girls safe?'

'The girls are fine. He wanted to take me away with him.'

'Where is he now?'

'We called the police and he's been arrested. Inspector Christos said he would be taken to the airport and under police guard. The Inspector said they would shoot him if he tried to escape'

'Pity he didn't try,' remarked Marianne as she walked from the kitchen out onto the patio, having deliberately waited so Nicola could greet John first. 'Let me look at you.' She scrutinized John's face. 'I was expecting you to be all battered and bruised, but there's hardly a mark.'

'I'm more handsome than ever.' John kissed his mother happily. 'Where's Dad?'

'Telling Uncle Yannis about this afternoon's events. Go and interrupt them. I haven't even said hello to Saffron yet.'

'I want to see my babies first.' John took hold of Nicola's hand. 'I've brought them some presents. I just hope they'll fit. I had to let the sales woman guide me on size.'

'I'm hot, sticky and dirty,' replied Saffron to Marianne's enquiry. 'We would have been here hours ago if it weren't for the incident at the airport which I now believe was due to that stupid American boy. We'd planned to deposit John and then come back later. We didn't want to spoil his home-coming.'

'You certainly wouldn't spoil it, and you'll stay now, won't you? We're so grateful to you, Saffie. Without you John would have kept quiet about his problems and they would only have got worse.'

Saffron shrugged. 'It was nothing. I just happened to know the right people. It would have helped if we'd not had the taxi accident.'

'How much longer do you need your plaster?'

'A couple of weeks. I'm used to it now. I've become quite good at using my left hand for everything. How's Grandma?'

'She's having a rest. She managed to get involved this afternoon and I think it frightened and tired her more than she is willing to admit.'

'How did that happen?'

'She walked along to the kitchen expecting to find us there. She could see we were on the patio and tried to open the door. Nicola had put the girls in the kitchen and locked the door so she had to walk back to her room and use her chair to come round. She'd realised something bad was happening and brought a carving knife out with her. She threatened to fillet that man like a piece of fish!'

'Trust Grandma.'

'That was the problem. I felt she was quite capable of carrying out her threat. She seemed rather shaken when I wheeled her back in. She kept saying, "Oh, dear, oh, dear, what have I done?" I insisted she lay on her bed and within a very short while she was asleep.'

Saffron smiled to herself. Her grandmother was a crafty old lady. She might well have feigned sleep so that Marianne would leave her alone.

Once Annita was certain Marianne had left the room she opened her eyes and raised herself into a sitting position. She picked up Elias's photograph from the bedside table and shook her head at it.

'Oh, Elias, I don't know if you would have been proud of me or horrified by my actions this afternoon. I know I used to get very cross with Anna and threaten her with all sorts of dire punishments, but I never felt violent towards her, well, not really violent. I gave her a good slap now and again. Not that it had any effect on her. She still did just as she pleased without regard for anyone else,' Annita sighed. 'This time I really was prepared to be horribly violent. I threatened that awful young man with a knife and I was quite prepared to use it. I was not going to have him hurt Marianne and I could tell that Nicola was terribly frightened.'

Annita gave a little chuckle. 'I couldn't really have filleted him. I would never have had the strength to hold him down, but I could certainly have stabbed him with that knife and done plenty of damage. I'm pleased I didn't have to, of course. Giovanni and Marcus arrived quite quickly and the police came not long after them. It's a wonder they didn't arrest me. I'm sure it's a criminal offence to threaten someone with a carving knife. I could have ended up in jail even at my age although I would have pled self defence.

'The police placed handcuffs and leg restraints on the young man before they took him away, so they must consider him to be dangerous. Apparently he was going to be taken to the airport under police guard and is being deported back to the States. It's a shame we don't still use Alcatraz or Elba, where they sent Napoleon. We could do with an island where criminals could be placed without any hope of escape. I suppose that was why they used Spinalonga for the lepers. They weren't criminals, though. I know Yannis managed to reach the mainland on a number of occasions. I wonder if anyone else did actually escape and avoided being found by the authorities? I must ask John. He seems to know more about that island than anyone else.

'I don't know why he and Saffie aren't here yet. They should have landed hours ago. I do hope they haven't missed their flight. Nicola will be devastated. She was terribly upset when they had the taxi accident and John had to return to hospital. They certainly haven't had the best start to their married life, but I'm sure they'll work their way through all their problems. We managed to and for a long time we didn't have my family to help and support us.' Annita placed Elias's photograph back on her bedside table. 'I will have just a little rest before they arrive.'

August 2009

'Uncle Yannis,' John waited whilst his elderly uncle lowered his newspaper. 'You know old Uncle Yannis wrote a book about his life on the island, do you still have it?'

'There's a copy on the bookshelf. You know that. You've read it.'

John shook his head. 'No, I mean his original notes. In the book it says his life story is based on the short stories he published and the notes he made. I'd like to see some of the material that wasn't used.'

'Why?'

'I'm always saying I know more about Spinalonga than anyone else, but do I? I really only know what I've read in Uncle Yannis's book and odd things that Aunt Anna told me. What about everything that was left out?'

Yannis frowned. 'There are some things that his wife didn't want published. She considered it was too personal and private.'

'I'm not planning to publish any of it. I'd just like to read it and find out more about the way they lived over there. They are definitely going to make a film from that book that was set on Spinalonga and I want to be able to correct them if they get their facts wrong.'

'It doesn't matter if it's authentic. It would be different if it was to be a documentary.'

Yannis dismissed the subject, but John persisted.

'In his book Uncle Yannis describes how he used his bath tub to float over to Plaka and simply says that some of the others did the same thing. Who was the first person to use his bath tub as a boat? What happened to him? Grandma asked me a little while ago if anyone reached the mainland and was never found. I didn't know the answer. It's probable that Uncle Yannis wrote about many things that occurred but then decided they were unimportant so he didn't bother to publish them. I'd like to know about everything that happened over there.'

Yannis lifted his newspaper. 'I'll think about it.'

Yannis tried to renew his concentration on the article he was reading about the Greek economy and the deepening financial crisis the country was sinking into. At least their immediate financial problems were solved. It had been a stroke of brilliance by Marianne to ask for compensation for their ruined season from the boy's father. He was surprised the man had agreed so readily; there had to be something in the boy's past that his father did not want disclosed.

Was that why John wanted to look at old Uncle Yannis's notebooks? Did he want to find out what he had not revealed about his life on the island? He had not looked at the original books that his uncle had written since he had helped Dora to get them published. He had agreed with her that no one needed to know that Yannis had fathered a child whilst a student in Heraklion; nor his deepest feelings of grief after the death of his wife and natural daughter, but what else had happened whilst he was on Spinalonga that had been suppressed?

With the making of the film that everyone seemed to be talking about there could be a ready market for a sequel. Maybe it would be a good idea to get Uncle Yannis's hand written note books out and let John read them.

If you have enjoyed reading John, you will be pleased to know that the next book – Tassos – is planned for publication in December 2013.

Read on for a 'taster' of what is to come.

TASSOS

September 2009

John had finished reading most of the notebooks that his great uncle Yannis had written after he had left Spinalonga. He was not surprised that Yannis's widow had asked for certain details not to be included in the publication of his memoirs. To have such intimate thoughts and feelings disclosed to casual readers was a violation of his privacy and John felt guilty for reading them.
In the published version of his life Yannis had glossed over his childhood and the time he had spent in Aghios Nikolaos living with his cousin, Annita and her family whilst attending the High School. In his notebooks he had described how he had disliked the work on his father's farm, preferring to search for pottery in the fields or sit and read.

Whilst living with Annita's family he was expected to go to sea at the weekends to help his uncle who was a fisherman. He confessed to being frightened of a rough sea and the night time trips his uncle made to Spinalonga to collect the smuggled goods that had been stored there, petrified that he would come face to face with one of the incarcerated inhabitants or be inadvertently stranded on the island.

His indescribable joy when he was told he had gained a scholarship to the Gymnasium in Heraklion and the relief of knowing that his teacher, Yiorgo Pavlakis would join him there and they would lodge in the same taverna. He described his journey up to Heraklion, the excitement he had felt at making the journey and also how nervous he had been when he had first arrived alone in the bustling town, as Yiorgo had missed the bus.

There were details of the friends he had made at the Gymnasium, his visit to Knossos and the discovery that the girl his teacher was enamoured of was one of the town's prostitutes; his horror and disbelief when he had been diagnosed as suffering from leprosy when he returned from a prolonged visit to his family, destroying his hopes and dreams for the future. He had contemplated returning to his family or hiding in the hills along with other outcasts who had been diagnosed, but he also knew that eventually he would be discovered. The doctor at the hospital had held out hope of a cure, so he had surreptitiously crept away from his lodgings, telling no one of his destination.

His initial meeting with Father Minos had not been documented in the published book and John found it fascinating to read about the compassion and understanding the priest had shown to his parishioners. Yannis had expressed his utter disbelief when Father Minos had joined them voluntarily on Spinalonga. How the priest had later told Yannis that he had suffered from a guilty conscience due to lack of knowledge of the fate of the leprosy patients and finally decided he had been called to Spinalonga to live amongst them.

John found Yannis's description of the conditions endured in the hospital in Athens unbelievable and was not surprised the patients had demanded better conditions. That their requests should have been met by being forcibly placed in strait jackets and sent to Spinalonga to fend for themselves was inhuman.

Yannis had described in detail the conditions he had found on the island when he first arrived. All the houses that were habitable were already occupied, with people using the churches and the tunnels for shelter from the burning summer sun and the freezing rain and cold winds in the winter. His determination to make life bearable for himself and the others shone through as he related how he had cajoled and threatened until, with his friend Spiro's help, he had organised the rebuilding and repair of the buildings.

Although John knew this had taken place he had never fully appreciated the amount of work that had been necessary and how they had begged the boatmen who delivered their supplies of food and water for materials.

Doctor Stavros had made a difference to their well being when he began to make regular visits offering rudimentary treatment and basic medication. With the pension Yiorgo Pavlakis had arranged with the government came a modicum of independence and pride and Yannis had described the various trades and occupations the islanders became involved with.

Their suffering during the war was unimaginable, and on every page of the notebook, covering the second year of deprivation until Crete was liberated, were the names of those who had succumbed to starvation. John had tears in his eyes as he read of the death of Yannis's wife. It was no wonder that after his daughter also died that he took to drinking.

There was a gap in Yannis's writing then, no doubt he had little memory of events that took place during his dependence on alcohol. There was so much he had wished to forget. When the notebooks continued he described the improvements the government implemented, but his greatest joy was finally being able to receive visits from his family.

The wedding of John's grandmother, Marisa, was described in detail and John wondered if she would like him to read it to her. She and Ourania were the only people left now that he knew had visited the island on a regular basis. How he wished he had asked Aunt Anna for more details of life over there before she had become senile.

Yannis's protracted fight with the Government for the new medication for the treatment of leprosy to be made available to them had been a part of his life story, but along with the notebooks were the original letters and articles sent to him by Annita and Elias. John found them fascinating, despite having little knowledge of medicine, and his respect for his great grandmother grew. He was sure Saffron would be interested in looking at them.

After four weeks of reading the neat hand writing John now returned most of the books to his uncle. The ones he kept were labelled with the name of an islander and the event they had been directly involved in. Yannis described how he had used a bath tub to sail across the short stretch of water and visit the mainland. He had not been alone in this venture and John was curious to find out the fate of the others who had attempted such a hazardous trip.

He read first the book labelled 'FLORA', having met the shy, reclusive woman occasionally in Aghios Nikolaos and was touched by Manolis's devotion to her. That she had survived the amputation of her arm without anaesthetic was nothing short of a miracle. He would have to ask his father and uncle for more information and wished the old fisherman was still alive.

The next book he tackled was entitled 'ADONIS'. It described the argument that had taken place between Adonis and Christos over a piece of cheese. Christos finally hit Adonis with the length of wood he used as a crutch and Adonis had retaliated by knocking the man to the ground. Before either could do any more damage to each other they had been separated. Adonis had become sulky and morose. Christos taunted him daily with references to cheese until Adonis decided he could no longer bear to be on the island with the man. One night he had taken his bath tub down to the jetty, climbed inside and hoped the current would take him across to the mainland.

Yannis described how the bath tub could be seen wedged amongst the rocks just along the coast from Plaka and was immediately spotted by the men as they brought the barrels of water out to the island. Having deposited the water barrels they made a detour, sailing as close to the rocks as they dared, looking for any sign of the man.

The information that an inhabitant of the island had escaped to the mainland was passed to the other boatmen who delivered supplies, the fishermen and finally the authorities in Aghios

Nikolaos. From his vantage point on Spinalonga Yannis could see the searchers combing the area, but it was not until a week later that Adonis was found and returned to the island. He had hidden in one of the caves, but without easy access to water or food he had finally been forced to emerge and make his presence known.

John frowned. He would have liked to know how the enmity between Christos and Adonis was settled or if it developed further. He searched through the books, but there was not another that bore either man's name. He had to conclude that there had been no further animosity between the two men and therefore nothing that Yannis had felt was worth recording.

The next book recalled how Theo had tried to leave Spinalonga. His freedom was short lived as he did not reach the shore until daylight and was seen by the boatmen and returned. Apparently he had been philosophical and declared he would not bother to make the effort again.

The description of Yannis's own journeys across the stretch of water had been published in his book. He had not planned to escape, merely wishing to visit his family, particularly his mother who had suffered a stroke.

John opened the final book, marked TASSOS. This was far more interesting. Yannis had described in detail Tassos's plan for returning to the mainland, evading recapture and the occupation he intended to pursue. Yannis ended by saying that he wished the man well and hoped one day to hear he had been successful.

John closed the book in frustration. What had happened to Tassos?

To be continued .....

Beryl Darby

YANNIS

A continuing saga

Beryl Darby

ANNA

The second book in a continuing saga

For up-to-date information about the titles in this continuing saga of a Cretan family, see the website:

www.beryldarbybooks.com

Beryl Darby

GIOVANNI

The third book in a continuing saga of a Cretan family

Beryl Darby

JOSEPH

The fourth book in a continuing saga of a Cretan family

CHRISTABELLE

The fifth book in a continuing saga of a Cretan family

SAFFRON

The sixth book in a continuing saga of a Cretan family

For up-to-date information about the titles in this continuing saga of a Cretan family, see the website:

www.beryldarbybooks.com

NICOLA

The seventh book in a continuing saga of a Cretan family

MANOLIS

A supplementary title to the saga of a Cretan family

CATHY

The sequel to Manolis

For up-to-date information about the titles in this continuing saga of a Cretan family, see the website:

www. beryldarbybooks. com

VASI

The tenth book in a continuing saga of a Cretan family

ALECOS

The sequel to Vasi